W9-AAD-678

Praise for
A Wild, Cold State :

"Debra Monroe writes like a razor—like the blade of an ice skate carves the surface of a frozen lake. Her voice dances between the rhythms of fearlessness and patience. She allows her characters their hard truths and contradictions, then she dazzles us by making them shine."

—Pam Houston, author of *Cowboys Are My Weakness*

"The stories in *A Wild, Cold State* are all about love's hunger and are scary and wonderful, honest and troubling. Debra Monroe can rattle you with an image and chill you with a word."

—John Dufresne, author of *Louisiana Power & Light*

"These stories are downright wondrous and triumphant and it's because this writer is smart and shrewd and her eye is true, wits are sharp."

—Robert Olmstead, author of
*A Trail of Heart's Blood
Wherever We Go*

"There are some real people in this book, and Debra Monroe knows how to make them think and feel. She recreates life on the page, and the troubles of the human heart, and she gets it right."

—Larry Brown, author of *Big Bad Love*

"Debra Monroe's voice, like that you hear from all storytellers inspired by the truths about our wickedly ordinary kind, is as spooky and thrilling to hear as are those noises that wake you out of Dreamland."

—Lee K. Abbott, author of *Strangers in Paradise*

"Nobody knows how to make a reader sit up and pay attention to language the way Debra Monroe does. Her characters, like her prose, have hard edges, big hearts, dark humor, and purely unique ways of opening themselves up for our inspection. Like the best books, *A Wild, Cold State* makes you want to take the author out for a drink and tell her all your troubles."

—Antonya Nelson, author of *Family Terrorists*

"Debra Monroe's work is layered, textured, intertwined on it-self . . . Monroe and her characters . . . have humor and wit, have gumption."

—Leigh Allison Wilson, *The Washington Post*

"The brilliantly written stories are sorrowful, based on characters whose lives are drab and empty. In all the stories, the characters . . . seem very real, as do the sorry situations they find themselves in."

—Ravina Gelfand, *Minneapolis Star Tribune*

"This outstanding second collection offers a series of short stories united by the common characters that inhabit a bleak Wisconsin landscape. . . . Even when cold, these characters are hopelessly charming."

—*Kirkus Reviews*

"Appealing fiction from the author of *The Source of Trouble.*"

—*Booklist*

"Fine and funky second collection of stories . . . these stories are marbled with warmth and romantic confusion. . . . The telling—and the seeing—are absolutely clear-eyed. There's plenty of emotion in these interlocking stories . . . but not a hint of sentimentality. And a quite wonderful (dare I say Prous-tian?) ability to see the world from a child's-eye perspective."

—Geoffrey Stokes, *The Boston Sunday Globe*

"Monroe . . . writes stories that have a bite to them."

—Darlene Trasherwhite, *San Antonio Current*

"This collection takes a well-deserved place alongside the author's Flannery O'Connor Award for Short Fiction winner, *The Source of Trouble*."

—*Library Journal*

"Whether she's describing a sleazy bar, a small-town cafe or the Big Muskie Museum, Monroe's evocation of the Wisconsin milieu is always convincing and entertaining."

—Timothy Hunter, *Cleveland Plain Dealer*

"Monroe . . . fully succeeds in following her triumphant debut. . . . Monroe lays claim to a strangely inviting land and the people who inhabit it. Let's hope she takes the reader there again soon."

—Jean Blish Siers, *Charlotte Observer*

"Debra Monroe's real talent in *A Wild, Cold State* is to plunge us into the bloodstreams of her female characters."

—Paul Swenson, *Salt Lake City Tribune*

"The interconnected stories . . . create a vivid culture with its full mix of yearning and dread, its individuals searching for something true, deep and lasting in the land of . . . real, cold weather that cuts through the bone and down to the soul."

—Jerome Stern, *Tallahassee Democrat*

"Monroe switches deftly from one character's voice to another and spins a complex web as the characters drift in and out of each other's stories. . . . Monroe has the gift of knowing her voice as a writer and marrying it to her clean but dreamy style of prose and dark humor."

—Nicole Crews, *News & Record* (Greensboro, North Carolina)

"These are ambitious and believable stories, written in a sparkling prose...."

—Steve Brock, on the Internet

"Monroe has the gift for real-people writing."

—*Kansas City Star*

"There is much to admire and much to enjoy..."

—Althea Romaine, *Dallas Morning News*

"The author's characters are true to life, in a deadpan way, and they'll be instantly recognized by anyone who's lived in a town where everyone knows everyone else."

—David J. Marcou, *Pioneer Press* (St. Paul, Minnesota)

a wild, cold
state

d e b r a   m o n r o e

Scribner Paperback Fiction

Published by Simon & Schuster

New York London Toronto Sydney Tokyo Singapore

For Sharon, *Shen*,
without whom . . .

SCRIBNER PAPERBACK FICTION
Simon & Schuster Inc.
Rockefeller Center
1230 Avenue of the Americas
New York, New York 10020

This book is a work of fiction. Names, characters, places and incidents either are products of the author's imagination or are used fictitiously. Any resemblance to actual events or locales or persons, living or dead, is entirely coincidental.

Copyright © 1995 by Debra Monroe
All rights reserved, including the right of reproduction in whole or in part in any form.

First Scribner Paperback Fiction Edition 1996

SCRIBNER PAPERBACK FICTION and design are registered trademarks of Simon & Schuster Inc.

Manufactured in the United States of America

1   3   5   7   9   10   8   6   4   2

Library of Congress
Cataloging-in-Publication Data

Monroe, Debra.
A wild, cold state/Debra Monroe.
        p.   cm.
1. Wisconsin—Rural conditions—Fiction. 2. Country life—Wisconsin—Fiction. I. Title.
PS3563.05273W55   1995   94–31913
813'.54—dc20   CIP

ISBN: 0-671-89717-9
          0-684-81511-7 (Pbk)

The following stories first appeared in these magazines: "The World's Great Love Novels" in *Quarterly West* (First Place, the semiannual novella competition); "Crossroads Cafe" in *The Gettysburg Review;* "Have a Ball" in the *Cimarron Review;* "Plumb and Solid" in *The New England Review.*

Fowles in the frith,

The fisshes in the flood,

And I mon waxe wood:

Much sorwe I walke with

For beste of boon and blood.

—anonymous medieval lyric

Acknowledgments

Thank you to my wonderful agent, Colleen Mohyde, and my editors, Judith Regan and Cynthia Gitter. Thank you to the following people for their help in the otherwise solitary process of writing: Susan Anderson, Francois Camoin, Lourie Frigen, Ann Hood, Steve Heller, and Blake Maher. Thank you Paul Zimmer for your lovely poems, from which I've plundered three lines and used here as story titles. Thank you D. C. and Sim Wilson (wild ones!).

Contents

The World's Great
Love Novels

A T A MUSEUM just off Main Street you enter a
door in the middle of what—if your imagination
leaps—is the silver underbelly. Inside, a display of
antique lures, tackle boxes, outboard motors, stuffed spec-
imens of not only muskie but bass, perch, walleye. Lights
glow in glass cases, and the imitation marble floor exhales
a scent, cool and dank, I associate with church basements,
VFW halls, school auditoriums, and, by extension, a list of
sacred abstractions. This is a museum, after all. Patriotism,
health, education, piety—a currency I didn't value because
I didn't see I'd ever spend it, which was the point. *They can
never take that away from you,* my mother said about patriotism, health, education, piety, but also about sewing
skills.

Photos of the world-class muskie this museum honors,
and the man who caught it, hang on walls in every bar in
town, which is plenty—ten on two blocks of Main Street,
another dozen not on Main but still within city limits. In
1960, John F. Kennedy used the men's room in a bar when
he came through on his whistle-stop tour: JFK USED THESE
FACILITIES a plaque says on the door, also above the urinal.

Another museum on the edge of town, the Gallery of Woodcarving, shows the life-sized story of Christ and other biblical figures. An old man carved them. I liked the subterranean *Daniel in the Lion's Den:* a ferocious king of the beasts, and Daniel, puzzled as to why God would put him through this, but gentle and wise as he approached the lion to take the thorn from his paw. People tossed money in. My brother, Davie, and I leaned over the pit. I loved the vertigo, the steep cement walls, like I could fall. "Louisa," Davie sighed, "if we could just get down there." He flailed through the railing toward silver and copper coins, green bills which seemed to have wafted down. My mother's black patent leather purse, as hard as a suitcase, bumped my head. "Children," she said, "it's not about money." To prove this, she gave us our allowance right there and helped us toss it. "Other people have less," she said, tossing more.

At the city bank there was a stuffed albino deer, its backdrop a replica of the Wisconsin forest hand-painted by a local woman renowned for spiny, smoke-colored trees, starlike flowers, and yellow skies. An albino has pink eyes. Someone had hit this one with a car and the state patrol officer thought it too beautiful to waste. As my mother made a deposit, Davie and I stared at the deer, its glass eyes. "Look at his toenails, Louisa," Davie said, meaning its hooves. I tried to understand. "It gives you a chill," I told the loan officer. He looked at me over his glasses, which had slid down his nose. "It does at that," he said. He sorted documents on his desk into significant piles.

Next door was Mike's Railroad Bar, which had train memorabilia—switching, tooting, flashing. Next to it, the Buckhorn Tavern—dead rabbits, squirrels, raccoons, wired up to sit at small tables, to play small cards, tilt small mugs. The Chatterbox had strippers on a platform in front of a window. Davie and I leaned against it, peered up. We could see legs, tall as trees. We aspired to upper branches. Davie wanted to see breasts. I wanted to see the face of a woman who'd strip. A man yelled, "You kids scram," and we crossed the tracks to the Depot Hotel to look at whores. I remember one started a fire in her room once by making a grilled cheese sandwich on a steam iron. The whores were older than my mother, not so pretty. My mother wore her hair in a French twist—on hot days, a white eyelet midriff top and navy Capri pants—and my father kissed her hard when he came home at five.

Whores were necessary, people felt, for railroad crews, for fishermen. "They've got to make a living too," my father said. My mother looked solemn as she acquiesced. Matt Dillon had said the same thing about saloon girls the week before. My dad liked *Gunsmoke* for drama. I liked Miss Kitty's beauty mark, her deep cleavage.

From the balcony of the Big Muskie Museum, a balcony which is the fish's mouth, the railing his chalky teeth (a design feature based on the Statue of Liberty's torch), I saw for miles: a bird's-eye view that dwarfed the landscape. The population was 2,493. 2,492, without *me*, I thought. And I attributed any failure to comprehend the order at which symbols hinted to the fact I wasn't adult.

By hanging upside-down, I'd picture the house I wanted to build: my hair dusting the floor, blood pulsing in my ears, I'd trace the ceiling, the sections of wall above doors that—in a house upside-down like I wanted—you'd step over to get to the next room. The chandelier in the dining room, a saucer on a chain, was a mushroom-shaped tea-table sprouting from the room's pale floor.

I'd hang a sampler on every wall:

X XX HOME IS WHERE YOUR HEART IS XX X
X XX CAST THY BURDEN UPON THE LORD XX X

(A lady I knew had this last one above her commode.)

One day, walking with my mother, I smiled at a drunk on the corner bench. All men are created equal. Children are God's sunbeam. My mother hissed: "Stop it." He heard her and hurled spit on the sidewalk. I looked down and noticed his shoe, the sole and lace-up section intact, the part that covered his toes ripped away like an illustration in the encyclopedia: the cross-section of a bum's foot. His toenails looked subhuman, like claws, which thrilled me. "Why shouldn't I smile?" I asked her. "You don't know where he's been," she said finally. She also said—we had two drugstores in town, Rexall and Wiggie's—Never go to Wiggie's.

The power of the number *two:*

Two nations, Russia and America, only one was free.

Two drugstores, one reliable, the other a hotbed. I pictured hell: pale bodies shoveling coal to a furnace, red snakes, their two-pronged tongues writhing. A vision based on the idea, I suppose, that hell was a factory where they made lava, and lava was the earth's bile. My Sunday School teacher actually said this. Wiggie's Drugstore, I thought, sold coal, snakes, bile.

When Aunt Celise came I saw the inside of Wiggie's against my will.

Aunt Celise of the Hairpieces, my father called her. Also, with white shaving cream puffed out on his face, he'd dance and sing in the bathroom every morning, falsetto, "I'm so pretty, and witty . . .

and gay . . . ,"

the song the female lead sang in the deserted bridal shop in *West Side Story*. My mother's smile was complicated, two-sided: embarrassed for his masculinity but happy he loved his kids enough to risk it. She also wished he liked sports. He didn't. She asked him to fix things even I knew he couldn't, as though some day, miraculously, he'd dredge a drain without cracking a pipe, hinge a door without slamming the hammer's heel into the soft wood.

In 1969, Aunt Celise had two hairpieces, one a long

ponytail that fanned out from a knot she pinned to the top of her head, the other a "fall" she attached behind her bangs. Years later, when she'd married a semi-cosmopolitan airline pilot, his friends thought he had routine love affairs because Celise wore her hair so many different ways no one noticed she was just one woman. She had fake eyelashes too but she never wore them in Bremmer—the sticks, she said, the boonies. She was from a smaller town, Lesterville, but she'd lived in Minneapolis—a Licensed Practical Nurse in search of a bachelor doctor—and had her eyes set on Chicago or Los Angeles. She'd been first runner-up in Miss Wisconsin, and I remember how my sister, Helen (who's four years older, practically another generation, as Helen says), sat with me in my grandma's milk kitchen and watched Aunt Celise in a sparkly red swimsuit toss fire-tipped batons at the ceiling. This was her talent, a liability; she scored higher in evening gown. She miscued that night on the porch, lost control, and a baton hurtled end over end—a flaming cannister of kerosene on each tip—and thudded on the gray-painted floor next to me. *Don't play with matches.* I waited for the the house-leveling fire to start. I cried.

Helen pinched me. Aunt Celise picked up the baton, twirled on.

One virtuous, industrious sister, Cinderella for instance, or me. The other mean, like Helen.

Was Aunt Celise a whore? I considered it.

There were two kinds of men, ones you'd marry, ones you wouldn't.

Aunt Celise, an expert, watched *The Dating Game* and called herself and girlfriends "bachelorettes." She'd given up on the doctor idea and felt now, in the space age, that good men piloted planes—she'd train to be a stewardess. She thought Johnny Carson, young and natty in a plaid sportscoat and short hair, was perfect.

There'd been a boyfriend in Minneapolis—no doctor but a wealthy patient. We took the family car to go meet him. Seven years old then, I remember his feet. He was on crutches, his bad foot in a maroon sock with something that looked like hay stuck to it. I wondered why, what the purpose of hay was, until Aunt Celise noticed it too and said: "Where on earth did you get those weeds on your foot?" He shrugged, "The parking lot, I guess." His family owned a factory that made neckties. He was an heir—a storybook romance, my mother called it. Then he turned out to be married, or at least engaged, and my mother said, "She was gaga about him and he didn't care boo." This was my first experience with her words "gaga" and "boo," which—in this coupling, I came to realize—meant Aunt Celise gave it away too soon. Like giving prize money to jockeys before the race is over. Some men just want one thing. The opposite is true too, but rare: my Uncle Leo on my dad's side was gaga for a red-haired welfare mother who didn't care boo either. As my mother said: "She liked his cash-flow."

My dad said, when I was in college: "Some boys will date you for your car." I had a stately Pontiac one year, a sassy Rambler another, a revved-up '65 Mustang once that reared when you let the clutch out—all of them compliments of my dad, who bought and sold cars.

Aunt Celise never lost her nurse-way with men.

My reckless boyfriend in college did press to drive my car—to jolt its shock absorbers, mash dents in its once-perfect fenders. When he wanted to make love, to emphasize how urgent and painful desire was, he'd lie naked on the bed, drape his hand across his brow like it was fevered, and say: "Nurse, Nurse, please."

I saw the inside of Wiggie's the summer Aunt Celise was done with nursing and waiting to go to Chicago to stewardess school. By August, she'd be licensed to say: "Fly with Me." It was also the summer we moved to a cabin on Sunfish Lake, a second house, my dad's dream. He said, when the weather turned warm and we packed up the van and car to move there (I was in the van with him): "I'll have to get a new dream, Monkey, since this one came to fruit." Which was a way of saying a ten-year dream of having a place to fish and swim with his kids was like a sapling he'd watered and fed, and his bank account grew until he made a down-payment and blossoms appeared, promised harvest. When fall came—and behind it, winter—we'd move back to town and have memories, preserved.

I looked in the side-mounted rearview mirror at the reflection of my mother's car behind us, a mint green LTD: Helen in the passenger seat, Davie in the middle, my mother driving, stressed.

She wanted Helen to get a summer job. "It's time," she'd say. "She needs to learn to pay for her own clothes and makeup." Helen resisted. My dad too. She has the rest of her life to work, was his line of logic. She doesn't need makeup. Helen agreed with him on the first account. But she already had four colors of eyeshadow, including silver, some of that frost-white lipstick girls wore then, and an eyelash crimper that scared me. I'd clamp it down and imagine someone bounding through the door, Davie for instance, and that I'd end up yanking my eyelashes out. Helen liked Aunt Celise—specifically the blue patent leather cosmetic case she carried each morning from the guestroom to the bathroom and back.

At the cabin, we unpacked. Once it was a bunkroom with a fireplace and screened porch, someone's fishing retreat, but they'd added on summer after summer, so that when we bought it at an estate sale after the old people who built it died, it had unexpected nooks, closets, porches. Its pink dining room was separated from its navy-and-pink kitchen by a wall of white-trimmed French doors. Davie slept in a cedar-paneled porch that didn't have windows, just canvas sheets that rolled up and were battened down with wing nuts. I shared a room the size of a dogpen with Helen, so I slept everywhere, on a couch one night, a chaise lounge another, on the braided rug on Davie's porch floor while outside the big trees whispered. Old-fashioned towels and blankets sat in neat piles in the closets, pink Depression china and real silverware in the navy blue cupboards, life jackets and tackle boxes in the boathouse. It smelled good—the water in the sink like pure, healthful minerals (water in town smelled like water), the closets like they were built from rare, aromatic lumber.

Helen hated it. How would she meet anyone?

She'd taken a class ring from Terry Kappmeyer which came in the mail with a letter. He lived ten miles east of town, he wrote, and we were living twenty miles west of town until August, and he wouldn't see Helen until then. She wouldn't see anyone so she didn't write back, and wore his ring with a rubber band to make it fit, also to mark its size. She'd say, pleased: "He has big hands."

"The idea of going with someone," my mother said, "is to see them."

"Exactly," my dad said, loading cheese puffs and ginger ale into the cupboard. Helen was looking in the mirror—she had on an orange bikini with a belt across the hips and a buckle in the shape of an elephant. "I've got to move on this tan," she said. I appreciated her smooth waist, her shadowy cleavage, all of it new.

We met Mr. Waverly that night when he knocked on the door, drink in hand—something clear, vodka or gin—and said, "I'm Bin Waverly."

Our lights shone against the glass windows that faced the lake—a brilliant glare. Mr. Waverly told us he was our neighbor, up from Chicago for a week but his wife and kids would live here all summer. I considered the outdoors: the patio with its mosaic bricks and matching umbrella, the dark waves slapping the silver pier. "I'm in construction," Mr. Waverly told us, "an independent contractor."

"Well, hello," my mother said. She's a good person who

thinks too much about money. She gestured at a chair. "Sit down."

He looked at a lamp with ferns on its base. "Nice place."

My dad explained how we bought it furnished.

My mother interrupted: "What's your place like?"

"Modern," Mr. Waverly said. "The A-frame two doors down. My wife's not a housekeeper. Indoor-outdoor carpeting throughout—kitchen, porch, bedrooms. I tell her she needs to vacuum maybe twice all summer, but what with the bon-bons and fingernail files and movie magazines, hell, I'll be lucky if she gets around to it once."

We were quiet, then we laughed. It was a new kind of joke, I decided, a city joke.

My own mother's cleaning schedule, inviolate, made for the constant smell of Pine-Sol I noticed only when I came home. When I stayed overnight at friends' houses, I had trouble sleeping, thinking of dirt. My dad told Mr. Waverly how she did dishes when she was in labor with Davie, contractions every four minutes. "She washes her hands every hour," he said. "We kiss through Saran Wrap."

"Joe," my mother said. "We do not kiss through Saran Wrap."

"I see that," Mr. Waverly said. "You have a fine family."

"You," she said, giving him a sideways smile—like a fish, considering bait.

"Well," he said, "I have to get home to the delinquents."

"Then they're teenagers?" Helen said. "Your kids?"

We turned around. She was wearing a bathrobe over her swimsuit. "Helen," my dad said. His laugh sounded empty, funny. "You're not going to get much of a tan here. Go put your pajamas on."

"More or less," Mr. Waverly said. His kids were more or less teenagers. After he went home—and left his highball glass on our coffee table—my mother and dad talked about how much money he made. "Flashy," my dad said. "He makes it but he spends it, and borrows."

My mother said, "I think he seems entrepreneurial."

"I take it that's based on your experience with enterpreneurs," my dad said, setting Mr. Waverly's glass in the sink.

In the morning, my dad wanted Helen to help him stain the pier while Davie and I went to town with my mother to pick up Aunt Celise at the Greyhound. "Come on, Gooch," he said, "you can wear your swimsuit." Helen pouted but she loved Dad. How couldn't she?

Bremmer was in heat. My mother's LTD lurched and idled through two crowded blocks of Main, through tourists with cameras and strange shirts you knew we didn't wear at home. Fudgies, my mom called tourists, because, in addition to plastic pins shaped like world-class muskies, Bremmer was famous for fudge sold in booths along the highway. Aunt Celise was the only person to get off the Greyhound except a long-haired man, a pre-hippie, the first I'd seen. Aunt Celise had four suitcases, one of them with just shoes, and my mother scowled. When she shut the trunk she said, "This is the time to ask, when Joe's not here—do you have money?"

Aunt Celise said, "It took everything for this trip. You know I can't ask Mom for more." My mother handed her green bills, and Celise said, "I'll do anything—babysit, work at Joe's car lot."

My mother said, "Right now, watch Davie and Louisa while I do bookwork at Joe's office."

We drove around with the radio cranked up. Aunt Celise had her hair pulled back in a puffy "do" and her fingernails clicked a lilty rhythm on the steering wheel. She sang: "Going to the chapel and we're gonna get married . . ." Also "The Age of Aquarius" and a song that went: "Try to love one another." She said, "It's a good time to be alive, so much love." She'd confused brotherly love with romance, an easy mistake. Romance is a woman's province, and to love indiscriminately is democratic and fair.

Aunt Celise parked the car, and we walked down the street. The taverns—the Buckhorn, the Chatterbox, Mike's

Railroad—were just opening. As we passed them, janitors swept their salty smell to the street. We went to Woolworth's, Smith's Gifts, Ben Franklin, Rexall Drug. "I want to get your mother something," Aunt Celise said, "a token. I'll know it when I see it. I haven't found it yet." She steered us to the door of Wiggie's Drugstore.

Davie skidded to a stop. "No."

"We're not supposed to, Aunt Celise," I told her. "Mom said."

Aunt Celise answered, "She won't care if you're with me."

It wasn't clean—the hardwood floor, its narrow slats silty. Two battered fans blew dingy streamers into spirals. A gaudy jukebox. Playing what? It was the first wah-wah pedal I'd heard. I thought someone had bumped the jukebox. *Mama told me, Mama told me not to come.* I gripped Aunt Celise's hand as I saw on a shelf next to me one of those flesh-pink rubber douche bags that—though at the time I had only nightmare ideas about its function—you're supposed to hang on a high hook and let gravity push the water down. "Ugh," Aunt Celise said, "who'd use that?" People in hell, I thought. (*This is the strangest party I have ever seen*, Three Dog Night). A burly man in black leather sat at the soda fountain and gave Celise the once-over—a biker, I've since pegged him, a man who goes by the name of "Tiny" or "Bull." And so it was. "Bull, you need another Coke?" Wiggie yelled. He approached us. "Looking for pharmaceuticals, Miss?" he asked Celise, his smile curving in odd symmetry with his center-parted toupee, the reason for his nickname, the store's name. "No," Aunt Celise said. She bought a toadstool-shaped cookie jar for my mother and goony sunhats for me and Davie which, at first, I liked.

When we got home, Helen was sunning herself on the boathouse roof with Zoe Waverly, one of the more-or-less Waverly teenagers, and also a sullen boy, Zoe's brother, I supposed. His name was Brad. He turned out to be Zoe's boyfriend. Her brother was named Brad too, and he sat on the beach. Brad-the-boyfriend had streaky, white-colored hair and skin the color of tea. But he had scary aspects—his cool gray eyes, also a ridge of blond hair that rose like an arrow from the top of his pants. Brad-the-brother was blond too, with freckles. Davie and I walked down the driveway toward the lake, my mother and Aunt Celise behind, my mother saying the impulse to give was praiseworthy only when you had money. "It's hardly a gift," she said, "when I end up paying for it. I gave you money for necessities." I tried to think what necessities were and I came up with the idea of sanitary things—that my mother gave Celise money for tampons, napkins, so on. Aunt Celise had the same confusion: "What's a necessity?" she asked.

My mother said, "Well, suppose you wanted an ice cream."

Aunt Celise said, "Well, suppose I wanted a cookie jar or sunhats."

My mother said, "What if you run out of shampoo?"

Aunt Celise didn't answer. My mother said, "Anyway, it's nice, the cookie jar, the hats too." This was her discipline style. First she yelled, then she felt bad for yelling and agreed to the excuse or gave you the compliment you'd expected all along. When she saw Zoe and Zoe's boyfriend, Brad, and Helen in her orange bikini, stretched out on paisley beach towels, she hesitated, moved her sunglasses down her nose. Brad-the-boyfriend stared. She moved her sunglasses back up. "I don't like his eyes," she said.

Zoe's swimsuit shocked me. She had on boy's swimming trunks—each longish leg from the center seam over cut from different fabric, one leg bright red, the other in blue-and-red stripes like the jaunty swimsuits men wore in the gay nineties with straw skimmers and handlebar mustaches. Only a sissy boy would wear that swimsuit and no girl should, I felt. She had on a red brassiere top, which didn't look like a swimsuit—it looked like underwear. All three of them stood up. I walked over. "What are you wearing?" I asked Zoe, who wasn't taller than me, not much older either it turned out. She made a sound like "Pffft," tossed her hair over her shoulder. "What are you wearing, yourself," she said.

She meant my straw hat, I guess, and my immature clothes, a top that left my back bare but looked like a pinafore, and matching shorts. My hat had a pink-and-blue squid on the domed part whose tentacles curved down to the brim in circles that held inserts of transparent green plastic—the idea was you had built-in sunglasses if you wore your hat low enough. Davie's white hat had Popeye with a corncob pipe that protruded, waved up and down.

"Those are so ugly," Helen said, which also shocked me. If she hadn't been showing off, she would have said: cute, cool. "I like Zoe's outfit," she said. "It's cool that she took Brad's swimsuit and hers and put them together." I remember a magazine ad that year showing a limber girl rubbing baby oil on her thighs: Innocence Is Sexy. Helen introduced Zoe, Brad, and Brad. Brad-the-brother looked at us from his sandpile. Davie stuck his tongue out.

"You're wearing your boyfriend's swimming trunks?" I said.

"I'm not," Zoe said, "they're my brother's."

I was figuring out if that was better when Mrs. Waverly walked up. "We do wash them," she said. "Geesh, you're a stickler."

"Oh, you should see her," my mother said. "She'll make a nice wife." She had my motives wrong, I felt, as she described to Mrs. Waverly my makeshift playhouse in the yard at home—a red boulder next to a lilac bush and retaining wall I'd turned into my house. By shifting rocks around, I'd built a window seat into the wall. The boulder was my table. Until maybe only a year before, when I'd grown embarrassed to be caught playing with her, my doll slept in a bed of leaves. When I saw wilderness I saw my place in it. "One day I couldn't find my canning jars," my mother said. "I found them outside by the rock, holding lilac leaves pickled in vinegar."

I didn't explain that I wasn't mimicking her, a wife. I didn't dream I'd grow up and sweep floors. The green leaves—heart-shaped and silky—had transported me. Before I knew it, I was in the cellar looking for jars, lids, seals. As for the rest, seeing beds in rocks, houses in trees, I just wanted to see myself, to draw a line out from my heart to my vicinity, my rich premises.

My mother, Mrs. Waverly, and Aunt Celise sprawled in patio chairs and got acquainted. "Is anyone else around here fun?" Mrs. Waverly said. She gestured in an obvious but covert way at the cabin next to ours, a shingle-covered frame house where a thick old lady named Belle lived. She said, "But I guess it's good to have a next-door neighbor who won't keep you up with loud music." My mother nodded, like we lost sleep over the idea of Belle or any neighbor in our neck of the woods having wild parties.

"It's odd how you hate someone else's fun," Mrs. Waverly said. She was perfect-looking, no vulnerable quiver, no uncertain mobility in her expression—like my mother and Aunt Celise, whose faces shift in the process of listening, reception. You speak. They hear, complexly. Mrs. Waverly's eyebrows were ideal. Plump, round-edged commas lying at perfect angles in relation to her eyes. Her black two-piece swimsuit was both matronly and chic.

"That's a cute outfit you've got the littlest girl in," she said then, meaning me. When my mother explained how she'd made it herself, Mrs. Waverly went on about how wonderful women are if they sew, and my mother made excuses: she only sewed because she couldn't get cute clothes here, which wasn't true, we had JCPenney. Next Mrs. Waverly said she hadn't thought to bring any reading material, which made it hard to work on her tan, and my mother rushed in with her enthusiasm for *Christy*, a novel about an Appalachian schoolteacher who gave of herself to the poor, contracted cholera, and witnessed the death of her best friend, Miriam.

Mrs. Waverly looked skeptical. "I like love stories." My mother said, "Oh, this has that too. She moves out of a foggy tunnel of fever and illness into bright light, and you can't tell if it's heaven. The doctor who cures her cholera is at the end of it and they get married and she has purposes left here on earth."

Aunt Celise said to Mrs. Waverly, "Is that what you meant?"

She said, "Nothing that complicated—a brave man who's gruff at first, a woman who's shy. Like she's a secretary and he's in business."

I was disgusted. "I'm going fishing," I said. I went to the lake.

I opened the boathouse and got a pole with a hook lodged in its cork bed. Davie and Zoe's brother watched. "You don't have bait," Davie said. Helen, Zoe, and Brad-the-boyfriend hung their heads over from the boathouse roof. "I can't believe my sister's going to fish," Helen said. I opened a tackle box, and its drawers stood up in tiers. I picked carefully through the feathery lures—dangling, sparkling ornaments with wicked hooks. "Those are for trolling," the boyfriend said. "You can't use them off the end of the pier." I ignored this. Everyone was jealous, I felt.

"The brighter the lure," Brad said, "the quicker you have to be."

Zoe came downstairs. "Cool," she said, and hung a yellow-and-red feathered thing with beads and a silver oval by her ear. "I like the box too," she said, opening and shutting it so the drawers folded, stood up, folded. "Mom," Helen said, "Louisa's going to hurt herself with fish hooks." I got mad then and opened a jar of salmon eggs and slid one—a soft, pink sphere—onto my hook and dropped my line off the pier. "These look like corn," Davie said. Zoe's brother pulled one out of the jar and squished it. But crappie and sunfish bit. Brad-the-boyfriend taught me how to take hooks out, to avoid the crappie's sharp fin. He sat on the boathouse roof and watched while I baited hooks for Zoe's brother and Davie. Aunt Celise was inside, unpacking. Mrs. Waverly and my mother sat in lawn chairs in shallow water, talking.

"We practically raised Brad," Mrs. Waverly said, "since Zoe brought him home. And now that I'm used to him, Zoe's sick of him."

I looked up and Brad was gone.

She said, "He stays around because he's like one of our own now."

I looked at Zoe, a year older than me, eighth grade: already a vamp, I thought. She'd peaked early. She looked sunny and unconcerned. Everything I'd been taught led to one conclusion—she'd come to no good. They talked about Helen's ring next, how it came in the mail after she'd sat with Terry Kappmeyer at a baseball game and she hadn't seen him since. "Joe thinks that's best," my mother said. "She has the *idea* of a boyfriend but none of the complications." Mrs. Waverly laughed so hard she choked on her iced tea. "I'd say," she said, "that's why I love Montgomery Clift."

My mother smiled.

So startling, so much truth. I tried to see what prompted it. But I was just a kid, no adult with events gauged and regulated.

By nightfall, my dad had events gauged but not regulated. His influence, his sovereign prerogative as father, waned. But that afternoon he had bliss, walking down the sun-washed driveway with Mr. Waverly and Aunt Celise, arms linked. All three of them carried highball glasses with pictures of deer and trout on them, and leather sleeves—containing Mr. Waverly's clear liquor. My dad kissed my mother and exclaimed his favor for me, a daughter who fished. "A man doesn't get luckier than this," he said. "Here, Monkey, I'll show you how to clean them." So we

went behind the boathouse to a shelf built expressly for
fish cleaning, and he showed me how to scale, gut, to cut
off the fins, to leave the bones intact. "They're too small,"
he said. "We'll eat around them." Brad-the-boyfriend fil-
leted the bigger fish, a good-sized crappie and a single
perch. "That's good," my dad said, "and your knife's not
even really sharp. Where'd you learn it?"

Brad pushed the hair out of his eyes. "One of my
mother's boyfriends."

Davie and Zoe's brother sorted rocks. "This is a dime,"
Davie said about a rock, "and these over here are dollars."
Mrs. Waverly watched us. "You're a pip," she said, "a Flo-
rence Nightingale."

I said, "Florence Nightingale didn't clean fish. Rebecca
Boone maybe."

I liked my role models precise.

My dad cleaned on, whistling. He stoked the grill with
coals and my mother rearranged dinner plans, postponed
T-bones she'd had in mind for that night to the next day,
threw bratwurst and hamburger on with the fish. And she
invited the Waverlys. Brad-the-boyfriend and my dad
dipped the fish in flour and turned them over and over until they were gold, and we ate them with cool potato salad,
carrots my mother took the time to cut in lacy strips.
Cheese Puffs and grape Kool-Aid. Our dinner was a party,
Davie standing on the picnic table bench to wave food in
the air and recite TV commercials he'd learned by heart—
until he got scolded, cried and snuffled through the rest of
the meal. Mr. Waverly kept the grown-ups' glasses full of
sparkling liquor, and when the food was gone, and the sun
level with the trees, Mrs. Waverly gestured us away: "You
kids go play somewhere and leave us be."

My mother frowned like she might impose rules, where
we could go, where we couldn't, but didn't. "Helen, you're
in charge," she said.

We went to Cyclone Beach, a strip of sand that tumbled
down a hill to the lake on a lot no one seemed to own. Inter-

esting things could be found there: bottles, charred wood, a harmonica once. Davie, chastened by the crest and crash of his mood at dinner, lugged Mr. Peanut along, a replica of the spokesperson for Planter's he'd sent away for after saving proof-of-purchase seals. Brad, Zoe's brother, muttered and looked unpleasant. Zoe and Helen led, Zoe casting new light on Bremmer: "I love it, very cool. I bet the boys are cool." They sat on a log as she said this, and Helen reconsidered, ventured to guess, after all, they were. "I'll bet they wear flannel shirts, boots, all of that," Zoe said.

I slowed down and sped up to make it easy for Brad-the-boyfriend to stay near me. He did, pelting big rocks at the woods.

Zoe said how she went to shopping centers for fun, and her friend had lifted two portable hairdryers by strapping them to her shins under bell-bottoms. "They were really big bell-bottoms," she said. She waded across the creek that fed the lake and stood on a rock, the cones of her swimsuit poking out from her torso, her legs tubular in the striped trunks. "I watch these shows on TV," she said, "and I like the outdoorsy types." She grinned like a wild-hearted soldier. Brad fooled with a rope swing hanging from an oak branch, and he flexed, the veins in his arms thick. The last amber light of day shone below the trees, through branches. Brad—entwined, hamstrung—backed up, scaled a tree, paused. "I mean," Zoe yelled from across the creek, "I just don't know anyone like that." He hurtled through the air so fast I felt wind.

He slammed into her. The rope crooked in one elbow, both arms yanking her near, he kissed her. She rearranged her hair and swimsuit afterwards and smiled across the creek at me and Helen, pleased.

Helen tried one last time to keep rank. A carload of teenagers pulled up to light their campfires, to drink beer and sweet wine. As car doors slammed, voices rang, Helen said: "I wonder if Terry's with them," meaning Terry her phantasmic boyfriend.

"Oh, right," I said, "like he's not at home getting ready for church." Which was cruel, yes, but he gave guitar lessons, changing nouns and pronouns in pop-songs to make them religious: "God's love is warmer than the warmest sunshine, softer than a sigh."

"You're probably right," she said, and we headed back. We met my mother on the way, who'd probed the trees and ditches with her flashlight, yelling, "Kids, kids." She said to Helen: "You know better, you should be home." Helen walked beside her as she explained Aunt Celise was on thin ice, too sassy. Brad walked next to me, long strides. Sometimes he'd look my way—embarrassed, I felt, at how Zoe had him leap through hoops and swing like Tarzan. Zoe sidled up next to me. "Brad's not my brother," she said.

I thought she meant this one. "I know."

She said, "*Him.*" She pointed at the Brad I thought was her brother. "He's my half-brother," she said. "My brother lives with my real mother in Oak Lawn. He's so handsome, you'd fall in love."

"Then who's that at home?" I asked. "Mrs. Waverly?"

"My stepmother," she said.

I nodded. I thought for a minute about whose swimming trunks she had on.

At the cabin they'd moved back inside, to the table in the pink dining room. My dad's glow was gone, a confused grimace in its place, his curly hair tufting high above his head. Mrs. Waverly stood up. "I've got to get home and put the kids to bed," she told my mother. "Keep on eye out, he likes your sister."

My dad talked about church in the woods in the morning. "Two miles on County Trunk 70," he said, "the first left past Lampson. For campers, tourists—a retired minister does it. Benches in the woods, you wear shorts, whatever. No swimsuits." He looked at Helen.

His words floated empty, no consequence. A dull lamp glowed through the French doors. I flipped the wall switch and overhead light bleached the room, everyone in it. For the first time, I saw someone I loved—Aunt Celise, my initiation—drunk. She looked startled and hilarious, like she'd been poked in the back with a stick. "They have a special hymn for the big muskie," she said.

Mr. Waverly laughed: "Ho ho."

Aunt Celise's eyes got wide. She said, "They re-enact Jonah in the whale."

She lost Mr. Waverly here, who seemed not to know who Jonah was. A few years later, when I knew Zoe Waverly better, she mentioned how Christ rose from the dead on Ash Wednesday, and her first winter in Bremmer she mistook hunting season for a religious festival. "Those must be the Mennonites," she said about the herds of men wearing Day-Glo orange from head to toe, overrunning every bar and cafe in town. Really, the Mennonites wore gray clothes—the women, those nice hair nets. Other than that you couldn't tell them apart except at school when they didn't pledge allegiance.

My dad frowned. "Celise, slow down."

Mr. Waverly said, "She's so cute, though. I'd do what I could for her if she came to Chicago. She could answer the phone at my construction business, but no one would see her. What a waste."

Mrs. Waverly said, "It was good enough for me."

He said, "Hell, Madge, when we got married I let you stay home."

"What a deal," she said. She left, the kids in tow.

My mother said, "All three of you, Helen, Louisa, Davie. Hurry up."

We got ready for bed. Mr. Waverly, my dad, my mother, and Aunt Celise sat in the dining room, so I bedded down with Helen. But a strip of light came under the door. The air was still and thick. Helen rolled over, poked me, complained about sand in the sheets, so I took my pillow and went to a daybed in the pink alcove off the kitchen where light still intruded, sound too—the clunk of fresh ice cubes sliding down glasses, Aunt Celise's antics, Mr. Waverly's laugh—but a breeze wafted by and I realized with a start I'd lived a day at the beach and I hadn't gone swimming.

I vowed to.

I dreamed this:

Under a yellow sky, deer with moss on their horns and rabbits watched as I walked to the lake where waves curled: *whitecaps*, a word that still makes me search the water for hats. Brad waited. He thought we had plans to fish. I convinced him to swim, to roll the thick inner tube my dad bought from a tractor salesman off the end of the pier, to plunge. We had a game, Brad on one side, me on the other, rocking. The aim was to tip the other first. You both fell, to win was to tip second. In the veil of spun water, the rhythm of cooperation, Brad became Zoe's handsome brother, the one in Oak Lawn she said I'd fall for, but he was also Brad because when I won—and he toppled down, down to the deep, weeds fluttering like banners—my arms curved around his chest, his tea-colored skin. His silver hair flashed. You could get hurt, scraped by the pressure valve. You could stay down too long. We should respect the water, my swimming teacher had said, not fear it.

I woke, wetness and vertigo locked in my hips, the sheet draped like a sail from a lost boat named—let's say—*The Happy Chance*.

Voices droned, trilled, like a radio:

"A hunter values squirrels because they're small."

"A girl like you should move to Las Vegas, you'd make a killing."

"No lights like footlights." Laughing. Laughing. "Put that down, Celise."

"You've had enough."

"You've had enough."

The clap of the screen door, Mr. Waverly leaving. My mother wobbling Aunt Celise past me to bed. And I broke at the sight of her, her expression no more polished than in the dated school photos of her we'd hung on the walls, no older, no wiser after all than me or Helen. Twenty years later, as I sat reading magazines in a doctor's waiting room, I saw pictures of Queen Noor of Hussein, who was really only a girl from Connecticut: in khaki and silk, visiting Kuwaiti refugees, or shopping at Saks in mink, saying, "It is awesome, just the concept, me, *Queen*." A stagey Joan of Arc and Marie Antoinette too, wanting to give, yes, but more than that to get. I thought of Aunt Celise, who confused *agape* with *amore*, love with different love, love with money. The last sound that night was Belle, our fat neighbor, sneezing—unlike a thin person's sneeze, I noted. "I hope," my mother whispered carrying glasses to the sink, "she doesn't think we had a wild party."

I meant to accord the sense of buried treasure, water locked in my hips, the slight significance it deserved. But the gloating idea that I'd invented desire or experienced it better than anyone held sway as I meanwhile told myself all organisms, non-mammalians even, who don't have hips, have desire: crickets, snakes, the muskie in deep water harking to cold blood. I watched a pair of birds, the male brilliant, pursuing; the female demure in gray with a pretty beak, flying away. Driving thirty miles to the orthodontist with my mother, I distracted myself from forthcoming pain, the wrenching of wire in my mouth, by remembering the dream, which seemed real, a secret Brad knew too, because the difference between *time* and *time with Brad* was the difference between water and water in a sealed jar charged with bubbles.

One Sunday—not the Sunday of Aunt Celise's legendary hangover in which she moved from one official position to another, in the sun or out, taking exercise or taking ease, taking food, taking none, falling asleep finally in the thick grass by the back door, not that Sunday, but another—we drove to town because my mother promised we'd go watch her friend's son be baptized at our regular church in Bremmer. The sun sliced through stained-glass windows. I smoothed my sailor dress, tried to stay cool, watched the baptism which—relative to the rest of the service—seemed novel, esoteric, the stainless-steel font, the suspense as to whether the baby would cry and cast out demons or not cry and leave them till later. The sermon started, of its own volition, it seemed, and I counted seconds to make minutes, minutes to make quarter hours, then quit my impatient prolonging (a watched pot never boils) and returned to my dream, willed it to grow, to finish.

My imagining: after the sinking in water part we'd surface, hook our arms over the inner tube to float while we pushed our wet hair back, reconsidered each other in the wake of our collision: *special*, of like species, unique. We'd swim to shore, say words, not many—they were utilitarian, so daily—and lie down. In the sand? Near the cabin in broad day? I cut suddenly to a bedroom, Brad's I suppose, with blond, Scandinavian furniture, sunshine through square windows. I backtracked—we swam to shore again, walked to Brad's bedroom. I had another practical breach here because I didn't understand sex—no one had explained erections yet, and the reputed interplay of energy and matter seemed unlikely. But I skirted the physics, sure, like mute animals, we'd manage.

I felt warm, dizzy.

We filed out of church. My mother said, "Are you all right?" But she watched Helen, who'd decided to give Terry his ring back because she wanted the romance to seem real, dramatic. She wanted a scene. She walked toward him in the fellowship hall where people drank Hawaiian Punch. He smiled—he'd thought he wouldn't see her till August. He started to speak, to say hello, and she yanked the ring off. In her plans, I suppose, his hand was open. But he held the Styrofoam cup with one of them, had the other in his pocket. Finally, she set the ring on a table and stalked to the car.

My mother, appalled, said so.

My dad said, "Well, he sent it in the mail."

My mother said, "She should have sent it back in the mail."

We went back to the cabin, passing the Waverlys' patio where they drank Bloody Marys or plain, spiced tomato juice (Virgins, Mrs. Waverly called them), depending on how Saturday night went. Aunt Celise had tomato juice there on the Sundays Bin Waverly wasn't up from Chicago. "Thick as thieves," my mother said about Aunt Celise and Madge Waverly once they got past the rivalry. When Aunt Celise left for Rome, New York, for her stewardess training in the fall, Madge cried, took Celise's address, promised to write.

Another Sunday that summer, or maybe the next, my mother's LTD burned.

We'd been to the church in the woods, the benches, the mosquitoes, tall pines making it gloomy, a place to leave behind. We were curving toward home, bogs and cattails on either side of the road, and my dad said (or said he'd said in the later accounts he gave): "Hmm, I smell gas. I wonder if some spilled in the trunk of that car in front of us." My mother looked puzzled. My dad stepped on the gas. Nothing happened. He coasted to a rise, opened his door, and flames leapt out from under the car. My dad, Davie, and my mother all slid out her door. After panic and my mother's shrill command—probably five seconds in all—Helen and I fell out the door on that side too, my side already orange, a furnace, hell. The whole car went, flames twenty feet high, and vehicle after vehicle passed. "Damn Fudgies," my mother said, blinking back tears at citified tourists who didn't have community sense enough to stop. Belle, our neighbor, stopped. My dad went to a nearby house to call a fire truck. We rode with Belle. "Yah," she said to Helen, who sobbed, "that's a good girl, go on and cry."

Years later, drinking a margarita in a bar called the Cantina in San Ardo, California, my mother said that the marriage went terminal that day. "It was my favorite car," she said, "the cool green. But worse, it made your dad preoccupied." True, the near-calamity.

"It makes you think," he said. Brad went with him to watch—a son's place maybe but Davie was too small—as the tow truck hauled the remains in for inspection. A bad gas line, so arbitrary. "Hell, I'm a mechanic," my dad said. On the Fourth of July that year, at a party at the Sunfish Inn, I lit firecrackers with Brad while Zoe and Helen watched. Davie and Brad-the-half-brother played nearby. Brad lit the firecrackers. I held them. Then I threw them. Sometimes he'd yell, "Throw it at the lake." Or: "At the woods." Once he gave too many directions and I waited for him to decide, and the firecracker blew in my hand, stunning cold pain, but I wasn't dismembered. Helen ran for ice, saying, "Don't tell, don't tell." But Brad, clamping the ice down hard, led me to my dad, who stood by himself in the parking lot. Brad explained his mistake—his, he insisted—showed him I wasn't hurt, how small the firecracker was. My dad winced in the telling, our family so near treacherous rocks again, foundering. He shook his head.

Bin Waverly saw my dad as his connection, the man to initiate him in northwoods mysteries, hunting, rapid water, how to eat red beans from smoke-blackened cans. My dad responded with lore about hunting he'd heard at the car lot, Chamber of Commerce statistics about nondeciduous trees or spawning habits of fish. One day, he told Mr. Waverly his theory that big game were small trophies; only foxes, squirrels, and rabbits, in terms of marksmanship, significant. My mother said, "Of course, Joe doesn't hunt." Then, "It does make sense, though," loyal. My dad intended for the touristy facts to befit Mr. Waverly, his likes and dislikes—protocol—but Mr. Waverly found them remedial, proof we thought he was soft. He offered to get White Sox tickets, to buy drinks at the stadium, but my dad didn't like baseball either, though my mother did, particularly the idea of a trip to Chicago. In compromise, my dad bought two snowmobiles after Mr. Waverly asked about thrilling winter pastimes and because my dad hoped, I guess, like fishing, he'd find it not a sport exactly but a way to be outside.

When he fished, he read books, neglected his pole. When he ice-fished, he admired the winter sunrise, the desert of snow. He set tip-ups, then forgot them while he cleared a spot for skating.

One Christmas vacation, Mr. Waverly came up to his A-frame with Zoe, Brad, and his oldest son, Willy. Madge and the half-brother stayed home. We went to our cabin too, an exercise in fortitude because neither cabin got warm enough to turn the water on. Helen, shaken by the prospect of minimal personal grooming in front of Brad and the alleged good catch, Willy, stayed home. Zoe stayed with me in Helen's room, and when we went to the bathroom in the middle of the night we stuffed our layers of sleeping gear—long underwear, flannel nightgowns—into snowmobile suits and trudged to the privy. One night when the plank door slammed behind us, in my aversion, my haste to go back inside, I spun, and my long hair caught in thorns. Zoe tried to disentangle me, giggling. She went inside where the grown-ups and older kids played cards. Her dad and Willy tried to cut me loose while she held the flashlight and laughed, making it wiggle. So Brad held the flashlight, and Willy and Mr. Waverly cut the branch off. Inside, my mother snipped it out of my hair with scissors. Helen, seventeen, had driven out for dinner—to assess Willy, no doubt—wearing her Christmas presents, a green sweater, boots, pink lip gloss.

Zoe and I got up later to drink water from the five-gallon vat and Brad was asleep on the couch, wearing his boots. My dad, Mr. Waverly, and Willy played cards, drank schnapps. Helen stood in the kitchen and whispered to my mother she'd stay overnight if she could go to Belle's in the morning—a year-round house—and bathe.

"I brought an overnight bag," she said.

My mother said no: "N. O." Helen looked at Willy. He looked at me and Zoe and waved. My mother put a blanket over Brad.

The next day Davie drove my mother's Skidoo into a snowbank. I rode shotgun and let him drive because with Brad-the-half-brother in Chicago he was bored. He buried the skis and we hopped off to tug them loose, but Mr. Waverly yelled at us through his snowmobile helmet, his face turning dark red, not exactly a winter athlete himself. We went inside where my dad worried aloud about his brother, Leo, who had a bad marriage. The radio played a song: "So many times I've let you down, I tell you now they don't mean a thing." "To whom?" my dad said, turning around, glaring. The next song went: "Is this a lasting treasure or just a moment's pleasure?" My dad said, "They've got that wrong." I thought to myself, Geesh, and I walked to the kitchen, past Brad and Willy playing cards, to make hot chocolate. Davie wondered where our mother was. In town, I supposed. I stirred the hot milk, my snowmobile suit unhooked at the top, draped at the waist, my hair covering my face as I leaned into the steam. I heard Willy say, above the clicking, shuffling cadence of the cards, "The little sister's real cute." My heart pounded. "Uh huh," Brad said, "for sure."

Helen never aimed for Willy again. She liked boys aloof but accessible—they should meet her eyes in crowded rooms. So she called Willy overrated despite how the local girls liked him, different from boys in Bremmer, tough. Even Zoe liked Willy's version better than Brad's, a category of appeal I link with Bruce Springsteen, or this poet I met years later who wore black T-shirts and motorcycle boots where most men wore sportscoats—too invigorated, like a male bird who flies into glass in mating season, mistaking his brawn for his rival's. Mr. Waverly too. He moved the family members who were willing north the next year, bought a trailer house for less than the cost of winterizing the A-frame, and lodged his eighty-year-old mother in it to keep on eye on the kids, who turned out to be Zoe, and Brad, Zoe's ex-boyfriend who wasn't even a Waverly; Madge and the half-brother disappeared. Bin, and Willy, who was eighteen, lived in Chicago, vacationed here.

Zoe was my best friend since the night of brambleberry thorns in my hair. She dropped the effort to impress me with juvenile delinquent experience, and we shared clothes, jewelry, in the end, the letter Z. Zoe noticed my name, Louisa, had the Z sound though not the letter, and I asked my parents did they mind if I changed the spelling. My dad said, "Whatever you want, Monkey." My mother didn't care; she'd changed her name from Arlene to Arleen to Arlyne. So the year I went feminine—a skinny high school freshman, Zoe a year ahead of me, Brad two—I was Louiza. Helen worked the cosmetic counter at Rexall Drug where she got a discount, also a plate-glass vista of Main Street where singles cruised.

Zoe, Brad, and I rode the schoolbus to their trailer parked by the A-frame on Friday afternoons, and I'd stay till Sunday. Their grandma watched TV, smiled, reported what food she'd stockpiled in the cupboards. We ate our meals and took showers at the trailer. Zoe washed sweaters and bras in the bathroom sink with shampoo. I thought what my mother would say—detergents are scientifically formulated for specific dirt. The trailer, cozy but a little rank too, needed detergent. We used the A-frame for our clubhouse. Under the high ceiling, gray sunlight reflecting off the icy lake through the windows, we lay on the bed in our coats, smoked cigarette butts we'd confiscated from ashtrays, and read a chapter in the novel *Airport* where the air traffic controller yields to lust.

Zoe, her curly hair tumbling over her red ski-jacket collar, tamped out her cigarette butt—a stub, really—and set the book down. "It moves me," she said. Given its subject, impending explosion, the book's sex was tame, waves lapping shores, like that. But Zoe and I staggered with it and sank—no better, finally, than the debased air traffic controller. A man tries to resist fornication but sometimes job pressures build and he can't. He says later, like pillow talk, like Bogart: at least we had that. At least we had Paris. They had the air-conditioned motel room with pictures of clipper ships rocking above the bed. I wondered about the seductress, her motives. "How about Brad?" I asked Zoe.

She said, "How about what?"

I struggled for a way to say it, a euphemism: "Love's hunger."

She threw herself into her laugh, shaking the bed, wiping her eyes. "Sometimes I still let him kiss me," she said. "That's it."

Helen meanwhile hooked up with a plump girl named Cheryl who worked at the soda fountain in the same drugstore, and Zoe and I called the pair of them the Weepers' Club because they chose men they knew slightly and then got lovesick. "He walked past me to buy a magazine," Helen said. "I don't think he usually buys magazines." Or, "He couldn't meet my eyes when I served him ice cream." Cheryl, having read the book *Love Story* they made into the movie, cried hard. She'd given herself to a man named Steve S. who loved a chaste woman, not Cheryl. So she knew him but not really. If I died, Cheryl said, he'd see what he lost. She was on the edge, I thought, but exactly how? I went for the obvious. "She'll get pregnant," I told Helen. Helen said, "He uses a sheath."

"Where does he get a sheath?" I asked.

"Wiggie's," she said. Of course.

My dad said to me: "Helen's mind is unoccupied." He frowned. "Maybe *preoccupied* is a better word." Like Helen's mind wasn't on cosmetic sales because it was full, tenanted: John M. lived there.

I told my dad, "She loves John M."

The Snow Dance came in January and a B-squad foot-

ball player asked me by phone. Helen and Cheryl pro-
moted it—what better could I expect? He wore braces too
and Davie made the standard jokes about how we'd lock if
we kissed. Zoe said, "There might be a problem with
Frenching." Most people no doubt find out about French-
kissing when someone sticks a tongue in their mouth, but
hearing about it like that, I worried: the braces, yes, also
whether I'd know how. When the time came I did. Later.
Not the night of the Snow Dance with Danny Delgaddo
when we double-dated with Zoe and her new boyfriend,
the potato heir, her phrase. Four years older than Zoe, already graduated, someday he'd inherit the biggest potato
farm in the state. It struck my parents funny he was going
to a high school dance, but not Helen and Cheryl, who expected John M. and Steve S. to attend at least the after-
dance party and meant to go too. Zoe suggested the
double-date, proof she had the upper hand with the potato
heir who wanted her all to himself.

"What about Brad?" I asked.

She said, "What about what?" He wasn't her boyfriend
now. He still lived there, she said, because his mother
couldn't afford him.

We'd been at the dance for an hour when the potato
heir wanted to leave. We drove around and around the
same block so we'd end up on Main, deserted by tourists in
winter but at night—my insight grew—teeming with cars.
We idled. I stared out the window. Once I saw Brad in a
car with boys his own age and I wished I was with them instead of in the back seat with Danny Delgaddo holding my
hand so it cramped, the potato heir in front telling Zoe he
must be crazy, crazy stalking her: jail bait. "Sixteen will get
you twenty," he said. At the time—how fortunate—I didn't
understand. "Why are we leaving?" I'd asked at the dance.
I liked the candles, the tinfoil on the walls, the shadowy
basketball hoops draped with streamers, a pretty girl on a
wicker throne in a white dress and crown. Zoe acted impa-

tient, like Helen. "No one stays at the dance," she told me, rolling her eyes.

I liked it when Danny D. kissed my neck. But when it came to the mouth, he mashed his jaw into mine, teeth clenched, very painful.

In the front seat I heard Zoe's dress rustle, a plaid taffeta pioneer-woman style, part of her new image, quirky like the mismatched swimsuit two years ago. She wanted to blend in here, seem plucky and rugged. Or maybe she did favor the outdoorsy type. She'd say, even when you didn't ask: "I'd love to shoot a gun." She took lessons from a local artist and hung her sketches of deer on the trailer walls, flat and stiff like cartoons, like graphics on tourism brochures. I backed off from Danny Delgaddo's kisses and heard the clunk of shoes falling to the floor, the taffeta rustling, and I thought about why, in Zoe's scheme, Brad didn't count but the potato heir did. I considered my dad's idea that big trophies are small prey and decided men like Zoe's boyfriend or John M. and Steve S. liked girls slippery, small, wily, whereas Helen and Cheryl were tame and sturdy like cows you led to slaughter or breed. (This was right for Cheryl, who ate too much ice cream at the soda fountain, but hard on Helen, I knew.) And Zoe moaned, making her dad's mistake, thinking: biggest, best. I felt like praying—for a good life, right choices.

I remembered the legend of my parent's first date, the five dollars he borrowed or stole to take her, her silver dress, green net bursting out from the waist, trimming the sweetheart neckline too, the song: *May this fire in my soul, dear, forever burn* ("Pledging My Love," Fats Washington). When I was little I'd wear the dress around the house, hold the top up to my skinny torso, totter in heels six sizes too big. I held a pair of Aunt Celise's false eyelashes in my hand once, a charm, as my mother retold the story. Later, when she thought I was old enough—we were in a bar in San Ardo—she revised, addended. He'd pressed to make love, sure if she succumbed she'd never leave, and it was his only chance, a poor boy, for a pretty, well-to-do girl. The rest of the song: "Making you happy is my desire. Yes. *Keeping you* is my goal."

But I'd heard only the pristine version that night as my date sat on the other end of the seat, pretending to look out the foggy window. *Generation gap*, I thought, *sexual mores*. I saw these words in newspapers—Walter Cronkite said them, characters on new, bawdy sitcoms. Somewhere people had stuck flowers in guns and stayed in bed to protest war but we got backwash here, the license to say words like *dick, fuck*, or, more innocuous, I guess, *pervert*. Zoe sat up in the front seat, yanked her dress in place. "You pervert," she scowled. She meant me, in the back, silent. We didn't do less, my mother told me later. We talked about it less.

"I'm bored," I said.

Complaining, adjusting his clothes, the potato heir started the car. We cruised Main Street once more, and he pulled up behind the Buckhorn. "I'll be right back," he said, and he went inside. Danny Delgaddo said: "You know, I'd like to go home and get a good night's sleep." I paused, nodded. "Well, sure," I said. "Training," he explained lamely, football season long gone. "That's fine," I said, and he opened the car door and walked away. Zoe laughed hard. Afterward, she wiped her eyes and said, "Come on." She wanted to see the Buckhorn. So we inched the back door open and she pointed at the rows of stuffed animals. I told her about the Gallery of Woodcarving and she was interested for a minute, then shook her head, wrinkled her nose, no. The potato heir stood by the cash register, a bottle in a paper bag next to him, nodding, putting bills in his wallet. The bartender pointed at me in my pale yellow dress with red flowers, at Zoe in her swishy plaid. "Get the small fry out of here," he said.

In the car, I put my coat over my dress and shivered. I asked Zoe, "What did your boyfriend mean when he said,

'Sixteen will get you twenty'?" I looked across the tracks at the Depot Hotel, ex-home of old whores, slated to be demolished. "Statutory rape," she said. I thought for a minute about statues and rape, what that meant (vandalism?), then skipped it. I learn fast. Zoe's boyfriend got back to the car and asked me: "Where should I drop you?" Zoe was staying with me because of the dance. "We have to come in together," Zoe said. "Her parents are strict." This was less true now; we hardly went to church. Zoe said, "And we have to breathe in her mom's face when we get there, alcohol check."

"I've got breath mints," he said, slamming the gearshift down. We drove eighteen miles out of town to a party at someone's hunting camp, a log building with a potbellied stove. Zoe sat in the middle of the seat next to her boyfriend as we took the winding, slick roads too fast, her ski jacket over the shoulders of her formal. I sat alone in the back seat in my long dress, thinking of jokes: "Home, Jeeves," I said once. Zoe smiled, rolled her eyes. Her boyfriend drove faster. At the party there were people in jeans and people in tuxes, the Snow Queen in her silky white dress waving sloe gin, saying, "You know, I was so surprised. Me, Queen." Helen sat on a bunkbed in cords and a dark sweater. ("Don't overdress," a magazine said that year, "try to look like you've been to another, better planet and Earth isn't worth it.")

Helen stared at me. John M. stood next to her. She said, "My sister has my earrings on," and she made me give them right back. Brad stood by himself, staring at Zoe. She took her jacket off, moved around the room, goosebumps on her bare arms. Her old-fashioned dress, the log walls, the potbellied stove—I thought of *Gunsmoke*, Miss Kitty who was really Amanda Blake and in the news because she championed animal rights. Brad and the friends he ran with looked like hippies, Army surplus jackets, hair that hadn't been cut in a year, its old outline still visible, long in back, jaw-length in front. Some of the high school teachers wore their hair long now. Our new minister embroidered his jeans, rainbows and birds. What did it stand for? It was economical, the only fashion statement available to Brad. My mother didn't like his eyes, the color of ice, the big glacier that passed over the state, forging subterranean lakes, rivers. His eyes turned dark, normal, gray. "Louisa," he said, "are you coming over tomorrow?"

"Yes," I told him. I had my good coat on—frumpier than a ski jacket—and no earrings. I sipped brandy and chewed breath mints.

"Time to go," Zoe said. The potato heir followed the two of us to the car, scowling. *I feel he hates me*, I muttered to myself like an actress. On the way home, he asked Zoe why she didn't have the same last name as Brad. "We're not related," she said, "he's like my foster brother." Then she said she couldn't sit in the driveway and neck. "We got that out of the way earlier," she said.

We went through the back door, into the kitchen—its clean smell, the pilot lights on the shiny stove top glowing like a small, familiar town. We tiptoed through the hall and tapped on my parent's door. "Did you have a nice time?" my mother asked, her voice sleepy-weak. "Come and say good night." Subterfuge—a cunning alcohol check. I blew her cover; I walked in and blew in her face. She said, "You *have* been drinking, something minty. Schnapps?" My dad sighed. I bumped into the doorframe, rushing away.

Zoe's dad and Willy—on their way north from Chicago the next day—picked us up and drove us to the trailer. Willy asked us, "How's school, girls? Breaking any hearts?" When we got there, Brad was watching cartoons with the grandma who looked at us and smiled. He avoided Zoe, but to me he said, "I got to thinking this morning—where did your date go last night? Didn't you have a date?" I blurted, "He ditched me." We laughed about that. "A fool and his girl are soon parted," Willy said. Mr. Waverly went to the Sunfish Inn then—to sit in front of the TV screen and drink—and the day dragged. We went outside and the wind passed over the lake. Willy talked about chopping a hole in the ice, setting tip-ups, but didn't. I walked to our cabin, ice hanging from the eaves, the white clapboard dull as snow without green, quivering trees. Belle, wearing a wool shirt over a housedress, tapped on her living room window and waved. I went back to the Waverlys', where Willy, Brad, and Zoe stood between the trailer and A-frame.

Zoe stomped her feet. "Let's play cards," she said, "or Chinese Tag."

Brad looked at me. "It's too cold."

Willy said, "We could play indoors but we don't have enough people."

"What?" I asked. They explained about Chinese Tag, a game Madge Waverly had played at parties when she was young, an athletic spin-the-bottle: boys caught girls and kissed them, vice versa. "Well, why is it called Chinese?" I asked. Everyone looked confused. "It just is," Zoe said. She ironed out the details—ours would be intensive, no partners to switch. "I'll kiss Brad," she said, "no big problem. Willy, you kiss Louisa." He put his hand on my shoulder as we walked into the A-frame, big and cold like a church that sits empty all week and then they turn the heat on Sunday morning. "Also no big problem," Willy said about kissing me. I hoped I'd be good enough. The leftover chase element was that Zoe and I hid in the living room while Willy and Brad waited in the kitchen. "Yell when you're ready," Willy said. Two closets stood on either end of the sofa. We each took one. "Ready!" Zoe yelled, and Willy and Brad came in. A closet door opened. "Shit," Willy said, "my sister." He slammed it, moved on.

Then Willy opened my door and led me to the master bedroom—Madge and Bin's, I realized—and looked around for a blanket. My heart thumped, from nerves, or love. Our coats bulky around our arms and shoulders, we lay on top of the bedspread and knocked our boots to the floor. "Let me finish this," Willy said, because he was eating an Oreo, and he chewed fast, like when someone asks you a question at the table and your mouth is full. "I have braces," I apologized. He smiled. He kissed around my mouth, then on it. I gave up on the difference between nerves and love, and I remembered the dream of rocking with Brad in deep water I'd perfected by adding a bedroom where sunlight passed through square windows and voices murmured: a chorus fostering action, consequence. I opened my eyes—the windows white and frosty—then shut them again and thought of Brad's summer-colored skin, his silver hair. The lurching began, reciprocation. I fell. "Hey. Hey."

It was Willy, pulling me back.

"Careful," he said, but his eyes were glassy and the smell of his breath in my face was like seaweed, wet like the bottom of the lake, and he let himself go for a half-minute before he stopped. "Enough of that," he said, and he gave me a quick, plain kiss and led me by the hand to the trailer, where we made pizza and watched TV with his grandma. "Geesh," he said looking across the table at me. Me: I loved Brad now. I was sure. Willy smiled, ate pizza. Then Zoe and Brad came back, slamming doors, and everything changed.

Everything.

In ten days, it seemed.

I took a trip to California with my parents and Davie—Helen stayed at home to date John M. We went to meet Aunt Celise's fiancé, a divorced pilot with grown children. Their house had straw mats for rugs, indoor gardens with trees growing from the floor to ceiling. Aunt Celise kept *Jonathan Livingston Seagull* on the coffee table and listened to old music. She didn't like what the radio played now: "Every night I go downtown, looking for *tush*."

My mother and dad argued:

Him: You just can't make marriage a career anymore.

Her: Shhh. She is going back to nursing, after all.

They went to Las Vegas for two days—to rekindle the fire, Aunt Celise said—my mother in her pale green dress with white shoes, my dad in white shoes too, uneasy. They posed for a photo in front of a big horseshoe with a million dollars inside, under glass.

When I got home and talked to Zoe, she hated Brad already. "He's moving back to Chicago," she said. "My dad, who was kind enough to raise him, will give him a job if I say so." We were on the phone. "What did he do?" I asked. He was messy and rude. The inexactness of these offenses depressed me. The Waverlys, with their oblique family tree, prodigal where my family was thrifty—my alter-family, I spent half my time there—was undone, undoing it-self. Zoe said, "And it's weird but cool too, Willy loves you. He says, 'I'm hit, I'm hit.' " I said, "He said that?"

She said, "He did."

And Helen had landed John M. (I wondered: did he say "I'm hit, I'm hit"?) Zoe said, "She needed to be more hard to get." I noted she said *be* hard to get, not *play*. John M. was friends with Zoe's boyfriend, the potato heir, so they double-dated. Cheryl, in spite of the sheath from Wiggie's, was pregnant by Steve S., who was engaged to a virgin, and Steve S. was also friends with John M. and Zoe's boyfriend. "I feel bad for her," Helen said, "but she played with fire." Her official, public response. Zoe wasn't *not* my friend now but I shared her with Helen. Both of them were with me the night I got lewd knowledge, very important. How would you know a reputable drugstore if you didn't know Wiggie's? How would you know love if not for jangled nerves, lust? Eve (carved in pine), thick-waisted, standing next to a snake-wrapped tree, didn't know she was naked—she'd never heard of clothes. Some boys will ask you to prove love, my mother said: don't.

One night my parents went out of town and I was supposed to stay at Zoe's, though Helen—an adult now—could stay alone. Zoe had a date, so I offered to stay home with her grandma. But since John had declared himself (his title, "Helen's boyfriend," we only called him "John" to his face) my mother enlisted him, put him to work: "I'm sorry, John," she said, "but you'll have other nights with Helen. Drop Louisa at the Waverlys' at the same time as Zoe." She wanted to get me out of the house, available; like Granny on *The Beverly Hillbillies*, who worried about Elly May's marriage prospects, she worried I'd shown so little interest in boys, vice versa. My dad said to Helen: "Keep track of your little sister, Gooch." They drove away, Davie in the back seat. So we went to a party at the hunting camp, a double-date, me a fifth wheel. At the hunting camp, the drop cloth that hung over the door separating the bunkroom from the main hall—white fabric with swirly ferns, red berries—fell open and shut as people passed through it. "What are they doing?" Helen asked. "Wishful thinking," John M. said. Helen, Zoe, and I were the only females there.

Then Brad and his friends came in with a girl, her hair long and dark against her olive-colored jacket. A law of nature: no unpretty fifteen-year-old girls. No homely puppies but everywhere you look, ugly dogs. Because she seemed unattended, no date—like me—I felt connected, as if she were the twin I'd hoped for when I was little, someone on the other side of the planet where it's day when we have night, winter when we have summer, but her life a duplicate of mine, the same series of events, accidents. She was from Lampson. "Hey," someone said, a fat type whose dad owned the camp: "Who let the freaks in? If anyone smokes Wacky Tabacky here, I'll bust his head." So they left. I hadn't seen that happen yet. Given the size of Bremmer, its remoteness, invitations were moot, parties like old-fashioned bees: everyone welcome. No factions or gangs, Sharks or Jets. They talked about the girl.

Who was she with?

"Ha," the fat one said. "Everyone. She bangs them all."

Zoe said this wasn't true. "She goes steady with one of them."

"Well, they should have left her here," someone said. And the talk started—I can't remember, don't want to, its details, the precise expression of camaraderie by way of proposing gang rape. Or, in the local words for it, the train they'd pull, who'd get a turn, who wouldn't, who'd go first, who'd take—a phrase I've been unable to obliterate— sloppy seconds. "I'll take sloppy seconds," the fat one yelled. There *was* a girl from Lampson, someone said, that liked it, didn't have to be raped. At this point, Zoe's boyfriend and John M. said this kind of talk was wrong in front of ladies, theirs. Sexual mores: it showed disrespect to the potato heir and John M. by implying they didn't have courage enough to shut anyone up. "I want Louisa to go home," Helen said, tugging on John's arm. He agreed, the ratio unnerving.

I didn't understand.

The fat one said, "But that girl is gone. We should find another."

His eyes, other eyes, fell on me.

My mind forced pictures, a series of men a train, a girl below—a generic girl, not me, not anyone I knew—her limbs sloped out like railroad tracks leading to a specific stop. I knew, and I refused to know, they were considering me, all six of them. Could they tell, I wondered, that I'd kissed Danny Delgaddo and Willy, that I'd lusted for Brad? I had love's hunger? I also knew it had to do with groups, false, swaggering courage, six of them, one of me. "What about you?" I asked Helen as she handed me my coat.

"I'm fine, I'm with John," she said. "Besides, they're kidding."

"Then why do I have go?"

"Louisa, never mind," she said. She got a nice boy, her phrase, to drive me back. I don't remember being afraid. I only remember the weather—false April, more snow coming but the promise of spring—as we neared Bremmer and I broached safe topics: "Calling it an early night?" I asked.

"What? Oh. I'll probably head back out. I'm doing this as a favor to John." (Later Helen told me John had threatened him: you lay a hand on my girlfriend's sister, I'll kill you.) Another topic, he was graduating. We passed the water tower, his mark on it, his year, 1973. "Must be exciting," I said. He said, "Yes, I turn eighteen and get to go to the bars. Mike's Railroad's my favorite." We passed the Big Muskie Museum, the gates around it, the door on its pale underside. We passed the Gallery of Woodcarving. "Did you hear they're tearing the Chatterbox down?" he said. "First the whorehouse, now the strip joint. Where do you live?" I needed to go to Zoe's, I explained. I realized when I said it he'd be inconvenienced.

"Can't you stay in town?" he asked. I thought of the last time my parents were supposed to be gone and Zoe and I drank liquor in little glasses and tried on my mom's old formals. ("I can't believe she sewed these," Zoe had marveled. "She's really good." Zoe was taking Home Ec herself, also Bookkeeping, thinking it a good idea to keep close accounts.) My dad came home from the trip a day early, his face pale. "Your mother decided to stay at the hotel alone," he said. His glasses were broken right across the bow, one lens gone. I can't, when I try, imagine my mother hitting him. Another time I came home in the middle of the day and found them in bed. "We were a little cold," my mother said, her shoulders naked above the blanket. "We needed to warm up."

"I've got to go to the Waverlys'," I said. He didn't talk again, twenty miles. "Thank you, good night." I slammed the door. Slush spit on my legs when he drove away. I stood there and looked at the lit, cozy trailer with the grandma inside, the cathedral-shaped A-frame beside it, the lake in a thaw behind me, solid, shifting. Two headlights snaked up the road, a car stopped. Brad got out. "Please," I begged him, "go for a walk with me." We ended up on the boathouse roof in front of the cabin, my dream beginning: the deep lake, Brad beside me, his bedroom

not far away. The weather was wrong, that's all. We'd im-
provise.

I veered, moved nearer.

Brad said, "I liked it here." How sad, how quiet his voice
was.

Past tense: *liked* it here.

I started to cry, hating Zoe then for loving someone
new and not letting Brad go too, for manufacturing reasons, distance. "You're really going," I said, "back to
Chicago to live?" And I thought of all the events in a line,
my Aunt Celise wobbling, drunk, desperate for love to
start her life, my mother's shiny dresses and high hopes,
my dad's broken eyeglasses, the two Mrs. Waverlys, and
Mr. Waverly still sullen, hard-drinking, alone in a bar. And
Helen—though I didn't know it yet but how it fits—be-
trothed to John M. in two years, drunk at her engagement
party, her thin legs knocking together in the bathroom as
she slid against the sink. "I don't love him," she'd tell me.
"How is this happening?"

"Do you have a key?" Brad asked me. "Do you have a
key?"

I stopped crying.

"Please, you're making me nervous." So I told him about
the key under the mat, and we walked though the mud and
snow to get it, Brad patting me: there, he said, there. He
wanted to build a fire in the cabin's fireplace. I pointed at
Belle's house and said, "She might see the smoke and think
it's a bum and call the police." Then Brad told me about
the bums in Chicago, street people he called them. He'd
be one himself if Mr. Waverly wasn't so generous. We lit
the space heater instead and sat on the couch by the big
window. "I liked your dad so much," Brad said, "I did."

My mother in San Ardo, twenty years later: "Do you remember the year he bought the Depth Finder? You're supposed to use it to find fish and all he did was putter around
in a boat, looking for depth."

"They fight," I said, "my parents." I stared at the space

heater, the orange and blue flames under glass. "My hell," Aunt Celise always said, a way of toning down the curse word "hell" by making it small, personal. She'd taken Davie and me to Disneyland when we went to see her, all three of us uneasy at the high-tech of it, provincial and spooked. A lady hit Davie with her purse when he butted line for a ride called The World of Tomorrow.

Belle's yard light flicked on, then off, like she knew we were there, staring at the small fire. I leaned into Brad, sleepy, rallying for a last minute against the heaviness, my exhaustion, with a vision of trouble I'd reap if we didn't leave now. The rumors.

I remembered the health class lecture where we separated into rigid twos, boys, girls, and learned life's facts, quelled the folk tale one last time about sperm that lived for days on someone's pants leg then swam vigorously upstream, the poetry about menstruation boys were no doubt spared, *the weeping of a disappointed uterus.* Suddenly, in my mind's eye a red heart with white beads—a valentine, or a purse meant to match a fancy dress. Next I woke, my neck sore from the angle it bent to Brad's shoulder, and a dim, recent dream crowding my proximity to him: a Home Ec class where Helen and Zoe gave a presentation on the significance of purses, the right one doing for you what no other accessory can, and this flowed, bled, to a lecture about finance, the difference between stocks, bonds, CDs. Brad stood, rubbed his eyes, stumbled to the daybed in the alcove where I'd dreamed of him one hot night, and I put a blanket over us, my arms in my coat cramped as he reached around me and we settled, lay like spoons, our extremities (hands, feet, noses) cold. My summer dream, its stunted, lean fruit. Brad fell back asleep while new light passed through the window, a chilly winter sunrise, washing the room pale.

• • •

My night with Brad, the morning after as we skulked past Belle's window, down the road to the trailer, discussing briefly our corroboration, our alibi. "Nothing," Brad insisted, "we fell asleep in your cabin." I knew, though, the multifarious shades of gray between what really happened, truth, and what we should say, falsehood. "If we don't lie," I said, "they'll think the truth is worse than it is. I'll say I stayed in town." But Zoe had called Helen, and John drove her out to the trailer where all of them lay in wait: John, Helen, Zoe, Zoe's grandma. Helen's relief was simple, Zoe's grief complicated. Love, I saw, dies piece by piece. "You," Zoe said to me, her face red, taut. Also to Brad, "*You.*"

Brad's departure therefore hastened, he left to finish his last year of high school in Chicago, to enlist in the Coast Guard the next spring. Helen told on me, to my mother who didn't tell my dad—the shock would kill him, she said—so I got sent to an appointment with the minister, the one with embroidery on his jeans who'd had courses at the seminary in family counseling, a new twist. He didn't believe my version, the truth: nothing happened. But I didn't act chaste or outraged either, the heroine in a story of errors because, given the chance, I would have. I just didn't. "Do you love the boy?" he asked. Again and again I said yes, I loved my parents too, and Helen, Davie, Zoe, all the Waverlys.

Zoe and I fell apart, away. I took to my schoolbooks, my ability to make grades. I got my eyes tested and rejoiced at the verdict, glasses indicated. I ordered the only horn-rimmed pair available (wire-frames, the norm) and showed up in yearbook photos in strange clothes, for instance in front of a row of students who worked on the newspaper, me, the editor, wearing gym shoes, men's safari pants, Davie's plaid shirt, my hair pulled back tight.

Willy said, "What happened, you used to be, still could be, so cute?"

The next and last time I saw Brad—except I dream

about him still, a variation, let's face it, on the archetype of dreamboat who got away, my legend, my own big muskie—when I came back to Bremmer six years later in a Mercury Comet, my college boyfriend behind the wheel. I was reading a thick anthology, blue cloth-bound with silver-edged pages, *The World's Great Love Novels*, antique, collectible. A professor, a besotted, philandering type you find on campuses everywhere, gave it to me after class one day. "I thought of you when I saw it," he said. I nodded, flattered, uneasy. I was navigating my way through Camille's deathbed scene, her fainting, Armand's regrets, the explication of hypocrisy, when my boyfriend hit the brakes, down-shifted with a grind, and said, "Chrissake, where do these weird people come from?"

"Fudgies," I said, because the streets, bars, cafes were overrun. Lines queued. I thought of Camille, also Mary Magdalene, the first noble whore. Was her statue in the Gallery of Woodcarving? "Look," I said, because the Chatterbox and Depot Hotel were really gone, a city park in their place, a historic train engine in its center, a testimony to whores after all, their livelihood.

"And don't try so hard with my dad this time," I reminded my boyfriend, Tom, a city boy who, like Bin Waverly six years earlier, even Zoe, presumed the men here, with their flannel shirts, guns, life in the woods, were prototypical, mythic. He swaggered, initiated conversations about northwoods sports, and neither my dad or brother really liked him. "He's an asshole," Davie always said, "and he's going to ruin your perfectly good car."

We stopped at the gas station Davie had worked at ever since he was old enough, amassing huge savings for a high school student, at the same time, low grades, contempt for school. He nodded at Tom, gave me a hug with his wrists, hands splayed out, worried, I guess, about smearing grease. "I took the things I wanted," he said, "just some tools. You're supposed to pick up the key at Dad's car lot." I'd come home because the cabin was sold, property that needed to be divided in my parent's divorce, the deal about to close. I wanted mementos, some glassware, a blanket, a lamp. So we left the car at the gas station and walked down Main, bumping and nudging tourists. "I'd like to go to the Big Muskie Museum some time," Tom said, holding my hand because he loved me but also, I increasingly felt, he worried I'd get away. "Not me," I said. "And look at antique lures, motors for old boats?"

I saw Brad.

In front of the shiny Rexall Drug which sprawled over two or three lots now, took up most of one block, he stood with his long legs in washed-out jeans, hands in his pockets, hair close-cropped. I hesitated—what if it wasn't him?—then yelled his name. Next? (Like a Clairol commercial: "The closer he gets . . . ," slow motion throbbing as we loped nearer, near.) We stopped short. "You look . . ." I paused. "Great," I said, boiling over.

"You too," he said, "really." This was true. Done with my willful homeliness now—or it was in style, at any rate horn-rimmed glasses were—I wore a straw hat, cut-offs with a black tank swimsuit my boyfriend had helped select in a department store the week before by standing guard outside my dressing room, visibly approving, swelling up over, certain styles when I cracked the door. He walked up to Brad and me now. "Old home week," he said.

I introduced them.

I told Brad why we were in town—and to meet us at the cabin later.

We found two or three hired salesmen milling around the car lot, my dad alone in his office reading a book about primeval forests. He shut it and said, "Monkey, this makes me realize we human beings are a small dot in the big picture." He kissed me. "How's the car running?" He offered his puttery old boat to Tom. "No sense in letting it go to strangers," he said. "I don't have a place for it. I know you like fishing." Tom would have liked to like fishing—to date, he'd never been. "Thanks," I said. Dad was being sweet.

Later it got to be a joke, the boat. When Tom and I broke up, it sprung leaks and Tom almost went down, bailing.

When my mother drove the five hours to see me and say in person she was moving to San Ardo, California, with an auto parts distributor, my response was sensible—people get divorced, children adjust. My roommate, who had a Saab from her dad and a ruby pendant from her mother, said: "Really, it gets simpler. You get to know each of them separately—not a unit, parents." So I smiled, said, "Well, on to new vistas." But I hadn't expected my mother to seem so shallow, my dad so shadowy and deep. He handed me the key. "Of course there's one in the garage," he said. "Would you like to have dinner later?" And when we hesitated, made excuses—homework, jobs—because it sounded depressing, to eat and sink low, he said: "Yes, you kids go on. You have your lives."

Sometimes he talked about natural order, selection: "I've had my span," he'd say. "God's been fair enough." Like God was also Charles Darwin. But everyone rearranges God; Tom, for instance, calls marijuana "the Lord's weed." "Are we going to visit your sister?" Tom asked as we walked back to the gas station to get the car.

"No," I said, "she lives forty miles west." The last time I'd seen her, her first baby was born. Zoe also had a new baby, Helen said. She and John saw a lot of Zoe, her husband too. I'd seen Zoe once since I left, at a distance, in a plaid maternity dress stepping out of a 4-wheel-drive truck at the bank parking lot.

We drove out of town. Tom talked about John F. Kennedy, who was in the news again for new evidence of sexual prowess. ("He didn't have no bad back, I tell you," an old stripper named Blaze said.) I told Tom, "You don't want to stop at the bar he used the bathroom at—it's just a plaque above a urinal." Then I felt bad, having forgotten how earnest Tom's face looked one night when we first met and lay in bed after sex resplendent and beamy as firecrackers—our pillow talk—and he told me all Catholic boys grew up with JFK's profile an emblem, his example a measure. I moved across the seat next to him, turned music on, not the radio, radio limited and limiting now, no single station a pipeline to the national mood. I picked through our cassettes, options, choices. I hated disco, avoided the new, raw punk. I liked blues, big, muscular women vowing: "I ain't gonna be your sugar mama." And I watched the roadside, cattails, ponds, familiar landscape.

At the cabin I put pink china in a cardboard box, also a navy blue vase, the lamp with ferns on its base. Brad knocked on the door. He was on leave, vacationing at Bin Waverly's houses, the A-frame and trailer. "It's run down over there," he said, "no one to tend it for years. Pretty sad. Here too." He angled his head as he walked through low doorframes. I knew what he meant, our salad days gone. "Remember," he said, "we caught those fish and your dad cooked them on the grill." Tom said, "I'll leave you two here to reminisce. I've got a boat to load." He walked down to the lake while I stood next to Brad, thinking I had insight at last—that growing up is ceasing to see yourself outside, the trees, your trees; the sky, yours. A rock a table, a cave a home. You feather the nest inside four walls, that's all. I looked at the daybed where Brad and I had slept like storybook lovers once and surprised myself by wishing aloud I had room to take it.

Brad said, "Can you get away later?" He looked sideways at me.

I thought, how? Ride back with Tom, turn immediately around? Blurt the truth: I have always loved Brad and need this one night?

"When are you leaving?" I asked.

"Tomorrow." He put his cap on. "I hear about you from your Aunt Celise," he said. "I stay in touch with her through Madge Waverly."

I said, "You do?"

He said, "She wrote me a real nice letter when my mother died."

Aunt Celise—a nurse in the end, no stewardess—told me at Davie's wedding rehearsal years later how good it is to let your looks go, also that a nurse's real job is preparing everyone, survivors too, not just terminal patients, for death. I looked at Brad. "Another time," I said, "next time." We agreed. We hugged good-bye.

Late that afternoon, halfway back to the city where Tom and I went to college, he veered suddenly off the road by a sign that said PUBLIC ACCESS. He wanted to try the boat out. My dad had told him to take a fishing pole, a few lures. We slid the boat into water and rowed, no life jackets or license. I told Tom about game wardens, the $200 tickets they'd issue, and his resolve increased. So I sat staring at the boat bottom, thinking of a summer day years ago when it was covered with fish, their silver sides and sunny bellies glistening as they parched, writhed, forestalled slow and torturous death. But that wasn't an angle I'd considered when I was twelve, my brother next to me, Brad on the adjacent seat with Zoe's half-brother. We whooped each time we caught another—each one that perished in the boat bottom one more we wouldn't have to knock in the head with a stick when we cleaned it. Tom shouted at me to hand him a piece of tackle right now.

I did; then I picked up my blue-and-silver book. I was done with *Camille* and pushing forward into *Carmen*, Carmen swathing a wake of blood as she quested for the most brutish, violent mate. The strong contender is viable. Power is hard to measure: muscle, sometimes money. I looked at the table of contents, *Daisy Miller*, Turgenev's *First Love* in which—having read the last chapter first—I knew the smart-talking Zinaida would die. Consensus on great love, I decided, is like consensus on God, some elements static—God is omniscient, for example; great love unrequited. Tom cast clumsily. I lay back, dipped my toe in the lake, adjusted my straw hat and pictured Tom as my old-fashioned suitor, his cravat neat, his back straight as he pushed oars through glassy water, lily pads passing us by, yellow wisps of twilight overhead. He became a perfect lover and—since this is a love story about love stories—opened a picnic hamper, poured tea, his eyes ancient and tender as we spread napkins and dined. Then Tom cast his line and was just Tom, and me simply me, in a boat on top of deep water, rocking.

Crossroads Cafe

AT THIS TIME, I understood sex? No. I didn't drive a car either. I had rage. This got me places. Away from Jump River, where I'd graduated fifteenth out of twenty-nine. My dad cut timber. We kept chickens. Our furnace—which used to be in the church and they gave it to us when they got a new one—I kept going by scraping its wires with a knife. You don't know a furnace is out until you're cold. One teacher said, "You should learn a trade." She had thin yellow hair, like corn, a fat Norwegian face. I said, "Everyone should." She said, "True." She meant I needed to worse than my sister, Corrine, who painted pictures of birds, had a job at Super Valu and a boyfriend, Randy. She meant I was ugly and queer like, come to think of it, her.

Miss Stitt, her kilt skirt, her beige purse. Her eyes, close up. *There*, I thought, in the hazel and gold. When I was little, my dad, who was lonely, would take me on walks in the woods. "What does this say to you?" he'd ask, pointing at a rock. *I never got what I wanted.* Miss Stitt's eyes said that. Besides, because she told me what to do, I didn't. I moved to Menominee and got a job.

I answered an ad: Roommate Wanted. Above a bait shop by the tire factory and Smith's Go Get 'Em Bar. A guy answered the door who needed a bath. Beer cans everywhere. "A female," he said, yawning, rubbing his eyes. "What the hell. I need help with the bills."

I didn't take that.

I got my job when I pedaled my bike over the bridge to answer a different ad: Female Roommate, Quiet, Non-Smoking. The Crossroads Cafe sat at what used to be the bridge intersection before they started rebuilding. A sign in the window: HELP WANTED. Kristine, the owner, moved her black plastic glasses down her nose. "You'll do," she said, a German accent. I didn't know she was wearing a wig, only that her hair looked shiny as embroidery floss, black to match her glasses, her suit, and the wallpaper with its silhouettes of movie stars: Marlene Dietrich, Humphrey Bogart. The uniform she gave me was black with white triangles on the top and hips. "Good for the busts," she said, "No?"

I had it on when I rode my bike to Ella's, and she stood outside next to her pale blue convertible. She showed me the house. I had my things sent—doilies, painted teacups that belonged to my grandma. One that came from Dresden has a picture of a dog tearing a doll's arm off. And my clothes, homemade. The trouble with sewing is that by the time you try a dress on, you own it. I never look like the pattern picture, slender girls. Ella was in my room when my boxes came. She picked up a teacup, held it to her mouth. (You're not supposed to do that. It's for looks.) I had on my waitress suit. She said, "That is so bizarre." I said, "It's easy to wash." She said, "It makes you look like a voluptuous robot." My dress that's the color of mints they serve at funerals and has gathers, shirring, at the waist, Ella liked. It looks like how I am in my mind but not how I am. It fit me bad. "Keep it," I said. She looked pretty, like something in one of those gift shops with a sign on the wall: BREAK IT, IT'S YOURS.

What does Ella have besides money? Time. She paints her fingernails every Monday, Wednesday, Friday. If it was May, she'd dance around a pole. After I moved in she said, "This is the perfect day, Janet, for ice cream." We went on our bikes, mine with flat handlebars so I sat straight like a ramrod, which didn't seem odd until I saw Ella. "It's a racing bike," she said. It had thin tires, went fast. It tipped over when she jumped a curb. She landed on that crossbar which meant her bike was a *boy's*, not *girl's*. In the old days, see, boys wore pants. Girls never did.

Ella stood, the bike so light, bouncing. "Janet, I'm hurt. I'm bleeding," she said. I left her there and rode home to call her boyfriend, Ray Silka, no answer. So I drove Ella's car, slow, back to where she'd tipped. It's not like I can't. I don't want to. Drive. She drove the rest of the way, blood turning the back of her dress rusty. The doctor gave her a shot there. I sat at the other end, her head. He looked through half-glasses and stitched. "How long will it take to heal?" she asked. "Do you have a boyfriend?" he said. Ray Silka teaches band in Love's Peak, Illinois, but then he was just sending his résumé out. They have problems now but not then. "It's none of your business," I told the doctor, who frowned. "Abstain," he said, "until a scar forms."

One day we went to Appleton, the town where Ella grew up. On the way there, she pulled up next to a paper mill. We sat outside, watching gray sludge climbing a belt and landing in heaps. Ella said, "This unsettles me." Her parents were in Ireland. In winter, they go south. We had tinned shrimp and crackers. Wine, pink and red. Then we got dressed and went to the fair, Ella wearing a brown dress and jeweled combs in her hair. We went on a ride, a red cage swinging back and forth. We should have planned ahead. Ella's combs slid out of her hair, through the mesh of the red cage into the night. She hugged her dress to keep it from blowing up. My money fell out. On the way back to the parking lot, we walked past a car. Ella said, "Janet, look."

It had a hatchback window which was steamed up. I felt like I'd lifted a rock—all that sorry business underneath. A man's fat butt moving up and down. White skin that looked puffy and sick. Ella said, "They got carried away and couldn't wait." This was months ago. "Don't dawdle," I said. Because I'm a good roommate. For instance, this morning I cleaned the kitchen from last night's dinner, meatloaf. "I'll leave the pans to soak," Ella had said. If I cook she washes, but sometimes she puts it off.

Next I answered my sister's letter which came on the back of a card—people skating with stovepipe hats, furry muffs, ladies' skirts swelling like kites across the ice. I wrote, CORRINE, I WILL BE HOME AT CHRISTMAS, RIDING THE GREYHOUND. O.K.? My ink, blue-purple. Outside, the sun was behind clouds, the sky wet. Snow.

I turned a lamp on, and the phone rang.

It was Chuck. I imagined him with the receiver pressed to his face, his winter ski jacket, red and black, an arrow on his chest pointing down. But I was making pictures in my head. He wouldn't be wearing his dumb ski jacket on the phone. Maybe his white apron, its tag with his name in big letters, CHUCK. He said, "Janet, I thought you might like a ride to work." I met him at the meat counter at the store across the intersection from the cafe. I said, "No. But a ride home. That's possible." I got ready.

Cotton underclothes. Support hose. Uniform.

I put on my red coat with the big plastic buttons, my muffler and mittens. I walked to work, fifteen blocks swerving beside the river.

Gray and secret, the winter sky. Snow fell down. The cafe windows glowed yellow. I opened the door, heat. I'd been cold. Everything black-and-white again—the wall, floor, Kristine's hair and clothes. Her husband. Sometimes I went to the basement for ketchup or soup mix, and he was down there holding a match to his pipe, his hair black in the half-light, skin white like a root. She met him when he was in the Army—he'd looked like Clark Gable and brought her flowers. Now he hardly talks. "Good afternoon," Kristine said. "How is our poetess?" My glasses fogged.

"Janet is a poetess," Kristine told a lady at the counter. One day Kristine found a napkin I'd put words on: HER RAT-A-TAT FINGERS TAP. MOUTH A-GAPING. HARPSTRING HAIR UNFURLS. There was something about MORNING GLORIES too. It wasn't a poem. Kristine said, "Have chocolate or hot coffee, then begin working." I hung my coat in the kitchen while Joyce, the cook, hopped between the stove, pots boiling, and the grill, meat sizzling under a weight to keep it flat. You're not supposed to talk to Joyce. "Her life has become a wreck," Kristine said. "Exactly how, we don't know."

I served dinner to the old people, All U Can Eat. Not much, they pick like birds. One man wanted more dumplings, and Kristine said, "More? Hmmph. He should watch it." She gave him one. "Thank you." He was grateful. Then Kristine changed for dinner, which she always ate in the booth next to my station, her eyeglasses gone, her wig too, her hair long and red. She was wearing a sheer blouse with a black bra. In Germany they do that. Her husband was handsome, but then he'd smile. I served them, Kristine beaming at me from above her breasts—we don't dress like that here—and correcting me, one finger with its long nail on my wrist. "Janet, hold the plate like this. Civilized. Yes."

Her daughter came in, banging her keys against her leg.

Kristine said, "Tamara, see how nice Janet has her hairs. Held back by the rubber band, very sanitary, and curls on each side."

Tammy said, "Janet's *hair*."

Kristine said, "I wish you had her manners, or you vacuumed so good."

Tammy said, "Adopt her."

Hiram came into the cafe from the back. He lived in one of the rented rooms above the cafe. So did the dish-washer, Dennis. And Tammy. They all shared the bath-room at the end of the hall. Hiram had to have his larynx removed—something to do with World War II—and he talked holding a beige plastic box to his throat, his voice buzzing. Kristine's husband went home. I gave Hiram a menu, but he wanted to talk to Kristine, who slid across the room like a ship. "Hello," she patted his hand. Once they had a fight and she wouldn't tell me why. "His colos-sal nerve," she said finally. "What?" she asked Hiram now, bending to hear what he said into the box. They left, Hi-ram tottering, holding Kristine's arm.

I put the sign in the window, CLOSED. I plugged the vac-uum in. I said to Tammy, "I can't help what your mother said. I've always had nice hair." See, I love Kristine. Tammy I'm polite to. This is a favor. Then she snubs me. Because she has bad hair, a Lilt Home Wave. Mine is naturally curly. She knows that. "Where did you get your perm?" she asked. It pissed me off. Besides, words come out of me fast. I never know when they're about to. "From God," I said. (See what I mean?) "You're a bitch," I said, "and you probably have sex with Hiram." I switched the vacuum to Low Pile, and when I looked up Tammy was swinging the hose extension like a club. I might have hit her back.

But Kristine walked in. "Oh," she said, "Tamara. No." In the kitchen, Joyce slammed pans. "Why can't you be friends?" Kristine said, sitting in a booth, holding her head in her hands. "I had a friend, Giselle, I went to all the places with girls should. Please, I'll give you pin money to take Janet somewhere nice."

Tammy said, "What a bargain."

"Maybe Dennis too," Kristine said, thinking.

Dennis, the dishwasher, had a bad temper because he was lonely.

Tammy looked at the dishroom door, then at me. "Why

don't I take Joyce too?" she said. "And Hiram?" It was a joke. I could tell.

Not Kristine.

"No. Dennis tonight, alone," she said. "With Janet."

In the time it would take to tell Kristine I didn't want to go, I didn't want to spend Tammy's pin money, I could, I decided. And be home, sleeping. I called Ella from the kitchen phone. Joyce, the cook, watched from a dark corner, wearing her winter coat and hat, smoking a cigarette, her eyes shiny as the lit tip. "Hey," she said, "tough, huh?" When she says that she means work. Ella answered the phone: "Oh. I was hoping you'd be Ray. I won't wait up." Then I crossed the intersection, sawhorses, pipes, holes, piles. Snow too. Like crossing the woods, not a street. They didn't get the bridge done before winter. Business hurt. I went into Peter's Meats which also was doing bad, one customer. "Chuck," I said. He smiled, his face crinkling like a fold-out greeting card—like first he was the sun, and this was the sun shining.

I said, "I won't need you to drive."

He looked like Chuck again, plain.

I said, "I'm going somewhere with Tammy."

"Where?"

I should have asked that myself.

But I got mad. "M.Y.O.B.," I said.

Across the road, Tammy was waiting in her Dodge Charger, a car shaped like a wedge. "Aren't you going to change?" she asked. I looked at my uniform. "No." Then we went to Kmart because Tammy needed new pants. Once, when my dad wasn't around, Corrine and I drove his car forty-three miles through a snowstorm to the new Kmart in Bremmer. We almost went in the ditch. I love Kmart. Longs aisles with potholders, spark plugs, birdcages on one wall, hoses on another. All you'd ever need!

Four kinds of ice cream scoops! Twenty pairs of black pants! Tammy sawed the tag off hers as we walked back to her car. Her butt had a definite shape now, a wedge. I said, "Those pants make you look like your car."

She smiled, suspicious. "Thanks."

We went to her boyfriend's house, and inside were Sam, Rick, and Jerry. Tammy's boyfriend was Jerry. Either Sam or Rick looked like the guy who lived above Smith's Go Get 'Em Bar where I'd answered the ad for a roommate and he said, "A female, what the hell." But men, they all look the same from a distance. "Dennis will meet us here," Tammy said. A carburetor, which is what ignites a motor, was laying in pieces on the table. "Hey, chicks," Sam or Rick said. Tammy stood in front of Jerry, lifted her elbows, turned—showing him her pants. Sam or Rick gave me a beer. "You a waitress?" he asked, pointing at my uniform. My glasses fogged. "A poetess," I said. I don't know what I thought he'd say back. He said, "Have a good time," and walked away.

Dennis came through the back door. He stalks in small circles—it has to do with being lonely. "Evening," he said, stalking. He looked at me. "You want to go for a ride in a car I built from scratch?" We were under a bare light bulb. "No." In the living room, something tipped. The music got loud, a sound like traffic pushing past. Whoosh. The lights dimmed. Dennis stalked to the living room door. "Figures," he said, "the dirty deed."

I thought of shovels and gravel.

"Dirty deed?" I said.

I looked through the door. I expected to see something, but not Tammy kissing Jerry, who was sitting down, and Sam or Rick in a shirt that said MOTOCROSS rubbing her from behind. The other Sam or Rick was touching himself. All of them moving together like a big machine, running. But rough. I took my glasses off. I put them back on. "Stop," I said like I was yelling. The song ended.

"What?" Tammy said.

Dennis said, "Let's blow." We went outside and got in his car.

"Who would have thought Tammy was such a dog?" I said, strapping myself in. The car revved and stalled. Did I have a defect, I wondered, that made me see things bad, evil? The blower sent hot air to my face. "Turn it off," I said, unbuttoning my coat.

Dennis said, "I've got a veritable bar in the back seat." I turned around and looked at a box with bottlenecks sticking out. "Schnapps," he said, "has a nice mint taste like toothpaste." Laying on the seat next to it was a magazine called *Jugs*. On the cover a woman held her breasts like they might fall. I thought of how I'd staked my tomato plants once, and autumn came and the tomatoes got big, but stayed green. My dad took the stakes out. "They ain't going to be ready 'til you let them drop," he said. I tried to picture a naked woman that wasn't a picture, but real. Real breasts. All I could think of was my own. Dennis parked the car. "This place is called the Top of the World," he said. He pinched me.

"Quit that," I said.

He shoved his hand between my legs, through my support hose. He yanked on my uniform and the front zipper popped, the streetlight shining on my white bra. "You've ruined my waitress suit," I said. A knot in my chest, like poison, leaked out my eyes, burning and freezing. I jerked the door open. I forgot my muffler and mittens. I ran. Dennis followed, the car chugging in first.

"Janet," he said, "I'll take you home now."

"Go to hell, Chuck or Rick," I said, confused. "You son of a bitch. Dennis. Alien." I walked, pulling my coat on. He drove away.

The stars were icy, seeping light.

The sky. What was behind it?

I pictured Miss Stitt like a signal or planet, her eyes flickering. *Life is a dirt sandwich*, my mother used to say. It's all I remember about her besides that she smelled like rain. I walked to town. A truck pulled over, and the driver said, "Are you exercising or do you need a lift?" His headlights flashed, making my glasses white disks. My hair slid out of the rubber band. My bun fell. "And throw myself out of the pan, into the fire?" I said. "I'm really not interested," he answered. Pulling away.

I opened the door and Ella sat on the couch reading *Leisure*, a magazine. A Christmas tree lay on its side, the red-and-green metal stand in pieces beside it. "Janet," she said, "what happened?" Because I'd slammed the door. *My hairs.* My hair was on my shoulders. "The dishwasher ruined my zipper," I said, opening my coat. My uniform gaped. My bra gleamed. "I lost my mittens."

Ella said, "The dishwasher ruined your zipper?"

"Dennis," I said. "And my support hose, four dollars a pair."

"The dishwasher attacked you?" She was wearing a yellow kimono. "Four dollars is the least of your worries. You can't keep walking home." She'd been saying this since the days got short.

I try to ignore the weather—low clouds, sun flat and gray as a dime. "This wouldn't happen in Jump River," I said. It could, though.

Think.

The doorbell rang. Ella said, "That must be Ray."

But it was Chuck, wearing his red-and-black ski jacket, his apron dangling below like a skirt. He said, "I wondered if you got home."

I looked down at my uniform, wrecked.

Ella said, "The man who washes the dishes attacked her."

I put the afghan over my shoulders.

Chuck said, "I thought you were with Tammy."

"Dennis gave me a lift," I said.

He said, "Until we find you a car, you ride home with me."

"What a deal," I said. Thinking of his name: *Chuck*.

He sat down, his apron hanging to the floor between his knees. "Janet," he said, "I'd like to drive you home for Christmas. And meet your family. Then you won't have to ride the bus."

"Go to hell," I said.

"Goodness," Ella said. "You must be distraught."

Chuck's face went stiff, a permanent smile.

"She must be distraught," Ella said.

It pissed me off. I looked for a way to say so, an excuse—some gap, dent, flaw. "You're not using a damn coaster," I told Ella.

She smiled, pale. "Maybe I should fix you a nice cup of tea."

"I'll get it myself."

I put the kettle on. It made that humming noise, water boiling. Ella whispered to Chuck: "Maybe she doesn't want you to meet them—they're a little odd." The kettle blew. "A broken home," she said. I walked back into the living room. "Yes," I said, "first the roof fell down. Then we couldn't keep the walls up."

Ella blushed.

"You're acting like a freak," I said.

She said, "I'm sorry, I had a bad day."

"Then you need a cup of tea." I handed her mine.

Chuck touched my arm. "You're sweet."

"Hell," I said. I turned to Ella. "What kind of bad day?"

She has a beauty mark above her mouth. "Oh, nothing," she said. Her skin is milky—you can see through it, blue veins. "Waiting for hours is all. What for? What's he doing," she said, "Ray?"

• • •

I rode the Greyhound, stopping for every town. LAMP-SON. BREMMER. By COUDERAY, the bus was almost empty. A man got on, looked up and down, then sat by me. I smelled his Vitalis, his Juicy Fruit. Hard luck. *Diffa, Dorfa, Flecka, Blah*, that's how his talk sounded to me. Two ex-wives. His beautiful daughters, Sarah and Diane, did I want to see their photos? He visited them as often as dead men see daylight. He was coming back for their love now. Would they let him have it? The bus stopped in JUMP RIVER, and he grabbed my suitcase. "Give you a hand," he said. I yanked it back. "Give yourself a hand." The colored pencils I'd bought Corrine for Christmas but hadn't wrapped yet fell out of my suitcase, rolling, making music on the depot floor. "Scram," I said.

Corrine was waiting. "Was that your boyfriend?" She frowned.

"Ugh." I picked up pencils.

She shrugged. We got in her car. She drove me down the snowy road to home, the trees peaky and blue-colored. "Dad isn't around," she said. "But we'll celebrate Christmas Eve tonight anyway." She parked in the barn. I went to the chicken coop where the water pan was frozen over. I said, "For Chrissake, Corrine. Everything's going to hell. You're going to have dead chickens."

She said, "They're not dead—notice." And went inside.

I decided to rig it, to fix it. I found a Styrofoam ice chest and cut a square hole in its lid so the water pan could hang down. I poked a hole for the cord and put a light bulb inside. Right away the light bulb got hot and melted the ice. Too many watts.

Corrine came outside. "Telephone," she said. "Your roommate."

My roommate. What did Ella want? The house smelled like fuel oil. I held the black phone to my head. Ella said, "I'm at a pay phone in Jump River." She started crying, making a noise like wheels spinning. "I can't get ahold of

Ray," she said. "My parents are in the Bahamas for Christmas. I don't have anywhere to go."

Corrine was making a venison roast with gravy.

"Come on," I said. I gave Ella directions.

I set up the cot in my room. I scrubbed the floor. Outside, snow bloomed down. Ella pulled up in her pale blue convertible with its matching ragtop. Even the hubcaps matched. I went outside. She stomped her boots with the fur tops and said, "My car was so cold. I had to scrape ice off the inside of the windshield."

We went inside.

"It's sweet here," she said. "Where'd you get the doilies?"

Corrine, stirring gravy, said, "I make them," and smiled.

We dressed for church. Corrine backed the car out of the barn. I checked the Styrofoam thing-a-ma-jig, and the water was fine, cool. We were going to early service so Corrine could go to Randy's afterwards. We sat in the front seat, Corrine driving, Ella in the middle with a sparkly scarf, a *fascinator*, under her chin. All of a sudden, Corrine pulled onto a gravel road and underneath a beer sign, the Ponderosa Bar. "What the hell?" I said.

Corrine said, "I want to get Dad so we can take him to church, then you bring him home and feed him. She's not so bad, Janet."

"Who?" She meant Merilee Croft, though. "Things get rotten fast here," I said, slamming my door. "Next you'll invite *her*. Next we'll have Christmas dinner at the dump." We went inside, and Merilee Croft was leaning against the knotty pine bar, her fleshy hips and breasts floating loose under her dress. "Merry Christmas," she said. There was one person at the bar—an Indian in a camouflage cap. "He's not here," I told Corrine. "Let's go."

Ella was looking at stags' heads, the mounted fish. She went to a display table and picked up one of the necklaces Merilee sells.

"Put it down," I said. "It's filthy. It's deer turds."

Merilee said, "Each one's been baked, then painted."

Ella said, "You mean these are deer turds strung together?"

Merilee said, "I've got silver ones too. It keeps me busy."

"Not busy enough," I said.

Corrine said, "Hush. Merilee, where's Dad?"

Merilee said, "Take a look-see. Doomsday trumpets couldn't raise him." She pulled back the curtain that separated the bar from her living room. My dad was in a heap of blankets on the couch. She had ugly things on the walls too—a calendar with pictures of tools. A shelf with empty perfume bottles. Jars of pickles.

"Come on," I said. I yanked his arm. He slid out of bed, bare-chested. On his pants was a wet spot the size of a coffee saucer.

Think.

Merilee, who was behind me, bent over—her knees creaked—and covered him. "He's an old man," she said. "Leave him." He groped at her legs through her dress. "One thing's for sure though," she said. "When he's sober I don't have to ask him twice."

I walked through the bar. Outside.

Ella said, "We can still go to church."

Corrine said, "Janet, tell Ella about the nativity pageant." I didn't. I got in the car. Corrine said, "Well, one year I was Mary, and Janet was a Wise Man. They used my doll for the baby Jesus."

I said, "A plastic doll with ratty hair. Forget it, I'm not going."

So we dropped Corrine at Randy's parents. She walked up the sidewalk shoveled down to where the snow was packed, the heels on her shoes—she'd spent eight dollars for them at Payless Shoe Source—poking holes. Inside the window, the Christmas tree lights blinked, red, white, red. "I hate Randy's family," I told Ella as I slid to the driver's seat. "Thinking they're high-class."

I drove home, slow. I went around the driveway loop, letting the car slide. Ella put her feet against the dash. I slammed the brakes. Inside, the furnace was out. I fixed it. We ate. We got ready for bed, Ella winding a music box. "Poor Janet," she said.

"Poor nothing," I said. "I always act like this here."

"It's good you moved away then."

I couldn't tell how she meant it.

She said, "It's not a criticism."

I sat in front of a table Corrine had made into a vanity by tacking on skirts. The ballerina in the music box twirled, Tra la, Flowers in Spring. I took the bobby pins out, and my hair fell. I brushed, a hundred strokes, with Ella behind me, and for a minute we blurred, my hair a dark cloud, Ella pretty as a pink-and-white cup. And I thought of Kristine's face, a secret behind square glasses, and Miss Stitt's eyes like wandering stars. And my mother—I must have stood beside her once as she brushed her hair, elbows angling, her face as sad as ditchwater. Something prickled.

Ella.

"Your hair"—she touched it—"is lovely."

"What happened with Ray?" I asked finally.

She sighed. "First he said he wouldn't marry me because his brother was divorced. Now he won't marry me, period. Janet, remember that day we went swimming, and my swimsuit top came down, and Ray tripped over a rock trying to pull it back up? I think things like this over," she said, "and wonder if I would have acted different, like a lady, if he'd marry me now. Do you remember?"

Yes.

Another time she was wearing a short, yellow dress. I was laying on the floor watching TV. "Oops," she said, stepping over me.

I'd kept my eyes stuck to the TV.

"I wish it was simple," she said. "Like I'd catch him with a slut."

"Don't wish that," I said.

Ella lay on the cot beside me. I pulled my blankets

around snug. I thought of the empty house. The blackness of darkness. Dumb with silence, the ticking clocks. I closed my eyes, imagined a window. Moonlight through icicles hanging on eaves. Ella rising from water. *Blue skies with birds singing. Singing,* I thought. Like a poem. Not exactly. *I wanted to be there with my mouth.*

I came through the back door into the steamy kitchen. Around my neck, my muffler was wet with breath. Joyce hopped, a cigarette in her mouth. I punched the time clock. "You picked a bad day to come back," she said. "Shit is flying into the fan around here, yes sir. But it's not my place to say so." She threw a pepper steak on the grill. I hung up my coat and went into the dining room. Hiram sat at the counter. He said something into his plastic box. *Buzz.* "What?" I asked. He waved his hands near his chest. "I'm so sad," he said. "I can barely eat."

Joyce rang the bell in the kitchen. Hot food. A pepper steak.

Hiram's.

Too sad, my foot. I set the plate down. Then I saw Kristine in the black vinyl booth next to my station, holding her head in her hands. "Kristine, what?" I hung my towel in my apron pocket and sat down. She blew her nose, shoved the Kleenex up her sleeve. "Tammy is P.G.," she said. "This would never happen in Germany."

The cafe was almost empty.

She said, "The doctor already knows it's twins. Have you seen perambulators for twins? So strange. Flat and broad. Wide, deformed."

Hiram was speaking.

"Just a moment." Kristine walked across the room and held her head near Hiram's throat. And nodded. "Janet," she said, "will you please help Hiram with his bedsheets? He is—" she walked back across the room and whispered—"incontinent. This too would never happen in Germany because people take care of their own."

Hiram and I wobbled down the hall, up the creaking steps. He talked the whole way about mothballs. "What about mothballs?" I asked, rolling his bedsheets into a bundle. We passed an open door, Tammy's room. A teddy bear in a T-shirt. An unmade bed. I pictured Tammy's face, which looked like her father's except on him—his moustache, dark eyes—it looked good. Was it here? Her limp hair, her naked shoulders? Then I remembered Jerry's house, motor parts on the coffee table. Sam. Rick. Jerry. Not here. There.

Or in her car.

I dropped Hiram's bedsheets into the laundry sack. In the dining room, Kristine was spraying tables with ammonia. *God is soap*, she said once, *hot water, forgiveness.* "My husband is with Jerry," she said now, "planning a marriage. He is the father, yes?"

I pictured Sam and Rick in tuxedos. Can twins have separate fathers?

"I guess," I told Kristine.

She said, "I'm going to eat a hard-cooked egg and go home."

A new dishwasher came to work.

"At Christmas," Joyce said, "Dennis vamoosed. No notice."

Then it was rush hour and old people came for chicken and dumplings, a couple of servings. Also hot coffee and strudel. Afterward, I carried plates to the dishroom. I vacuumed, and the kitchen phone rang. It was Ella, who'd been crying about Ray Silka. "Janet," she said, "Chuck called. I told him you were working. But if you don't mind, could you come straight home tonight? I'll pick you up." I looked at the jars of tomatoes on the shelf, remembering the day Joyce stewed them, the way they fell apart in water. "O.K." I said. I put the CLOSED sign in the window.

Across the street, cutting meat, Chuck.

What would I say if he called?

No thank you.

I polished flatware, my white cloth bobbing. I remembered my mother's good silverware in its mahogany box—she didn't take it with her when she left. When Corrine and I were little, we'd pretended spoons were round-faced women, their flared handles like old-time skirts. They walked across the table and had conversations with men, knives, the sharp, blank blades their faces. We ate applesauce and mashed potatoes then—spoons were reliable. But someday we'd need knives, also forks, short-haired boys.

Ella parked in front of the cafe.

The graters and plows stood silent. When the bridge was done—everyone said so—business would boom. But this was hard to picture. Ever since I'd been here, the corner was out, traffic stalled. Across the way, Peter's Meats was locking up. I got into Ella's car. She said, "Thanks. Sorry I made you come home." I said, "It's fine." She pulled up in front of our house. Inside, she said, "Ray and I broke up. He went back to Love's Peak."

"Broke up?" I said.

She nodded.

I said, "It's about time." But I didn't know what I meant. That Ray was mean? It was a good decision? What decision? I got ready for bed, tucking myself in. Sometimes, before I sleep, I see pictures. For instance, I saw big, gray piles. Iron filings, I think. Children sat on top. Across the pit where they'd dug the iron from, men and women were having arguments, and it was none of the children's business. But what could the children do except wait? Next I saw the wallpaper from the cafe. Black, white. Boys, girls. Ella. In my room. She said, "Can I sleep here?"

I sat up.

She said, "Move over. I'm cold."

She got in, her back toward me, elbow under her head. I could smell her nightgown. And I remembered how Corrine's boyfriend, Randy, told me about queers—we were smoking cigarettes behind the barn. Sometimes, he said, men love men. Girls love girls. I'd thought it was a story. Lately I read in a magazine, *Glamour*, that people touch themselves. (Myself! I thought. Why not kiss myself?) I'd showed it to Ella, who said "Healthy" and "Self-esteem" and even this: "It's good to know yourself so that you can communicate with your lover." Then I couldn't sleep, smelling Ella, thinking about how Joyce, the cook, got new bedsheets for Christmas and had to exchange them for plain white because the stripes made her dizzy. At the end of my arms, my hands felt like giants.

Next there was loud rapping at the door.

Ella sat up. "What's that?" And fell back down.

I shoved my glasses on, went to the door. Chuck.

He said, "I stopped by because the lights were on."

He was talking about a car. "A Plymouth, he said, "a fair price. I can lend you the money." I put my mouth over his, making his words smothered and flat. I unbuckled, unzipped. Arranged his clothes this way, that way. Lifted up my nightgown. *Horsepower*, I thought. *Friction. Steam heat.* I bent over backwards. My glasses slid off. I rode him, see? I remembered Christmas Eve, the spiky pines, icicles hanging from eaves. And Ella. *I never got what I wanted.* I never wanted to be alone either. "You're crying," Chuck said. I shivered. What else?

Royal Blues

I WAS SITTING in the backyard with Raoul and Big Daddy drinking gin and lime when I saw that life as I knew it was about to change. If my weeping willow story has a first line, beyond *I was born into misery thirty-six years ago*, then this is it. I was in a lawn chair. The voices of the two children Raoul and I (by some miracle) had produced tinkled like silver. For good measure, I yelled, "Travis, don't break anything. Honey, quit that bad habit this instant." I was having two thoughts, one specific. The way Walter "Guitar" Dumas, who is the best blues player in Wisconsin and the star of Raoul's band, had looked at me when I was wearing jeans so tight you could bounce a Ping-Pong ball off them. I'm a big woman. The second thought, constant and repeating, a song: *I'm a fraction of myself, You won't take all of me.*

Raoul once said, "Toni, I love you more than I can say." A long time ago, before we became man and wife through thickness and through thin. Then he said, a few years later: "It's none of your business how late I come home," or "I don't give a damn about the toilet seat. You want it down, put it down." It wasn't hard—not a supreme affliction like I could have mastered. I prayed to God, also Mary, who'd been inseminated by a bird and then married Joseph, who had the bad taste to ask who she'd been with. I admired them for making a test to match my weakness, the big ordeal so infinitesimal that my life with Raoul seemed like a quiet room in hell. A switch involves shattering. A rip. Gin helps.

I marked time, noted the loggy smell of a breeze skitting across the river, the unkempt trees, mustard blossoms on the edge of the yard. Big Daddy was telling about how his mother and dad couldn't live in the same house and saved their marriage by buying a duplex. He's a talker. Give him two drinks and an audience and his expression changes, his posture. On bended knee, he told us how his father moved out of the house the first time, crying, blowing his nose in a blue-and-white hankie, going into the children's bedroom to hold the little clothes in his hands and weep. This was 1935. "But then," Big Daddy said, "we started going to restaurants, the movies. Mother and Dad called each other Dear. He moved back just to move out. We bought the duplex."

Honey, who was seven, said, "I like the 'Love in a Duplex' story."

"Because it has kids in it," Big Daddy said. People call him that because he's wise, also the oldest customer at the Idle Wild. Raoul's band is named for him, Big Daddy and the Roadhogs, though Big Daddy isn't in it for any reason but to shout "Take it away!" "Sing that thing!" Or strum an electric guitar that's unplugged.

Next Travis threw his kickball on the hood of Raoul's car, and Raoul hollered that he'd throw a rock at Travis's bike and dump it in the river. This was how Raoul kept discipline, making it clear that revenge exceeds the foul-up. Even when he was playing with the kids, which is to say lying on his back and letting them poke him or throw the dog's ball so she had to leap over him to fetch it, he sounded like one of them, but bigger: "We watched Mr.

Toot yesterday, Bonehead, so we're watching Ironsides to-day." Or getting on Honey's case because she took up too much room on the couch and yelled, "Mom, Dad's kicking me. I was here first." When I'd mention to women I worked with or drank with my fear that nothing would ever change, the unlucky ones told their own stories, worse, he hit her or spent the money. Some said, "You knew what you were getting into." Still, the sense that my time with Raoul was past and my arousal about to begin came in a flash with rumblings: a car door slammed, four people trudged up the driveway. The car was Tramp Cleveland's ambulance, which he drives because it's big enough to carry his drums.

Tramp was the first person.

The second was Janet, wearing a poncho and a man's hat, carrying Walter's two guitar cases, one on each side. Walter was pulling up the rear. A woman was with him I knew I wouldn't like. It turns out I'd already met her—I didn't remember, too drunk.

Have you ever been high in a swing, pumping hard and coming down so fast your stomach lags behind? It felt like that except that what I left in the wild blue as I descended was my womb, which seemed at the time like a hive of swarming bees. Walter smiled.

He was Janet's lover. Mine, he would be.

He had his eye on the other one too. Big Daddy said, "Let's play."

In twelve years with Raoul, I'd had one infidelity. I de-served it. Raoul had his. I didn't confess mine, though I did once tell Raoul I'd kissed someone I hadn't if only be-cause we were in the car on the way to a Sunday afternoon pig roast, and Travis was a babe in arms. It seemed like a condition, bad weather, that no man would be interested in me again, whereas Raoul, good-looking in that half-

French way, and conspicuous because he was always behind a microphone, made it clear he'd had offers.

I said, "Well, I kissed Peter."

Peter is a blond man who makes iron swivel poles to
hang windsocks on so they blow hard no matter how much
the wind shifts. Since he doesn't make money this way, he's
also a carpenter. The Northwoods Arts Catalogue won't
let him advertise the poles because it's for arts not crafts. I
told Peter he needed to engrave the poles, put a lep-
rechaun or a frog on top, and he said, miffed, "That's not
my genre." He has big lips, very pink. I'm sure that's why I
chose him for "man I kissed" because there's nothing else
about him besides his straight teeth. He's neat but frumpy,
dragging a comb though his frizzy hair, worrying his belt
won't match his Pocket-T. Later, after I'd split with Walter,
I get ahead of myself, Peter had this plan to introduce
himself as a suitor out of Walter's league but willing.

What he said was, leaning across the table at a restaurant: "Ever since I saw you in that dress that looks like
cobwebs, singing 'Empty Bed Blues,' I knew you were for
me." I'd been singing with Walter at the Idle Wild on
Tuesday Is Bluesday ever since he'd heard me singing with
records around the house and called me Intonia, Queen of
the Blues. I haven't sung since. Peter went on to say that
he'd be a good lover in every way I could imagine, but he
couldn't compete with Walter in the contest of . . .

"Well . . ." He spread his hands on the table. "Size."

I was eating a sandwich. I choked. "What?"

He explained that once he'd been on a canoe trip with
Walter and everyone had gone swimming naked. Peter
said, "I'm not built like that." As though length and
breadth was a measure of what Walter had. Peter later
made the same pitch to Janet with the same qualification,
he wasn't built like that, though he explained the circumstances by which he'd seen Walter's dick differently. He'd
gone to smoke pot with Walter on a hot day and Walter

answered the door naked. "I'm not built like that," Peter said.

I don't understand Walter. He has long, black hair and a beard shaped like a spade. A man in a bar in Minnesota once said, "You're as ugly as sin." And Walter unraveled some of his whiskers and said, "But I have the longest side-burns you've ever seen." Once I was washing dishes and told him to take money out of my pocket to buy ham-burger for dinner and he put his hand in, passed the money by, squeezed *me* and said, "I feel the riches."

But the day I told Raoul I'd kissed Peter, though I hadn't, we were getting out of the car at the pig roast. I was reach-ing for the diaper bag and Raoul was opening the trunk to get his guitar. Peter waved. Raoul sniggered. This is the only time I've ever used the word *sniggered*. Raoul said, "You can do better than that if you hold out." He went to talk to Tammy, a woman who wears a bandanna on her head, leather pants, and low-cut blouses.

I took my vow, adultery. Once.

I thought of it as money I'd spend with an eye to making the occasion memorable—like saving the cash relatives send you for First Communion to buy a watch or ring so you have something to show for it other than six nights at the roller-rink and a new lipstick. I looked at men. I should have hung a sign out, Now Taking Applications. I had anx-iety unlike any except the kind I had when my granny gave me $600 to buy a washer and dryer and it took me two years to decide what model. But Raoul made my decision regarding who and when automatic. He left. Four days later he wanted to come home. His band wasn't booked and he'd been lonely in the bachelor pad he was sharing with Tramp Cleveland. I knew he missed the attention—a small throng of women rushing a small stage—and I told him we'd wait until the morning after the next gig to dis-cuss the conditions of his return.

I called Elton, who's been my best friend since sixth

grade—he doesn't even live here now, he moved to Alabama. He invited me to a party at the Unitarian Church so I assumed it was a church party. This was my first mistake: the Unitarian Church had rented their basement to the ACLU for a fund-raiser. What I thought of the ACLU when I found this out—on the way there—was that it was for high-brows, and I hoped they had parties worth the price of a babysitter. Elton had told me that people would be wearing costumes so I was dressed like Dale Evans in a white hat and red dress with wagon wheels. I tried not to think of Raoul. I met that woman I knew I wouldn't like— though I've never remembered, too drunk—and shook her hand. "Pleased, I'm sure."

This is what she tells me.

I gazed through the black air in which cigarette smoke made curling, ghostly spirals. That was the theme of the party Elton hadn't explained: black and white. Everyone wore black and white, and drank champagne from Spain called Negro. The bottles were black, the champagne white, sparkly. They served it at the Sunday School tables. The other splash of color in the room besides my red dress was the beaks on the penguins, yellow. There were nine women dressed as penguins. I said, "Well, they look like a softball team. That big one looks like Suzie Crusoe." I must have been talking loud because Elton said, "Shh, it is a softball team. You've seen them play. That is Suzie Crusoe."

"Oh, the lesbian team," I said suddenly. They came into focus. Once I'd seen them just plain whip the team from the Idle Wild.

Elton said, "Gay. People say gay now, Toni."

I felt bad. I work hard at being polite. Elton said, "Shh." That's the last thing I remember well, though I stayed for hours. I danced with Suzie Crusoe, who recognized me from high school, and I was sorry about saying she was a lesbian instead of gay, though she didn't know that. I danced several dances. At one point her girlfriend ("lover," Elton said) joined us. So there were the three of us. Then

Elton joined us in his black-and-white tuxedo, his hair slicked back like a vampire. Elton was the only person I knew well and I looked around and got that circling-down feeling, like a bird, that feeling I get from drinking. I told myself to account for it. Under those strobe lights, I was steamy. My dress throbbed. The music wasn't that good. After that I met Louisa, shook her hand. "Pleased, I'm sure."

Next I was lying in a bed of leaves, and the moon was white, tree branches faint veins across it. Elton said, "Get up. For Christ's sake, Toni. I'm not Hercules." He pulled on my arm and I went to cooperate, to throw my weight that way. I dragged him down.

Next we were in a tunnel—the eye of a needle.

"Big gold thread coming this way," I said.

Elton said, "That's your yardlight. We're almost there."

It was the end of autumn.

I dropped my purse. There was snow in the night. I brushed it back in the morning to find my hairbrush and wallet in the driveway.

The headache. Aspirin. The desire for a cold, sweet drink. Travis and Honey leaning across the bed more excited than worried to see, not Raoul, not my half-empty bed containing me, Raoul missing. But Elton. Honey, in her white pajamas with the red hearts, jumped up and down, up and down, jogging my stomach and Elton's, though I don't know if he was queasy. "It's company," Honey said. "Travis, we have company. Uncle Elton is here."

Elton's vampire hair was sticking up like a rooster's.

"A rooster doesn't have hair," he said.

The babysitter was asleep on the couch.

Elton was naked except for socks. "You passed out," he said. "Not before—like Sleeping Beauty. And not after. But during."

I said, "Have you noticed how red your lips get if you have a hangover?"

He said, "You broke the light on the living room ceiling."

I remembered. The babysitter had been watching, smiling. I'd said, "Good to be home." I kicked my shoes off. And the glass shards rained down and lay like stones on the living room floor.

"I cleaned it up," Elton said. Then he got dressed to take the babysitter home. He stepped into his magenta underwear carefully, his skin with the beauty marks stretching tight across his bones. I'd only been with Raoul. I explained this to Elton. The changes I make are safe, reversible. Then I reverse them so they're not changes. "Besides," I said, "I've been with you now." He picked up his car keys and shook his head, but he was laughing.

Elton came back from returning the babysitter that morning and we ate breakfast. We took Travis and Honey for a ride, going north, upriver, to a place where it wasn't still and muddy but fast and white, especially with winter coming, water falling like ice over the falls, onto rocks, black and sharp. I shivered, remembering the dozen people who'd been said to die in that water. We drove to Menominee, to Show Biz Pizza. It didn't feel different that day, but like any Sunday Raoul would watch football and I'd call Elton and he'd come by and, before we left—Elton and me and the kids—Elton would walk in the living room and shake Raoul's hand. Raoul would jump up, tuck his shirt in, and say, "How're you doing, man." They'd both say this and shake, shake their hands. It was Honey, wise as Big Daddy, who said about the handshake: "Enough already. I think we get the idea."

When we got back the sun was setting and the light I'd left on in the kitchen shone through the windows like eyes, the house waiting up for us. "We should have stew for supper," I said as the car doors slammed. But no one was hungry. When Travis and Honey were in bed, this feeling I get twenty-four hours after I drink—say I started to get drunk at eleven o'clock Saturday morning, well, I'd get depressed by eleven o'clock Sunday, no matter what. This feeling started, part guilt, part fear about how far I'd gone. I missed Raoul. What, exactly? That I knew him well, what he looked like, what color his underwear was bound to be. I was lying with my head in Elton's lap, him playing with my hair, giving me the shivers. "Blow on me," I said, meaning blow on my skin and make me shiver more. We were watching TV, the two stations you get out here. One was showing a documentary on people in comas, the other a movie about a woman in hostess pajamas who had to admit to her husband and children she was a drunk. I looked at the broken light fixture. "Whoa," I said. Like: woe.

Elton patted me on the butt. "You better get some sleep," he said. He kissed me good-bye on the back porch that always smells like mice and the LP gas tank. I stood there, hand on my hip, a big woman as I've said. I wondered if we were having an affair.

Of course Raoul came home right after that and I didn't hold him to anything, conditions of his return, but the first day he was back the van from Ferg's Flower Shop pulled into the driveway; we were in the kitchen. It was the morning after one of Raoul's gigs. He was eating Cheerios, his post-Cheerios Alka-Seltzer fizzing itself out in a highball glass next to his bowl. I saw the boy coming up the sidewalk with the tissue-paper sheaf, and thought, Flowers from an Unknown. My heart unhinged. Raoul was turning over an old leaf (Toni, I love you more than I can say). Or Elton had refused to cede in the contest for me. Which is saying there'd been one. But when I got the envelope open and found out the flowers were from my granny who keeps a Hallmark book with everyone's birthday in it except she's got them down wrong, I was disappointed: "Happy Birthday, Antonia, Love, Granny."

Honey was standing in the doorway. "Are they from El-ton?" she said.

I looked at Raoul. "No."

Raoul kept eating.

I put them in a vase. Four days later I took a job as a fry cook.

The only job I've ever had was frying—chicken, corn-dogs, fish. At the A & W. I'd rather be a waitress or bar-tender, something where you'd learn interpersonal skills and go on to a better job. But now that Honey and Travis were school-age, and Raoul a husband who came and went without marking it on the calendar and didn't notice if someone, anyone, sent his wife flowers, I needed diver-sion. It used to be—Raoul working at night, home in the day—fun. Chinese checkers, ham sandwiches. Sex on the floor. But now he played solitaire in his bathrobe wearing headphones, okay, but I hate that tin sound that overflows from headphones. I also took the job because when I was on the verge of telling Mr. Tip I'd think it over as he walked me through the kitchen to the back door, I saw Suzie Crusoe in an apron and a chef's hat, standing there with a spoon. "Hey, Toni," she said, and then to Mr. Tip: "If you're thinking of hiring Antonia, you're doing the right thing." So I took the job because of that. Raoul said, "You told me you'd never fry again."

It was like the words my cousin and I had used when we were teenagers and first heard of sex: fry, singe. Also the word for sex so powerful it left a mark: to burn. I'd been brave, burning with Raoul, whereas my cousin had just singed. To Raoul, I said, "I'll leave that up to God." He said, "Whether to take a job at the Tip Town?" I didn't an-swer. At work, everyone talked about sex.

I fried potatoes and fish, minced vegetables for the other cooks, men all of them, except Suzie, and they'd ask me how often I made love, how good was I, like that. I kept my answers short, good-natured. "They like you," Suzie said. About Mr. Tip, she explained he used to date most women he hired and then had personnel problems and took Valium. But now he'd lost thirty pounds and had grown his hair into a ponytail—not casual and sloppy like Raoul's or Tramp Cleveland's, but gelled and styled. And he was careful not to fraternize with the female help, so careful he seemed rude. "You're so womanly," Suzie said, "he can't let his guard down at all." We were in the kitchen when she said this, and a cook swung a rope of sausage in a suggestive way.

I arranged for my regular babysitter to stay over Saturdays so I could go out late and she'd be there in the morning. Her boyfriend came too and I noticed the difference between them and us—they were glad to have the privacy to sit on the couch and hold hands. Of course Raoul wasn't in love with me now, that fades. But neither was he running with a woman, I thought, nor—it follows—interested in privacy. But in publicity. In being somewhere where people listened when he said how stressful it was to be a musician, also that you could draw a parallel between Rome before it fell and the United States now, enamored of bad music.

One Saturday night at the end of my shift, I was waiting for Suzie, sitting at the bar with Big Daddy, Elton, and Peter. Elton was in the habit of waiting for me then, also Peter, who'd done carpenter work for Mr. Tip and was taking it out in trade. Mr. Tip had drawn me aside to say that if I curled my hair and wore a bra, I could bartend. "I am wearing a bra," I blurted, shocked. Suzie walked out of the kitchen then. "I thought you'd put sexual harassment behind you," she said to Mr. Tip, who blushed and disappeared. We stayed for another hour. I wasn't used to thinking about my looks but sometimes, by accident, I had to. "What did he mean?" I said, looking at my breasts but thinking of my hair, how I'd slept with sponge rollers in. Peter said, "They hang lower on you than most women." Big Daddy said, "You're built like a brick shithouse. A buxom woman is never out of fashion."

Suzie said, "Actually, buxom women have been out of fashion in many eras. That's why we have anorexia. But Toni looks fine."

Peter said, "In a big way."

Elton sat there.

We went riding in the car—on a maze of backroads, Elton driving, frost sparkling in the ditch. I sat next to him. "Are you all right?" he asked me once, above the din of Suzie yelling at Big Daddy, and Peter telling the both of them to hush. "Why?" I said. But I was blue, like a streak of light fading.

Was a change coming?

Elton cleared his throat: "Have you talked to Raoul?"

We pulled into the parking lot at the Idle Wild. "Have I talked to Raoul about what?" Someone punched someone. Suzie and Big Daddy bickered their way to the front door. Peter was peeing and lighting a cigarette at the same time. Elton said, "The old flame."

I said, "Twelve years old." I thought he meant Raoul's and mine.

"Coals," Elton said. He's a sucker for that, the right word.

I went inside and Suzie called me a prick-tease. "Not that women are responsible to pricks," she said, "but I feel for him." She was breaking up with her girlfriend. "Elton," she said. I looked for him while Suzie talked about the phases of love. In the morning, I remembered only bits and pieces of her speech—too noisy, people talking, Raoul singing, Walter stretching his strings. "Love is economics and religion combined," Suzie said. "You pay. One lover loves the other more," she added, "never equally."

She took me down to the river . . .

Raoul sang this, but the guitar, Walter's. Erasing, easing.

"Love is acute when it departs." *Her hair shone like gold in the hot morning sun.* "To note power is to exert it," Suzie said.

I drank gin.

"Throw yourself at his feet."

I considered it. All the magazines, *Reader's Digest*, *Woman's World*, and every talk show you see now, say that women should take the initiative. I should go to Elton. That was the plan, also the hitch. I couldn't. Raoul's sister, who's four years older than Raoul, remembers her childhood as when she wanted hats like Jackie Kennedy's, and Raoul remembers his as being so angry he broke things, windows, jaws, six washers at the Washateria once. That's how they still are, but adapted—Raoul's sister to a soap opera star's fashion statement now, and Raoul to this day still breaking rules. And me, a coward but loyal to an old idea: a woman in a fairy tale, sleeping, locked up. Flat on my back—at the most hanging my hair down a wall to facilitate entrance. The hero's reward. I'd adapted too, neither Raoul nor Elton much like a prince, and me—I held my hand to my hair, considered my low-hanging breasts—no Rapunzel, but a well-fed queen.

I went to say this to Suzie, that patience was a female virtue. The band went on break and the jukebox kicked in with its hard pulse. The bar looked more than ever strange, the stage empty and the gray cinder blocks revealed, smoke circling the shoulders and heads of patrons thronging, the bartenders mysterious and athletic. All of it reminded me of the bar scene in *Star Wars* where they stop off for a drink between planets and it looks like every bar I've ever been in, and the creatures look like *my* drinking friends. Big Daddy. Tramp Cleveland. Peter. Tammy in her bandanna and black leather pants. Janet sitting on the edge of the stage in her striped poncho and man's hat, rubbing Walter's sleek Stratocaster with a rag. Over the heads of drink-seekers, Suzie gestured. I couldn't tell what she was saying, something about Elton. The smoke-eater above my head crackled.

I thought it was Elton behind me.

I prepared myself for entrance. Let love slide through my mouth.

My hand gave me away, fluttering like it was wired until it rested in a hand behind me. The jukebox thudded. Suzie yelled, "Stop."

I turned.

Walter in a purple jumpsuit with a long zipper squeezed my hand.

He's burly, but not tall.

He looked at my jeans, the way they stretched. I shifted my weight. My hips rolled. "That," Walter said, "is the seat of power."

I pulled my hand away and—just like in adult fairy tales, Harlequin Romances—it smarted as though battery acid had spilled where Walter touched me. Suzie was saying, "Elton's gone, I tell you." Walter's brown eyes shone like copper. Suzie dragged me away. "He's got nerve," she said, "going around in that jumpsuit with the hole in the crotch, like to say he's uncontainable."

Then Suzie, Big Daddy, and I went outside to mill around while Peter and Janet smoked a joint under the light pole. Across the lot, we saw Tramp Cleveland's ambulance, muted lights glowing through the paisley curtains in the back window. Big Daddy said, "Well, I wonder." Suzie went home. Big Daddy and I wandered over and he rapped on the double doors. "Yoohoo," he said, "it's us." We heard scraping and shifting noises, tap-tap. Something closed. Tramp Cleveland let us in. "Come aboard," he said.

Raoul nodded at me, sniffed, pinched his nose and looked at his fingers. He'd been doing coke. Tammy sat next to him, her brown hair under the bandanna wiry as a scouring pad, that pointed nose, those thin hips with as much curve as a scrap of eggshell.

Tramp said, "How are you, Lady." He calls me that.

Big Daddy settled in. I gave Tammy the evil eye. When no one said anything, Big Daddy rambled. "As I was saying, it's a cliché, but largely true too . . ." Raoul interrupted him. "Oh, shut up. You never said anything in your life that wasn't a cliché." This is unlike Raoul, who has great patience for Big Daddy, though the reasons why are dim. "Furthermore," Raoul said, "why lead off with 'As I was saying' when, for the first time ever, you weren't—*saying*, that is, jawing. Silence is golden."

"That's a cliché too." Tramp said this.

We went inside and I thought about how I'd have to go through Raoul's pockets now when he passed out, which is hard, given, first, that he passes out less when he does coke and, second, I feel like a bitch. But the idea of my rent money going to pay for Tammy's bills, her habit, her low-cut blouses, made me mad. The band cranked up and I danced with Big Daddy. Remember, Walter played with B.B. King once. I know this, I have pictures. I moved around the dance floor like one of those big turbines you see in movies, steam blowing out my top, my hips and feet thrashing what got in my way. Cigarette butts. Barstools. "Anger is aphrodisiac," Big Daddy yelled. Everything he says isn't trite. "I could lift a car," I yelled back. Walter pulled strings, slid a bottleneck down them. The right pressure, pleasure.

He ran me down, his eyes headlights.

I'm going to Kansas City, they got some pretty big women there . . .

At the end of the night, Janet packed up Walter's guitars while he stood on stage. Tammy wandered over: "How about a nightcap?" she asked Raoul. She jerked her head at me. "She can come too." Raoul put his arm around me and said, "We have to take the babysitter home." We didn't, of course—she was spending the night. "Right," Tammy said, "and they're the light of your life."

"Who?" Raoul said, when she left.

We went outside. "Honey and Travis," I said, "the light of our lives."

This was February.

The car wheezed and turned over.

The stars were bright and hard. Raoul scraped the windshield. I tried to imagine sunshine, sweet and sticky, like honey.

B ut first there was the spring, rain leaking through the seams in my boots, no matter what boots, how much I paid for them.

"Give it the boots."

This was Suzie's plan. She said it about my marriage of course, also the things I hang on my walls: a calendar with a photo of Dale Evans, a coconut shell painted to look like a lizard.

We were having coffee in that hour after the school bus drops the kids off but it's still too early to eat, too early to shut the curtains because it's light out, but inside the lamps glow. Honey was counting the *M*s on her report card—*M*, a high grade standing for Most of the Time as opposed to *S* for Some of the Time, or just plain *N*. Travis was watching cartoons. Raoul had walked through with a brown-and-white cowboy shirt on a hanger, like he meant to iron it. "Is that an eyesore or what?" Suzie said. I couldn't tell if she meant Raoul's shirt or a vase shaped like a woman's head she'd just picked up and set down. Then Raoul wasn't there anymore. We noticed it a few hours later.

"Where did Raoul go?" I asked.

Honey said, "To work."

I said, "Daddy doesn't have a job, sweetheart."

She said, "I mean he went to play songs." But it was the wrong night.

Suzie said to Travis, "Do you know where your dad went?"

He didn't answer. It could be his fifth time through the same TV show, and you'd yell "Fire!" and he wouldn't budge. When I finally got his attention and asked, "Did

Dad say where he was going?" he looked up but stared past me. He scuffed his shoe. "No."

It turns out Raoul was at Tramp Cleveland's. He came back for his things a little at a time. A change of clothes first, a deck of cards and frying pan next, his tool box and fishing pole later.

"Of course," I said, "where else?" He'd gone to Tramp Cleveland's last time. But this time he didn't want to come home. "Why?" I said. I was sitting on Tramp's couch. I'd hurried through the door and plopped down still wearing my coat, my boots leaking on the floor. I was sitting on my purse, which hurt. I surprised myself by starting to cry. Tramp walked past in a sweatsuit that made him look thin. He had a rag and a can of Pledge and was moving things around, magazines and ashtrays, dusting.

Raoul said, "Well, I was watching *Donahue*, and a marriage counselor said if a couple can't compromise they should split up."

"No one said *that*," I said. "Besides we don't argue. How can we compromise?"

"A counselor on the same show," Raoul said, "said that couples who don't argue—they're the ones whose marriage is over."

I hit him with a newspaper. "We either argue or we don't," I said. "You can't have it both ways." When I left, I said, "You don't have to have a reason." I meant it sarcastically—a zinger.

Call me rash. Suzie did later. I drove to Elton's.

I pulled over and yanked the emergency on. I'd parked two blocks from his house. I started to go back to move the car, then turned around and kept going. I clumped onto the porch—a Victorian house with cupolas—and knocked. When the door opened, I rushed in, making puddles, swinging my purse. "It's over," I said.

An old lady in a white sweater said, "What is, dear?" She led me to the kitchen and gave me some juice. Elton, who was on the phone, waved at me, then frowned. He hung up and said, "Toni, you remember my parents." He was introducing me to the lady, also a man in a Pendleton shirt who was walking around with his hands in his pockets, whistling. "They're here for a visit."

"Yes," I said. "We met once."

Elton's mother said, "You got Elton drunk in church."

I turned red. I didn't know what she was talking about.

Elton said, "She means graduation, Toni. Remember?"

I remembered three things. A song playing on the radio that day about a line to toe. The frosty, round feel of the bottle's neck in my mouth as I tipped it back. The sweet smell of my skin in the hot sun. We'd been parked by the lake, sitting on the roof of Elton's car. Later, when I sat in my cap and gown in his mother's kitchen while Elton showered and changed, I'd blurted something. She was doing dishes, making conversation. She didn't like me. I'd always seen her at a distance in a crisp dress, a striped marketing basket on her arm. What I'd said, *I wish you were my mother*, was stupid, since I had Granny and—at the time, though she's dead now—Raoul's mom, who was nice to me. Elton walked in, his hair slicked back. "What's going on?" he said. No one answered. Later, during the ceremony, he snored. I nudged him when it was time to stand up and get his diploma.

"It wasn't church," Elton said. "It was graduation."

"It was church," his mother said. "I remember the robes and praying."

Elton shrugged.

"It wasn't church," I said. "I could never be drunk in church."

Elton said, "Toni's traditional. She has vestigial religion."

His mother looked interested. "What did you say when you came through the door, dear?"

I hesitated. "I came to tell Elton I'm getting a divorce."

"You are?" Elton said.

His mother's face turned pale. "Are there children?" she asked. Before I could answer—Yes, Travis, Honey, the light of our lives—she started to cry. "The world," she said, fumbling in the sleeve of her sweater for a Kleenex, "has changed so much."

Elton frowned.

"It'll be okay," I said, patting her shoulder.

She said, "In my day, no one divorced. Marriage today, I tell Elton, is perilous. I want him to come to Alabama—we live there because of our asthma. But Elton stays here because of his girlfriend."

"She isn't my girlfriend," Elton said.

"That was her on the phone," his mother said, "begging him to stay."

"She's active in the ACLU," he said. "I've helped with fund-raising."

Elton's father cleared his throat. "Seems to me if you have so much money you don't need a Civil Liberties Union here. People just sitting around waiting for something unjust to happen. What good's a Civil Liberties Union if no one's got a lawsuit?"

Elton's mother said, "I'm sure there's an ACLU in Alabama."

Elton walked me to the door.

"Do I know her?"

He said, "She's not my girlfriend."

I said, "You're going to Alabama?"

"I don't know," he said. "Maybe."

When I got home, Suzie was watching TV with the kids—I'd left her there to tend them. Janet had dropped by. "She's having a bad day," Suzie explained. "Things are going poorly with Walter and you know how it is—slim pickings. If you break up with someone around here, it's years before you get laid again."

I thought this must be especially true for Suzie—living in the northernmost part of a wild, cold state. I said, "Are those women on the softball team the only gays here?

Don't you want to live in a city?" I tried to picture myself in one. I couldn't.

"They're probably not the only ones," Suzie said. "I met them through Elton when a friend of mine, Michelle, had a lawsuit."

I didn't pursue it. I'd heard enough about the ACLU. "I don't remember Michelle," I said. "You had those penguin suits on."

Suzie said, "You love someone because they're available."

Janet looked sad—like a TV Indian in her striped poncho.

"I think Tramp Cleveland would be a good choice," I told her. "He could use love, home cooking. He's thin." She perked up.

Suzie said, "You have to work tonight, Toni."

Honey, who'd been listening, said, "You better take a nap, Mom."

I went into the bedroom where the March sunset bled through the lace curtains. A plant that hung near the window—too cold—and at the same time near the floor furnace—too hot—was withered and gray, dusted with residue from the LP flame. I burrowed under the quilt. In the next room, Suzie read "Aschenputtel" to Honey, a German version of "Cinderella" she found more suited to Honey's development, less negative, with better role models. I plumped up the spare pillow next to my torso, something I'd begun doing since Raoul left to get used to the size of the bed without him. I fell into sleep, cold like snow. I dreamed I was in a box, a dungeon, and to survive meant not to spend, my body a country, each colony staggering to contribute, not to squander. But creaking and tapping, someone wanted in.

Suzie, Travis, and Honey stood in my door.

I sat up. The room was dark, the sun gone, light from the hall angling in.

I said, "What?"

Time for work.

• • •

The night before Easter, at midnight, after fry-cooking at Tip Town, I pulled into the yard and found Raoul. We sat in the living room, and he asked me, sweet, to make a ham the next day, potato soup, peach pie. Easter is important to Raoul because his dad left his mother for a woman named Effie Swanger on Easter Sunday, 1969. I let my mind wander. To where I'd be able to get a ham on short notice. To what Raoul's mother made for dinner in 1969. How long would Raoul stay? Did I want him? Was repairing a sprung marriage for the sake of the children smart? Months passed.

Mother's Day.

Father's Day.

Memorial Day. A picnic with ants. Raoul snapping at Travis, at Honey who won't take it: "Get an Alka-Seltzer and pipe down."

A hot day in July. Travis mad at his dad, cursing, kicking. Honey stringing dandelion chains. Big Daddy going on, "Blue skies . . ."

Honey: "I like the 'Love in a Duplex' story."

Big Daddy, wise: "It has kids in it."

I drank gin. Tramp Cleveland said, "Lady, you should try quinine."

"It sounds like poison," I said. I made eyes at Walter.

Tramp introduced me to the woman I thought I didn't know and wouldn't like. "Have you met Louisa? She writes for the *North Tribune*."

"Pleased, I'm sure."

"We've met," she said, "at an ACLU party. You had to leave."

"Something came up," I said. Thinking this: the urge to lie in a bed of oak leaves in moonlight and topple Elton. Raoul stopped playing his guitar and looked at me, eyes narrow and bored.

Tramp Cleveland's drumsticks were in Janet's purse.

Big Daddy said, "The blues are ancient."

Louisa, who wanted to write an article for the paper, said, "The blues celebrate poverty—they make the best of limited means."

"Like making straw into gold," I said. I was thinking of "Rumplestiltskin," the captive princess, the miracle of *inner resources*. I held my glass to the light. My ice cube was beautiful—the clear block and, inside, the starburst of caught air.

Tramp said, "Who rented the house up the road?"

I smiled at Walter.

And Travis said the most complicated thing he ever did. "You better go ahead and tell everyone, Dad," he said, "about Tammy."

I opened the door of Tramp Cleveland's ambulance where Walter was alone, smoking a joint. I took him to the river. He said once, making love to me on a table in a deserted greenhouse by the lake, "The heart is a muscle." I opened his mouth, his hands. "I wondered when you'd get here," he said. "Finish me off."

"You blew it," Suzie said, sitting in my kitchen. "That one night at the Idle Wild—and Elton gave up." Honey was making a cup of tea. "I wasn't there," she said, "but looking back, I'm not sure Elton was right for Mom. He's so little and she's big."

Suzie said, "That shouldn't make a difference."

"Maybe not." Honey sipped tea.

I said, "What do you have against Walter?"

Suzie said, "Does he have speech skills? Can he talk?"

"Of course," I said. Walter talked about the blues. About the collapse of civilization, the need to build shelters, stockpile real wealth and preserve our teeth. Also about *Mad Max*. Of course he didn't follow this advice—he was concerned with a good meal and sleeping. I told him that the end of the world wasn't about scrap metal and guns, but trumpets. The earth cracks open. Lava spills. The souls of the dead float on a red tide. I repeated this conversation to Suzie, who said, "That's sick."

My granny, on the other hand, was unaffected. She'd ask Walter to do the chores Raoul always had—testing antifreeze, lighting the pilot light. Travis said: "I think Granny thinks Walter is Dad." He asked her, "Granny, do you know the difference between Walter and Dad?" She said, "Walter is short."

"That's better than I can do," Suzie said.

But there were differences between Walter and Raoul.

You could see it in the way Walter held a long note with one finger.

The other difference was that Suzie liked Raoul now. So did I. It couldn't have been easy living with a woman addicted to coke. I'd drive by and see him in the yard with Tammy—they lived in that house a mile down the road—and she'd be wearing a bathrobe, clutching the lapels at her throat with one hand, flailing with the other, Raoul leaning against his car like he was ready to go. "She makes him feel alive." Big Daddy said this.

"Celibacy is sensible," Suzie said.

Raoul walked in to pick up Travis and Honey for a visit. "Right," he said, "I saw that on *Oprah Winfrey*." When he came back for his things the last time he didn't go into the kids' rooms and hold their clothes and cry. But he went through the photo albums so he could have a few snapshots, and he fumbled with the adhesive paper, got the snapshots he wanted, then went in the next room and shut the door. I heard him—blowing his nose—and looked at my photo albums, snapshots gone, white space, gaps.

The only photo of me that year, I clipped from the newspaper. I'd been singing with records around the house until, by habit, I got the timing right on "Empty Bed Blues." I sang it at the Idle Wild.

I never had an empty bed 'til I met you.

I'm wearing a black dress with a neck I converted to a *V* by pinching its folds into a brooch to make my cleavage deep. Walter told me to think of the song, not the audience, and I stood there with a row of light bulbs from the hardware store mounted on a two-by-four glaring in my face. I felt transparent like an ant farm, like a pane of glass. ("Is a soul the same thing as a ghost?" Honey asked after she went to Sunday School.) I fixed my eyes on Peter and thought for the umpteenth time of his beautiful mouth wasted on an otherwise irredeemable mind and body. The flash went off. The caption read: Queen of the Blues.

At the annual pig roast, I had Peter install one of his swiveling poles. He said, "It's a good investment, Toni. In a year, you'll want to use an emery cloth on the ball and socket, but if you do routine maintenance like that, I guarantee it'll last."

"Great," I said. "Now I need a windsock."

Suzie said, "I have one."

Peter said, "Let me put a pole in your yard too. Louisa would like that." He leered. I've never used the word *leer* before.

We sat there, Suzie and Louisa on the fold-out end of the chaise lounge. Suzie said, "You'll have to ask Louisa yourself what she likes. You could put a pole at her place." It was Suzie's way of saying Louisa wasn't her lover and hadn't ever been.

"I get it," Peter said. "You like Toni."

Suzie said, "Christ." She walked away.

Louisa said, "Does everyone have someone they went to bed with, and they spend the rest of their life regretting it?" She moved her chair away from Peter, away from the fire, into the cold.

Walter came out of the house with Travis and Honey, who were spending the weekend with Raoul. Raoul pulled into the yard. Travis and Honey kissed me. Raoul kissed me on the cheek, Tammy watching.

I found Suzie in the woods. She explained that when she made friends with a woman, people sometimes thought she had ulterior motives. Peter always had ulterior motives, so he thought everyone did. "It's sad," she said when we got back to the yard, "but Peter's motive isn't sex." No one was there. "He doesn't have friends," she said. There were slabs of meat gone from the pig and you could tell that someone, hungry, had eaten it raw. We found Peter on the couch, his arms around a pillow. I noticed for the first time he had freckles. "Hey," Suzie said, gently. When he woke, she said, "Get up, you bag of shit, you're drooling."

Big Daddy was outside by the water.

I thought of my granny, of Raoul's dad before he died, neither of them hard to have around—mixed up, but not sad like Big Daddy, who cried when Raoul and I told him we were getting a divorce.

"Did you eat?" I asked Big Daddy.

"I lose my appetite," he said. "Everyone's at the bar."

Suzie drove Big Daddy and Peter home.

I threw plastic over the pig. It was lying above a pit of coals on a bedspring we used for a grate—it gleamed tough and shiny where the meat was gone. I remembered Walter and I making love in the greenhouse, when he said: the heart is a muscle. I'd based the future on that, the idea that my heart needed exercise, strenuous love. Walter, I thought, riding through thorns and sand, to take me away. I repeated what he'd said (the heart, the heart) to Suzie, who said, "Okay, so you're in love. You're doing quotable quotes now." But what Walter meant was that the heart was a muscle which pumped blood to extremities and when it stopped we'd die. He didn't have a plan. He didn't think that far ahead with an apocalypse coming, his apocalypse after all a projection—Walter with his bad liver, sure the world was failing fast.

Tramp Cleveland's ambulance pulled in the yard. I heard them—laughing, drunk. I went inside to put the rest of the food away. Tramp and Janet drove off. Walter and Louisa came in the door.

"Did we miss dinner?" Louisa said, nibbling lettuce.

I slammed cupboard doors.

Walter said, "Smoke a joint. Sit down."

I stayed in the kitchen.

I heard Louisa say: "Is she mad?"

I pictured Walter, blowing smoke. "No."

Louisa, drunk, said, "She doesn't think I want to sleep with you?"

I walked in. Louisa saw me. Walter didn't. He said, "Will you?"

I got rid of him. Around 5:00 A.M. I was sitting in the kitchen with Louisa. "I have a hangover," she said, "and I didn't have fun getting drunk." The phone rang. Walter was calling—in case someone wanted him, he said. No one did. I thought about the time we'd spent together, mostly in bed. A hot place. "He didn't mean anything," Louisa said, talking about Walter.

A week later I was in front of the bar at Tip Town, and I saw my face in the mirror behind the tiered bottles. I startled myself, finding an expression I recognized but resisted—the same look I'd seen in my granny's face when she was younger but not young, and in photographs of my mother, who's dead. I was pale. My expression? Forbearance. A face I wouldn't have claimed but a face, after all, Elton and Walter had made a pitch for. It wasn't the girl Raoul had wrangled with on a truck seat, not even the woman he'd reached across the bed for. Hell, it's dark in bed. We never turned the light on. I looked past the liquor bottles—brandy, whiskey, gin, Triple Sec, Galliano, schnapps. Behind my reflection—the restaurant dining room, the snowy field of tablecloths, the picture windows overlooking the gray, frozen lake.

The other day, folded into a quilt and sleeping, I got that shifting feeling, the floor going out. If I was with someone, not alone, they'd tell me it was a dream, the world was holding fast.

I headed to the kitchen to fry.

Chicken wings.

Smelt. Which is a tiny fish the men go to Lake Superior for, standing in cold water after sunset, dragging the deep, carrying the silver buckets home. I was cutting the heads off, and the guts out, saving the meat. I decided to change the way I looked. I walked out to the bar carrying my cleaver. Mr. Tip, who was on a bar stool reading a TimeLife book about space aliens and high on Valium, said, "Toni, don't come out here looking like that."

I said, "I want the name of the guy who does your hair." Mr. Tip looked at himself in the mirror, his sculpted forelock and ponytail. He scowled. But he wrote the name down.

"Thanks," I said. "I'm going to get one of those bras that'll make my breasts look like missiles, and I want out of the kitchen."

This inspired Suzie to suggest to Mr. Tip that he turn the management over to her. So we went through a personnel shift that involved hiring a few new good-looking cooks. They had qualifications too. Suzie hired Michelle, her friend from the softball team, to make desserts— Baked Alaska, bread pudding. Peter took over fry cooking, though he didn't have experience. Travis, who was thirteen in November, cleared tables and washed dishes. I cut my hair. I bought a new bra and a red dress. I went to work tottering on heels across the snowy parking lot, but I had boots in case of car trouble. I went inside, put quarters in the jukebox, and played a Cyndi Lauper song my granny likes because (I don't understand) it reminds her of the Vienna Boys' Choir. I looked in the mirror—my hair flowed down over one eye. Peter walked in. "Hey, *trés* sexy," he said, "like Veronica Lake."

"Except more buxom." This was Suzie.

They went outside because Suzie had decided to re-landscape using windsock poles. They couldn't wait until spring so they were out there, the temperature fifteen below, screwing brackets into deck partitions so that Tip Town—sitting on the tip of a point that juts in the lake—would look like a castle, surrounded by swiveling windsocks, puffed wide open, each of them, by blustery wind.

The door opened—Michelle, our dessert chef. She headed to the kitchen. And Louisa, who drank plum wine at the bar on weekends. "God," she said, her hair crackling with electricity as she pulled her beret off. "Winter is so long it makes me gloomy."

I was thinking of fairy tales—the princess who sets out to make the beast docile. And that one princess—what's she supposed to do with the straw she spun into gold when she was locked up? Or that princess whose father gave her away for a leafy vegetable, and she weeps on the prince and her tears heal him? The womb, I think, gets confused with the heart, with inner resources. We give it away. I thought of Elton, his letter from Selma, Alabama, where he's taking care of a lawsuit and counter-lawsuit, helping a man who's both a plaintiff and defendant, Selma a prison town with lots of injustice. Elton's mother broke her hip and he has to tend her, an invalid. This is what Elton does.

I told Louisa, "I heard from Elton."

She said, "I used to think he might be a good boyfriend."

Then she told a joke about a man who reads self-help books and tells his girlfriend she needs to find her center, she needs to find her center. And she says: No. You need to find my center.

"Not funny." Suzie came through the door.

Peter said, "Suzie's in love."

Suzie said, "True." She helped herself to Michelle's bread pudding.

I said, "You love someone because they're available."

She said, "Sometimes you love someone. Period."

Travis walked in. "You love someone," he said. "That's great."

I thought about Raoul living in the house down the road without Tammy, who'd gone off with a bartender. I worried if he was doing coke, and I asked Travis once, who said, "Why don't you hire a detective?" Honey chimed in. "I don't think it's coke, Mom. I mean, how can he afford it with Tammy gone?" I looked outside at the frozen water, the dark sky and spiky pines. I wanted to fly past this cold place. Which is impossible—flying. But not impossible to imagine. The loft. Whir. Big wings.

Love lasts in a duplex.

The blues has a limited number of chords.

Love lasts.

The Plow Got
Through, Too Bad

I PLAY GUITAR but my fingers mash down two strings instead of one. Dis-chord. I sell dope—a little, I'm cautious—and deliver it in a van I painted to say "Get Naked." I wear my tool holster, a loincloth, as I stand at the bar and drink, suds in my whiskers. "Would her ladyship care to break bread?" I asked a woman named Toni who carries a torch for a man named Walter. He plays in a band, the Roadhogs—he's ugly but gets good women. And one night I watched this scruffy fellow, a tree surgeon with tattoos, Al. The women sat on porch chairs talking about biological clocks, why artichoke dip is surefire for potluck. Al crunched his beer can, said, "The ladies' voices sound sweet with the tree frogs." One, then another, turned her head. Like ballet.

And I was sitting in a dark watering hole called the Oarhouse, staring at sunlight through the doorway, the mystery of dustmotes swirling, when a woman flashed by. Sweatsocks, brown legs, cutoffs, a leotard (a "Danskin"). Two days later I was standing in front of a house. I'd just delivered a quarter pound. She pulled up in a Mercury Comet and yanked the emergency on. She made her way

up the sidewalk. Legs. Skirt. A white criss-cross something
or another covering her torso. She had these Dairy Queen
Bags—red-and-white logos, pictures of Dennis the Men-
ace. She bought the quarter pound from the guy I'd
dropped it off for, but for sixty dollars more. "Notice," he
said later, "I could handle some volume." I held my peace,
wait-and-see. She asked to use his scale to portion out her
ounces. "I have to collect on them right away," she said.
She put an ounce in each bag.

I saw her next at the library when I was checking out
Chord Progressions for Starters. She was in that glass cubicle
for serious brains, an egghead with ink stains sitting beside
her. SILENT STUDY AREA. NO SMOKING. I opened the glass
door. It made that sucking noise, air tugging out. I sat
down, crossed my legs, cracked a book. "An Art major," I
said, "right?" Her face looked washed out, lavender half-
moons below her eyes. Like she'd been repairing a motor
with tweezers, delicate parts. Or embroidering under a
dim bulb, an irksome passage in the big design. "You're an
Art major," I said, "I can tell." It was the Danskin again,
her jewelry with cornucopias of semiprecious stones, bells
dangling from her ears. "Nice try," she said, "but no." She
was an English major. I said, "I like to read." She glanced at
my book, "Really?" I ran a string-search through memory:
book, book, book. "*To Kill a Mockingbird,*" I said, "my favorite." She smiled. I'd never read it. I made a motion with
my thumb and forefinger, inhalation. "How about taking a
break," I said, "the pause that refreshes? We've met, you
with the Dairy Queen bags."

"Right," she said, "your van. 'Get Naked.' "

The egghead was staring us down.

Outside by the pond, I lit up and said, "You should get
your quarter pounds from me. You'd save sixty dollars." I'd
have donated them—I'd scale towers and whack away
lizards. She said, "Thanks, but I don't really deal. I kept
one ounce and sold three to break even."

"Savvy," I said.

She held the joint to her mouth, the smoke in her lungs. One, two, three. Exhale. She said, "Lovely." It was autumn. A chill wind passed by—my skin and clothes felt fresh like I'd been hung on a line by the shoulders with clips. I stared. "You look like the Bionic Woman," I said, "Lindsay Wagner." She looked at the sky, at an imperfect speck in the canopy of light. She said, "I get my pot from my boyfriend now." This made her sad.

So I said: "What did one man-eating lion say to the other after a night on the town?"

"I give."

" 'I warned you about that bar-bitch-you-ate.' "

She smiled.

Trees shook. Leaves fell. "Thaes ofereode," she said, "Thisses swa maeg." A poem from the eighth century, she explained. About heartbreak and desolation. And she had to get back to her studies.

She worked at a Dairy Queen, maybe. I haunted the two in town, ate corndogs and ice milk. I stood in line behind a semi-beautiful woman in a pink dress with white palm trees under her fur coat. She stuck her hands in her pockets, pulled out fistfuls of sand, and said: "*Mi amoroso*, Antonio." She looked at me. "Excuse me, I just came back from Acapulco. You have no idea, the beaches, the passion, the sun." In my other life (before love) I would have bought a pair of flip-flops and made a conquest.

I looked for her at a roadhouse, the Idle Wild, where biker chicks and groupies sat together every night, drawing from the same small pool of men but buying each other drinks. Janet, Toni, Tammy. I'd asked them all out once and they made it clear I wasn't ready. Suzie, a gay woman, said: "Peter, you're gentle." Had she aspersed my masculinity? "It's not how deep you cut the furrow," I said, "but the number of rounds you make." She said, "Sex is the least of it." The most of it, I think, is that women from that bar, that crowd, play hard. They idle wild.

Love galls.

But one hoodoo evening I held her, a breast in each of my hands as snowy as beach sand, the outlines of her suntan sloping away. She sat up, picked her backpack off the floor, yanked a book out, *The Norton Anthology of English Literature 1:* "The small rain down can rain. Christ, that my love were in my arms, and I in my bed again." I kept my hands in place as the earth shifted.

But first, autumn turned to winter. I took a class, Life Drawing. Di Ann was the model, lumbering and heavy-bodied, her hair the color of mice. Later she said she cut it herself. You can see that. My reservations about Di Ann? Well, you aren't supposed to look at the model like a piece of flesh but at its planes and angles. No one said so but we caught on when one student drew Di Ann better than she is—a slender body, charcoal on the rims of her eyes like eyeliner on a Hollywood slut. The prof, bald on top with a long fringe of hair, held the picture up. "Pornography," he said, "altering what's real to make it match a conventional definition of perfection." I concentrated on elbows and knees. I looked up and Di Ann stared—I looked around, I doubted, me, yes. Her eyes softened like milk chocolate. I'm free, she seemed to say. Or inexpensive. Not dear.

She slipped behind her screen to dress, and when I packed up she stood beside me, buttoning the plastic buttons on her wool coat. "We know the same people," she said. And she explained how she knew the women from the Idle Wild, Janet, Toni, Tammy. Suzie. How she'd been at that dinner party last fall where they'd talked about artichokes and biological clocks. Al, the blue-tattooed tree surgeon who looks like Dennis Hopper, was her ex-lover, the father of her daughter. They had joint custody—Clara stayed one week with him, the next with Di Ann. "How about a cup of coffee?" she asked me. (Clara was staying with Al.) In the morning, waking in Di Ann's bed, I wondered how I'd got there.

When Di Ann asked me in, she'd suggested wine instead of coffee. I thought about how to say no. At what point? No wine. Or before that? In the yellow-lit classroom, snow coming down in clumps in the black sky outside. No coffee. Or later: "No spend the night," brief and authoritative, brooking no argument. Or tactful: "I like you too much. Tommorow comes early." Women have experience in the gradations of *no*, reserving enthusiasm, assent, until they feel safe. Di Ann felt safe. There's a difference between the way you make love to a woman you like and a woman you adore. With one, you spend words and phrases establishing common interest. Intercourse. With the other you pitch woo. News. Late releases: a meteor crossed my heart.

Actions speak.

My tongue on her throat: i.e., the loveliest throat in the kingdom.

I like Di Ann, but I felt bad. First of all, about her apartment. The only bed and bedroom belonged to Clara, and Di Ann slept on the couch the weeks Clara was there and not with Al. So the weeks I made love to Di Ann, I made love to her in her daughter's bed. Also, her pitiful salary at the bookstore. Her self-cut hair. Her clothes. "Accessorize, accessorize," she'd say, words from a fashion magazine, as she put a necklace of zebras on top of a sweater from the Church of Christ Thrift Shop. She sewed windsocks. Her best—a yellow cluster of grapes on black silk with a turquoise bolt of lightning—inspired me to design a swiveling pole, a contraption of steel that gives the windsock loft. It's no art. It's "arts and crafts." I'm sensitive to that. My poles are sold wherever Di Ann's windsocks are.

That first night Di Ann empathized, her eyes round and wet, about the labor a carpenter exerts, his exposure to wind, rain, snow. She gave me wine, also Red Zinger tea.

She rubbed my shoulders and remarked how noble it was I spent winter nights—when my body should refuel for the grueling carpentry season ahead—studying art for no visible reason or profit. In the morning she made an omelet with avocados. I'd thought love was a barter system. (I put a roof on a fellow's house, he rebuilds my engine; I build a hot-tub deck for Al, he trims the trees in my mother's yard.) But I was wrong. I invited Di Ann to my house for the only meal I can make, Eggplant Lasagna, a way to say: Look, the omelet was great, even Steven. But Al couldn't tend Clara that night, so I had to bring the lasagna to Di Ann's. We made love on the couch, the streetlight shining through the window. In the morning we ate pancakes at the drop-leaf table, Clara staring us down. Don't ask me about the third time, or fourth.

You eat with a selfless woman, her daughter a witness, you're stuck. Di Ann was stuck in her life, its paltry limits. But like the man in the story who grew up hungry and later never stockpiled enough food, or Imelda Marcos who went without shoes until she was sixteen, Di Ann cultivated fantasies about champagne and, she confessed to me once, coke. "It's nothing," I said, but there was something particular about the idea for her. Numbing, chilling, the desired effect: invulnerability, an Artic soul.

"It's not like that," I said, "it makes you selfish."

She said, "Good."

I went to hunt some down to prove her wrong and—when for the first time I wasn't looking in every corner, under every stone—I found her. I knocked on this guy's door, Tom, a schmuck who grew up in a Milwaukee suburb famous for juvenile delinquents. She answered, jeans tucked in her mahogany boots ("Frye boots"), a Danskin under a jacket made of fuzzy, ribbed stuff like bedspreads. "You," she said, "what is it?" In the next room, wails, crackles, Tom practicing Hendrix-style guitar. "I came to see Tom," I told her. I thought: Shit, she's a coke-whore. Why else is she here? And she toppled down from where I'd placed her, which seemed at the time like a ski hill she wasn't ready for, never had been, end-over-end, a header. A fall.

Tom turned his guitar off, laid out a line for me to sample. "You're sure you don't want any, Louisa?" he said, his face like mine. Yearning. She sat on the couch, elbows on her knees, a book in her hand. *Seven Old English Poems* with Commentary By John C. Pope. "Of course not," she answered, an involuntary shudder.

"You don't like it?" I asked, hopeful.

She said, "It makes me feel awful."

Tom snorted across the mirror, his babyish face gelling hard.

"I have to go," she said.

"Are you coming back later?" he asked. She had homework to do, she said. She went out the door. Snow blew in and settled on the shag rug. Tom was wearing black sweatpants, no shirt or shoes. "I just woke up," he explained. "Want to do another line?"

A few days later, in the shingle-and-clapboard neighborhood by the tire factory, I saw Louisa shoveling her car out, a Mercury Comet. I pulled over. "Go away," she said. "Who do you think does my shoveling the rest of the time?" I stood there. "You live here?" I asked. A prim white house, shallow picket fence, black trees, snow clustering in V-shaped branches. "You mean 'Not with Tom,' " she said, wiping her eyes. The wind blew hard. It bit. She said, "I can't. He practices his guitar too loud."

Of course Di Ann didn't like the cocaine, more numbing and brilliant-like-diamonds in her imagination than in fact. She said, her nose twitching, "It's low-key, isn't it, for the high price?"

In my heart-country, Louisa thrived. Once I knew where her house was, I drove past. What was she doing? What coast or peninsula did she tend? And the Dairy Queen bags, what could they mean? I bought an ice cream freezer, the kind you use with rock salt, cream, and eggs. Oh, irresolution, dark windows. One night her living room light shone, a benevolent, amber square. I knocked on the door. She opened it, chain in place. She said, "What?"

I said I'd made a hand-cranked bucket of Praline French Vanilla, did she want any? "It's too cold for ice cream," she said, "but I'd go for a drink." I happened to have a bottle of Pouilly-Fuissé in the van, but I didn't want to be obvious. I said, "I'll just run home and stick this French Vanilla in the freezer."

"Can't you leave it here? I have some wine."

"Come to think of it," I said, "me too."

Inside, we sat down, light from the space heater shining blue and orange. I wondered: Where was she born? What was her favorite color? Her worst fear? Why him? I looked at the wall.

"Nice place," I said.

She said, "You don't say what you feel."

I looked at a piece of furniture. "Is that a sewing machine?" I asked. And then—the memory shames me—I couldn't converse. I didn't. I had a spasm. I said, "My clothes need mending."

She said, "I keep the machine because it was my mother's. But I'll mend your clothes. That's simple." She pointed at a stack of textbooks on the floor. "I like keeping busy," she said.

I reached for her hand.

She stiffened. Her eyebrows arced. I rubbed away the friction. She relaxed. "I love him," she said. "I can't break up. I've tried." I don't remember how I answered. I thought of saying: "Forget the mending." I spilled my wine. As she mopped up, she asked me to go with her the next night to an airplane hangar where Walter's band, the Roadhogs, was playing blues, her favorite. She said, "But I'll drive. You've got to repaint your van."

When she picked me up, I was waiting at the front door. "Is this a good time to get your mending?" she asked. I said no, worrying the phone would ring. Di Ann was at home with Clara—her week of custody—and hadn't liked the idea I needed elbow room.

On the way to the airplane hangar—where there was a wedding dance for a couple who was taking their honeymoon on Harley-Davidsons—Louisa drove through new snow, the dashboard lights flickering, her neck scarf filmy and iridescent as cobwebs, her hands trim in leather gloves. She asked who'd owned my van before me and gave it the bad paint job. I didn't tell the truth, how one year I'd lived in Colorado and a guy like Al or Walter—with girlfriends coming out of his ears—had painted his van to say Get Naked. I came home and painted mine too. Sex appeal. I'd wanted just one girlfriend. That was then, this is now. I want Just One. "I bought it from a guy in Colorado," I lied.

She said, "A good deal?"

"I don't think so."

The airplane hangar was dark except for the band's homemade stage lights and the glow from the potbellied stove. Music careened off the tin walls. The bride and her attendants wore long dresses that looked like shrouds. The groom and groomsmen had black T-shirts printed to look like tuxes. Toni and Walter were together—with Walter making passes at every other woman, including the bride. Also Tammy, a snaggled-haired barfly. Also Janet, who polished Walter's guitar between sets, her face as sad as that Indian on the TV commercial who cries about polluted rivers.

We walked in and heads turned.

Al, schmuck, pulled me aside. "That's one high-strung, thoroughbred filly. Lucky son of a bitch. I wouldn't turn it down."

I would have hit him, but Louisa walked up and smiled. A few minutes later she said, "He's nice, isn't he—that Al?"

We were standing a few feet from the tool bench where they served drinks. Because of the shadows, the noise—my cover—I pulled on her arm and whispered in her ear, fierce. "Where's Tom? What gives?"

She answered in a speech:

"He wouldn't come because—you know he plays guitar—he's jammed with these guys before and Walter thinks he's good. And he is for that violent, grinding kind of music, stretching strings. But the rest of them think he's a hot dog, no group spirit, which is obvious if you consider he only plays when he's alone."

She was drunk. She walked around a table, naming food: "Baba-ganoush, tabbouleh, pesto, guacamole. What, no Vienna sausages?"

Suzie, this hefty woman who is sometimes nice and sometimes not, said, "Peter, you have a lot of nerve. Or a hormone imbalance."

I led Louisa to the car.

I drove. She came across the seat at me. "I know you have pot in there," she said, pressing her hands against my breast pockets. "Do you know I used to like pink cigarette papers—I was that intent on making people notice." The car skidded. She thrust her hands in my pockets. "At last," she said, lighting up.

I'm thinking, Keep This Car on the Road.

Also, What does she ever *do* with him but drop by in the middle of the day like a social worker to see if he's dressed yet?

She answered my question when we were in my living room. "Watch TV," she said. She hiccuped. "Sex, of course. Which is hard, given the people coming and going all the time. One guy even banged on the bedroom window. It wasn't always like that." She took her jacket off, her boots, clunk, clunk. She unhooked her belt. "Stop," I said, but I was in her face, her hair. My tongue in her mouth, her sharp teeth. A miracle, her curving jaw.

"Peter," she said, "your bed." My bedroom has an overhead light, 150 watts. I left it off as we landed on the springy double mattress in the middle of stacked clothes, shirts and pants I'd tried on for my date with Louisa, then discarded. They fell as we burrowed, the smell of laundry softener thick as I felt myself lucky, a dog, a ferret, a French boar uncovering truffles.

She froze and said, "Can we turn the light on? Then I would know it was you at least, not a stranger." But once the light was on, she turned her head and looked at a photo of my mother, then at a table I'd made in shop class in high school. Wearing only socks and a forest green Danskin, her hair spread across the pillow like Lana Turner's, she said, "We can't now," the word *now* private and significant. She'd remembered Tom. "It used to be heady," she said. "Like when I was a kid and spun until I was dizzy—it made me sick, but what a diversion. Did you ever rub your eyes until you hallucinated, the world turns red? We can't."

I said No, the word in my mouth like a swollen thing, an insect bite, a bad bone. I lay next to her, my love adamant and durable.

She looked at the toppled clothing. "Am I supposed to mend all of these?" I told her she didn't need to mend any of them, but she insisted. So she put a pair of gold corduroy slacks that were too long, and a flannel shirt that needed a patch, into the back of her Mercury Comet when she drove away. Di Ann had lent me the shirt—who knows who had it before me, Al? It was plaid with pearl snaps, and I'd put a three-cornered tear in one sleeve.

Then five things happened at once, synchronicity.

Also cause-and-effect.

First, Louisa broke up with Tom. So he bought a used Pontiac, got up early, showered, dressed. He tailed her. She'd come out of class and he'd be in the hall. Did she need a ride? Or course not, she had a car. One night she ate dinner with an ageing English professor with baggy pants, the son of a bitch, and he kept pulling his dining room curtains back to keep an eye out. Louisa told me about it. "I guess I've seen too many swashbuckling movies," she said, "but I found it irritating he was nervous." Tom busted in and slammed the prof against the wall. Another time she came home late at night and found Tom inside waiting, a smashed window. Next he went skydiving and broke his leg and three days later—driving drunk with a cast on—rolled the Pontiac. She visited him in the hospital. She couldn't *not*.

Second, Di Ann used the Life Drawing class to wear her heart on her sleeve, on her bare arm like a glow-in-the-dark tattoo, and the bald-headed Art professor reprimanded her for inattentive modeling. He did privately at first, but in the end snapped at her in front of the students, and she started crying, silent, naked, wet. I took her out for coffee. I said, "I handled breaking up badly. I admit it." Al had told her about seeing me at the bikers' wedding dance with Louisa. Did Di Ann answer me? She said, "When you wash your sweaters, Peter, they have to be blocked."

Third, Al made a pass at Louisa. He came by for a quarter-pound when Louisa and I were watching a nature program, the reproduction of songbirds. I went to the pantry where I keep my scales and Ziploc bags, and when I came back Al had her in a corner. She couldn't leave, caged. She moved her mouth but didn't speak. He said she needed to take better care of Tom, who was hurting himself. He was pathetic. He scared Al. Louisa nodded, Tom scared her too. Al said, "You must be bodacious to make a man so desperate." He stuck his chest out. "Someday when Tom is better off you'll be free, and I'll lick your perfect ankles." She listened, looking dreamy and faraway. I mean, she bit.

And I thought about what men tender up and women fall for. Baggy pants. A Fender Stratocaster. A painted van. An ugly coke habit and a personality to match. The Art professor, stringy-haired and bald-headed too, to whom female students deferred like apostles of Gandhi. Was it pheromones, a sexual smell? My mother once explained she fell in love with my dad at first inhalation, even though she knew he was a bastard, that sneering, superior face. But she was slavish to his dangerous scent. Another theory I have is that some men get just one woman and are so well-made, so ample, their reputations grow, word-of-mouth.

Fourth, Suzie hit me.

We were in the Oarhouse, and Al was in the next room playing pool with Tom, who'd propped his crutches against the cigarette machine and hopped on one foot to make shots, his leather vest flapping open. In the best of times, Tom looked tense—like he expected late-breaking catastrophe, an official messenger arriving to say Live or Die. "Relax," you wanted to tell him, even if he was calm. I saw him bend over the table to shoot, Al behind him, and I thought about getting away before words turned to fisticuffs. Suzie sat down next to me. She said, "What you do is obscene." At first I thought she meant carpentry, or my poles. I said, "Making swiveling windsock poles?" She said, "Putting her on a pedestal. How can she act sane when you think she's a vestal virgin, a centerfold, and a genius rolled up in one?"

"Who?"

"Good question," Suzie said. "You're fucking up a lot of people."

I said, "It's not your concern."

She looked worried. "Maybe you're right," she said. "I'm working on that in therapy—wanting to control other people." Then she chewed her lip, stared at me, drew her arm back. Hit me.

Last of all, Di Ann broke the window in Louisa's Mercury Comet to steal the corduroy pants and plaid shirt Louisa had taken home to mend. Steal *back* is what Di Ann said, like Louisa had stolen them in the first place. This is rational regarding the shirt which was Di Ann's at one time, or at least Al's. But the corduroy pants always belonged to me. Louisa told me how her car had been parked in front of a bookstore. She didn't hear a thing. "Safety glass," I explained, "very quiet." She said, "It was Tom of course," and she worried how she could afford to fix it, what her father would say. "He's obsessed about cars." Di Ann had already called me, taking responsibility, saying: "Peter, I know who she is now, your mistress, the poor little rich girl. I'm cutting your corduroy pants up for rags." I arranged to have Louisa's window fixed by a guy in a glass shop who owed me. "Now I owe you," Louisa said, "I do." I didn't tell her it wasn't Tom who'd broken the window, thinking she was through with him forever.

An error.

I heard it from Toni and Walter, who'd spent a evening at Tom's, eating lobster and drinking tequila: Louisa was back with Tom. "She doesn't eat much," Toni said, "or snort blow. But he's crazy about her for sure." (Did she seem unhappy? Did she say my name? Does she love him?) I wondered all of this, but what I asked was: "Did she have a Danskin on?" Toni gave me an odd look, but she wears wool ponchos and men's hats. Walter said, "One of those slenderizing, scoop-necked ballerina shirts? Yes."

I spent the next forty days and nights asking: What did Tom give her? The answer seemed like a ship arriving through fog.

He gave her grief.

Di Ann was hopeful about a reunion, my pants probably not in rags but safe in a drawer. Me, I hated the weather, my sporadic carpentry work. I picked up my guitar and swung it like a club. I thought about painting my van but the memory of Louisa stopped me, too futile. I returned to my poles because they're what I do best, and I'd been thinking about making them ornamental since Walter's girlfriend, Toni, suggested it. "Put an acorn on top," she said, "or a toadstool." (You can tell she'd be good in bed, not uptight.) I'd tried to advertise my poles in an arts catalogue, but they wouldn't let me. Not artistic, they said.

Too crafty. I used my Life Drawing tools to make sketches. But I didn't make any new poles. I walked the streets, my Sorrel boots beating dull rhythm as I stared into windows, plumb and solid. I haunted her neighborhood. One night, walking to my van, the bartender's words in my ears—"Last call"—I kept going until I ended up in front of Tom's, his windows slit-like and low-browed. If I meant to be a lovesick voyeur, I realized, I'd have to get a dog, a leash to yank on when people looked out windows, wondering.

Inside, Tom was playing acoustic guitar, his leg in its cast propped on pillows. Louisa sat on the couch. I listened through the sounds of the winter midnight, icicles dropping, cars slushing over roads. Flamenco guitar—loverly, Spanish strains. Tom stopped playing. She looked angry, then cried. Then she looked angry again, and startled. I wondered if she'd seen me. It was dark, of course, but as I rushed away I imagined her at the window, remarking on my familiar shape. I felt jealous about the fraction of her life she hadn't reported—that Tom played guitar not just like Hendrix, but like a swain, and it made her weep.

A daydream, not a night dream, takes over your life. I remembered the dance at the airplane hangar, Louisa's face, her voice. Fiddle players. The Blues. I wanted to come home and find her. We'd eat. She'd like what I cooked. Red wine was winter's bounty. She'd read out loud: "Oft him an-haga are gebideth." (The one who dwells alone waits.) Our hearthside would shine.

L ouisa called me. She said, "I owe you." I looked outside, snow sifting down. She said, "I'm taking you to dinner. I'll drive." I said, "No, I'm driving—last time you got drunk and I had to anyway." She agreed. " 'Get Naked,' " she said, hanging up.

We ate at a Japanese restaurant. I asked where Tom was. How he was. His fractures? She toyed with her food, her hair falling onto her shoulders like a cocker spaniel's ears. She was wearing a cardigan sweater over a black lace shell and I waited for her answer (Tom? What about Tom?), tapping my foot on the floor, no, the base of the table, because the whole thing shook, the plates, the snowy linen, ice in water glasses making a melodious tinkle. I pulled my foot away. The table stilled. Louisa said, "He rented a log house in the country. He's moving today."

I said, "So you sneaked away?"

She wiped her mouth on her napkin. "Maybe it'll be easier to break up now. He doesn't have a phone yet. He's safer there. He's storing his coke in the trunk of a junked car in the woods." She looked at me, worried. "I shouldn't have told you that." The waitress came by with sake. Louisa sipped, her fingers curving around the bone cup. I pictured her prim, white house connected by phone wires to Tom's—to his bad temper, to the strained, mysterious protocol of drug deals. She said, "I could never date another dealer." Like that was the problem. "But you could quit," she asked, "couldn't you?" I said, "I would."

She smiled.

We drove to the Idle Wild. Snow came down. When we pulled into the parking lot, she asked me: Did I have all-season radials? Had I heard the forecast? "Don't worry," I said, and I held her hand as we went in. Tammy, a tacky, thin woman, danced alone. Suzie pulled me aside. "Sorry about that time I hit you," she said. "I was out of line." Al had Louisa cornered, showing her a wallet-sized photo of Clara, making poetry out of the fact she was his daughter. "My life's work," he said, "my daughter." Di Ann danced, her hips bumping under a skirt that looked like a tablecloth. I stared at it—gingham print with berries and bread loaves—and realized it *was* a tablecloth, or had been. The last time Di Ann called me, she'd said the most insulting aspect of the fact she'd been betrayed was that I'd given Louisa my mending. "She can't sew," Di Ann had said. "Anyone can tell that by looking, the prima donna." But who cared, not her. I could ride around naked in Louisa's car for all she minded, she said. She had a boyfriend, the bald art professor.

Unlikely.

But who knows? I thought of the English professor with the baggy pants and—if Louisa was my lover for now and ever—would he back off? I turned to her, not to ask questions but looking for a love signal, a cue. I heard her say, "Al, tell me about your work. I saw you in my neighborhood, hanging by your harness from a tree. It was autumn, the smell of fresh-cut wood just lovely."

I said, "We have to get out of here." I pointed out that Di Ann was snubbing us. But Louisa had no idea who Di Ann was, thinking Tom had broken her car window. And still she went back to him, still would. Someone is in love here, I thought. We went outside. Snow came down in clumps. I found my message on the beer sign, bold print: Idle Wild. I said, "I'm not taking you home."

She said, "Good."

I didn't want to go to my house—jinxed by the last foiled attempt. I drove on, and Louisa worried. Didn't I know the roads were slick? Did I have a bag of salt? A candle and a blanket? "Relax," I said. And she said she always got nervous. I kept going—away from Tom's old house, Tom's new house. Away from Al, Di Ann, Suzie. I ended up in the yard of a cottage I'd been doing work on. I thought of Tom, miles away, and I tried to picture him maneuvering on crutches to sit in a chair by the fire. I said, "Let's go in." Louisa said, "We'll get stuck here."

But she followed me.

I turned the heat on while she stomped her feet in pointy-toed boots, her breath puffing out in clouds. She put her hands deep in her pockets and stepped around the mess—tools, lumber, a mattress dragged down from the loft, a bathtub in the middle of the kitchen hooked by a hose to the sink. We stood by the window eating canned peaches. "If we do get snowed in," she said, staring out at the sky, the chalky snow, "we have food and books." She nudged her backpack which she carried everywhere like a purse. "It could be a rite of winter," she said, "like in the spring I always buy May wine. It has an unusual herb, woodruff."

I thought: woodruff? I reached across the cold room for her.

She said, "Peter, you know how people say coke is bad but pot is supposed to make you spiritual? I'm starting to think it's bad in a different way—it makes you obsessed with nuances, like you're living in the bottom of a well, enthralled with the view."

I thought: She must make a list of possible topics before she leaves home. But suddenly I remembered the first time I saw her, how as she came up the sidewalk carrying Dairy Queen bags, a flurry of speed and motion. I said, "Remember those Dairy Queen bags you used to have—what did they mean? That you liked ice cream? You used to work there?" I put my hand under her sweater, under her lace top. Her nipple was hard as marble.

"I found them in my house when I moved in," she said. She tipped her head back, her voice quavering. "You're only the second person I'll have been with." The sound of our clothes falling to the floor seemed loud. Lovemaking was a game. I touched her. I gave her an *X* and she gave me back *O*, which I took as permission. "I'm grateful," she said. "I owe you. I do."

I closed my eyes and thought—I don't know why—how Di Ann had felt safe. Then I had a vision. Snow fell like velvet and sealed the cottage, made a haven with its bright furnace and bed to lie on. I also pictured—though I willed myself not to—a row of snowplows coming over the hill to dislodge us, big white sprays arcing out from blades. The End. I opened my eyes and came back to the dim room where Louisa had moved to a far corner of the bed. She had to study, she said. I fell into hard sleep. When I woke, she was in the bathtub, the hose snaking from the tap to the tub. Gray light shone on her hair which sometimes looks gold, but didn't. And I realized she'd go back to Tom, that I'd been the bridge out, only the first one. I was about to tell her I understood, I'd be fine, don't worry. She rose, water beading on her skin as she reached for a blanket or towel. She grabbed her sweater, wrapped up, took herself away. Up until now was easy. I'd arrived like a storm, violent and temporary.

The Petting Zoo

I T WAS AN "ENSEMBLE," a navy blue coat with box pleats and a matching pillbox hat made of polyester spongy enough it could stand by itself, vertical, in a corner. Our neighbor's daughter had outgrown them, the coat at least, but what good was the Jackie Kennedy–inspired hat without the coat? My mother thought they were cute. She wished they'd fit her, she said. I was playing with a Barbie doll and one of my mother's floral handkerchiefs, wrapping it around the doll's busty torso like a sarong. I hated that stupid lid for my head, that stiff, wide coat designed to look like everyone else's, its foamy backside too ugly to be revealed. As I looked at it, I shuddered as though I'd seen someone's underwear hanging on the line or, worse, used for a rag and stuffed under the kitchen sink. When my mother asked me to wear them to school, I pitched a fit so melancholy she called a babysitter to give me toast and 7-Up because she had to go to work at my father's car lot, keeping the books, the close accounts. I wanted my things eccentric or daring, but beautiful all the way through.

The first time I applied this criteria to a friend was when I became enamored of a Mennonite girl named Rosemary:

her hair knotted in an old-time chignon, her little white net-hat, her calico dresses, her name that reminded me of a fairy tale, her beauty (she had Snow White's pale hair, and Rose Red's vivid skin). All of these quaint details whorled together to make me take her on. I waylaid her in Gym, in the hall outside History. I invited her to stay over. Her parents, with their eleven children, couldn't be bothered to worry where one of them might be for a day, and they thought it wasteful to drive from their farm to Bremmer— forty miles round-trip—to pick Rosemary up. They decided, Rosemary said, that she should stay with us all weekend, until Monday, then business again as usual, the school bus ride home, chores that lasted into nightfall, homework shoved into the last, lamplit half-hour before bed. I pictured her bent over her arithmetic, a pewter cup on the table beside her. I thought how naive, how reckless, for her parents to let her come without finding out if we were worthy. My own mother conducted investigations before I could visit someone for even a day.

The weekend, my infatuation, fizzled away. Rosemary's coat, though not her regular, indoor clothes, smelled faintly of barn. But to hate Rosemary for that would have been to judge a book by its cover, to be snobbish and cruel, a sinner. Plus, my father, who'd been raised on a farm, always said the smell of manure was sweet and fertile. No, we fell out over tennis. I liked tennis not for the athletic rigmarole—though I'm only guessing that's why people like it, I've never understood sports—but for the idea of myself dancing across the court in a bell-shaped dress, lobbing a yellow ball to victory and, later, sipping lemonade on a sunny pavilion. Never mind we played at the school court which was run-down, needing nets and new paint, no pavilion within miles, and we wore sweatshirts and jeans. I figured if we could get the ball going, my imagination would supply the details. But Rosemary was clutzy. I wasn't rude, just quiet, as we walked home. That night, Rosemary ventured her first opinion all weekend.

She said, as we laid out clothes and schoolbooks, "You got upset about that tennis."

I couldn't help it.

You see, I'd thought she'd be my complement and accessory, my opposite and twin too. Her hair was blond, mine brown; her skin rosy, mine ivory. City light. Country star. Why couldn't she send the ball back when I landed it in her corner? I ditched her.

And I started playing with Danielle Thompson, who lived across the railroad tracks. When we played "House" she manipulated the assigned roles to give herself excuses to ask my brother and me to strip. She'd be the parent, for instance, giving the kids a bath: "Okay," she'd say, "now get undressed." And once, playing "Dentist," Danielle sawed on Davie's teeth with a fingernail file; she sprayed my sister, Helen, with a garden hose and one of those attachments that makes the water come out hard. Though I couldn't help but admire her household, its deranged rituals—the way her mother worked five to midnight while Danielle ate malted milk balls for dinner and her sister made out in the next room with a boy—in the end, I decided Danielle was strange but not smart or beautiful.

I dropped her.

I picked her up fifteen years later, hitchhiking. I was headed back to college in my '68 Pontiac, and I let her drive because I was tired. I sat and stared, at her wiry body, fringed hair, her mascara-black eyes. She looked mean and pretty, like she could hurt you, and you'd let her. I'd seen only the ugly duckling all those years, not the swan—if you can picture a tough swan. She answered my questions with monosyllables, my punishment, I guess. She said, "This is my exit. I'm getting off."

I met Zoe the summer I turned twelve, and she already had a boyfriend, Brad, and secrets: she had "dirt," the kind you "get." Then she fell in love with someone new while she kept Brad on a string, and this was uncharitable, I thought, a sin of omission. I was undergoing catechism at the time. But Zoe didn't think it was wrong to let Brad wither while she took up with a new boy whose parents farmed 750 acres of potatoes. She got some of her ideas about religion from her dad, who got them from country music. Kris Kristofferson, nursing a hangover and feeling gloomy, "Why Me, Lord?" Zoe's grandma, who raised her, believed in a voice in the clouds, a God with standards, but not rules. I found this lack of rules superior, even noble, because—think for example of Pharisees—rules get warped by misappropriation, abuse. Still, I felt secure for having my navy blue book of rules, Luther's Small Catechism.

I idolized Zoe and begrudged her.

And I wanted her discarded boyfriend for myself. Our love triangles collided: Zoe's attraction to Brad and to the potato heir pulling her two directions; my loyalty to Zoe and my adolescent desire for Brad, a temporary desire, but impossible to forestall. It pulled us apart. I remember Zoe's face, red with anger, with loss. "You," she said. But the way she said it: *You!* As in *false-hearted, untrue.* We weathered the rupture. It took years.

One day—after I'd left Bremmer to live in Menominee, a college town a hundred miles away—I thought I saw Zoe in a factory outlet. I went out of my way to head down the aisle she'd staked out with three kids, a purse, a diaper bag. I was shopping for beads and rhinestones to sew on a vest I'd bought at a thrift store. Maybe it was the fabric Zoe was buying, washable cotton with choo-choo trains, or what she wore, a striped top, matching slacks. I decided it wasn't her. When she'd first moved to Bremmer—she was thirteen—she'd wear her brother's jeans, her dad's belt, her own shoes, putting it all together to look like someone from a planet where the concept of coordinated outfits was quaint. But Zoe took on local habits like camouflage; after six months of dating the potato heir, she wore plaid, checks, or dots, neatly paired with harmonious solids. I turned around. Maybe it *was* Zoe after all, I decided. "Louisa," she said, "of course. It's you."

We ate lunch at one of those restaurants with a salad bar and thirty-two entrees. Zoe talked about the way the year divided into planting and harvest, how "crafts" were important because she did them for herself. About me, she said, "You thought you were too good." I smiled, but it was true her lack of rules had scared me. I'd gone back to myself, my own kind. She sat across from me, incognito, a farmer's wife, just one year older but matronly and wise, it seemed, since marrying Dick and bearing children. And me, defying convention through appearances, I was wearing a lace dress with combat boots. I showed Zoe the vest I planned to embroider with gaudy beads and she didn't get it—pairing poor people's clothes with rich people's accessories. One of her kids smashed a cracker on the table and banged his spoon. One slept. I stalled, remembering my sister, Helen, telling me, years ago, that Zoe had four children in all, one of them dead, stillborn.

I wondered: For all my surface alterations, for all of Zoe's reserve (*Hands Off,* her face seemed to say, *No Trespassing*), which of us had changed the most? "What?" Zoe, said. "Finish." She stopped her son from banging his spoon. I returned to the story I'd launched into, an episode from my life, some fire I'd played with, thin ice I'd walked on. When I left home for college, I'd remade myself. I worried that, socially, I'd fail, I'd be a wallflower, that no sophisticated coed from a rich suburb would ever befriend me. So I set out to be aloof, resilient, foolhardy. As I served this version up, I didn't lie about the hazards I courted, just the fact that, every single time, I wanted out, too late. For what? And the story I told? It might have been this:

W̶e had to go to Chicago before the semester started. Despite his earnings, my boyfriend, Tom, didn't own a car. Of course *I* wouldn't have had a car except for my dad who, by way of owning a car lot, bought me these mint-condition sedans previously driven by proverbial old ladies to the bank and church and back. He warned me—handing over keys, let's say it was Christmas and a blue '64 Rambler was in the driveway with a plastic bow across its windshield—never let anyone drive. Well, Tom drove. We left for Chicago with a mongrel set of passengers, first, Tom's roommate, Bert, and his girlfriend, Sue. Once Bert dropped out for a whole semester—he was intellectually fried, he said—to go to bars, do coke, sleep late. No one noticed, not even his parents. The other thing about Bert and Sue is that they came home late from parties and made love with Neil Young turned up, that wailing, braying business about gold hearts, lost highways, and Sue calling out in an amorous pitch: Oh! I sat next to Tom in the front seat, and on my right, a stubby, unwashed guy, our contact. I hated him.

One day I'd brought my dad to meet Tom, a ritual event. I was wearing a pale, feminine dress and my hair wafted in the breeze, its shampoo-scent like green apples. I loved my dad, I loved Tom. Where was the conflict? (I hadn't figured on the Freudian stuff. I read it because I'd be tested on it, that's all.) I'd drunk wine at lunch—the first time in front of my dad—making a fuss as I ordered, settling in the end on Liebfraumilch. As I stepped out of my dad's car, the sun beating down, he put his arm around my shoulder and, as we crossed the street, asked: "Which one is your boyfriend's house, Monkey?" I froze and recovered, like when you're giving a speech and something goes wrong but you have to finish anyway. Because the short, dirty guy was in Tom's yard, handing him money. Tom—in jeans, no shirt, his hair wet from the shower—looked at us, waved, shoved the money in his pocket. And the short guy vanished. Tom ran across the yard, athletic.

He stuck his hand out, apologized for not being ready. "People dropping by," he said. My dad pushed his glasses up his nose, trying not to look at Tom's hips as his jeans slid low. Tom loped into the house to get shoes and a shirt, and came back looking like he should have the first time. We went for the drive we'd planned, my dad handing Tom the keys to his late-model Riviera, white with a sporty vinyl roof. "You know the way, son," he said, a gesture Tom appreciated. Tom loved cars. On a country road winding though pasture land, he made polite conversation. I started to relax. My dad said, "Why did that oddball give you money?"

Pause.

"Lawn-mowing service," Tom said. "I put an ad in the paper to find guys to do the mowing. I line up the accounts and collect the money."

"And this guy collected one of your accounts," my dad said, helping out. When it comes to hard questions, he'll settle for marginal answers as long as they're not sarcastic, flaunting artifice.

"Well," I said, making a joke, "if you think that guy was odd, Dad, you should see his brothers—all of them look like trolls."

"A lawn-mowing service with trolls," my dad said. "Funny."

Zoe wiped her mouth on a napkin. "Dick's friends are jerks too," she said.

Dick is Zoe's husband.

"So is Dick, of course," she said, "when he's with them."

On the way to Chicago, I sat between Tom and the short guy, wondering if the cloth seats in my car would absorb dirt, his residue. "Can we roll the window down?" I asked. "Are the vents open?" I complained at gas stations, pulling Tom aside: "Get rid of him." "I can't," Tom said. To him, he said, "I'll pull over at the next truck stop, buddy. We can all use a shower. It's a hot day."

"Thanks, Tom," he said, "but I'll hold off 'til the A.M."

Meanwhile Bert and Sue lolled in back, thinking—I saw Sue pulling her shirt up to her nose, wiping her forehead with a languid hand—that they were too good. But they wouldn't say so, hoping to get freebies, samples. Tom, on the other hand, thought he was better than Bert because he paid his own way—his tuition, his rent, his recreational drugs. I knew from the snarl in his voice when he talked about Bert's semester-long vacation, Bert's credulous parents. Still, Tom was embarrassed about the affiliation—the short guy's name was Mick—embarrassed about having dealings with Mick. Me, I thought I was better than everyone. But I loved Tom and therefore couldn't rank him, love being classless, distinction-free. If I forgot, even for a minute, and brushed close to Tom like a compass next to a magnet, I went haywire, my needle swinging: love everywhere. Love was hot but—coupled with disapproval, my growing sense I wished I loved someone else, not Tom—love was cold too. Like dry ice. "Can we stop up here for a Pepsi?" I said. I made Mick sit in back.

I'd pressured Tom to be more painstaking about alliances—for safety but for dignity too. Like my mother telling my dad, years ago, he couldn't make any more deals with the Swangers. They'd order a transmission through us, or he'd let them have a car on credit and they'd never pay, and in the end he'd take a used refrigerator too dilapidated to be of use, or a rusty, three-toned travel trailer built in the thirties which sat in our yard until my mother's outrage forced my dad to sell it for less than the debt. "Next," she said, "you'll trade a privy for a Ford LTD," her ultimate insult since the LTD was her favorite car. My dad loved his business, match-making, like a horse trader finding the right mount for the right rider: "We Find Cars for People," his advertising slogan. But my mother complained that *she* ended up scouring the Swanger's refrigerator before it could be sold, or cleaning their travel trailer, or serving them coffee in her Melmac cups. "This is a nice patio you have," Mrs. Swanger said, except she pronounced it *payshio* and blew her nose in a paper napkin.

I objected to Bert and Sue because, Tom was right, they treated us like we were Swangers and they were respectable. I objected to the troll in the back seat next to Sue—I gloated—and to his short, ugly brothers. I had careful approval for a guy named Horse who Tom only recently began to have joint ventures with. He was stoop-shouldered and had one of those mustaches that hung past the corners of his mouth. But he wiped his feet when he came to the door, and once I offered him a piece of cake and, when he was done, he thanked me, rinsed the plate and set it in the sink. I couldn't help but see how my dad would like him if he met him somewhere else, for instance on the lot, talking in a well-mannered way about cars. One day he brought along his girlfriend, Amy, who was frail and blond, but her eyes looked wise. I threw myself into a demonstrative friendship. We needed friends, after all.

I was thinking about Amy as we exited I-90 into the Chicago suburbs, Elk Grove, Oak Park. Horse had once said, "I wouldn't have much truck with Mick, Tom. He's sloppy." He meant that Mick didn't cover his tracks. Hygiene was beside the point. But what about hygiene? And the desire to keep someone like Mick out of your living room, away from your loved ones, your dad? I'd looked to Amy for advice. "He smells bad," I told her. "He's stupid." She had pale, pale hair. She was petting my dog, Pearl, a black Lab who stared up at her with loyalty, love. She said, "They were in my grade school, Mick and his brothers. All of them got held back." That was it, no clue or signal about manners, about *etiquette* which, as Emily Post says, keeps us from revealing our feelings too soon. I shifted angrily in the car seat. I jabbed Tom. "I hate him," I hissed. His answer? "Strange bedfellows," he said. We dropped Mick off in a run-down neighborhood called Eden Park.

"And I worried about the dogs," Sue said. When we'd planned this trip, we talked about bringing the dogs along—Pearl, and Tom's dog, Angel. But Sue had complained: "With this heat, the panting, the car will stink like dog breath!" We left them with Amy.

Mick had disappeared into a building with a knapsack. "Will that be big enough?" I asked. We were supposed to come back for him. "Yes," Tom said, frowning, pulling away from the curb. Then my nerves went bad, my thoughts into a confused spiral. It was my car. Horse had warned us. Would they arrest *me?* I crossed my legs, smoothed my light blue sundress I'd made myself—my mother thought every nice woman should learn to sew. Lots of people did coke—I'd been amazed. I hoped the arresting officer would see I was nice. How unfair that people bought drugs but condemned the vendor. Everyone smoked pot—though not everyone, I realized, not me.

I'd tried it, then went back to my dreams and worries.

Just to love Tom wrenched my mind. I ran down the list of reasons why I couldn't help it, one reason but endless: we made love over and over. Once we took a shower so long that, near the end of it, the hot water started going cool, running out, and I said, Tom, we have to finish up here. But I couldn't finish even speaking. I slid down, down into the water—it was growing cold as pin-pricks. I came to with Tom leaning over me, scared but smiling, proud. I told this story to Sue once, who didn't of course like Tom, but all of a sudden started acting like she might. She could.

He hunched over the steering wheel, nervous. "I wish you did run a lawn-mowing service," I said.

"Right now," he said, "me too."

We'd planned to go to a rock concert to kill time. But the mob of people parking their cars and thronging toward the gate scared me. As we pushed forward, I hung on, afraid of being cut loose, set free. My purse got stuck in a swell of people pushing the other way, and I hung onto

Tom tight, who'd grabbed Bert, who held onto Sue, and the four of us pulled forward while my purse strap dug into my shoulder and snapped. My purse flew overhead—I yanked it along behind me like a kite on a string. But I got a headache as soon as the concert started, and Tom and I went back to the car where I lay still as he stroked my forehead. In a while, Bert and Sue wandered out. "Dumb shits," Bert said, "weirdos."

We were parked in. We sat in the dark and watched people. A few feet away, a group lingered, smoking, passing a bottle. Laughter tinkled like bells, like shattering glass. One girl was wearing a raincoat made of turquoise plastic that glimmered like cellophane. I wanted to be so conspicuous, gaudy like a queen. I wanted courage. At the same time, I wanted to go home. Tom left to go to the bathroom with Bert. Then the concert ended, the cars unplugged themselves from the congested parking lot, and we headed back to Eden Park to get Mick. I felt light-headed and giddy.

Mick got in the car. "Got it, buddy?" Tom asked.

Mick patted the knapsack. "You were nervous?"

"No way," Tom said. But sitting in the dark between him and Mick, I felt the flux, the easing out of strain, the calm current that flew in behind. Tom hadn't been worried about getting caught, I realized, and the ride home with ounces in the trunk seemed, to him, easy—he'd just thought Mick might run off with his money, that's all. I struggled with two thoughts at once. One, it was good Tom didn't panic. (He should marry Sue, I thought, furious, bristling). Two, I'd been dragged through this despite my reservations. (Please come with me, he'd said, I'll miss you. He wanted my car, of course.) I vowed to stay angry for days. Mick sat next to me—foul, odiferous, but in the context of a strange city at midnight, as dear as a pet who's run away and rolled in mud, and you're mad but glad to have him back safe.

We stayed at an apartment that belonged to an old

friend of Tom's—someone who was out of town. Living room, kitchenette, bathroom, that's it. I'd made the suggestion that Mick should spend the night at the apartment where he'd scored the coke, and Tom gave me a look like, Forget It, whereas Mick at least had the manners to explain: "I don't think that's practical, ma'am," he said.

I said, "Ma'am?"

"I don't think that's practical," he said, "Louisa."

Tom was sitting on the sofa bed, looking weary and perturbed as a father on a TV show with wisecracking kids. Bert and Sue spread blankets on the floor. Tom said, "We're sleeping in the same room and need to be mature about each other's privacy. Understand?" He could be firm and gentle; he loved children and dogs. He was majoring in sociology and wanted to be a counselor. I liked the authority in his voice. "You," he said to Mick, "take a shower."

It was pitch black, claustrophobic. Light wedged between the curtains. Tom and I lay on the sofa bed, high above everyone—I shifted and the frame squeaked. Bert whispered something to Sue. "Hey!" Tom said. "None of that." Mick was snoring. As Tom lay back down, I thought how I wanted a shower too. I couldn't sleep for thinking of it. I put my arm around Tom, so familiar. I didn't say anything. I didn't have to, all that electromagnetic stir. I felt like I'd blown backwards into a dingy, musty place where the only sound was a quiet murmur—like a puppy recently separated from the rest of the litter, begging to be petted, petted all the time. I froze. It was me. I pushed Tom away. "Stop it," I whispered. "We're not that bad. We're not *them* yet."

"It was a close call," Zoe said. Lunch was over, the story too.

"Which part?" I asked. She shrugged.

• • •

I didn't hear from Zoe again for weeks. But as I reconsidered the way I'd unburdened myself, infused our conversation with secrets, I remembered Communication 101—my worst grade ever—how I'd failed to understand the concept of self-disclosure: that people tell secrets in order to shame others into telling theirs. But Zoe never shamed. And I started worrying that she was back in Bremmer, laughing at how I'd turned out. Then she called to say she was coming to Menominee to visit me. "The back-to-school sales," she said, "but the kids' clothes can wait. Let's shop for ourselves." Amy was sitting in my living room when I took the call. "Good," I said, "I need new clothes too."

As I hung up, Amy said, "Boy, do I need new clothes." She'd just started back at the Vo-Tech, studying to be a veterinary assistant. "I hate shopping," she said. "Your things are so cute."

So were Amy's, but piece by piece—not how she put them together. For instance, she wore a sleeveless pink blouse tucked into jeans, and clunky brown shoes: a southern belle from the waist up, a lumberjack from the waist down. It was fashionable for clothes to go together unwillingly—satin with sheepskin, a tuxedo jacket with faded jeans. But to violate style, you have to understand it. To wear those shoes with that blouse, I thought, the rustic with the dainty, she needs to mix it up head to toe, not top-half, then bottom—she needs to *accessorize*. I said, "You look fine." I thought of Rosemary as I said it, the Mennonite girl I'd befriended and dropped. It was Amy's coloring, I guess, and her old-fashioned, floral-print blouse. I invited her to come shopping.

As we sat waiting for Zoe the morning of the shopping trip, the phone rang. It was my mother, who'd recently moved to San Ardo, California, with her boyfriend—her "fiancé"—and she'd come to rely on the phone and special weekend rates for expressing maternal instinct. "I just called to say hello," she said. "What are you up to?" I explained I was going shopping. "With my friend, Amy," I said, "and Zoe is coming down from Bremmer." My mother said, "How nice, your best friend from childhood and a college friend too." I couldn't explain with Amy sitting there that she wasn't from college. Besides, I liked the way it sounded.

In the department store, I noticed both Amy and Zoe had lots of money—from drugs and potatoes, respectively. Tom had tried to give me forty dollars the night before: "Buy yourself something," he'd said. I'd refused, insulted, but it was different for Amy, who lived with Horse: you wouldn't live with someone unless you could share money without worrying where it came from. Zoe bought matched outfits in bright colors, but all of them boring like something my sister, Helen, would wear. Amy followed us around. "That's cute," she'd say, but she didn't try anything on. We ended up in the lingerie department my mother had brought me to the summer before when she bought me all the undergarments ("foundations") she imagined a college girl might need. The same clerk—a grandmotherly type who'd come into the dressing room and put her glasses on to stare at my bosom and warn me never to consider a bra without underwire—waited on Zoe as she bought panties.

Zoe said to Amy, "Aren't you going to buy anything?"

Amy just smiled.

On the way out, Zoe stopped at a display of honeymoon lingerie and looked at a black lace corset—strapless, elastic garters dangling from the hem. "Dick would like that?" I asked, curious.

Zoe looked at me. "M.Y.O.B.," she said. I'd never heard that expression before. I thought maybe it stood for a kind of sex, like "69." Later, when I asked Tom and he explained (M.Y.O.B., Mind Your Own Business, that Ann Landers always said it), I felt let down.

Zoe bought the black lace thing, a merry widow. At the last minute Amy grabbed one too, followed Zoe to the counter, plunked it down, and pulled a wad of twenties from her pocket. Both Zoe and the clerk looked surprised. "I'm not sure that's your size, dear," the clerk said. It was the only thing Amy bought all day except—when we went to a discount store so Zoe could buy school clothes for her kids—a pair of beige corduroy slacks.

"Beige is ugly," Zoe said.

I said, "So is navy blue." Zoe was wearing navy. All day she'd been rude to Amy. And when we pulled up in front of Tom's house—and Horse was in the front yard, and Tom was on the porch wearing jeans, no shirt, even though it was September, already cool—Zoe sat with her foot on the brake, frowning. Tom was talking on the phone, the cord stretched through the doorframe. Zoe said, "I take it the guy with the Jesse James mustache is Amy's boyfriend, and the torso on the telephone belongs to you. Anyway, I've got to head out. Dick doesn't know where I am. Think of it." She put her car in gear, a Ford Bronco, and drove away.

Tom went back into the house.

Horse kissed Amy. "Tom's on a rampage," he said.

I was thinking about Zoe, how she saved good manners for formal occasions—that being her friend meant I was exempt from pretense and empty gesture; I should be flattered. But still. I sat on the step. "Why is Tom mad?" I asked. Before Horse could answer, Tom came outside, jabbing me in the back with the edge of the screen door—I almost toppled into the yard. And he yelled at me: How long could I possibly shop? Was I an inconsiderate shopping idiot?

At first I thought he'd been worried, jealous, he'd missed me. Should I be mad? Should I say: there, there (which is how you talk to children)? Then Tom said he needed to use my car, right now, he was sick of waiting. I remember the details, the blue sky, the flaming red-and-orange trees. Someone across the street carrying groceries into their house, stopping to watch, curious, aloof. Bert pulling Sue back inside because she was staring, eyes wide, mouth open. Horse and Amy walking discreetly away. The dogs bounding toward us, then milling in confused circles as they slowed, noses quivering, sensing blood-heat in the air.

I spoke through my unreliable mouth, insults as astringent and toxic as bleach. *You. Drug-addled. Sleep with me— fuck me*, I said—*because of my car. Everyone is amazed. Stupid. My dad hates you. You don't have friends, just customers.* I'd thought some of this before—complaints, worries—in those treacherous, skeptical moments when I realized Tom and I would never last. We were ill-starred, ridiculous. Some insults I invented on the spot, and yet how accurate, how stinging. I said them in the front yard on a fall day, clutching a Herberger's department store bag. Did saying them make them true? Last and ultimate: *I hate you*, I said. Something failed, essential power. In the stalled-out aftermath, I felt relieved. How lucky Zoe hadn't stayed, after all. Horse and Amy came back around the corner. Tom—glittery-eyed, exhausted, his shoulders rolling. I loved him still.

I followed him in the house—past Bert and Sue getting ready to leave—through the kitchen, the living room, into the bathroom, where he splashed water on his face. I searched for outward signs of damage, loss of function, confidence. Was something broken? Or were we, together, durable like heavy plastic? I laid my hand on his arm. He pushed me into the wall—the jagged sound his lungs made, *in-out in-out*, like a motor with a bad lifter turning over. To indicate it was lust making his heart pound, making him sob, he kissed me. If we kissed long and hard enough there wouldn't be time for anything else. To come or go. Leave. Split up.

Horse tapped on the door. "Sorry," he said, "but we'd better get going." Then Tom tried to apologize by saying he'd asked yesterday to borrow my car—I was supposed to have dropped the keys off. It sounded like one of Tom's plans, except it wasn't. "I didn't see you yesterday," I said. "I was studying for a test."

Tom said, "Well, maybe the day before. Maybe I forgot." He left with Horse—they jogged the six blocks to my apartment to get my car.

Amy and I watched them huff away. Then we walked to the grocery store to buy food for dinner. In the clean, well-lit aisles, we talked about Stouffer's Frozen Spinach Soufflé, which Horse liked, and Broccoli with Cheese Sauce, Tom's favorite. We bought steak, lettuce, baking potatoes, and dog food—all of it with Tom's money. How easily scruples melted away, I realized. What had I meant anyway, lending my car, but refusing gifts, bounty? "Amy," I said, in the kitchen at Tom's house, doing dishes to free up the sink so we could cook unimpeded, "do you and Horse ever fight?" I meant: do you hate, every day, the drug deals?

"Horse isn't a fighter," she said.

I could see that—he jollied Tom out of his moods and tantrums.

"He writes poetry," she said quietly, scrubbing potato skins.

I said, "Really?"

"About his feelings," she said.

I tried to think what Horse's feelings might be. I remembered the Barry Manilow song, my sister's favorite: vague, unprovoked "Feelings." I thought of the boys in my high school English class, the poems they wrote when the teacher asked them to, a combination of science fiction and rock and roll, like: "Dungeon queen, perchance to dream, all that glitters isn't gold." I'd been studying poetry myself, some of it five hundred years old. *Fowls in the frith, fishes in the flood, much sorrow I walk with* . . . Once, when I was half-undressed, my figure enhanced by the undergarments my mother had bought me at the most expensive department store in town, I'd circled Tom's neck with my arms, imagining them white and slender, and myself, the poet's muse. I quoted my favorite sonnet: *Dearheart, how like you this?* "Not very much," Tom had answered. He was mad, punishing me, holding back.

"He's high-strung," Amy said. "He loves you so much. He can't help it."

"Help what?" I said.

"Loving you." She frowned, reconsidering. "Or being high-strung."

Then Tom and Horse came back and turned up the stereo. I remembered how my mother used to serve dinner to some of my dad's friends—she was pretty, a good cook, an asset. "Delicious," Tom said, patting me on the butt. The loud music—its thudding bass—made eating a chore, conversation difficult. When dinner was over, I turned the stereo off, made coffee, and served pie. I shut the windows because, outside, the temperature fell; winter loomed. I looked at Amy, her corduroy pants and plaid shirt, her clunky shoes—Pearl's head was in her lap. Angel, Tom's dog, slept. Horse lit a joint. This was home, I realized. Times change.

Horse said, "Do you still have that blotter, Tom?"

No one spoke.

Horse said, "I didn't trust Mick, but he came through. I guess that's fine."

"What are you talking about?" I said. I thought of desk blotters—those nice, cushy surfaces. Of course, Horse was talking about LSD. But I couldn't imagine anyone I knew doing it. When I was a kid, Art Linkletter's daughter had, and—thinking she was an orange about to be squeezed and turned into juice—she jumped out a window. "No one does that anymore," I said.

Horse shrugged. "An odd fellow here and there."

I looked at Tom. "Then this is what Mick got," I said, "in Chicago?"

He nodded. "I didn't think you'd want to know."

I didn't. But what difference did it make, I wondered: One illegal drug or another? All of them cargo on a train that sped toward us from who knew what sordid point? Who, for instance, were the people in Chicago Mick had bartered with? And before them, the source of the source, who did they get drugs from? Ethics, I saw, required constant attention, fine-tuning. First, I'd drawn the line with marijuana, the "Lord's Weed." Then—with such lucrative business from the fraternities, even a city councilman—cocaine. But this hallucinogenic throwback to the sixties? "Don't worry," Tom said, "it's almost gone. I won't get anymore."

"I'll take the rest off your hands," Horse said.

I looked at Amy. "Do you"—I tried to remember the lingo—"trip?"

"When I'm out in nature," she said. "Never when I have to be indoors."

I didn't understand the distinction.

I stood up, crossed the room, and sat down again. Tom watched me, preparing his excuses. But I surprised him by saying nothing. I let my mind wander—my eyes settled on the bathroom door, standing ajar. When Tom first moved into this house, I'd helped him unpack, arrrange furniture. We were new lovers—summer stretched ahead. We drank wine on the front porch. At nightfall, I took a shower. Because there wasn't a curtain on the window yet, I hurried as I dried off. Then I looked up and saw a face—a window peeper—and screamed. Tom rushed into the bathroom and, when I told him what I'd seen, he ran into the backyard, his dog snapping and growling behind him. He never saw, or caught, anyone. As I retold the story later—to Tom, to Bert and Sue—I thought how indistinct the face had been, the blur it became as it slid away. A face belonging to a "bad" person had moved in, close to my own, then faded. Was it my reflection? What did I know for sure?

"Louisa?" Horse asked. "Is everything okay?"

I looked up.

Tom sat across the room, waiting. And Horse and Amy—my friends.

For a moment, the word seemed unfamiliar.
Friends?
"Yes," I said, deciding.

The next time I saw Zoe, it was February, very cold. The car tires crunched, rolling over snow-packed roads. Tom and I were driving to Westly—a town north of Bremmer—to find a guy named Geet who'd been Tom's link to the fraternities, a brisk business until Geet started acting like a drug abuser on some TV program, pale and nervous, telling obvious lies, even banging on Tom's bedroom window once when we'd been about to make love, the doors locked, music playing softly. Tom had put his bathrobe on and opened the window. "Chrissake, Geet," he said, "I'm with my girl." I was on the bed, wrapped in a blanket. Geet waved at me. "I've got a quick favor to ask," he told Tom. Now he'd disappeared, and we were driving to his hometown to find him. Tom hunched over the steering wheel and said, "What was he thinking of, running away? I need to talk to him and work things out."

The car heater was on high. Angel and Pearl sat in back, panting. We drove through Bremmer—one stoplight—and continued north.

As we passed the Swanger farm, I pointed it out to Tom—an old barn with a Pillsbury Flour logo on its side, junked cars and rusty appliances in the yard. I was struck by a memory having to do with one of my dad's car deals. I was continually struck by the way my love affair with Tom seemed like my parent's marriage except for ironic details. For instance, when the Swangers reneged on debts, my dad felt bad about the way he'd meant to help them, then got treated like a sucker. Geet's disappearance caused the same emotions for Tom—self-doubt, anger. I was confused. How would my mother have reacted? Once, when she was mad about yet another deal with the Swangers, she said: "Never mix business with pleasure." Then she stopped, confused. She couldn't see how contact with the Swangers was pleasure. At one point, I'd complained to Tom: "Geet talks weird," I said, "and his personal grooming is lax." Tom explained how everyone he did business with wasn't his friend. Still, he sat Geet down and told him that some dealers did lots of drugs, but none who lasted. "You should have cut him off," I said now.

He said, "Hindsight is twenty/twenty."

All day, we'd been fighting. Tom's grades for fall semester had come in the mail that morning: a D, two Cs, an Incomplete. "You can do better than this," I'd said, waving the grade report. He could. One semester, a sociology professor had hypnotized Tom, instructing him to improve his grades. It was the power of suggestion, I suppose, and the fact that Tom wanted to help a professor who'd taken a special interest—he wanted to validate the professor's research. And Tom was smart. He made the Dean's List.

I said, "I still can't believe your grade report."

He said, "Easy for you to say. My dad doesn't send me money." Tom didn't have a dad—at least he didn't know where his dad was.

I said, "Other people work their way through college without breaking the law." Which wasn't the point. What was? "You can't concentrate on your studies," I said. "Drug dealing is too stressful."

We pulled into the edge of Westly, a small, farming town. WILLKOMMEN TO WESTLY, a sign with flowers and scrolled letters said. Tom parked in front of a white clapboard house with snowbanks packed against it, its sidewalk shoveled deep. I waited in the car as he knocked on the door. I couldn't see who answered it—just Tom in his three-toned ski jacket, nodding and smiling. I assumed he was talking to Geet's mother.

"What did you say?" I asked him when he got back to the car.

"That I was Geet's friend. He's down at the shop—just off Main Street."

In a moment, we pulled up in front of it. GIEDT'S SMALL ENGINE REPAIR.

"Look how Geet is spelled," I said.

"Are you coming in?" Tom asked me.

I hesitated.

"Yes," I said. We opened the door and stepped into a hot, luminous room. Engine blocks rested on platforms, but no one was working—it was Sunday afternoon. Men with gray whiskers, smoking pipes and wearing coveralls, sat around a potbellied stove. A younger man came through a door in back, closing it behind him. Everyone was quiet as they stared, at Tom in his new ski jacket, at me. I was wearing boots with high heels and pointed toes (yet made of rugged leather, a nice incongruity, I'd thought at the time I bought them, worth the price). And a fur coat I'd bought at a thrift store. A lot of college girls wore furs then. They got them from rummage sales or great-aunts who'd packed them in mothballs. No one worried about animal rights yet. But the old men didn't care about dead animal pelts, or whether I'd dressed the coat down by wearing it with jeans. What they saw when they stared was extravagance, money. I looked around.

I smiled.

No one smiled back. In an instant, I realized they thought I wasn't *nice*. Or maybe that I used to be—they looked me up and down—and then, how sad, I'd run with a bad crowd and got corrupted.

Tom said, "I'm a friend of Fred's from school."

Fred, I thought: Fred Giedt.

"He hasn't been around," Tom said. "I've been worried."

He *was* worried—not just about money. He liked Geet. He wanted to work things out. Once when I'd complained how pesky and stupid Geet was, that I couldn't imagine why he went to college, Tom had answered: "Lighten up. You're a snob." Like my dad might have said.

The younger man ignored us, scrubbing his hands with a rag. "Fred's not here," he said. Then he stared. "You're his friends from college?"

Tom nodded.

"What in hell are you doing here?" He walked away, slamming the door to the back room.

I suppose that's where Geet was, hiding.

And the old men knew it and thought I was a new-fangled gangster's moll, that I satisfied my taste for fancy clothes with tainted money. (Thou shalt not, I thought. Not what? "Take thy neighbor's money nor goods, nor get them by false ware or dealing.") I thought about Fred Giedt, who was no doubt the first kid in his family to go to college, the great hope, and now he was in trouble. And the Giedts couldn't tell I was from down the road, from Bremmer, that I knew Luther's Small Catechism by rote, that I had scruples. "You tell him I said hello," Tom said, disheartened. He wanted people to like him. He wanted a white clapboard house and a brother who'd stand up for him.

He walked out to the car, wearing that ski jacket, no hat or gloves. This was my territory, the northwoods—I'd grown up here. "You must be freezing," I said. We sat in the car, letting it idle, the defroster clearing the windshield that fogged up because of Angel and Pearl clamoring in back. Tom put the car in gear. He lit a joint. He'd promised me that we could visit Zoe if I rode along on this trip. "You still want to go?" I asked him. He shrugged. "Why not? She's expecting us, right?"

He was quiet as I showed him which road to take to the potato farm. We turned down a driveway a quarter-mile long. A farmhouse sat at the end of it, a row of immense silos glowing blue and silver as the sun sank below the horizon. Zoe served us weak, amber-colored coffee, and crumb cake with cinnamon icing. We sat in the living room, our plates perched on our knees. Zoe's husband, the potato heir, Dick, I've never called him that, had better manners than he used to in the days I first knew him when—irritated at the way Zoe dragged me along on their dates—he'd make jokes about how I was undeveloped, un-womanly. "You're looking good," he said. "You grew up real pretty." The kids ran around, two boys I couldn't tell apart except the oldest seemed moody, like he'd been pam-pered those first years he was an only child.

I remembered again about the stillborn baby.

I studied Zoe's face.

So she'd had that, I thought: misery. I don't mean I found misery picturesque. But for a second I envied Zoe's adult stature, her wisdom-through-experience conferred by pain. In one of my classes, I'd been studying catharsis—how you cleanse yourself of negative emotions by watch-ing someone else's tragedy. Of course, you're supposed to get the tragedy from a play, a story, something fictional. But how instinctive, I realized, how easy, to see someone's life as tragedy, to appropriate fury and grief.

Or not easy. Like I said, Zoe never self-discloses.

"So you have two boys," Tom said. Small talk. He was stoned.

But Zoe grinned and told him more than she'd ever told me. "That's right," she said to Tom. "But we keep try-ing for a girl." She slapped Dick on the knee for emphasis. "Isn't that right?"

Then she asked how my family was.

I explained we hadn't seen them.

She said, "But I saw your sister last week and we talked about you coming—at least I did. I assumed you were coming to see family."

Tom and I looked at each other.

Zoe said, "You came all this way just to see me?"

I said, "Tom has this friend in Westly—"

Tom interrupted me.

All I'd intended to say was that we'd stopped to see Tom's friend in Westly—I wouldn't have said *why*. It was conceivable, but not likely, that we might have stopped to see Geet, a social call. But later, when I explained this to

Tom, he got angry: "You don't understand small talk," he said. "When Zoe asked if you came to see her, you should have said yes. You put too much stock in sincerity." Meanwhile, he said to Zoe, "Of course we're going to visit Louisa's sister. Her name is Helen, right? How far is it?"

"Too far," I said.

Zoe said, "Not by back roads. But they haven't been plowed today."

Dick spoke up. "You could take the Bronco," he said. "It's four-wheel drive." Zoe gave him a sharp, critical glance. But Tom didn't notice. He said, "We could?" He loved cars. He had lost time behind the wheel to make up for—he hadn't gotten his license until he'd met me and borrowed my Pontiac to take the test. So maybe because Dick offered the Bronco. Or because the Giedt family had treated him like a thug. Or he was sick of his own childhood and wanted mine. But he was dead-set on visiting Helen. Me, I wanted to go back to Menominee. I didn't like being an ambassador between my people and Tom, our customs and his.

County M to 25. Left on Y, six miles.

The road was snowy, phosphorescent. Angel and Pearl hadn't been fed since morning. "It's just that I've never met your sister," Tom said. Sometimes, at night, he'd ask: What was the worst thing I ever did and how had my dad punished me? Did we take family vacations? Did my mom get up in the morning and fix breakfast? Tom's accounts of his own childhood were incomplete—when they got depressing, I changed the subject. I wanted catharsis—someone else's tragedy—in small doses. Not in bed, pillow talk.

I said, "They'll wonder why we're so late."

Tom said, "Is that your dad's car?" His Riviera was parked in Helen's driveway. We pulled up next to it, and my dad came outside.

"You made it," he said. "We thought we had the dates mixed up."

We went in—to Helen's living room with its beige carpet and orange sofa. Helen, wearing slacks and a blouse, stared at my fur coat, luxurious, wide like a bell above my spike-heeled boots. She wrinkled her nose. "John had a Snowmobile Club meeting," she said. "I held dinner as long as I could. You should have called." She stared at Tom. "Are you spending the night?"

I said, "We're just out for a drive."

Helen said, "Fine. I could make meatloaf sandwiches for you to eat in the car." She turned on the TV, *The Barbara Mandrell Show*.

My dad sat down on the couch. Barbara Mandrell was wearing a sequined tunic with a sash. "What are you driving?" my dad asked me. I explained that we'd borrowed the Bronco from Zoe. "Nice piece of equipment," he said. "Zoe turned out to be a smart farm wife."

Tom said, "Smart? They're loaded. Those silos? A hundred grand a piece. I read somewhere they're a status symbol for farmers."

"Interesting point," my dad said. "How's the lawn mowing?"

Tom said, "Obviously not too great in the winter."

"I figured that," my dad said, nodding.

Was he sending a message, I wondered, implying he'd never believed the line about the lawn-mowing service? Was this small talk?

Helen said, "It's a funny time of year for a Sunday drive."

My dad said, "You could invest in a snowblower."

A snow-blowing service with trolls, I thought. Funny.

Helen said, "Well, do you want those meatloaf sandwiches or not?"

Tom said, "We'd better head out. I have homework."

In the Bronco on the way back to Zoe's, I said, "What an excuse, homework. Like you're going to do homework at midnight." We pulled into Zoe's yard, the blue-and-silver silos (the status symbols) gleaming in the dark sky. (Was this some sociology idea, I wondered, like that business about church steeples really standing for penises?) As

I herded the dogs out of the Bronco into the back of the Pontiac, I looked up and saw Zoe in her kitchen window. Tom gestured that he was leaving her keys under the floor mat. She gestured back, waving and nodding behind the yellow-lit pane of glass. I said, "She's not coming out to say good-bye, I guess."

"I need to get back," Tom said. "I have an appointment."

I said, "It's late."

"Late," he said, "exactly."

We pulled onto the highway. Already the rhythm of the car lulled me, the tires churning snow to slush, the dashboard heater whirring, the dogs settling to sleep. I burrowed into my coat and slept too, the silky feeling of fur against my face. I had one of those dreams where I knew it was a dream and I could have forced myself awake, but didn't, riding along—a passenger—to the end.

It was a noisy dream, people talking. My dad and I were at the Bremmer County Fair, looking at 4-H displays: a jar of pickles, a skirt with flat-sewn seams, an embroidered sofa pillow. Then we went to a pole-barn to look at animals that had been scrubbed and combed, the pigs especially, their pink skin. My dad said, "Monkey, let's see what's happening at the arena." Anything was possible—a tractor pull or fashion show, a tug of war. But when we followed the crowd through the gate and sat in the bleachers, we found ourselves watching a demonstration of Rototillers. "Imagine," my dad said. Short, stumpy men with long hair—even at a distance I could see it needed washing— were churning up dirt with Rototillers. Mick, I thought, Mick's brothers. What were they doing in my dream? My dad was talking to someone. "These are a few of Louisa's friends," he said, "from college."

I woke up. We were in front of Tom's house.

The dogs scrambled out of the car, racing zig-zag across the yard. I knew as soon as we got to the porch, the house shaking, that Bert and Sue were making love. A Neil Young song was playing not just on the tape deck Bert kept in his room but on Tom's stereo in the living room, Bose 901 speakers. Tom turned it off. There was a moment—like in cartoons where the coyote runs off the cliff and doesn't look down—when the song stopped but Bert and Sue continued. Oh oh, Sue called. Then silence. Bert came out wearing his bathrobe. "That wasn't nice," he said to Tom. I was feeding the dogs, and he smiled at me. "Louisa, *c'est la vie*." More and more, he implied we were two of a kind, long-suffering. Sue stood next to him, wrapped in a yellow bedsheet. It was hard to tell from her bored, sleek expression—the way she didn't blink when Tom stared—if she was mad, or curious. And willing.

Tom sorted magazines into stacks. He moved a plastic bong into a closet and wiped the coffee table with a rag. "I have an appointment. Go back to bed. Sorry to interrupt," he added, "buddy."

Bert shrugged. Sue followed him into his room.

Then Tom and I had a fight—a re-run of a fight—about where I'd sleep. "I have class at nine," I said. "I hate going out in the cold and driving home, just to go out again." Tom said, "I'll never understand why you don't bring more of your stuff over. Live here." He'd said this before. "Where would I study?" I asked.

Again, he didn't answer.

Someone knocked. "That's it," Tom said. Al came through the door.

That's not to say that Tom introduced Al. "This is my girl," Tom said, "Louisa." And in the pause where it would have been customary to say Al's name, Tom said mine again: "Louisa." Al said, "Pleased to know you." He had blond hair, a flat nose, and cheeks that were plump and rosy like a cherub's—and looked oddly sexy with his black leather outfit, a silver chain dangling from his belt to his thick wallet. "Call me Al," he said, helping Tom out with the introduction. Years later, when I read about his arraignment in the paper—Al Jakubowski, 501 Spruce

Street—I realized how well I'd known him, how long, his last name a quiet secret.

I said, "I better go."

"Sit down," Al said. "This is important."

He looked at Tom. "Rules," he said. "I make deliveries late at night. I don't want to meet, or see, roommates. Except of course the girlfriend." He nodded at me. Tom said something enthusiastic about my character. "Don't sell small," Al said. "Sell quantity to a few people. Let them develop traffic, the penny-pinching idiots who want an eighth of this, a sixth of that. Then tell everyone where they got it." He stared at Tom, at me. I stared back like one of those students who sits in the front row, a teacher's pet. His speech sounded familiar, not the words but the gist— for success do this, not that. Like catechism, I realized, like finding out that the way you've always done things isn't strict enough to get you to heaven, to keep you safe. I sat on the couch, exhausted and worried. What if they were the wrong rules?

Later, in Tom's bed, the streetlight outside the window brilliant because of new snow, I tried to sleep. But words ran through my head. *This is my exit, I'm getting off. Strange bedfellows. Mind my own business.* "Al seems abrupt," I said, finally.

"Businesslike," Tom answered.

"The people you sell to, who will they be?"

"Friends," Tom said, rolling over and kissing me. "Like Geet, Geet used to be. Horse." Tom touched me. My apprehensions flowed out. "You love Horse," Tom said, touching me again, "and Amy."

I never saw Al, only evidence he'd been there. "It's not unthinkable for Al to mix business with pleasure," Tom explained, "but he'd have to really like you. He discriminates." As for the two or three people Tom sold to, I didn't see them either, because I chose not to. I'd pass someone on the sidewalk who'd say hello. I'd be on my way in, he'd be on his way out—and I'd walk right by. One day I came to get Tom because we were going to the mall, and one of these guys I knew-and-yet-didn't was in the living room. And Sue, without Bert. And Horse, on the couch. I was wearing a red plastic raincoat that crackled as I sat down next to him. "Long time, no see," I said, demonstrating I wasn't a snob. But I also wasn't going to be nice to every Geet or Mick who passed through this living room which, if it used to seem like a retail store, now seemed like a wholesale outlet, more efficient, less amenities required. Besides, did my dad make friends with everyone he sold cars to? "Horse," I said, "how's Amy?"

"Man," he said, "depressed."

I saw the coke mirror on the coffee table. "She is?" I said, looking at Tom rubbing his nose, at Sue in a chair beside him, blinking.

"I told her to talk to you," Horse said. "You're a brain."

A brain? I thought. Depressed? The guy I didn't know left. Amy came through the front door. She said, "Louisa, I hoped you'd be here. I don't know what to do. I'm failing one of my classes."

Sue sniffed. "At the Vo-Tech? You actually studied for a class at the Vo-Tech, and you're failing?"

Horse said, "She's getting Cs in her other classes."

I said, "She's putting herself through school—loans and grants. She's under pressure." Still, I thought. Cs, Ds? How hard was it? What did she want me to do? And why had Tom done coke before we went shopping at the mall? "Did you talk to the teacher?"

Amy gave me a trembling, crooked smile. "Should I?"

Dumbkopf, I thought, which is my dad's word. Dumbhead, my own. In the span of a minute, my interest in Amy vanished. I always remember the moment: I serve a tennis ball to Rosemary and she lopes toward it and misses. I spend the night with Danielle Thompson and, washing my face as I get ready for bed, decide it's her fault she's not clean because, like my mother says, soap is cheap. Though I remember the precise moment a friendship ends, I never know why. And I don't see it coming. I didn't know until Amy smiled, embarrassed, asking for something. What could I give her? I stood up. "Don't worry, I'll call you," I said. "We have to go."

In the car on the way to the mall, I thought how, again, I'd been snobbish and cruel: I'd have to change. But first I'd extricate myself. I'd act bored and remote. Amy would notice something was wrong. But she wouldn't know why. I couldn't tell her. I didn't know either. She'd stare. I'd flinch. "What classes do you have to take to be a veterinary assistant?" I asked Tom.

"Who cares?" he said. "She's no rocket scientist."

I said, "You should talk. Your brain needs to be dusted off and used." Tom hardly went to class now. His grades at midterm were bad. "Burn-out," he explained, sounding like Bert. ("I'm intellectually fried," Bert used to say. "You're fried," Tom had answered.) "When Bert got bad grades," I said, "you made fun of him."

"I never made fun of Bert," Tom said.

"You did." I reminded him of one day we were in a liquor store and Bert was buying Midori, a green melon liqueur, for special drinks he made in the blender. And talking again about needing the semester off. "I've been tense," he said, handing the cashier a fifty-dollar bill. "You're a spoiled jerk-off," Tom had said. "I never said that," Tom said now. But I could tell by the way he walked fast, losing himself in the crowd, he remembered. He went into the Ye Olde Smoke Shoppe and bought imported to-bacco. He'd taken to smoking a pipe with a sloped stem like Hugh Hefner's as he paced around in his bathrobe, listening to music.

A home-and-garden show was going on in the mall corridor—"Spring Fling" a banner said. Tom stopped at a

hot-tub display, nodding thoughtfully as the salesman described deluxe features. I watched him, gaunt and muscular, running his hand through his hair, laughing at the
salesman's joke. Looking at someone you love is like looking at your reflection. It's yours, you want it to last. But
you know its imperfections. His head is full of cocaine, I
told myself. He wants too much. To be rich yet altruistic.
To work nine to five as a social worker, yet spend evenings
in a hot tub, nights in bed on satin sheets. I looked at a display of garden tractors, at a fat-bellied salesman in a
Hawaiian shirt sitting in a lawn chair under a fake palm. If
I were a heroine, now would have been the moment of my
conversion. I understood in a permanant, instant way: it
was over. Using things up, throwing them out. Where do
people go when you cut them loose?

I yanked on Tom's arm. "Where's Geet?"

"What do you mean, where's Geet?" Tom said. "He's in
town—avoiding me. Why are you talking about this?"
Shoppers milled around us. I couldn't help myself.
"Where's Mick?" I said. I'd hated Mick, short, foul-
smelling, not having sense enough not to hand Tom cash
in front of my dad. An inopportune fact, Mick. But facts
don't disappear. "He's around," Tom answered. "Horse
sees him."

"Horse said Mick was sloppy," I said, remembering how
at the time it seemed like a character defect: Mick is
sloppy, not our kind.

Tom said, "He is. I can't afford it with the volume I do."

"But where is he?" I said. "Who does he hang around
with?" I meant what is the rest of his life like? Where does
he live and breathe?

But Tom was talking business. "I'm not responsible," he
said.

We left the mall—with me behind the wheel—and I
dropped Tom at home in the cold rain. I sat with the car
idling as he looked at me through the wet, beaded glass. I
smiled and waved broadly, a reflex: increased, effusive

manners. I didn't self-disclose. Etiquette keeps us from revealing our feelings too soon. I drove away as Tom stood in his yard, holding a bag. Then I remembered Pearl—I'd left her at Tom's. I did this a lot so she could romp in the yard with Angel. But this time I wanted her home. I parked my car and went to get her. I shooed her into the back seat. "I've got to hurry," I said, waving. "Homework. Lots to do."

At my apartment I sat for a long time in my rain slicker, Pearl curled warm and damp at my feet. I knew I should call Amy and say something helpful about her grades. Instead, I thought about the moment of resolve I'd had in the mall corridor while looking at shopping carts and fake palms. Did I think I'd defect from one group of friends, Bert and Sue, Horse and Amy—in the end, Tom too—and transport myself to a new group, reformed, sincere at last? Would, someday, what I felt and what I said match? I picked up the phone and called information for Zoe's number and dialed long-distance to Bremmer, to talk. But—I reminded myself as Zoe picked up the phone and said hello—Zoe doesn't talk. She fires off sarcastic comments while lighting a cigarette, downshifting a car, washing a sweater in the bathroom sink.

"How's Tom?" she asked me.

"Fine," I said. "How's Dick?"

"Buying a tractor we don't need. I'm pregnant," she added.

I pictured Zoe the last time I saw her—behind a pane of glass. "That's great," I said. "I suppose you and Dick feel very close."

"The night I got pregnant we did." A joke. "How's your friend?" What friend? I wondered. "Amy," she said. At first, I couldn't figure out how Zoe knew Amy. The shopping trip, I realized. Zoe sounded like my mother, who used to duck her head into the rec room and say: "How are you and your little friend doing?"

"I don't see her much," I admitted.

Zoe said, "She was such a dork."

I didn't know what to say.

But a nice dork. She keeps herself neat and clean (this is what my dad once said about a friend of Helen's named Cheryl who ended up marrying a Swanger). I said to Zoe, "I feel I can talk to Amy. She shares a lot." This was corny, even inaccurate—though I'd hoped Amy would turn out to be a close friend, the most intimate conversation we'd had to date was about Horse's favorite foods. But I kept on. I was trying to tell Zoe something. "I like a person who opens up," I said. Zoe said, "This is long distance. I better go." Even though I'd called her.

I hung up. I took off my coat and shoes.

I wanted to like Amy, still.

But I knew from experience I couldn't rouse my enthusiasm once—at some unremarkable point—it dwindled. I remembered Rosemary, the Mennonite girl, how after she'd spent the weekend with me I kept trying to send a message: *How can I miss you if you won't go away?* I'd chanted this silently, over and over, my eyes boring into Rosemary until one day we were walking to Chorus and I said it out loud. Her face crumbled. She never spoke to me again even if we were in a group and, guilt-stricken, I waved and called, "Rosemary, hello. How are you?" She turned red and looked away.

I tried to think why I'd first liked Amy, but I only remembered when. Tom and I had stopped to visit them at their old house that sat between a gas station and plant nursery. Amy had odd furniture, a sofa made of beige vinyl with an embossed picture of a saddle, and wooden armrests that looked like wheels. And in the built-in cabinets around the fireplace, plastic statues of animals. Horse explained that Amy loved animals. Her favorite book was *All Things Bright and Beautiful.* She was going to school to be a veterinary assistant, and they'd be broke in the meantime, but they didn't care. We'd just finished eating dinner. Tom and Horse smoked a joint. Horse put his arm around Amy and started singing that hillbilly song about not having enough money, your clothes look ragged and funny. But you have each other. "Side by side . . ." Horse danced and sang this. Amy smiled and blushed. These are the ones I want for friends, I decided.

It came to this. I pulled my window shades and locked the door.

I'd had disloyal, impulsive thoughts. I wouldn't have disloyal actions. Not yet. I'd call Amy. I'd invest more time. I might turn out to be wrong, and we'd be friends still. I thought this as I got ready for bed. Or we might not, in which case I'd put the friendship out of its misery. I'd make my detachment—I was tired, falling asleep—painless and gradual as sleep.

A few weeks later, I'd found excuses not to stay at Tom's anymore, but I hadn't yet decided why he shouldn't stay with me. I used to want him to, and he wouldn't: he was comfortable at home, he'd say. He needed to be near the phone. But now he'd left a razor and toothbrush in my bathroom and—imagine my surprise when I found this—a bag of pot, clean socks and underwear in a drawer where I otherwise kept dishtowels. He sat on the couch, smoking. "Nice to get away," he said, "from the phone, the pressure." He was polite, no demands. For instance, on the first day of spring, I set a limit on lovemaking. From here on out—I said during foreplay, my dress sliding off my shoulder, Tom murmuring as he kissed my neck—once would be enough. Then we made love and when we were done, when each of us was done, Tom reached for me again, and I nudged him away, the tip of my finger against his hips. "Right," he said, "once. I forgot." He fell asleep, his feet pushing the end of the bedsheet out.

I went into the living room and sat on the couch, reading *Madame Bovary*, about the love-starved Emma who, once she'd had an affair, saw that the color of her eyes changed, the arch of her foot had gone languid in the climate of luxury. In addition to true love, she wanted new clothes, jewels, cactus plants to sit on the window ledge. It was a matter of time before she'd be made to pay. Greed kills. But only in books, I told myself. The phone rang.

I looked at the clock—almost midnight. The phone rang again.

Someone sick or dying, that's what a phone call in the middle of the night is. Or a pervert. I wanted the ringing to stop. "Hello," I said. It was Amy, her voice ragged and sad. My first impulse was to invent reasons why I hadn't called. I'd meant to, but I'd been busy, homework. Tom and I hadn't been getting along—that kept me preoccupied. (My mother always says: when you make excuses, make just one, or you sound like a liar.) Amy said, "Sorry to wake you up, Louisa. I tried at Tom's and they said he was with you. I need to talk to him." Tom was in the doorway behind me, naked. "He's here," I said. He grabbed the phone out of my hand. I listened. "What the fuck?" he said. "You're kidding?"

"He still had some of *that?*"

"Try to get some sleep. I'll call tomorrow."

He hung up. He said, "Horse sold blotter to a narc."

My thinking stopped. Blotter?

Narc?

Next I considered myself—that Horse was busted, that was sad, but not my problem. Of course, Tom would be implicated if Horse talked. I'd grieve and worry. I'd been an accessory, riding along, loaning my car. But Tom, chivalrous, wouldn't say so. I might go to hell for loving a drug dealer, but here on earth I wasn't going to prison. I looked at Tom, holding his head in his hands. He said, "It was my blotter. Horse took it off my hands as a favor. It's my fault, passing off customers like Mick."

I said, "Mick?" I didn't like Tom this way, guilty, worried. I got mad. I saw white—the absence of color, color leaching away.

Tom said, "Mick brought the narc over to Horse's. Not intentionally, I guess. He's careless. But it's the same in the end."

I had a lot to say—that Tom had gambled and lost. It was his fault, yes. It was time to quit. I couldn't afford to love him. What I said in the end was clichéd and dull. "I told you so."

Tom said, "Chrissake. You didn't like Mick because he's uncouth. That's not the same as saying you thought he was a risk."

Yet it is. Good manners are logical. Mick was stupid. Amy was better—she liked manners and rules but couldn't always figure out what they were. It's not as if they're written down somewhere—even when they are, the Ten Commandments, Emily Post, you need to keep your wits about you as to the way they change with new circumstances. I thought of Amy, alone in her house with the funny couch and plastic animals. Did she watch as they put handcuffs on Horse and read him his rights? What did she feel? The only parallel I could draw was when our neighbor in Bremmer, Mrs. Belter, watched her husband have a heart attack and die. My mother brought a casserole over. "We don't know what you're going through," she said, "but you won't go through it alone."

Horse was in trouble. Tom, possibly. Amy.

Still, my thoughts traveled back to myself. If Tom was responsible for Horse, was I responsible for Amy? I wanted to be free. But I wanted to be kind and proper, to acquit myself. I saw myself apologizing: I'm sorry, I couldn't have known it would turn out this way. All my advice, my inside tips, couldn't save us from this. Amy would answer: It's not your fault—it's my life, out of control. I looked across the room at Tom, the streetlight outside the window making his face a mask, tragic planes and angles. He said, "We have to do what we can for Horse—the hard part is figuring out what that is."

• • •

I sat on the passenger side of my '74 Mustang—used, but new to me. My dad had traded me even-up for my Buick. He'd said, "I was awake one night worrying about you, Monkey, and I pictured that old car and thought, no wonder." I said, "No wonder what, Dad?" He said, "You don't seem like a normal college girl. Maybe it's the Buick. A college girl needs something sporty." Though I wasn't oblivious to social differences—there are people you have to rule out, I'd come to realize—I'd thought I was above vulgar distinctions like those implied by the model of car a person drives. And yet I felt different in the Mustang, lucky, typical. It's like when you change your hairdo and your old clothes and accessories don't flatter it. Tom— who let the clutch out fast and made the car kill at intersections while people stared, then popped it again until we lurched away—looked awkward behind the wheel. But he drove every chance he got, practicing, aspiring.

He did better on the highway—that's where we were, headed east, dressed up, Tom in a new shirt and polished shoes, me in a lavender dress I'd made myself. Amy—wearing white jeans and a beige blouse, those clunky shoes again, her pale hair flying—sat in back. Angel's head hung out the window, her ears flattened out. Pearl slept curled like a snail in the corner, her head in Amy's lap. The tape deck was turned up loud: the Rolling Stones, *Exile on Main Street*, jangling, bitter music. The wind whipped through the window. Amy pulled strands of hair out of her mouth with one hand and stroked Pearl with the other, careful not to wake her.

East, West, North, South.

The compass my dad had mounted on the dashboard bobbed. East. We were on the interstate, the signs saying: Exit. I'd never been here before. Only north, safe, home. Or south to Chicago. What would we find? I tried to picture it—gray cinderblock walls? My Religious Studies professor once explained that in the Bible the East stood for civilization, cities, decadence, but that in the modern

world the concept of evil was too vague. He punched the
air as he made his point, his gaudy necktie shaped like a
fish swinging as he enunciated. An action is more or less
moral, he said, more or less reprehensible. But still.

Exit. Exit.

Tom and I had met with Al. The three of us ate dinner at
a restaurant named Déjà Vu where they served stir-fry and
imported beer. We sat in a corner. Al never took his jacket
off. Tom spoke in a low voice. I saw my reflection in a mirror across the room, and I looked like myself, Louisa. But
in my mind's eye, the tables, the flickering candles . . . Suddenly, it wasn't 1978. I was named Lou, or Ruby. And it was-
n't Tom or Al across the table but a couple of bootleggers.
"So far out of the mainstream," Tom was saying, "LSD. It'll
look bad." I looked in the mirror again. Was there a new,
ruthless cast to my eyes? Once, in passing, my dad had said
that he felt a woman should never be a cocktail waitress because it makes her hard. Forever. My mother had answered:
hard or soft, good or bad, it's a matter of willpower, not sur-
roundings. But if that were true, I thought, why did she
hate the Swangers? Al turned the conversation to me. How
old was I? Where was I from? What kind of stone was in my
necklace?

I hadn't been here before.

Al turning the conversation to me was like Zoe small-
talking to Tom to keep me from asking questions that
crossed out of my territory into hers—questions about
Dick, her childhood, her mother. How much did she want
this next baby? When we were teenagers, I'd ask: Did she
love Dick? Or Brad? Did she love them both? Her face
looked stony and faraway. She didn't want my prying. But
she wanted me for a friend. At the time it seemed like a
cold choice, but from where I sat now—at a table with
Tom saying *raise bail, first offense, arraignment,* Al picking
his beer label and staring at the ceiling—necessary. "You
want to be selective," Al said, finally. "Don't have truck
with someone like that."

Truck, I thought. Dealings. Someone brings you some-
thing. You give them something back. The buyer bewares.
All around us, trucks carried goods. A yellow truck: *Dart*,
it said. I wanted to get there. I didn't want to get there.
When we pulled into Waupaca, it seemed like any town.
Feichtner's Auto Supply. Rehberger's Hardware. Friegen's
Electric Repair. Amy was reading a map. "Take a left," she
said, "on Forty-nine." The prison farm was made of bricks.
It had a fence with coiling wire, a tower with a guard.
Horse couldn't raise bail and there wasn't—the court-ap-
pointed lawyer said—a nearer facility for state prisoners
awaiting trial. We checked in at the gate. Could the man in
uniform tell we weren't the usual type? Our car was better
than some in the parking lot. I looked at other visitors—a
few looked like you'd expect, tattoos and dirt. The rest,
like us. They were.

We left Amy with the woman who'd search her. Then
she'd see Horse, after that, a social worker. Then we'd pick
her up. I tried to picture Horse—in a navy blue uniform, I
decided, his trademark mustache and long, curly hair
gone. He'd have that look: signaling I'm hit, down. Don't
hit me again. Then he'd get tough. Tom and I would pass
on, unscathed. "Now what?" I asked.

"Right now," he said, "a picnic. On the way back—I
don't know if you saw the signs for Wild Acres. It's a petting zoo. I thought Amy would like that. We can get a motel and stay over."

"No."

Tom shrugged. He pulled into a Dairy Queen and
bought foot-long hot dogs, Pepsi. We drove to a park and
ate, Tom saying that Bert was moving out. "He's a wimp,"
Tom said, "but at least we won't have to listen to Neil
Young in the middle of the night. Sue's not bad, though.
My point is . . ." He put his sandwich down and leaned
across the table. "You and I can live together."

No.

"Get married," he said.

Married, I thought. First, the electricity would have to stop. We'd have to break the circuit to keep from burning up. Then we'd start over with low, steady current, less friction and force.

Impossible.

"Chrissake," Tom said. "What?"

A man with a beard was taking our picture. He handed us his card. "I'm with the *Waupaca News*," he said. "Sometimes we run a seasonal photo—people in the park, kids swimming. Can I get your names?"

"Get the fuck away," Tom said.

The man left.

I said, "You're rude."

Tom said, "Like I want my name in the paper."

We drove back to the prison farm. Amy came outside as soon as we parked. She seemed happy, relieved. "They've set a court date," she said. "The social worker met with the lawyer, and they're hopeful because it's Horse's first offense. It's acid—that looks bad. But only eight hits. The social worker liked it when I said Horse was putting me through school. And he writes poems."

"The social worker writes poems?" Tom asked.

"Horse does," I said.

"What does Horse write poems about?" Tom asked.

Amy looked out the window, dreamy. "Oh, different things." The wind whipped her hair. Pearl nuzzled her. "Sweet baby," she said.

Tom said, "I thought we'd stop at this Wild Acres."

Amy said, "I'd love that. But I'm starving."

We bought her a sandwich, and she fed bits of it to Angel and Pearl as we pulled into the Wild Acres Petting Zoo and parked—bickering about Tom's plan to get a motel room and spend the night.

"I could get two rooms," Tom said.

Amy said, "I could sleep with the dogs."

I said, "No."

We paid admission in a lobby filled with trinkets—keychains, little beaded shoes that hung on strings, T-shirts that said "I'm with Stupid," or "I had Sex for Breakfast." It reminded me of a bar in the backwoods near Bremmer— I'd never seen it but I'd heard of it—where a man sold jewelry he'd made by sun-drying deer turds, which are symmetrical, and spray-painting them gold. One of my dad's friends told us this at dinner one night, and my mother got mad. "I won't have that talk," she said. Of course, it wasn't "talk." Even if she didn't want to hear it, those necklaces were there, a fact. Is it important to know every fact, I wondered, sordid or otherwise? I looked at an ashtray shaped like a buffalo. "You want something?" Tom asked. He shoved money my way.

"Don't we have a tour guide?" I asked.

"Beats me," Tom said.

An ostrich walked by. A peacock. A family was in the rabbit pen, looking at rabbits—the mother with long braids, wearing an orange poncho, the dad short and fat. One kid tipped the water trough over, another straddled a rabbit, lifting its tail to look underneath. The animals. They never get to eat, rest, or lead a normal life. For being petted. The humane thing would be to let them go. I looked at the landscape, weeds, a piece of tinfoil shining silver, an old wheelbarrow tipped over, a smoky shade of rust. Amy knelt next to a fawn. Beautiful, right? The sun shining, the musky smell. Out of the blue, I thought of the wild girl who'd lived across the railroad tracks, Danielle. And Rosemary, too tame.

"Why won't you stay over?" Tom asked.

Get married. Something tugged on my skirt. Then noise.

Me, screaming.

I'd stopped by the time I heard myself.

Tom said, "What the hell?" I looked down. A goat was chewing my dress, the lavender fabric crumpled and wet in its mouth.

Amy said, "A goat can't hurt you."

The dogs waited in the car. Angel, her eyes glued to Tom, hers. Pearl, jealous, looking back and forth, at me. At Amy, stroking the fawn. I wanted to leave. I saw, for the first time, Amy was crying. "I'm lucky to have you" she said, "for friends."

Have a Ball

THERE'D BEEN TALK LATELY about hypothermia—how your blood slows down like water in the Chippewa River, chunks of ice, and snow seems soft by comparison; you want to lie down. Walking to my job at Leinweider's Lounge, I was intrigued by the simplicity of the option. But not desperate, or *too* desperate for a peaceful end. So I continued, my boots making the snow shriek like it does when something heavy lands on it. What's snow for if someone's planning to die in it? It's an end, not a long alliance. I'm pale and thin too, easy to crash down on. Sometimes I try praying. I remember the picture over my mother's bed, Jesus on a rock in the Garden of Gethsemane, weak, saying: "If it's possible, let this hard time pass." Part of the apparatus of the hope that someone who loved you but put you through hell might rain down kindness again is the certainty that the one (or ones?) you love now is (are?) unacceptable.

Behind me, the tire factory pumped smoke. I walked through the slick parking lot, birds perching on the Dumpster. *The robin is our friend.* But displaced here, far from a birdfeeder or picket fence, thriving on peanuts, frozen scraps of pizza. As for me, I'm here because my mother came to town, bought me a red coat with raccoon trim, a pink nightgown and matching robe. *New things keep our spirits high.* Over shrimp with herb mayonnaise, soup laced with sherry, over *luncheon,* she said, "A job will put structure in your days. You have to move on—you won't meet anyone sitting at home."

I had a degree in Music, a C average. I got a job in the office of a wholesale food distributor. Someone has to ship food to stores and restaurants. Think hard, someone has to pick it, slaughter it, wrap it. But my skills seemed deficient to the office manager, who valued error-free business correspondence and came into my cubicle with the sign on my desk that said "Ella Gustafson" and told me she wasn't firing me, but I could have the afternoon off to look for a job. "And," she said, "you don't dress right for an office." I looked down at my V-neck dress, black with mauve flowers. She said, "It's better suited for a cocktail lounge." Sure enough. Gray-faced pedestrians were hurrying down the street, and I stepped into the darkness, red carpet on the floor and walls, the stage with guitars and drums, waiting. Mr. Leinweider smiled. I have straight teeth, also dimples. I smiled back.

On the phone my mother said, "Your father and I worry you won't meet anyone nice in an office. Still, opportunities snowball."

I opened the back door and hung up my coat. I sliced oranges and limes, set a candle in a red jar on every table. If Ray Silka called to say he's come to realize the way he used me up, I'd answer: In the way of news, Ray, I have a job. Amusing, the people-watching. I'd omit details, the new skills I'd acquired—balancing a tray, making change, vacuuming at 2:00 A.M. All those years I learned to be, what? Ornamental. I wanted to be practical. Here, ornamental *is* practical. For the tips. The customers who come to see me.

The other waitress, Tammy, washed tables. Mr. Leinweider walked in, looked at Tammy, then me. "Just the three of us," he said, putting his hand on my shoulder. "Fix me a drink, hon." I looked uneasy, maybe. "Seagram's and water," he explained. I found the bottle. I asked, "The little cap measures the amount?" Tammy and Mr. Leinweider looked at each other and smiled. "Hey, Snow White," Tammy said, "just pour it half-full and add water. Voila!"

Tammy and I are important to each other. "For contrast," she said once. She meant she'd had experience—lots of men, also two children she'd left for her mother to raise. But me, the only bar I'd been to until now was a table at a wedding dance where a waiter served drinks and, barring a single exception when I'd been confused and seeking pity, I'd had sex with just one person. Ray. But a hundred times and with great illusions. If I ask myself where I got them, I think—oddly—how our Lutheran minister used to stand in his pine pulpit, the guttering candles softening his face. How I sat near him after Sunday dinner—he was dressed in street clothes, slacks, a jacket—as he talked business with my father, collection plates, the fund for the new roof. Or later, when I was twelve, that I'd read an Ann Lander's column regarding a survey about whether women liked sex. Most didn't. One woman disagreed. Every night, she wrote, she gave herself to her husband like a chalice. Sentimental, yes (loving ourselves more than God could). But I thought of it when I made love, music playing. If I chose, *Mondnacht*, a woman's voice. If Ray chose, jazz fusion, a metrical assault.

Mr. Leinweider said, "Where's Jimmy Pagnuittch?"

"Late," Tammy said.

The door opened and Jimmy Pagnuittch came in. When I worked my first shift three weeks ago, I saw how fierce he was, bitter under the surface. I stood in the waitress station while he held the bottles high so the liquor arced. "Well," he said, " 'Ella'. Where does 'Ella' come from?" Appleton, I told him. He'd grown up on the Lac Courte Oreilles Reservation, he said; I should visit it some time. I set the drinks on my tray. I answered carefully. "Because you want me to see for myself the . . ." (I thought about inserting the word *deplorable* here and decided to skip it.) ". . . the living conditions?" He said, "I meant to people like you it's invisible." I tried picturing a reservation. Cinderblock houses near a river? Junked cars? A store that sold bulk food and hardware? Jimmy said, "I'll take you on a tour some day. Consider me the Native Guide." He was squinting. Or smiling. I couldn't tell.

Mr. Leinweider said, "Jimmy, get here on time or quit the other job." Jimmy's other job is at a home for alcoholic teenage Indians. Native Americans. A place called Ahm Dah Ing. Mr. Leinweider pronounces it like a man with a speech defect saying *I'm dying*.

Jimmy said, "I do my prep work in half the time as Ella."

"Leave Ella out of it," Mr. Leinweider said.

Jimmy said, "Why leave her out? I like her."

A thump sounded on the door behind the stage. Mr. Leinweider walked across the bar, his belt riding below his stomach, keys jingling. He stepped up, unlocked the door. Twilight flooded into the cavernous side of the bar where later on people dance. It's dark and deep here. I could get lost, strangled on the rungs of a bar stool, and lay helpless while a creature with traits specific to the habitat—this Loch Ness of red carpet and spilled cocktails—scurried across my face. Light shone through the open door; in it, long legs, an angular torso. Chill Billman. And behind him, his band. Chill said, "Have you heard the forecast?" The band members followed him in, wearing puffy-sleeved shirts. The last one, dragging a drum case, smiled at me. Chill Billman smiled too. Mr. Leinweider said, "Cold temperatures. Lonely hearts. Good business."

On a spring night, my phone rang at 2:00 A.M. I answered it. Ray. He said, "My paperwork for graduation is filed." I thought I heard his refrigerator door open.

Close. I pictured him in his apartment. A bottle cap came off. "My assignments are in," he said. Swallow. "I mailed my résumés." I'd been sleeping, having a dream in which a wrecking ball on a thick chain figured. I said the wrong thing. "When you go away, will you miss me?" He blew up: "Why are you so redundant?" But the force with which his words burst—the flash, spitfire—was exaggerated. Phony. Standing in the dark in my sleeveless nightgown, the lighted phone receiver against my ear, I pictured his bad temper like fiery, sunburnt skin, but underneath the vessels and organs pumping their daily business, no stress to report. He wasn't mad. He had to make an example. That way he seemed like God who will lash out—no telling when—after for centuries letting sin grow. Then, clap clap. Done for.

I thought to say, If asking if you'll miss me is redundant, then food is. Love is. Instead I said: "Is something bothering you?"

He said, "You wouldn't understand."

Again.

He said, "For instance, you don't understand Schopenhauer."

He must have just written a philosophy paper, I thought, looking out the window at the smoky trees, the streetlight's gold halo.

"You've always had money," he said. "Ella, I never did. I'm the first Silka to get so far. I'm financially invested. Ergo, my emotional investment. You don't have it." All the while he was saying this I kept my eyes shut. I thought of a hole in my roof, my head. I thought, *Patch it.* First, I thought, maybe vines. Over the hole. No, boards. Saw them. Nail them. I was also thinking it isn't fair I'm falling short. He picked me out of a crowd.

* * *

The bar started to fill with people. Fat and thin. Someone with a long nose and sideburns shaped like pork steaks. Someone who walked with a limp. A phase of the night I'd learned to distinguish. The overhead lights not yet dim. The arrival of a regular, Fluff. Once I said to Tammy, "Do you know what Jimmy Pagnuittch calls that big woman with the white dandelion hair and the polka-dot blouse? Fluff." Tammy laughed. I said, "It's funny, isn't it?" Tammy said, "But that's her name, Ella. That's what she goes by." Also, the jukebox still on, treble. The band tuning up. The lead guitar, twang. Bass, hum. Snap snap. Percussion. Men wearing their jeans that hang jaunty on their hips. Women who'd run out in the cold and snow last night to the laundromat so they'd have glad rags ready for tonight. The talk, someone saying, "Maybe we should fix you up a chair with a soft cushion. You're so old." Or, "You can't hold your liquor better than a tub that's sprung a leak." And talk about the weather. Tonight.

The wind gusted, twenty-five miles an hour. The thermometer would hit minus thirty. "These numbers add up," Tammy said. "That's how they get wind chill. It will feel like fifty-five below. You better not walk home."

"Last time it was this cold," the woman named Fluff told Mr. Leinweider, "my car tires froze in the shape they'd been sitting, flat."

Mr. Leinweider held his cigarette, smoke furling.

"When I drove," Fluff said, "they went around, clunk and clunk."

Jimmy Pagnuittch—pouring one of the brown liquors, making an Old-Fashioned—said, "Ella. You didn't walk to work tonight, did you?"

I looked across the bar, wondering if the band would play that one song. *My eyes are still blue.* "Yes," I said. I'd walked. The best part of the day. My hair, washed and styled, under a beret that wouldn't flatten it. I could sense my makeup: the scent of powder, my eyelashes thick with mascara, the waxy feel of my lips. The wind blew. The snow—my red coat moving over it—contracted under my feet. At the end of the night, someone gave me a ride. Tammy. Mr. Leinweider. Or I walked home, the sidewalk beside the river. I had a car, but I didn't like being behind the wheel.

Jimmy said, "Get a ride tonight."

I delivered the drinks to a table near the stage. Chill Billman's voice swelled as he sang about making love on the floor in a hallway. I thought for a minute about my spine knocking against wooden boards, about giving up under a man like Chill. What was sex if it wasn't that? Underneath, I'd bend my mind. Pleasure, a wish. Chill, I'd think. (Ray, Ray.) Closing my eyes, choosing how it could be. Arching my back, willpower. Sex is wedlock. ". . . Closer than we'd been before," Chill sang. But in fact it gets done separately. Like painting a house, planting a garden. You each paint a section, or bed six plants. Afterwards, you've accomplished the garden, the painted house, together. Shared pride. But I'd been startled to find how easy it was with a stranger, that I felt odd after it, not during when I was solitary anyway.

Someone yelled, "Hey, dolly, a drink. Over here." I'd never heard that before this job—there was even a song about loving a dolly.

Chill sang, looked tender. I thought of *Madame Bovary* which I'd read one spring break when Ray wouldn't tell me, and wouldn't tell me, if we'd be able to go on a trip. Then at the last minute he visited his brother alone; it would bore me, he said. My parents were in Sweden. My roommate at the time—the kind you get when you advertise Female, Non-smoking—was gone too. I went in her room, borrowed a book. I stayed up a day and night, reading. After having wished for a prince but making real love to Rodolphe, also Leon, Emma went to an opera and thought the singer sang only to her. *Even the arch of her foot had gone languid in this climate of steam.* I looked up. Chill wasn't smiling at anyone else. The drummer slammed on his snare, nodded. He played his drums to me, true.

At my station, Jimmy said, "When you get a minute, Ella . . ." he filled a glass, ". . . go to the stock room for schnapps. Also brandy."

I glanced at Tammy's section. I thought I saw—

Maybe not.

Sometimes memories pry themselves loose, finding prompts everywhere. For instance, another of my roommates once got attacked by a man she worked with—he gave her a ride, ripped her uniform open, then never came back for his shift. She hoped to avoid him forever but for months thought she saw him at the grocery store, the Kmart, the Allstate Insurance booth at the mall. Fear didn't have me burying this face from my past like a bone to dig up. The sense I'd done something wrong. Sin. The man whose face I saw in the crowd, no one could say he'd attacked me. Lust? No. Relief.

I found the schnapps but not the brandy. I heard Tammy calling, "Ella, you're filling up." Since I'd started this job my dreams were about drinkers, a thirsty, disappointed multitude. I brought the schnapps back. "I can't find the brandy," I told Jimmy and went to wait on my tables. "Ella," he said when I got back, "the brandy." I went to the stock room. In a minute, he came blustering in. "Fuck this," he said. But he couldn't find it either. He stood behind me. My back felt like it always does, except receptive. Defenseless. Jimmy Pagnuittch—storing up anger— put his hand on my hip. The difference between hot and cold is unclear. Coals turn white. Frostbite burns. Repulsion (when someone shoves me away, not the reverse) feels like attraction. Turmoil like heat. Mr. Leinweider stood in the door. "Get back to work."

We went out on the floor, and Mr. Leinweider told me Tammy would cover my section while I went in the restroom—"the women's head"—because someone was throwing herself at the wall. "Find out what the hell is going on," Mr. Leinweider said. He jabbed his cigarette at

Jimmy. His jaw dropped as he talked. "I don't care if you're the best damn bartender in the world. Rut on your own time." He looked at me, "Pardon my French." It wasn't the first time I'd heard him talk rough. Once he'd asked his son, who, in Mr. Leinweider's own words, was good-for-nothing, a bad seed: "You know how a yearling stud goes around with its dick out?" The son nodded. "Don't do that," Mr. Leinweider said. He turned to me. "Sorry."

There was nothing in the restroom except a girl—a woman—who'd folded herself in the corner, crying, rubbing her face on the sleeve of her sweatshirt. She had on laced-up boots with fur, Mukluks. Her hair, in a braid down her back, was pulled away from her face, which was wet, and pale like the moon. She was saying the same thing over and over. Him. Him. (Hymn?) I couldn't think what to give her besides the towel I kept tied to my apron. She wiped her eyes, then made a pitch, her expression both earnest and rehearsed, a cartoon version of sincerity—a snake-oil salesmen describing his great need, his widowed mother and ten starving sisters. It isn't a contradiction. You believe in what you sell. You believe in it because you sell it to earn your keep. Not to die. She said, "Please, I'm so hungry. A dollar would get me a sandwich."

The door thudded wide open. Mr. Leinweider came in, his jaw clamped down. Maybe because of the cigarette. Maybe because, guarding territory, he'd tapped into his adrenaline. He grabbed her arm. She pulled it back. He ended up holding the sleeve of her sweatshirt, and she thrashed around in the rest of it—four or five months pregnant, I saw. The empty sleeve flapped. "What the hell, a goddamn minor," Mr. Leinweider said. "We'll see about that." He hauled her out. I saw how he liked the audience, the parting of the crowd as he made her walk faster—stumbling and sobbing—than she possibly could. His eyes fixed on the door. He smiled, grim, pleased. *Necessary evil. Emergency.* That was the message.

"I'll do anything," she said. "Anything."

Jimmy Pagnuittch glowered. I understood for the hundredth time that a mixture is more accurately a description of a state of mind than a basic list. Dejection, Cheer, Fear, Ease. These won't do. Mr. Leinweider was scared, also elated. The girl from the restroom was beaten down but getting one up on whoever decided to help her. Jimmy was furious and suffering. "Fuck this," he said. Right then, it was the only difference between him and Mr. Leinweider, the choice of expletive, *fuck* or *hell.* The band kept playing.

"Where did he take her?" Jimmy said.

Tammy said, "So you know her?"

"I know her type," Jimmy said. "I know what she'll do." He looked at me. "Where do you think he took her—the fucking United Way?"

I said, "The police station, I guess."

Tammy looked at Jimmy. "I'd knock it off. You're already on thin ice."

I left for my section where I collected orders. Olympia. Budweiser. Brandy. Whiskey. A creamy drink called an Orgasm. "I'd like an Orgasm," the customer said. The first time I fell for it. Now I make a joke. "Me too," I say. "It's the human condition." I walked and took orders, and thought how Jimmy blamed me, that the difference between Jimmy and Mr. Leinweider was the difference between anger that was necessary and anger that lifted you into an orbit where you escaped hating yourself by hating someone else. I passed Tammy, who said, "Once he crushed someone's head."

Who?

"Leinweider," she said. "Who else?"

The drummer thumped. Chill sang. I let myself sway to the song which—if I thought about the words, "Baby, baby, he's no good"—I'd hate. Still, I needed lulling. I'd read somewhere that country music makes even rats drink, which is to say the meter, the lilt, not the exquisite, sorry lyrics, made me thirsty. Where did Mr. Leinweider take her, I wondered. To the parking lot for service, then he turned her loose? To the police station, social service?

"What did you do with her?" Jimmy asked when I got back.

"Nothing."

I saw immediately that was the problem.

"Have a shot," he said. It was gold and smooth, like honey. Except hot. I drank, and the song the band was playing lurched forward. *Baby, baby,* it sighed. The lights glowed. I said, "More."

Then out of the crowd—

I hadn't imagined him, after all. Walking across the room, his eyes like rocks. I thought what to say, what conversation to make, then dropped that line of logic because I might not have to speak at all. He stopped in front of me. Jimmy Pagnuittch watched. Tammy came up behind. "Al," she asked, "do you need another drink?" Then she saw him staring at me. "Christ," she said, "did you want an introduction?" He spoke to Tammy but looked at me. "Me and her have already met," he told Tammy. "Old home week."

Regarding the idea of amusement, fetishes, I've never understood why it's respectable to collect, let's say, antique beer tankards, while a passion for well-cut dresses, skirts, and blouses is shallow. On a fall day when the leaves were red, I was happy as a bird in a tree because I had on a blue dress, russet stockings, a lipstick called "Coral." As for a new dress: the first day is best. I'd been picked to march in front, carrying the banner. Because I had leadership skills? No, the ability to enhance a uniform. Besides, I wasn't a good flute player. Sitting down was one thing, but with the business of marching, moving my feet, I gave up and pretended to blow, to move my fingers, letting my eyes roam. We marched across the road to the stadium, the thud, thump, groan of football practice. The drum major, Ray Silka, had leadership skills. Barking orders. Keeping us rigid. He blew his whistle, told us to look senseless. Then he came over, dropped a rock on my foot and—without moving a muscle in his face—asked me out.

Six months later when I had to move, I saw every empty house as a place for Ray. I rented a two-bedroom white clapboard with a gazebo. I pictured us at the window drinking coffee, watching birds hover at a suet ball hanging from a tree. But he wanted me at his apartment across town, behind Kmart. A complex with one hundred units. His had tan paneling, carpet with stains shaped like Massachusetts, Texas, Iowa. Kitchen, bedroom, bath. A living room without a couch. I'd step over books, his trumpet in its black case. I'd sit, worrying I'd crushed something and think how, when I was little, my dad used to raise dogs and he told me never to forget I was a visitor in the pen. "It might not be much," he told me, "but it's the dog's home and we need to respect that."

Once I said something that made Ray raise his eyebrows. "I should send you on your way," he answered, joking. But once he really did throw me out. I'd complained about the stacked bundles of newspaper in his bedroom, the bathroom cabinet next to the toilet that was covered with—who wants to know?—soap film. I wanted to scrub it. I tried to keep the siren pitch out of my voice. Be clear, which siren. Not the kind that lures sailors to a pleasant death, but the kind that makes dogs howl. A look slid over Ray. Tolerance, shifting. To what? I remembered the two kinds of argument. One, you've got a point you're calm enough to make. Two, you're petty. I felt bad for Ray. Hating me was past his control.

He shoved my head on the floor.

I thought about the carpet. How dirty it was, but my face could be washed. I felt my skull—a miracle, really—a thin wall between the fragile place inside and the hand clamped outside, bearing down. I went limp. I smelled the mildew. I thought of a sunny day, yellow tulips. My dad wearing a muted tie under a sweater, smoking a pipe on the sidewalk outside church, listening to the minister talk in hushed tones about a parishioner who'd been arrested for beating his children. "I understand he's under pressure," my dad said. "But certain behaviors aren't, well, civilized."

Ray let go. "If you don't like it, leave."

He watched as I took my purse and coat.

He followed me to the parking lot to my car, stood outside, arms across his chest. What it meant to sympathize, I realized, is that at some point I'd felt as tarnished as Ray standing in front of me, almost grieving. But not that frozen. If loving someone is looking in a mirror—see them, see yourself—then crying for Ray because he couldn't cry, or even consider that he'd threatened to hurt me, is saying I didn't like what I saw when I looked in the rearview mirror. Pale skin, tiny mole on my chin. I was ugly.

I stayed away from my classes the next day. Outside, a chainsaw roared. The landlord had sent someone to trim branches away from the roof. I lay on my bed, staring at the pink-and-gray rugs, the polished floor. The kitchen cupboards with glass doors and, inside, teacups like inverted cones. The tree surgeon knocked on the door. "Could I get some water, ma'am?" I saw where the idea of TV cowboys came from. People existed who looked, spoke, walked like cowboys. In the confusion of filling a blue, fluted glass with water, I didn't consider that maybe Al watched TV cowboys before he got manners, that he wasn't a prototype but an imitation. He spoke in sentences that concerned now, this moment, but other lives and the future too. He looked at my eyes, no makeup, red-rimmed, a box of Kleenex on the chair. "A bad day," he said, "will hang you up." I had control. Then sympathy. Someone taking my pulse. He said, "For a hard time, I recommend a soft place."

I watched our clothes piling on the floor, my terry cloth robe, his T-shirt, jeans faded at the knees, black boots like chimney stacks. I curved my back like it was wired. I thought about looking out the window earlier, through the sheer curtains at the man in the tree—please, he said, my name is Al. He'd swung in a harness. His boots chipped at the trunk. I thought about what it means to be strung up. The bedsheets looked like gauze. I closed my eyes and pictured a man lowering himself on a cord, coming down from the green clouds of trees. I had a glass of water and he'd be there to drink it. A soft place, I thought. Will hang you up.

I stood between the chrome bars of the waitress station as Jimmy Pagnuittch slapped drinks down so fast they sloshed. I wiped my tray. He slammed down a bottle of Miller and suds bubbled. "Slow down," Tammy said. She stood next to me. On the other side, Al loomed, his face near. Words had nothing to do with it. For example, animals don't talk. But they make exchanges and deals. What do animals want? Jimmy lifted a bottle. Gold-colored liquor jetted into a glass. "Drink up," he said, sliding the glass to me. He pulled empties away from customers who were barely done. "Why is he mad?" I asked Tammy as I went back to my tables. She smiled, her mouth tight. I set a glass here, a beer there, thinking how everybody's anger seemed like my obligation. "You say 'sorry' too much," Mr. Leinweider told me once. A customer had taken his shoes off, put his feet on the table, then threw a drink at the wall. He'd phoned someone, he said, and she hung up. Mr. Leinweider told him to put his shoes back on and leave. "I'm sorry," I told Mr. Leinweider. "Why?" he said. "He's not *your* boyfriend."

I watched Jimmy. I sipped my drink. "It'll put hair on your chest," he said. He filled it. I thought of cough syrup, calming, soothing.

"Why is it slow?" I asked, looking around. Vaporous

smoke floated toward the smoke-eating machine. Two customers here, four there, three on my side. "You noticed," Tammy said, lighting a cigarette. The music rippled. Chill swiveled, nodded, grimaced—emotion on demand—and I realized the intimacy, the sense he sang to me, was talent. The drummer was lost in clatter. One of Al's arms draped itself across the rail. He touched my shoulder. Tammy watched.

"Because it's fucking cold," Jimmy said. "It's the coldest night of the year." He pitched an empty bottle in the trash and it broke.

Tammy said, "Why are you mad?"

"Ella," he said, "get drunk."

"I think," Al said, "that's the lady's prerogative, not yours."

Jimmy said, "I didn't know she'd hired a mouthpiece."

Tammy said, "Get a grip, Jimmy."

He looked at her. "Why am I mad? Do I seem mad?" I thought of the beer bottle, jolted and frothing over. Jimmy was stirred up, shooting off at the mouth. That's what Mr. Leinweider would say. "Well," he said, like he'd been considering the question a long time and finally hit on this. "Leinweider treats people like shit. Like he was put on earth to sell rats drinks. But if the rats get drunk, he throws them into the street: Isn't that right? Ella!"

Wasn't what right? "Yes," I said.

He grabbed his coat and left. Tammy took over behind the bar. She said, "I hope he's not tracking Leinweider and that girl."

Al leaned close. "Do you want to get together later?"

I looked at his gray eyes, his square shoulders, the spiky hair hanging in his collar. "I don't know you well enough," I said.

He stepped back, surprised. "Fine. Maybe you don't."

Mr. Leinweider came in, rubbing his hands. "It's colder than a whale's ass outside," he said. "I'm not paying a band to play for six people." He saw Tammy behind the bar. "Where the hell is Pagnuittch?"

"He had to leave," she said. Her eyes shifted to the wall behind her. "He got a phone call." She looked at Mr. Leinweider's face now. "From Ahm Dah Ing—the group home. They had an emergency."

"What emergency?" Mr. Leinweider said. "A drunk Indian?"

So he believed her.

"I just bought a bus ticket for a drunk Indian," he said, "who was knocked up." But it didn't matter, for Jimmy's sake, if Mr. Leinweider believed Tammy. Because he hated Ahm Dah Ing, the taxes spent. "I'm dying," he'd say, talking about the drain on small business. "I'm all for helping the other fellow who helps himself." A familiar ethic: Persevere. Sacrifice. Prosper. But I'd had a class, "The White Man's Indian," where the professor pointed out that traits people ridicule—Indians being passive or alcoholic—evolved because their livelihood had been appropriated. He also said that Europeans made up ideas about Native Americans that were—he poked the air with his finger—like science fiction, like ideas about extraterrestrials today, a projection of what we desire and fear. And don't own up to. *The women made lustful,* Amerigo Vespucci wrote, *by the biting of poisonous animals, causing their husband's parts to swell and fall off.* I'd made a B in the class.

Mr. Leinweider told Tammy, "Take down the bar."

He walked over to the stage and waited for Chill to finish singing. Chill bent over, listened to Mr. Leinweider, then made an announcement. "Belly up to your sweetheart for a last dance. Last call."

"I'm going to cash out at the restaurant," Mr. Leinweider said. He owned a Pancake House too. "I'll be back in half an hour."

I wiped tables. The band started rolling up cords until Chill Billman said, "Stop. We'll do this in the morning."

The bass and lead guitar players went upstairs to the apartment Mr. Leinweider keeps so bands don't have to stay at motels. All the customers were gone except Al, sitting at a table. Tammy finished stocking the cooler, walked over, put her arm across his shoulders. Her silvery permed hair fell over her face. I like the crafted way she looks—her hair shadowing black at the roots, her eyelids the precise colors of the shirt she has on. Gold. Cinnamon. Mauve. She said something to Al, who nodded. The bathroom door opened, and Fluff came out like a cloud in a fringed dress and sat next to Chill.

Tammy said, "Ella. I'm going." She nodded her head at the table near the door to let me know—I figured it out—she was leaving with Al. "He's an old friend," she said. "Do you want a ride?"

I shook my head. Not with them. I wasn't jealous. But I was shocked at how quickly Al had moved on from me to Plan B, Tammy.

She leaned over like she might hug me. But didn't. "Be careful." Al shifted his feet while she looked in her purse for keys. Then he noddded at me as if to say: Nice Meeting You. I wiped the bar one last time. I held my coat in my lap as I sat on a bar stool a few feet from Fluff and Chill and waited for Mr. Leinweider to come back, lock up, take me home. Fluff looked like a comedian. But she didn't mean to. It was the way her makeup emphasized . . . what? Not an intelligent or seductive curve of bone. Not that she didn't have intelligence, or the desire to seduce. I looked close, squinting. She did. But my first impression—I thought of Fluff's creamy body landing like an imprint in sealing wax—was the look of perpetual surprise that had to do with being fat, the flesh startled by the fact of weight throwing itself around, dragging her skin, her ordinary expression, down.

Chill was behind the bar, dropping ice in a drink. I went behind the bar too and poured myself a half-glass from the bottle Jimmy had been waving around. Fluff punched the jukebox and started singing. Because you couldn't hear the

record, just Fluff, it sounded like Karaoke, that microphone business where they have the old favorite tune, but
no one singing, and someone you know stands in for
Chrissie Hynde or Tony Bennett. For a minute it seemed
like Fluff was clowning. Hamming. Her big butt, the way
she made it roll. Then the look on her face, taking this
rendition to heart—*your body for my soul, fair swap*—eyes
closed, dimpled chin tilted. Chill said, "Are you ready,
girl?" He stood by the door that led upstairs. Fluff nodded,
a good sport, and followed him.

I heard a noise from the dance floor. Rustling, skidding.
Then a bar stool moved near me in the dark.

"Where'd Chill go?" It was the drummer, thin hair over
his forehead. His white puffy sleeves billowed. I nodded at
the back door. "Oh. With Fluff," he said. "He's got a regular gal back home." Like that explained it. "I mean"—he
grew expansive—"too serious a girl to want to get entan-
gled with someone as pretty as you."

"I'm waiting for Mr. Leinweider," I said.

I saw he thought I was waiting to go home with Mr.
Leinweider. Go upstairs. Go to bed. "For a ride," I said. He
nodded. We were drinking. Drank. Had drunk. The jukebox—I'd never noticed—had colored lights like jewels.
Like a carnival ride. A clanging streetcar.

"You sure he's coming back?" the drummer asked.

"This place," I said, "is not locked up."

Ray was on the outside, pushing. I'd had an insight. My
body was a house. I was obsessed with the cellar. Was
my soul there? Or reproductive machinery? Likewise,
words he said—"Bring your mouth over here"—signaled
commitment, his life forever welded to mine. Either that,
or lewd instruction. "Of course I love you," he said. I'd
asked. Once I had a roommate named Mary Dent whose
lover wanted to leave. She'd say, "Love me," meaning take

your clothes off, come back in. They made love under overpasses, by the river near the trees, but broke up still. I had another roommate, Janet, who was like a box, no doors or windows. No one got inside. The cords in Ray's neck pulsed. I was a machine after all. I felt the belts and fans moving, my feet floating, anchored by my legs. He said, "I'm sorry, so sorry." And he gave in like that, a puff of smoke.

Then lay on his back, one arm across me. We were in his apartment, the paneled walls. He'd asked me to dinner, but the groceries were still on the counter. Red meat under cellophane. An onion, pepper, potatoes. I didn't crave this food. But I'd turned hungry, waiting for him to unburden. He'd opened a beer, another, another. Budweiser—he had brand-name loyalty—is bitter. He'd been saying how scholarships kept him almost broke, no material distractions while he labored. "But I don't deserve to live like this." He slammed his fist on the cheap table. Then a question. "Ella, have you never noticed a state of unofficial apartheid exists between the haves and have-nots?" Had I never? Not how he wanted. By sneering at a suburban lawn or a new car in a stranger's driveway. By hating shellfish. He said he preferred hot dogs. "We're doomed," he said. Also: "Excuse me if I don't find the issues you worry about compelling. I'm concerned with a different hierarchy of needs, food and shelter." He opened another beer. I looked at the potatoes and meat, thinking we needed to eat now.

He set the beer down. "It might be . . ." he meant us, the fact of our passion ". . . dead." But he pulled my sweater over my head anyway. I let my mind skim details, wander to the far corner. He'd seemed aloof before. Now he seemed like a mass of dusty, trivial complaints that had settled on a surface I wouldn't clean. I thought—if Ray was the past and not the future—how would I live? I didn't wonder: whether. How. In what fashion. Like in a dream I have where my teeth fall out, even as I say the words, "How will I live without teeth?," the shards of enamel

falling like dust on my tongue, I continue living, in fact,
live as I speak. I stared at the fan in the window. Ray ex-
erted himself, moving his hands, his spine. A gust of wind
blasted in. The fan slowed. The blade reversed. Then
turned itself around. Persisted. This isn't a dress rehearsal,
I thought. A preparation for a day when Ray will get
enough tenderness to give some back. The fan never
stopped. My teeth were always in my mouth when I woke.
The meat on the table, still wrapped, I'd never eat.

A door opened. Light entered. On the inside of my eyelids, like a movie screen, I pictured who I'd see if I
opened them. Mr. Leinweider with a ring of keys. Jimmy
with plans for justice. Ray. Gone. My head ached. My
mouth tasted rusty. I felt if I moved, water would slosh my
stomach like the inside of a washing machine. Beyond
that, a familiar hammering in my hips that meant I'd
started my period. Tammy once said, taking a beer with
Midol, "Never have menstrual cramps on the same day as
a hangover." I smiled. I'd never had one. I expected to see
the wall over my bed. But this looked too big, too white.
Maybe I'd been asleep upside down. When my senses registered, it wasn't my wall. The drummer, next to me,
wrapped in bedsheets, an ashtray on his chest, smoking,
said: "Morning." I thought, God. I didn't know his name. I
remembered how at the turn of the century the word
"drummer" meant salesman, one who drummed up business, made a pitch. Snake oil.

   This stuffy room over the bar. Heat rising. My parents
called every Sunday morning, the cheap rates. They
thought it was a day of rest. I lay on Mr. Leinweider's
bed—a creaking, rickety frame—bleeding. I felt tacky
from the waist down. I thought—wanted not to think—
how it would look. Red. Blood is protein. On white. During deer season, a hunter in the bar had told me hydrogen

peroxide was good bleach. "When we butcher," he said, "we use it to clean knives and towels." I looked at the drummer's bony face.

"I have my period," I told him.

He said, "I thought you were a virgin."

What century did he think it was? "Of course not." I felt sick.

He said, "Well, nobody's perfect. I have a bad leg."

What did he mean? That virginity, like a good leg, was something you hoped to keep but didn't grieve if fate took it? Who was he?

"Where do you work?" I asked.

He frowned. "You don't remember?"

Of course I remembered.

He said, "You mean where do I work at home in Min- neapolis—what's my day job?" He seemed embarrassed to say. "I work in a cafeteria."

If that explained it. The servant class, I thought. But I was a waitress. A textbook heading popped in my head, bold print and all, *Sexual Mores and Socio-economic Status.* I thought of cool water. What had I done? Heartache, com- pressed. Compared to giving up Ray, this was easy. Or hard. Less sordid. More. I was confused. There's no such thing, I decided, as relative ease. Soft is soft. Hard, hard. Ice, always ice. Warm air, a reprieve.

Last night I'd gone upstairs because the drummer said, "It's not so cold. You can wait for Leinweider there." True, without the band's lights, the thronging customers, the bar was cold as the bottom of the ocean. I hated the damp smell of the aftermath. Upstairs, a semblance of a living room. Mr. and Mrs. Leinweider's cast-off end tables with slanting legs. A Ye Olde brass-finished lamp. The bar was still unlocked. I stood by the window, kept my eye out. "When he comes back," the drummer said, "you'll know." Then one lamp looked like two. The living room, not like an imitation but cozy. In the bedroom, in the dark, once he started, my substitute lover seemed real too. Still, I saw

Al swinging in a harness from a tree. Ray in a parking lot, arms across his chest, looking mean. If you knew him you were supposed to understand he was just proud but sorry all the same. Then I pictured Jimmy Pagnuittch walking down a street, a rolled-up parcel under his arm. A newspaper? The Declaration of Independence? Mr. Leinweider rapped on a door. Not really. Because it was morning. "If you want the truth," the drummer said, "you fell asleep in the middle of it."

The light from the window was white. New snow.

"I have to go," I said.

He sat up, draped in a sheet. "If you don't feel good, lie still." His hand was on my shoulder. The look on his face, a familiar promise. I pulled away as if in other lives, on other continents, I'd fallen into bed and fought to get out. I saw myself with a granite mattress, a rock for a pillow. Bed-ridden. I'd lain down looking for purpose. I said, "I need air." I took the blanket off the bed, wrapped up in it. Down the hall, I heard people's voices. Fluff? Chill? I shut the bathroom door behind me.

I washed with a bar of shaving soap.

Then I put on my floral-print dress, my nylons. I said, "I'll take these sheets home and wash them." It seemed fitting. It might be a custom somewhere. He waved his hand. "I'll go to a laundromat later." I put on my red coat with fur, my hat and gloves. "I had a nice time," I said. And hurried downstairs. Outside.

The parking lot was a white blanket. I walked, my boots sifting along. I came out on the sidewalk in front of Leinweider's as Jimmy Pagnuittch, in a green station wagon with big fins, pulled away from the gas pump at the Sack N' Pack across the street. "You want a ride?" It was the first time I'd seen him in daylight. He was smiling, or squinting. The snow and sunshine. I thought suddenly that I'd been out all night. I was wearing my Sunday best, rumpled. No better than a pregnant girl camped in a restroom. But I was intact. "Where do you live?" he said. He

put the car in gear. The tires gripped. He was talking
about how, in the old days, the Chippewa tribe did a dance
to thank the Great Spirit for thick snow, which made it
easier to track game. I nodded, staring out at the blaze of
whiteness, the glimmer. Great Spirit, I thought. He said,
"I know you think it's boring, Ella, or primitive—a religion that celebrates the hunt of otter and beaver."

I said, "You don't know what the hell I think."

He did smile. The tires spun. We were at the bottom of
the hill by my house. I thought of a time when Ray came
over and I'd cooked dinner—ham, pie, deviled eggs on a
platter—while he sat at a table and explained why this or
that opinion I had wasn't good enough. I was like a machine on a tool bench, under repair. If I was always in
pieces, I thought, how could I run? Then he wanted to
make love. I went along with it: the idea that, if Ray dis-
mantled me, a euphoria of pain would take over and I'd get
thrilled. "I'm no paragon," Jimmy said now, downshifting.
"But, Ella, isn't it time you got off?" I wondered for a
minute if he meant got off into a bout of pleasure. Love
me. I looked out the window at the street I walked to and
from work on. Or off this particular treadmill: Every
Night at Leinweider's Is Ladies' Night. The latter, yes.
The tires grabbed. The car lurched forward, uphill.

Cool, Trim, Quick
in the Water

ONE NIGHT I LAY NEXT TO MY HUSBAND, the window beside the bed open wide, rain pouring out a drainpipe fast. I knew this even though I was asleep, water abundant in my dream. A silvery wooden pier angled across a lake. I sat on it, my limbs foreshortened. I wasn't myself, not exactly. A boy was poised to dive at the end of the pier, and a girl in a swimsuit had one arm across my shoulder, the other arced over her head with comic grace. These were my children, I decided, the time and place real but also not: a photo of good times snapped for a family album. My eyes were glamorous, ideal, my lips red like a film star's. I was a spectator, removed. But I was in the picture too, and something was in the lake beside me. It was chock-full. My future was in store. Would it bite? My legs dangled. A plane flew low, and the big thing swam near. I woke in our house far from a lake but near a small airport, the rackety noise of commuter planes constant.

There are two ideas about dreams.

They tell the future. Or they record the past, still unresolved.

The past is big but not unfathomed, I would have said

then. Compared to the future, it's easy—dwelling on it is childish and low-down, like looking through someone else's diary. But wanting to know the future is practical: I'd stave off trouble. I'd meanwhile sabotage the now-revealed future and be back to where I'd started, which was here, sure the dream was from days-to-be, the children in it yet unborn, the time now: advent. I'd *be* happy.

Female trouble—my father's phrase for below-the-belt problems. It's a late affliction, late in the century and late for me, seeing motherhood that hasn't happened as the key to satisfaction so fundamental it can't be paraphrased. How many women did I know who'd had fertility therapy? Or laser surgery to remove tissue, vestiges of disuse? So I ignored how much the children in the dream looked like children I already knew. My sister, Helen's: her girl and boy. My friend Toni's—Travis, a teenager, but once sly-faced and wily, and Honey, her bored twelve-year-old. My friend from Bremmer, Zoe, had kids: a herd of boys. Or maybe in the photo I'm my mother and the girl is Helen and the diving boy my brother, Davie, all of us grown now, the dream-photo a testimony to my sense of my mother's failure to prepare us. Like the past wasn't done, a bad dress rehearsal. We'd do it again. I was a kid in a time when I felt free—we all did—not to honor parents but to point out they'd blundered.

Dale, my husband, said the day before, "That's bullshit."

We sat on the porch, a box of Kleenex between us. We both had hay fever—breathing useless, wasted pollen. All the earth's stale air. My old dog, Pearl, lay by my feet, flapping her tail, her eyes milky as she looked up to communicate something ancient and private only she and I knew, not Dale, who'd come into our lives late. "Your parents can't have done bad," Dale said. "You all turned out fine. Mistakes were made. What does it matter whose?"

He made it sound as if I'd announced I'd barely survived my childhood, when in fact we'd been talking about Dale's brother, Jack, Jack's wife, Marlene, who was hypochondriac about not only her body (chronic *organ* recitals, her liver and lungs, her heart and uterus), but also about what used to be called the soul. Every trauma ever reckoned to leave scars had. She was anorexic, her siblings were cruel, she'd been raped or seen rape, one parent had beaten her. I said, "Something bad *did* happen, so she tells these stories."

Dale said, "Bullshit."

I said, "The past has consequences. Believe it."

He doesn't.

He was raised by his mother, who suffered from a rare disease and once spent an entire year in bed, her house of sons running itself, Dale cooking and cleaning, his older brother bringing in cash, the youngest boys tending just themselves. When I met Dale I'd reached a point where I couldn't stand to spend time with the kind of man who always held a measuring tape or voltameter up to our life. Plumbed its depth. Carried our love around like a sick child, taking its temperature: I think we're doing better now, or worse.

Dale thinks we're doing fine. The one argument we have is that he lives just in the present. Me? I lay next to him on cool, striped bedsheets, a breeze wafting past as I considered my dream, the children, the big thing in the gray sky or water below that had nothing to do with now, nothing. But with what had happened.

Or might. See how we argue?

We're subject to different routines. It's Dale's goal—his thrill and desire—to be objective, faithless to any system but the practical. Imagination is a crap shoot. "Men have an undeveloped sense of the symbolic," my friend Zoe said after her husband spent the night at the house of a girl who'd jumped out of a cake at a bachelor party. Because he was drunk. Spent the night alone, I mean. The cake-dancer was with the groom. Zoe's husband apologized—his safe future was at stake. He bought flowers and chocolate. "I don't speak chocolate," Zoe said, before she acquiesced, forgave. When Dale and I got married he didn't want music at the wedding. "I'd like to be clear-headed," he said.

Like music is a drug. It is. Listen to it.

You'd think the story of life was love. But ask anyone about passion's brief spin, the collapse of love or marriage, and they talk about parents, in-laws, children. Also about the great love story they once starred in—all that misfired, badly spent lust. Gunpowder wasted on pyrotechnic display. The sexual appetite they mistook for permanence. Suffocation. Pain. Like the stand-up comic who said he was so moved he had to put his hand on his heart, and he grabbed his crotch. That was my favorite joke for years.

My story, a fish story: you should see the one I never landed.

A metaphor grounded in the rituals and seasons of the resort town I grew up in—the careful way we counted points on racks, laid fish on calibrated boards. A fish has to get away. If it doesn't, there's nothing to tell. I reeled it in. I hung it on the wall.

I ate it.

The last time I saw Tom, I was in front of his house.

My boyfriend at the time—Peter, I don't think of him often—had gone inside to buy drugs. A window curtain stirred, Tom peering out. He ran into the snow in his stocking feet and leaped around, thumped on my car window. "Open up, Louisa," he said. "Open up. It'd be so easy." A fish that swims away—through opaque water, to the end of the earth, to the polar cap, to death and back—carries with it the wreck of the lure, the mangled, seductive hook. So it seemed as the sky drenched the earth and Dale slept beside me, his lungs perpetual and steady as a clock.

One summer I moved to Menominee—an idyllic, civilized college town compared to my hometown, where the major industry was keeping tourists in liquor, bait, and guns. A storm blew through, four tornadoes in its wake, all of them touching down in the city and nearby district. Thirty percent of the trees fell. Businesses and schools closed because of power lines flattened by tree trunks as big as sofas. Trees also crushed retaining walls, turned ordinary sedans into mashed-top convertibles, blocked traffic. Looting took place and, for everyone but power company employees, it was fun. I went walking, my favorite part of the aftermath the way the neighborhood was drastically unfamiliar. I detoured usual routes, climbed over trunks, through branches, my new-made forest, wishing for luck, no crackling, lively power lines.

People clustered on a street where a hundred-year-old tree had sliced a house. The trunk had landed on a small, old-fashioned bed, the nappy blanket turned back, the percale sheets exposed, a picture of Jesus ("the Lord is my Shepherd") on the wall above, which was pink. The woodwork was white. The curtains needed washing. A cross-section of private life, a shell cracked open to show the pearly inside where the soft mollusk had made its home. The story: the woman who lived there didn't have a basement and was old and stubborn and wouldn't leave. She went to sleep and the phone rang—her brother begging her to sit out the storm in a cellar. When she was on the phone, the tree hit the bed where she'd lain so lately, praying. She had to go to the hospital for shock.

People said: But for the grace of God.

I pictured God with exemplary coordination.

The morning after I slept beside Dale, dreaming of water and children, planes and fish, I sat in my living room with Big Daddy and Toni, staring through the old glass in the window. I waited for Zoe. She'd called to say she was coming to stay with Dale and me in the hopes that her husband, who ran a big farm near Bremmer, would see the light. Her grievances were specific: she wanted a cleaning lady, a Florida vacation, and one of those "I'd marry you all over again" diamond rings jewelers market for couples who get married in hard times and then make good. Zoe's husband had always made good but he spent it: on snow-mobiles and cars; on an air-conditioned tractor with quadraphonic stereo; on expensive, unnecessary silos. Zoe started visiting me years ago. "I need time off," she used to say, showing up on the front step of whatever place I rented then. This time she said, "It's almost his last chance. But I'd be in your way, right? I should go to a motel."

I hesitated. I never mind the time and space Zoe takes, but the fact of her marriage, its tremors and rattles, its hot-and-cold state swinging through my wide, clean home I try hard to keep serene.

"Dead people are serene. A cow is serene," Zoe said once, ashes from her cigarette falling on a doily-covered table in my living room. "You'd make a great old maid," she said, blowing smoke.

Blowing her stack. That's what she does. I told her to come on.

I sat, waiting.

Dale was at work. Big Daddy was beside me talking about the past. When Dale and I bought this house—a fixer-upper, a good buy—we moved in next door to Big Daddy. "I loved just one woman," Big Daddy told Toni and me now, "but she joined this club that read books and had sessions to talk about their deep meanings, and I was jeal-ous. I laid traps. It's hell to be old and wise."

Toni said, "You were jealous of a club?"

Big Daddy said, "I thought some highbrow would steal her away."

Zoe pulled into the driveway. I watched her walk toward the house, her face resolved. When we were children I was fascinated by her surface. What does she *think*? Are her wishes and fears unrealized? Or secret? Is she practical enough to forbid them? She keeps me posted on who's divorced, rich or poor or recently dead. Who's been born but not *what*: what she suffers and resists. I always pay attention to her face, her clipped words, her stance. But that day—Big Daddy's story with its faint-hearted moral, Zoe striding to the house, a stubborn wife—I thought how her exterior might not be hard, just brittle. It could crack. What would spill? I opened the door. The phone rang. "Get the door, please?" I asked Big Daddy or Toni. The phone rang again. "Hello?"

I woke in Tom's bed one morning, two mattresses on the floor shoved together; Pearl, my black dog, curled beside me. I woke exhausted and surprised. Drug users are masochistic and self-destructive, yes. But for dabblers, middle-class girls gone slumming, the reverse is true. I wanted luxury in private, my glad, solitary mood unclouded by the need to respond to the beggarly world. I noticed Pearl, her cowering posture. I heard noise outside the window, Tom cleaning my car's interior. Vacuuming; soapy water in a pan. He made heaving noises as he threw trash in a can. His dog cowered too—Angel, a sleek, white female. She moved her head when Tom moved, worried, sympathetic. If dogs were children, ours would have grown up and gone to therapy, a bad home situation, they would have learned to say. Pearl let out a suppressed growl and thumped her tail. All of my scruples had wedged themselves into four areas. I did my homework. I kept my apartment—two rented rooms—clean. I belabored everything to do with Pearl, her health, comfort, and routines.

And I had the idea my car would last forever, that I'd be ferried across the river Styx sealed in it, its perfect chrome, clean vinyl, and oft-changed oil—pure and honey-colored—helping secure my place in the afterlife. Car care was exact and holy. Small imperfections were called "dings," larger ones "dents." Anything worse than a dent and you got rid of the car, forgot you'd ever owned it. One of my cars had slid downhill and slammed a curb. The welding unhinged; the body jarred. The linkage stuck. To drive it was to hear it wheeze. My father said, "Don't look back. Someday you'll see you didn't have a choice."

I traded it. Tom didn't understand. A city boy, raised by his mother, he didn't know jack-shit. He was Catholic. It's Protestant to count your shipshape material possessions as evidence of good work. But he was cleaning my car for a reason. We'd whirled out to the edge, the limit. I remembered the night before: Tom's face, the bang of my head against the wall, the instant sense I was a surly child punished for a minor crime. The scrape of the carpet against my skin as he pushed me out the bedroom and down the stairs. Grace—my elastic muscles reacting fast—broke my fall and knocked it out of the Emergency Room range.

Every fight we'd had before was diplomatic, me imposing sanctions, Tom heeding them or not. But this time I'd got my power because Tom had let his go; he'd let it spray. After he'd pushed me down the stairs and out the front door, I wandered through the neighborhood, back to my apartment, no shoes, a pair of jeans under my nightgown—I tucked it in like a shirt when I ducked through the hedge at the end of his yard. It was perilous. The sidewalk tipping to the street. A car whooshed. I sat in my rented rooms in the subdivided house, listening to the noise of other tenants, the hum of a radio, the thump of someone's headboard against the wall. I walked back to Tom's where the door was unlocked and he was sleeping. Angel stirred; Pearl licked my hand.

Love grew like a weed. I went outside that morning and Tom crossed his arms over his bare chest. I moved toward him as I let my face send warnings: how bad off he was now. Forever. I started to cry. I bit. Tom bit too. It was First Love, the First Let-down. All subsequent love—our own as well as rational, permanent varieties—would be chintzy, second-hand, frugal from now on.

• • •

"Hello," I answered the telephone, as Zoe neared the front porch, and Big Daddy opened the door. Pearl lifted her body off the floor and weaved toward them, her vestigial watch-dog impulse activated: *woof*, the sound of her bark distant as a foghorn losing power.

At the other end of the line, "Louisa? This is Peter."

I quelled the urge to send my spite down the phone line, silent and magnetic. If I didn't try hard not to, I'd hate him. "What is it?" I asked. Another car pulled into the driveway, Dale coming home for lunch. Pearl barked again, *woof*, knocking herself down. Toni stood up to calm Pearl, "There, old girl," she said. And Dale came through the door with Toni's kids, Travis and Honey, behind him. "Hello, everyone," Dale said, nodding. Honey asked, "Mom, are you coming home to make lunch?" Pearl barked. I didn't hear what Peter told me. "I'm sorry," I said, "there's commotion here."

"Louisa, I called to tell you bad news—"

But the call-waiting signal bleeped. "Just a second," I said and I took the call. Zoe's husband. "I know she's there," he yelled, "damn it. An animal takes better care of its young than this."

I called Zoe to the phone.

Toni put her coat on to leave. Pearl flapped her tail. Big Daddy sat back down in a chair. Zoe pulled the phone into the kitchen.

"What does he say?" Dale asked, worried.

"That animals take better care of their young than Zoe."

Dale said, "Even a negligent human tends its young longer than animals."

"Please," I said. "This isn't biology."

"Sorry," Dale said. That's when he told me he'd invited Marlene for dinner. He said, "Jack's out of town. I told him we would."

We do what we can.

Dale says this about recycling trash. About repairing Big Daddy's ramshackle house. About easing Pearl through her old age by grinding food, tending wounds. About seeing anything through to its end. I, on the other hand, paralyze myself, grief so cold and shallow. Once I was thinking of leaving. I told Dale, who said he could live without me but he'd rather not. Rather not live? Live without me? I ended up staying. But if I'd had to leave I couldn't have stopped for a dying man. I let Peter hang. I didn't call back. Zoe and I bought groceries for dinner. Time passed.

An aquarium gurgled in a dark corner, yellow, coral, red. Outside, the sun sank, the night about to start, festive. At last. After years of putting Barbie dolls in dresses for their prom, their hoe-down, their bowling-alley dates. After years of watching my older sister, Helen, prepare—tasteful turtleneck, matching slacks, flat shoes. Not that I hadn't had dates. But no stirring, emphatic interest in them, no reason for my heart to quake as I painted my nails, waited. I remembered the story my Girl Scout leader told: eat an apple on Saturday night in front of a mirror by the door and you'll see the face of the man you'll marry.

I'd seen Tom at my favorite cafe. At a head shop and record store, Water Dreams, where I immersed myself studying the wee, clever tools—paraphernalia—vaguely aware of the uses to which each one could be put. Rock music thumped like the heart of a whale. A woman in a beaded dress rang up Tom's purchases, a record, a pipe, a spoon. He nodded. He turned away from the woman to smile. One day he walked across a classroom with a hundred students in it—a lecture under way, the professor yelling, Hey you, Hey you—and wrote his name in my notebook, how much he wanted to see me. *Paraphernalia*. I looked it up in the dictionary. Trappings, clutter, gear. Property a woman brings to marriage.

What could he want, I'd wondered, staring into a mirror as I waited. I'd told him I couldn't go out until I was done studying. How could he tell by my profile at a distance I was worth stalking? We ate at my favorite cafe. We walked home across the footbridge over the river. I loved his living room, the eerie sky through the window, the fish tank in the corner, its silky *glub-glub*, my skirt patterned with jungle trees and birds, rippling across the sofa. And Tom, who said, "Have you smoked hash?" I'd hardly even smoked cigarettes. What was hash? I was from a tourist town in the woods. "Of course," I said, witless and embarrassed, a demeanor that could, however, get mistaken for contempt. "I didn't know," Tom said. "No reason to sound like that."

We slid into the cushions, Tom pushing himself against me. He has nothing to do with me, I thought. But I was stoned. He doesn't know me, I thought. I decided that what he'd seen in my face was himself. "Louisa," he said, my name in his mouth a threshold.

In the morning I felt wobbly, still high. When I say to someone now—my sister, Helen, or Zoe—that I loved Tom but I can't remember why, they have answers. I didn't love him, Zoe says. Helen says, You were young, the drugs, the loud music. I listen to Muzak at work now, torpid and hypnotic. My boss leans over my desk. "Louisa," he says about hard news that comes over the wire, "don't run anything unsavory. WAR ON DRUGS A SUCCESS, fine. NANCY REAGAN RED STILL A HOT COLOR. If you couldn't stand to think about it if you were hungry, tired, or lonely, it's not for us." The morning after my date with Tom I had an appointment with one of my professors to talk about my term paper on Saccho and Vanzetti. I listened to his suggestions, my throat tight, my eyes hot. "Your outline is good," the professor said. "Why are you crying?"

I blinked.

"I'm not," I said. But since he'd mentioned it—and the

sad, dead Italians, alive only in paragraphs and photos, their faces resigned as if to say a single breaker rolls in but the whole tide rolls out—I did cry. "There, there," the professor said, kindly, nervous. I walked home, my outline in my coat pocket, the gray weather unreliable, pending violence. People in cars rode the crest of the day as if they were dead. And Tom should have had intelligence to report: I worried about you, he should have said, how was your day? "I remember now I don't like hash," I told him. He said, "That happens if you're out of practice."

Once he made me cannabis tea for my menstrual cramps. Queen Victoria had sipped something like it, physician's orders; Tom read that in *High Times* magazine. My mind wandered. Light refracted. I sat on the sofa, averted from life's purpose, from holding my finger in the dike like the Dutch boy, bracing my shoulders against the ceiling or sky in case it might—could it?—fall.

Rain came down in sheets as Zoe and I drove to the grocery store on winding roads by the edge of the river. Zoe was talking about sex when she was young, how sometimes she wished she could have the kind of orgasm she used to before she met her husband. "Of course," she said, "maybe I can't now—physically. Maybe I outgrew it. I should ask a doctor." I pulled over to the side of the road, rain falling hard. "I'm sure if you could then, you can now," I said. "You had orgasms like *that* before you met Dick?" Zoe was fifteen when she met her husband. Her boyfriend before him was Brad. I'd been in love with him too, a far-flung dream. The windshield wipers slapped, swish. Zoe sighed, "Brad had talent."

"Sounds like technique," I said.

She puffed her cigarette. "Dale's not bad in bed," she said, "right?"

I put the car in gear. "You're going to hate this sister-in-law who's coming to dinner."

Zoe said, "Louisa, you won't get a social disease from talking about sex. Boinking. That's what your brother, Davie, calls it. My brakes went out and I took my car to his shop, and we boinked right there. When I was pregnant, I fantasized I boinked Davie on a kitchen table while outside the crops ripened. And he liked my pregnant shape, Earth Goddess, shit like that."

I laughed.

It was the picture in my mind of Davie—tending to a lot of brake-failures these days. On a table. Boinking. Ripe crops. Goddesses.

"Are you trying to get pregnant?" Zoe asked.

"Not systematically."

"Dale's fine," Zoe said. "You married him because you love him."

I sneezed. The car swerved. We tooled down the road. "Hay fever," I told Zoe. "I'll be in a stupor until the first frost."

The first time Zoe came to visit—to take a break from her husband, to put the fear of God in his heart, to let absence make him grow fond and malleable—I resisted. It was January, my apartment windows frosted over. Zoe chain-smoked, her pregnant belly on her lap, complaining first how cold my apartment was, next that the bathroom was across the hall. I said, "You can't walk away from your marriage for two days." She gave me that look like when we were kids—I still didn't know the facts of life. She said, "Why not?" I couldn't answer. My own parents had never fought and yet one day—as my dad says every Christmas, every Father's Day, every time I see him—my mother up and walked away, no warning. "I always assumed she was happy," he says. *She* says: "He dwells on bad news. Catastrophes. Hell, I'll die when I die, but I'm not going to spend twenty years thinking of ways to do it."

Zoe said, "I'm practical." She wouldn't come to the phone when her husband called. He started being nice to me, desperate, his first cordial words: "Louisa, tell her I love her. The kids and I love her. Tell to have a nice time, to go shopping." I hung up.

Zoe smiled. "See what I mean? Hell, let's go to a bar."

We walked downtown. Zoe ordered Kahlua and cream.

I said, "You're not supposed to drink."

She said, "Your mother did. So did mine. I turned out fine."

We sat in a vinyl booth, the window above the table facing out at street level, people's shoes and ankles treading past. I strained to keep my eye on Pearl, who waited for us at the front door, patient, skittish. She'd followed us across the bridge, leaping at falling snow. I wasn't careful, letting Pearl sit outside a bar in cold weather where someone could steal or maim her. But times have changed. It was less risky then. I'd wandered the streets unperturbed—Pearl, Zoe, me, everyone I knew, everlasting. Zoe looked around at the old men in undershirts, jars of pickled eggs, dice. She said, "This the nicest bar you know?"

I explained that bars with ferns, tablecloths ("A glass of chablis, please?"), left me cold. A man at the bar with a grizzled chin and fuzzy earflaps smiled and waved. I said, "This is part of life we can't ignore." I didn't admit I found it picturesque.

Walking back over the footbridge, back to my rented rooms, I marveled at the still, cold air, the black figure of Pearl cavorting and leaping on a snowy background—a comma, an exclamation mark—dashing back and forth, glad to have retrieved me and to go. I breathed into my woolen scarf, my breath wet, my boots squeaking on the frozen earth. Zoe said, "So you have a boyfriend. Where is he?" I'd wondered that myself: he hadn't called. Once he'd called at 11:45 P.M. "Interested in getting together?"

"You went ahead and said yes," Zoe said. "What a fool."

Life's a bitch, and you marry it. I thought this as we crossed the river. Someone on the *Tonight Show*, Doc Severinsen I think, said the coldest place on earth was a footbridge in Menominee, Wisconsin, raw air rising from moving water. We walked up the steps of my apartment house. "I take it this is another part of life we can't ignore," Zoe said about the dusty entry, the muffled noise of other tenants' lives. "You don't lock the front door?"

I said, "There isn't a key. I lock the door to my own rooms, sometimes not even that. People always coming and going—it's safe."

Zoe got ready for bed, rubbing her stomach with cocoa butter before she put her white nightgown on. "My anti-stretch mark regimen," she said. She wandered into the kitchenette, where my schoolbooks lay on the table. "What the hell?" She flipped through the *Norton Anthology*. ("With sorwe thou come into this world, with sorwe thou shalt away. Lullay, little child, this wo . . .")

"A lullaby," I explained, "from the Middle Ages."

" 'Death shall come with a blast'?" she said. "How upbeat. I think I'll read it to my kids. Christ." She pulled back the covers in the bed in my bed-sitting room, plumped a pillow. I explained to her about medieval life—short, dark days, early death, the half-pagan vision of heaven as a reward for pain. Apotheosis. She said, "Apotheosis, it sounds like a liver disease." She turned the light out. "I don't see why they think they had the market cornered on short, dark days," she said, her voice floating across the chilly room, "sounds like Wisconsin to me."

I didn't lock the door that night.

I went across the hall to use the bathroom—big and drafty. The claw-footed tub I scoured every time I used it because who knew who'd sat in it before me. The only pictures hanging on the wall—an Art major across the hall had mounted and hung them—black-and-white photos of

"The World's Most Beautifully Tattooed Man and Woman Contest," grotesque, swirly designs covering torsos, arms, legs. Zoe had said: "You look at this when you brush your teeth?"

She was already asleep when I got back and crawled into my corner of the bed behind her hilly shape. I closed my eyes and tried to relax without rolling into her. I remembered how—right after I'd first begun sleeping with Tom—I'd gone to my sister, Helen's, for Thanksgiving and had to spend the night in a double bed with my mother, who was visiting from California, and I'd thrown my arm across her neck, laid my head on her chest, and murmured how much I liked her. It. *Something.* I woke as she pushed me away. I thought about what Zoe would do if I accidentally hugged or kissed her—she'd tell everyone. She embraces what she likes about someone and throws the rest away. Suddenly, the door banged open. A rectangle of light sliced the room. Tom weaved drunkenly. Zoe sat up in bed like a fat ghost. "What?" she said, falling back down to sleep. She sleeps hard.

"Excuse me, I had no idea. Oh, shit." This was Tom.

I jumped out of bed. "It's my girlfriend," I said.

"Oh shit, really," he said.

"From Bremmer," I said, "visiting. I just have one bed."

I steered him downstairs to the entryway, to the sitting room in the corner with the musty couch no one sat on, the upright piano no one tuned or played. A window looked over the street to the park, the river. I moved my feet off the cold floor and tucked them under the folds of my nightgown. The streetlight shone like a silver moon, and Tom reached for me, liquor on his breath like perfume, the nylon of his jacket making silky whispers as he moved his arms this way, that way. "God," he said, "Louisa," my name in his mouth again. So intimate, I thought, to be in his mouth. I came. Salty. Brimming. Cold. On the couch in the hall, anyone could have seen.

Upstairs Zoe lay like a heap of exhaustion—I pictured her—sleep flowing out of her mouth like dust.

Yellow overhead lights, the clinking of metal carts— Zoe stood in the door of the grocery store bent over, pushing her hair into a rubber band. Someone bumped her. "Well, excuse me," she said, like it was normal to put her hair in a ponytail in midstream grocery-store traffic. "If I don't," she explained, "with this rain, I wouldn't have any curl left for the dinner party tonight."

My clothes felt steamy and woolen. I wheeled my shopping cart in time to the soporific music: ding ding, a Beatles song, sentimental violins. Trouble so far away. Yesterday. I put exotic, bitter lettuce in my cart, a head of cauliflower, which—as I remarked to Zoe—reminded me of a human head, a clean, white brain.

Zoe said, "You're so weird. I like iceberg lettuce. Who likes it bitter? Who was that old fart at your house, and the fat woman?"

"Zoe," I said, "they're my friends."

She said, "I remember the fat woman, her husband dumped her."

"She's big-boned," I said.

"And the old guy—"

"Big Daddy."

"If you like old people," Zoe said, "what's wrong with your dad?"

The wheel on my cart wobbled; it was out of whack. Big Daddy does look old, I thought. And Pearl, who bounds in the house like a puppy but misjudges depth, distance. She falls. Big Daddy forgets what he's talking about, to whom, the point he meant to make.

Zoe said, "Your real dad looks bad these days. If I had a family, I'd see them. Who's the sister-in-law coming to dinner? Not Dale's blood relative, I hope. One thing about a small town is you know the family you marry into—they can't keep it a secret if they're crazy and then you're already in love, too late."

Love love. Yesterday.

Sad, befuddling music made mulchy and easy to swallow. I put plastic-wrapped slabs of beef in my cart, eggs, olives, wine. Dog food for old dogs. I said, "If you don't shut up I'll make you eat bitter lettuce." And I remembered the phone call, Peter at the end of the line: "Louisa, I called to tell you," he'd said, "bad news."

Tom and I sat in a restaurant designed to look like lumberjacks ate there, axes and saws hanging on the wall above the jukebox. I hated my lunch, pale lettuce with ragged carrot sticks, murky salad dressing in foil packets that said: monocalcium steryl bromate. My car sat in the parking lot, Pearl and Angel in the back, their pink tongues hanging out. Tom said, "Admit it, you were wrong." The night before I'd run into a friend at the laundromat—she'd suggested we go for a drink. We ended up at a college bar, Pearl on the floor inspiring one-liners. Is that your dog? You three girls come here often? In the morning I woke, no sheets on my bed, my neat stacks of laundry nearby, Pearl woozy from eating pretzels. And Tom in the doorway ready to leave on this trip we'd planned, his suitcase packed. "Get up, you slut," he said. He didn't mean it. He tried not to lose his temper, and I tried hard to keep it monitored and steady, a heart condition exacerbated by stress. "I was inconsiderate. Sorry."

"Where were you?"

"Out with a friend," I said.

We pulled into his mother's yard four hours late. The last words Tom said (as she waved hello from the door, a

Kleenex in her hand, her ruffly apron flapping): "You didn't fuck anyone, I hope."

He put my suitcases in a room that used to be his brother's, toys and trucks in primary colors on the wall, a stale smell in the rug, slats of light from the street projecting through the venetian blinds, unsettling like bars. "You can't plan your life around kids," Tom's mother said at the dinner table. She hadn't seen Tom's brother in years. He was with Tom's father, who was insane, she said. And she herself had bad nerves. She'd lost her sense of smell and taste during childbirth. "Very rare," she said, "it doesn't happen to most women. Don't let that stop you from having children. Have a dumpling. My boys used to fight over who got the last dumpling and that's why I set this extra plate. I'm not living in the past, but hoping for a better future—that someday I'll have Tom, my loyal son, and the other one back too."

Angel and Pearl sat at the edge of the kitchen, eyes narrow, tongues hanging out, mouths stretched—dogs grinning. A crucifix hung on the wall. One day Tom found her passed out in the La-Z-Boy. "I sleep so hard," she'd said. Valium. A St. Francis of Assisi statue stood in the backyard: she loved animals. But when Angel and Pearl woke at 4:00 A.M., pacing, letting me know it was time, they needed to go, it was time please, I called across the hall to Tom, and we dressed and ran them, quick, down to the park on the corner. "Not there, not there," we'd whisper, "here." We walked back to the house at dawn, the dogs relieved, Tom silent, angry.

On the third day, we drove away. I loved a particular section of the Milwaukee Expressway, a miscalculation, a ramp that rose into the sky and stopped. "Has anyone ever driven off it?" I asked, sure someone had, a legendary and impersonal disaster. Tom said, "Louisa, how morbid." I'd drunk champagne that day. I loved it, also the slope of the freeway, my car a well-tuned machine, the dogs in the back, their faces serene. We stopped at a city park where Tom had once been arrested. His mother had called the police and said: "My son is out there, it's after city curfew, arrest him." "Wait here," Tom said, kissing my cheek. He knew the people hanging out, friends and enemies. He hated but respected them. He crossed the road. Cars went by, whoosh, stereo music thundering through open windows. Tom shook hands with everyone. He was in college now, he explained. (All *A*s one semester, all *F*s the next. Drugs. He probably didn't mention that.) Majoring in social work. Peter, my boyfriend right after Tom, had scoffed: Social work, he'd said. Hell, Tom *needs* social work.

I explained. A social worker had kept Tom out of prison. It's all he ever wanted to be. Besides rich. Loved by a beautiful woman, both surface and soul. He waved me across the street.

Angel and Pearl clamored to go too. I opened the car door and blocked them in until traffic lulled. Then I crossed the stream of cars, holding each dog by her collar, stumbling as traffic surged. Tom said later how he'd watched, impatient: Louisa, hurry, come meet these people. A scary bunch, I thought at the time. But I'd traveled so little. I'd left the state once, to go to Disneyland with my aunt. But that day I dodged traffic in Milwaukee wearing new clothes, a silky top tucked in my jeans, new boots. I used to shop while Tom stood outside my dressing room, brandishing money. I always felt like a peasant, protected and claustrophobic, collecting favors I couldn't repay except with service. I hung onto the collars of the dogs we were proud of, their quirks and manners, their magnificent health. I smiled. You looked good, Tom said later, hanging onto the dogs like that to make sure they didn't get hit, smacked. Louisa, I looked around at the crooks and punks I used to run with, I had no choice. I said to myself—looking at you—I made it out of here. Alive.

• • •

I stood in the kitchen, cooking.

I scrubbed bald carrots in the sink, their stringy roots falling away. I chopped cauliflower into chunks, seared the edges of the beef in a pan so when it roasted the juices would stay intact. Zoe sat at the kitchen table, flipping through the *Globe*, the *Enquirer, Star*. I said, "Well, I guess I better call Peter back."

She held up a copy of *Star*, pointed at its headlines: MY NIGHTS WITH KINKY KILLER TEACHER, PAM. KIEFER ON HEARTBROKEN HOLLYWOOD RAMPAGE. "For God's sake," she said, "For this you studied Shakespeare? Those gloomy poems from the Middle Ages? Where are your books? You work at a newspaper, but you read this crap."

I said, "I need a break. I read Emily Dickinson but not every night."

"Angie Dickinson," she said. "And you've been to college."

"I'm going to call Peter."

She said, "What a jerk."

I put the roast in. I picked up the phone.

Zoe said, "I know you needed to move on, to get a new boyfriend after Tom. You were looking for something safe and easy. The pendulum effect, over-correction. But you swung too far."

I dialed. The line rang.

Peter answered. "Long time, no call. Look, I know we've had bad blood, but I called like a friend to tell you something you need to know. Of course, it's old news. It's been true for days."

Tom was dead.

Peter went on to say that if I needed details I should call Tom's friend, Al, who'd been a pallbearer. There'd been a guitar mass. Tom's mother came. He was buried in Milwaukee, the family plot. It happened six days ago. He never got over me but I never got over him either. Did I? A truck with a load of logs had plowed into Tom's car, knocked it off the road. Logs flew in a bundle and landed on Tom, bull's-eye. It was raining, wind gusting. Imagine, Peter said, logs flying like that and landing, synchronized, on Tom in his car. Of course Tom wasn't a good driver, you know that. He used to beat the shit out of your Mercury Comet. It's hard, Peter said, but I thought you'd want to know.

"It was his fault," I asked, "right?"

Peter said, "The driver of the truck was drunk. Tom was on his way to work. He's been straight. He was a social worker, you know that, drug rehab. Otherwise," Peter said, "how have you been?"

Tom was dead.

Lovers survive when they're gone from your bed. Dead, but not really. Some people have lunch with ex-lovers, send Christmas cards and annual, newsy letters. But as long as Tom was across town, his heart ticking (a door, a window, a car ride away), I didn't go straight. I veered. I didn't make sense of our time together, regrets and paybacks, old pain. Old news, already true. Tom had been dead for years. "To marry you," I'd yelled once, "would be to marry the past." And when he'd tailed me as I went on new dates, trying to forget him, I yelled, "I hate you, I wish you were dead." It's the kind of thing your mother tells you never to say, you'll regret it. Don't make an ugly face, it'll get stuck like that. I explained this to Zoe as she sat at my kitchen table after Peter told me the old news, already true, Tom was dead. She said: "Louisa, lighten up. Who hasn't said that?"

It hadn't been easy, going on dates. Someone would call with plans, no corsage or box of chocolates, no hoedown or bowling-alley date. But we'd go to a restaurant or movie, not straight to bed. "Do you and Tom go out?" someone had asked me once in front of Zoe, who'd answered for me: "They go in and out." Once someone had called and said let's go to dinner at a restaurant in Fall City, twenty miles away, and we sat eating chicken and cole slaw and Tater Tots with old farmers, my date watching the street as if Tom might drive up. He might. "Come here often?" I wanted to say.

A date was public, official. The first time I went somewhere with Peter our appearance sent waves of information: Look, we're trying it out. Some busy, meddling person—let's say her name was Tammy or Di Ann or Suzie—would say: "So you're with Peter, how interesting." What could I say? Chances are, it won't work out? I'm dating him for frivolous reasons, I could care less? I defended my choice to the extent it was scrutinized, and ended up feeling as if I'd signed a binding contract as people said, Well, so you like Peter, how interesting. And I answered, Yes, yes, I do.

Once I went to a party in someone's backyard on my birthday where Peter had arranged for a cake and balloons, surprise. He held my hand. He put his arm around me when we walked to the house to refill our drinks. Someone stepped out of the crowd to ask me, "May I have a birthday kiss, please?" Peter looked abashed and polite: he wanted to forbid the kiss but, according to the rules, couldn't. As I tipped my cheek, many happy returns, I saw Tom. *Angry Young Man Figure.* (This is a set of terms from sociology. "He'll understand," Tom had said once about a professor, "he knows I'm an angry young man.") How will he age? I wondered as I watched Tom. The near-stranger kissed my cheek. It won't age well, I thought, Tom's anger. He was taking six years to finish college. He'd try to quit dealing and someone would show up with prices on pounds or ounces too good to pass up, and he'd turn a quick profit, then get back to the business of going straight. He walked across the lawn that night, the edge of the dusky sky turning violet, the smell of honeysuckle sweet and brief.

He said, "You look like hell."

He hated it that I'd cut my hair, traded my usual flowing, gypsy-type dress for one that was short—like a tennis dress except it was black. I'd just seen a movie about avantgarde artists in Paris who decide not to prolong modernism and cynicism, to get on with their lives, and they take a sleek plane back to the U.S. and even their paintings look cleaner, less private and fierce. Tom said, surly and violent, "I get a birthday kiss from you too," and he kissed me, clenching, biting, leaning hard. I fell backward into a shrub and he landed on top like a load of bricks.

Peter said, "Here." He tried to pull us up but in the end couldn't.

On the edge of the lawn, fresh-mown and sweet-scented—was Tom's date, who looked good but she didn't have "advantages." That's how we'd say it where I come from, Bremmer, where anyone who doesn't have practice in spending time and money on clothes, details, acessories, enters the race late, from a bad position. I stood up and brushed the grass off my dress. Tom dusted his knees. His girlfriend was dark-skinned, Italian. Catholic. I'd seen her from a distance, her sad eyes. According to Tammy or Di Ann or Suzie, she came from "a bad home situation" and Tom had more in common with her than me because I'd been an ideal—Suzie explained this to me once—Tom's love for me not love but blind faith. I never learned her name, Tom's girlfriend, but I thought of her as *Carmen* because of her dark skin, or *Camille* because of her disadvantages, or *Zinaida* because she made me think of any fiery-tempered, unlucky heroine from a Great Love Novel who attracts a man she aspires to, and of course she's pretty and young, and he bites, but in the end swallows her whole and moves on.

It's an old-fashioned idea: that just men sow loose oats on the wrong side of the track. That just men find themselves attached to needy, promiscuous lovers before they settle down to marry.

Later that night someone hit someone.

It wasn't Tom or Peter. I watched the man who'd suffered the worst blows—he drove away, holding a red-
stained towel to his head. And the woman he'd spilled
blood for watched, a new lover by her side. I felt odd and
guilty. "We've been going to the wrong parties," I told Peter, "hanging out with a bad crowd." I felt responsible, and
I didn't even know them, the men who'd fought, the
woman they'd fought for. But at least it wasn't Tom or Carmen or Peter, I told myself. At least it wasn't someone I
knew.

Rain turned to snow. "You want to cancel this dinner?"
Zoe asked. The light in the house turned dark. I
flipped a switch—a yellow glow flooded the rooms. Heat
swelled from the stove, pots boiling. "It's not good weather
for people to be out in their cars," Zoe said. "You should
worry about Dale getting home from work. I should call
Dick. Who all's coming? Why are we doing this?"

"Shut up," I said. "Set the table."

"Shut up," I told Tom. I'd asked him to keep Pearl while
I went to Bremmer, where Helen's baby was being
baptized. He'd said: "Is this a custody arrangement, or are
you making excuses to see me?"

"It's because she knows you," I said, "and Angel. I don't
trust just anyone." It was easy to be protective about Pearl
in front of Tom—he'd yelled at his friend Al once because
Al had dropped his dog off in Tom's yard so she could play
with Angel. "Your dog needs personal attention," Tom had
explained, pacing. "Understand? She needs to spend time
with you." Myself, I got to the point where I never took
Pearl out without her leash. I didn't like to walk to the corner grocery and leave her tied up without checking on her

through the window, my basket loaded with eggs, bread, milk. I'd see Pearl's leash pulled taut, meaning she was at the end of it. Still, I'd press against the window until I saw Pearl, anxious, peering back. If she turned up dead or missing I'd survive, if I didn't die of grief in the first five minutes.

"Okay, sure," Tom said, "drop her off."

I dropped her off, a suitcase in my trunk, my car refueled, its fluid levels safe and high. I knocked on Tom's door and Pearl jumped against it, hopeful. The door banged open onto Tom's living room—he didn't value the effect of sunbeams passing through windows enough to open his drapes unless important guests were coming. "Hello, Louisa," he said, opening the drapes. The dogs slammed against the coffee table, their tails wagging. Al was on the couch, and next to him this guitar player with tattoos, Walter. They stared, amused and suspicious. They were high, all three, at ten in the morning—seeds and stems bunched in a corner of a tray, drug clutter, paraphernalia, stowed on a low shelf. I looked for a mirror, traces of white powder, a smeared streak. It was progress, I felt, that Tom just smoked pot now, the Lord's Weed if you believe Rastafarians. Even I'd liked pot until I got worrisome. Who was I, what hypocrite I wondered, to complain about pot when I liked wine, quoting the Bible as I tipped my glass: that maketh glad the heart, for thy stomach's sake.

Pearl jumped over the coffee table to romp with Al's dog. Al said, "Dog custody arrangement." Tom's joke. Which meant Tom had told Al he thought I was just making excuses to come around and visit. Al grinned and stared, a leering consumer's look. Appraisal: Should I lay my money down? Is she worth it? My little brother, Davie, looks at cars this way, making offers even when they're not for sale. "Bullshit," he says, "everything's for sale."

Al said, "I see you couldn't stay away." Like I couldn't stay away from him. He'd put it to me like this once: You need time away from Tom. He had me in a corner, his arm against the wall. You need time away from Tom, Al had said, but you don't want to hurt him. You can trust me to keep your secret and I'm so good I'll make you forget your troubles. He wasn't. I didn't. And now I had the memory of Al's afterglow: satisfaction. The intimate part of sex— when you need to be in love or suffer through—isn't sex itself but later, when you put your clothes back on.

Tom went upstairs to get some things I'd left there months ago, he said. I waited for him in the dining room. I looked in the mirror above the table. I was thinking about the unfirm texture of my skin the night before—it had been late, I'd been tired. I'd looked in the mirror. I wasn't old but I could see I would be. The surprise I'd felt had made my eyes, my expression, unfamiliar, a stranger staring back. I thought about formaldehyde and vinegar, fluids that keep organic matter indefinitely young. Dolly Parton once said her favorite food was Wonder Bread and Cheese-Whiz, and some hunky Italian actor said no wonder she looks good, it's the preservatives. Which is a joke of course. Preservatives are unhealthy. But the idea is nice, like Ponce de Leon's fountain of youth. To live, to breathe, is to die. I'd seen the changes wrought on Helen's body by the gestation of a child.

Tom came downstairs. "Is this your hairbrush?" he asked.

"Yes." I put it in my purse. In the next room, Al talked, laughed.

"These?" Tom said. He held up earrings.

"I would never wear something so ugly," I said.

Tom turned red. He put them in his pocket. He smirked. It was part of the Angry-Young-Man package: smirking. "Then this wouldn't be yours either," he said, waving a filmy nightgown or slip.

I said, "If you're letting me know you won't take care of Pearl, fine."

The living room was quiet, Al and Walter.

"It's ugly," I said. "A slut would wear that. She probably bought it at Woolworth's."

"Louisa," Tom said, "let it go. Let's cut our losses." He threw the nightgown on the table. "Come pick up Pearl on Sunday night."

Zoe laid napkins on the table. "When my dad died," she said, "I bought a book that explains how there are things you hate about yourself that you've always blamed on this person who's now dead."

I poured ice water into glasses. "I hate self-help books. They're like tranquilizers. They don't cure you, they keep you sick."

Zoe said, "There's a questionnaire to help you process grief."

"A questionnaire," I said. "A grief processor."

Headlights flashed through the front window, illuminating a tunnel of falling snow, damp and bunchy like clots of milkweed. "Well, Dale's home now," Zoe said, sighing, "which is good. Isn't it?"

I pulled up in front of Tom's house on Sunday night. I knocked and knocked. Finally, I opened the door but it stopped short—the lock, four inches of chain stretching from the door to the frame. I called for Pearl, who shoved her nose toward me. Angel sat by the couch, her loyalty to Tom permanent and certain. Like death or taxes. Angel loved me but she loved Carmen too, who no doubt worked at it. So what was inside? Synthesized music. I'd heard it as I came up the sidewalk, its dull, emotional pulse like an organ, hymns played under water. And Tom and Carmen, whatever her name was, sleeping in a pile on the couch as if they were dead. "Come on, Pearl," I said, trying to get her to squeeze through. Tom woke and shuddered, shaking the cobwebs from his head.

He lumbered toward me, tall and frightening. Franken-stein, he had a heart but no skill for love. He opened the door and Pearl burst out. I backed up. "I hate you," I said. "I asked you to keep Pearl and you didn't stay straight." He was barefoot. Snow sifted onto the edge of the sidewalk. He moved toward me until my back was pressed against the car. He put his arms around me, opened his mouth and kissed me, his teeth clamping down. "I love you," he said, "that's it. I'm hungry. Let's eat."

I waited for him in the car while he put his coat and shoes on. We drove to a restaurant. We left Carmen on the couch. "She took downers," Tom said. "She was pissed off your dog was there." Tom stared at me as he said this. Pressed meat slid out of his sandwich onto the table. She'd said: "You'll never be through with Louisa." And slugged back tequila and red pills. Tom tipped his head back and ate the meat. "I never will be," he said, "through."

Peter tried to reach me. The phone rang and rang, he said. He kept in touch by driving past my apartment, look-ing for my car. "I know you're back with Tom," he said fi-nally. "Listen, if you're not in love with me, I'd just as soon get good prices on pounds."

I never saw Carmen again.

But I couldn't help remembering her as I slept in Tom's bed, ate meals in his kitchen, sensitive to her traces and relics, her liquor in the pantry, toothbrush on the bath-room shelf. At night I lay under Tom, his flesh mine. Ham-mering and chiseling, both of us, until we were numb and blunt. I considered her sad eyes, how she must have ached when she said: You will never be through. Peter, who'd said: Listen, regarding Tom, you'll never be through. A month later, I thought I was pregnant. I sat at the top of the stairs in Tom's house in my warm nightgown, thinking I'd tell Helen, and Zoe, anyone I knew who already had a baby, I was having one too. I thought about it in clear terms: If I was pregnant I'd marry Tom, at least for a while, and a part of him would connect to part of me and grow up and have a life of its own. We'd be all the way through, in twenty years. Or I'd turn out not to be pregnant and we'd stop now. I wasn't. We did. Forever.

"People shouldn't get married young," I said, "not because marriage is hard, but because divorce is. You need to be mature to split up." I heard footsteps on the porch as I said this, the chime and rumble of voices. "It's Marlene," I told Zoe, "the sister-in-law. Dale must have picked her up so she wouldn't have to drive."

Zoe said, "Who married young? Who's splitting up?"

I said, "Don't worry, Dale and I are in the pink." I turned the porch light on. I said, "Big Daddy and Toni will be walking over."

Dale came through the door, his skin and clothes damp. I brushed against his wool coat to kiss him. Happy as a lark, I thought. Happy as the day is long. Marlene was behind him. She's tall—six foot, two—with big shoulders and a flattened-out expression that has more to do with bones and genes than discontent. Still, she puts people off. Jack stokes her, sustains her appetite for pain, for noticing what's wrong, never what's good or right. As though love were unnatural, requiring effort. The effort is Jack's, not Marlene's, who's suffered already with her bad health and childhood, just ask. She was talking about her heart as she came through the door. "It has a murmur," she said. "I take a special drug when the dentist cleans my teeth."

That's what's good about Marlene, or a soap opera. You throw yourself into the trauma. "How terrible," I said, as I kissed her hello.

Zoe said, "What does heart trouble have to do with teeth?"

It didn't matter that Marlene hadn't been introduced. She's nervy, thin-skinned. She said, "Well, I could get bacteria in my valves."

Zoe was doubtful.

Marlene said, "If my gums bleed."

Innards and disease are unacceptable to Zoe. "Gross."

We laughed, Dale most of all, a hard, dry blast. He clears his throat when he's worried. These tics infuriate me. One day on the phone I told my sister, Helen—who thinks Dale is a great husband—all the reasons he's not. My list was short. I said, "He gets strung out in the grocery store if I put things in the cart in a messy way. He nags me if I leave doors open." Helen said, "So?" Meanwhile, I pushed away the memory of my anxiety when he laughs because he's relieved, or clears his throat because he's nervous, my flurry to speak and act, console, erase his disappointment. If serenity wasn't invented yet, it wouldn't be missing.

Toni and Big Daddy thumped onto the porch. I opened the door. "What's so funny?" Toni said, taking her coat off. Big Daddy's glasses fogged up. Zoe and Dale were laughing. Even Marlene was laughing hard. "Come to the table," I said, "and eat."

As I served dinner, I remembered my wedding day, the quiet vows, the reception at a friend's house where I'd refilled glasses, carried plates away from small tables where people clustered to talk. Dale stopped me on my way out the door with a trash bag. "You're the bride," he said. But all I saw was clutter. This time, I'd supposed—though I'd never been married before, not in a wedding—would be streamlined, no paraphernalia. Old pain.

I put meat on Big Daddy's plate. He said, "I loved just one woman."

Toni smiled and unfolded his napkin.

Zoe lit the candles. She said, "Who was the lucky girl?"

Big Daddy frowned. "It's on the tip of my tongue," he said. He tried to remember—who the woman was, what speech he'd been about to make. We smiled, patient, encouraging. Dale had put music on, something mellow, good for digestion. Big Daddy said, "Personally, I like Zamfir, that pipe music. It puts me to sleep."

Zoe smiled. Then she turned to Dale. "So," she said, "you had a good day?" My office, my responsibility. Of course, Zoe doesn't always ask her husband how his day was either. I do—on the scarce occasions I see him. It's required, a polite veneer. I passed the platter of cauliflower, the bowl of potatoes. How effortless, I thought, to ask a near-stranger about his day because he won't answer except in a fluid gloss. That's when Marlene put her hand to her chest and shrieked. "My God, has that dog had a stroke?" Big Daddy stood up. His fork fell to the floor.

I prayed: One, don't let this happen. Two, happen fast.

Dale cleared his throat. "It's just that her hips are bad," he said. "She sways when she's nervous. She probably has to go outside."

Big Daddy said, "Glad to lend a hand. Come on, girl." He headed out the back door with Pearl. That's when dinner slid to its halt, food on our plates growing cold, sauces thick and gelled like sap. We heard a crash, thump. Toni stood up. "Shit," she said.

A minute passed—that block of time after crisis. I didn't react. Grief is irregular, relief sweeping cleanly as I think: At last I can stop waiting. Meanwhile, new pain as I wonder: Will no one grieve more than this for me? Will I sit at a table, rambling about my past, my Great Love, and suddenly not remember what I'm saying, and young people will smile and think, She's not long for this world. Not that I sat there, having heard Big Daddy fall on the back stairs and thought to myself I'd die some day too. Or, Good, Tom is dead at last. But I considered my reaction, my leap to the conclusion that Tom had been drunk, inept, had killed himself, when in fact he was a victim this time. I thought how—even if Pearl hadn't had a stroke yet—she would soon. That my father grew more feeble every year.

Now Big Daddy had hurt himself, who knows how bad, a broken hip, a last decline.

Dale rushed to the door. Zoe looked at me and blinked. I've known her so long I understood the gesture: we should wait. Toni paced, hands clenched, because Big Daddy is like family, her own kids surly, her parents dead. I went to the door—cold air whistled in, snow fell. Dale said, "It's probably a sprain or fracture."

"It could hemorrhage," Marlene said.

"Hurry up, damn it, check the dog," Big Daddy said, "check the dog." I understood he'd fallen on or near Pearl—he worried he'd hurt her. I bent down and felt her ribs. I looked in her eyes but the yardlight glared, making their surface opaque, impenetrable. She rubbed against my leg and made a satisfied growl.

"She's fine," I said.

Dale brushed past me to get his coat, his keys. "I worry," he said, "the Emergency Room. He probably doesn't have insurance."

"Don't worry," Zoe said. "Keep the car on the road."

Toni and Marlene helped Big Daddy into the back. I stood in the doorway as Toni said, "I'd ask you to call Travis and Honey and tell them where I am, but they won't even notice I'm gone." Marlene came inside for a blanket. "He could get complications," she told us. "Once, my contusions got infected and I got cellulitis."

Zoe was scraping plates—limp vegetables, cold beef. She said, "You get cellulitis from picking scabs. My kids get it." I started to laugh. Zoe said, "Laugh or cry, it's all the same."

Dale pulled out of the driveway—with Big Daddy, Toni, Marlene. Zoe finished the dishes, scrubbed the stove top, folded towels into neat squares. She said, "Mind if I smoke?" I said of course not, even as I watched ashes fall to the counter and floor.

She picked up the cordless phone and dialed. "Phone home," she said—alluding to the movie *E.T.*, I suppose—

and she went in the pantry and shut the door. I stood in the living room in front of the window, the rippling glass, and stared outside at the squares and circles of light from houses along the highway and, for the first time, I understood Dale was on a slick road with a confused man and at least one hysterical woman. What if he slid in the river and died? I recognized this sequence of logic as panic, a train that derails every time the phone rings in the middle of the night, or Pearl wanders away, the speedy assumption news is bad, the second phase in which I think: then on with it, suffering, my solitary life. But this was the first time I'd panicked about Dale, grown appalled he'd driven away and I hadn't realized every time is possibly the last. What good is the knowledge?

Zoe came out of the pantry, and I said: "Did you call home? Are you done, for today, with running your marriage like a trade embargo?"

Her eyes brimmed up, for the first time in all the years I've known her. I waited for her excuse. That she was joking. She'd stood too near a bag of onions. Smoke was in her eyes. Or would she break down and admit to terminal pain? "Zoe," I said, "I'm sorry."

"I'm tired," she said. "Let's watch TV."

We went in the bedroom, Dale's and mine, where the TV was at the foot of the bed. Zoe said, "When you have kids, you'll have to buy another one for the living room. Of course, you won't have kids unless you get the TV out of here." She explained how she'd read that couples who have TV in their bedrooms have less sex. Jay Leno, nature programs, *The Fugitive*—none of it induces ardor.

"We don't watch much," I said. Stacked next to the bed was my selection for late-night reading. A gift edition of Emily Dickinson. *Seven Old English Poems.* Magazines that specialize in celebrity gossip. A copy of the newspaper I work for—Dale always complains about its lack of news, its trifling editorials. I blame it on my boss, who's not really an editor but a professional booster, a graduate

of the Norman Vincent Peale school of thought. But I'm
relieved every day the paper goes to press with no news
but what's palatable, even if it's a lie, omission. Besides,
there's rarely bad news on a big scale here: death, property negotiation, human interest. Once I wrote a feature
about a woman who watched her livestock be slaughtered
because she didn't think it was otherwise right to spend
earnings from the sale of the meat. I understood the ob-
session with knowing the consequences of your life, who
or what fails to survive because of you. At the same time, I
thought: Why dwell on what's necessary? I asked Zoe,
who answered: "That way you get used to it."

She flipped through the channels while I settled down
to read. It's for appearances or good intentions I keep serious poetry by my bed—as if I could stand the agitation so
late at night.

I skimmed the introduction: "*A perennial daughter, never
a wife or widow . . .*" No wonder Emily Dickinson wore
white, I thought, to keep from wearing black. Zoe was
watching a show called *My Generation*, videos of rock mu-
sicians who were love idols fifteen years ago. I read on:
"*Then came the death of her father, that strong Puritan who
communicated the vigor of nature.*" The videos blurred past:
heavy bass lines, lead singers with long hair and wire-rims.
A California band sang about fickle love, their faces mean,
happy, tense. One of them sniffed, brushed his hand up
against his nose. "Look," I said, "they're doing coke." But
Zoe swung her legs to the floor, talked about going to bed.
She stumbled down the hall. The videos—images, melody,
lyrics—evoked nostalgia. The memory of not an event but
a frame of mind in which it was possible that love would
streak from the sky and warm me all the way to the soles of
my cold feet. I read, the blurry words, "*Could you with
honor, sir, avoid death, I entreat you,*" until, too late, I slid under the covers to sleep.

One last question thrust itself forward: Tom's dog, Angel? I pictured her white shape, her appeasing, obedient

face. I wondered if I should call Tom's mother and ask if Angel was safe in limbo between her life and Tom's, if I should bring her here to live with Pearl? This made me think how the calendar year was headed to the winter solstice now, a day that always makes me anxious and defeated like I'm stuck in dark water under a frozen lake.

I dreamed about airplanes.

It was probably the sound of a commuter overhead. But maybe not, because the world was muffled with new snow. I dreamed I was in a silver jet with Zoe, its belly cavernous like a barn. We were flying to a sale on linens—a white sale—and I told her about Tom's plane, small like a van, lacy with rust outside but inside plush and red. Naugahyde, crushed velvet, a refrigerator, a wet bar, a waterbed. "Too luxurious to be believed," I said, "all those comforts inside, but outside, rusty and brittle as a tin can. A Catholic plane," I said, "it has to do with sacred hearts."

Then, steadily, a glow spreads from inside. My *basement*—because this is the word Zoe and I use as we sit, ladylike, and discuss the heat rising from our private parts. Suddenly it's clear this is no flight to a department store, because we're on a plane that exists for the purpose of reproduction. A brood plane. The seats are like benches, or stanchions. We're bred not by lovers but by holding still for the pleasant sense that—without marking the calendar, without stocking up on vitamins or buying a layette—a baby is on the way after all. One for Zoe too who sits beside me, motionless. It makes perfect sense then as I remember how my aunt, who used to be a flight attendant, once told me about an expert who'd compiled a list of the different sexual fantasies people have about planes, and also about her one roommate who'd dreamed she had sex with a jet, and it was the best, the plane swiveling its haunches, its landing gear, begging her to come on now. And she was glad, it was the best she ever had.

I woke, scared. But it was Dale making love to me, his skin fresh and cold, bringing the outside inside. Now. I

thought about my dream in which Tom's van—the last vehicle I'd known him to own—had become a plane that
floated like shrapnel in blood. I thought about the jet in
which Zoe and I had flown—and I had a split-second of
religious guilt that, even though I'd dreamed it, I'd had
aberrant sex on a plane. I thought at the same time that
Big Daddy, Toni, and Marlene must be safe in their beds,
or Dale wouldn't be here making love to me. Now. Then it
was over, the moment of planes and skies, Dale inside me,
the best yet. Still, I couldn't forget Tom, floating in a van.
Behind the sky, not in it, heaven infinite and dim like water. I'd never, never get through to him now, even though
part of me, the best part that had lured him my way, was
fastened down in muscles like jaws, years of my life floating like bait in the gut of a fish, like essential data in a misfired, orbiting rocket that has only a slim chance—a
prayer's breath, a snowball's in hell—to hurtle to earth.
And stop.

Plumb and Solid

CREW OF MEN inserted beams into the new-poured basement. How did I picture the house? From blueprints. A box for a living room, box for a bedroom, outlets, doorways, between. I thought of sewing patterns. But there you hold the tissue to yourself in front of a mirror; you get a vision. Bruno jumped in the air—he's the oldest, eleven—and said, "This is it, where we're headed." Wayne and Leroy started jumping and cheering too. Bruno slapped me on the ass and said, "You look like a fox, Mom." Dick's trying to teach him it's wrong to talk that way. But he got it from Dick. I pushed him, "Quit." Still, I smiled because I'm eight months pregnant—with a girl, please God—and Bruno is one of two people who like the fat way I look. I stood with my boys on the edge of the lot, smelling wood and mud, watching the contractor dangle a cone-weight on a string. I looked into the distance, past the blue hills toward Bremmer where Davie was at the gas station, I knew, in a pit below a car, wrenches flashing, a sound like a silver bell if he dropped one. I turned to the basement.

This is where we're headed.

If you watch TV, you'll hear about midlife crisis, when men get to a point of realizing they'll die someday, and they want to be happy first. For Dick this meant sex, also house plans that look like a maze on the back of a cereal box, the prize at the center a master bedroom with a waterbed and a big TV. Someone had talked him into a bidet, a washbowl French whores use. Now, we live in the house his parents had before they built their brick ranch-style— a clapboard two-story painted eggplant, with lacy pinwheels on the porch rafters. It sits in the middle of plowed fields. We don't waste land here, though I did insist on a handkerchief-sized yard with grass and a fence so the boys could play as Dick rounded the fields in a tractor with air-conditioning and a CD player, tilling, harvesting, counting potatoes, multiplying them into dollars and translating that into what he'd buy.

I've been confused. A pregnant woman is. Last night, Dick and I drove to town for pizza. The restaurant filled up with people from Minneapolis—men in ponytails, women in crew cuts—who'd come to film a movie that's a joke on murder mysteries, like *Blazing Saddles* with farting cowboys is a joke on westerns. They were using our town museum, a five-story building shaped like a muskie fish, for the backdrop. A woman who had snake tattoos and horn-rimmed glasses walked by. Dick said, "She sure as hell isn't an actress because no one would pay to look at that." Sometimes Dick says things I agree with. I'm quick to point them out. Once he said, "Not everyone is college material. Somebody has to do hard labor." I nodded, "True." But I looked at the person he'd made fun of. I thought how she looked the way I did when I first moved here from Chicago. Style had to do with shock. I was fourteen. I hadn't met Dick yet. I don't prefer how I look now, a purple shirt over purple maternity slacks. But I understand there are ways to live, to look, choices. "I never liked the pizza here," I said. Dick said, "You're pregnant. You don't like anything."

I took a bite of garlic bread. Dick paid the bill. I looked down the street toward the gas station. Davie was getting married in four days. Did I care? When he asked—I'd been sitting on a stool in his office—I answered, "No. I could be wrong, but I don't think you'll go through with it." I thought about Trudy, who he was marrying. "She's not even pretty," I said. I was six months pregnant then. He nodded and smiled. "Not compared to you."

Dick and I came home from pizza. I fell into a hard sleep, then woke at 3:00, the house still and dark. I ate cinnamon toast and watched the 24-Hour News. I'd been doing this for a month, and it occurred to me that maybe Davie couldn't sleep either, that he'd been awake at 3:00 for a month too. Do I believe in love? I love my children. Dick and I love each other. It happens when you live in the same house. I never meant to go to bed with Davie—go to car, go to couch—but once I'd had my nails done with acrylic stuff that gives off intoxicating fumes, and Dick had gone hunting, and my mother-in-law had Bruno and Wayne. Leroy wasn't on the way yet. This was years ago. I'd had a chef's salad and three glasses of blush wine. I bought gas. I talked to Davie, who's my friend's brother. I've known him forever. He put whiskey in his coffee. I don't like coffee. I don't like whiskey, usually. But next thing we had the radio loud. I woke on the couch in Davie's office, my head on his chest. He laughed—not at a joke—saying my tongue had been in his mouth, slick and deep.

It took us weeks. He'd say, "When you're ready, Zoe. I, myself, like the buildup." Once, nervous, I dive-bombed across the room for a condom in a wrapper that was sitting on the gray desk next to the accounts receivable. I had the guilt, I might as well have sex, I felt. And he said, "Where's the fire?" We finally did it on Dick's poker night, a Thursday, because I'd been to town to buy Holsum day-old bread at the outlet, and I drove my lavender AMC Jeep, gripping the wheel, praying at the sky: Don't let me. I filled my tank. I washed my windshield. I went inside to pay. Because I was intent on the fact of sinning, it wasn't so good. I got on top, letting my hair fall over my face like it does in old movies when the woman knuckles under. When I say I didn't get a kick, I mean just the first time, getting over the newness.

I won't say—as I stood watching a contractor and carpenters saw and nail a new house Dick called my anniversary present (though I liked the two-story clapboard), my boys playing beside me, and a bun, as they say, in my oven—that I didn't think of Davie. His skinny chest covered with hair. Creases beside blue eyes. Long legs. "Excuse me," I'd said when I first put my hand *there*. I'd paid to have my Tarot cards read the day before, in Couderay. I never believe them. So what? The woman in the plaid pantsuit who tells fortunes said I'd meet a blond man whose love would uproot me like a tree in wind, and he'd have money. In the dark, drunk on whiskey, I put my hand there. "Excuse me," I said, "this is remarkable." It turned out to be Davie's thick wallet on a chain. He took it out of his front pocket. I touched him again. This time I thought of the TV commercial that talks about a new-and-improved something, and the woman says: *What a plus!* No, I wasn't good enough to stand watching my house getting built, and not think of how Davie makes me—even when I'm pregnant—feel like a fish in fast water, fanning. Like it's dinner. We're hungry. Time to eat. You don't think I feel guilty?

I never had church like most people. No one took me when I was little. When I tried praying the day I'd gone to the outlet to buy day-old loaves for the freezer, I thought of my friend Louisa, Davie's sister, and this Bible she got for confirmation with her maiden name engraved in silver letters, a page in front with blanks for Births, Deaths, Marriages. And she wrote in her marriage to this guy named Dale. Everyone thought he was fine. He didn't talk much. He acted gentle with dogs and old people. He put up with her moods—she thinks too much. Turns out what no one knew—what Louisa couldn't say out loud until she'd decided to pack up—was he used to hit her when his job got tense. Once he threw a glass of orange juice and ice cubes, which slammed her in the chest. Once he smashed her antique plates. Once he swung at her in a motel in Washington state, an amber-colored ashtray up-side the head. That time, she couldn't sweep up. She drew a diagonal line through his name in the blank, *marriage:* Dale Henry. *Slash.* She'd sit with that Bible in her lap, flip through, eyes closed, open them, a finger on a verse, like: "They creep into houses and lead away captive silly women with divers lust."

Divers lust? That night in the lavender Jeep, I kept it simple. God of sky. Of woods. God of hay and cows and sorghum. Help. The dashboard lights glowed. The red sunset pooled like water behind winter trees. The message? Let light into secret places.

I stood by the new house with my kids. The hammering seemed like it would go on. That Dick, the boys, the new baby, and I would move in and try to sleep and we'd hear tap-tap. All night. Forever. I looked at the horizon and said a prayer for the baby. Let it be a girl. And born alive. Kicking. "Bruno, Wayne, Leroy," I yelled. "Round yourselves up." I wanted to go back to the eggplant-colored house, still home, and call Louisa, who, along with the rest of Davie's relatives, would get to Bremmer today, he'd said. Also, Louisa had a new love interest with impractical factors, a wife and two children. And in spite of her prim side—"She's a tight ass," Davie said—she was not sorry, swooning, swearing this time she was in love on all eight levels at once. Which eight? I wanted to know. I'd try talking to her, some sense.

• • •

I drove my lavender Jeep, with Bruno, Wayne, and Leroy, on back roads to Davie's other sister's. Helen's. I hit a low spot where the Jeep dipped fast and our stomachs flew. "Way to go, Mom," Wayne said. I thought of Davie, who was getting married in three days now, and my jostled stomach sunk to that other part, my lower level where I keep wishes and hunger, my sweet-tooth satisfied by, yes, Davie. Last week at closing time, a woman put Old Milwaukee and a cassette, *Gospel Favorites*, on her Texaco credit card, along with gas. She left. Davie said, "I worry about going to heaven. Seems like a rough crowd." And kissed me hard. I sunk my nose to his skin. His belt buckle clinked. The sharp points of hipbone. The miracle between. He didn't make that joke about angles. I'd told him once I liked it on my back, him sideways at an angle. So sometimes making love, he'd say, "Forty-five degrees? Or ninety?" And shift back and forth. But last week, he'd pulled my chin up, stared at my face. Afterward he kissed my big stomach and said, "You better get dressed before you catch a bad cold."

Remembering this, hearing Leroy complain his shoe was untied, downshifting, I said, "Bruno, help Leroy with his shoe," and I started crying. It seemed plain that if Davie was getting married we wouldn't make love anymore. That had been the last time. Why hadn't I noticed? Would I do it different? Take notes? Light a candle?

"Mom's crying," Wayne said.

Bruno said, "She's pregnant. She doesn't like anything."

I pulled into Helen's yard.

She came out on the step with her kid, John Junior. John Senior had taken a trip. The key to some marriages is time apart. The door to Helen's house got stuck. I saw Louisa through the diamond-shaped windows, twisting and yanking. Finally, she pulled the door open and came running outside. "Zoe," she said, "my oldest friend in the world." I don't trust these displays. Louisa always wants something she's figured out ahead of time. She reads too much. For her, everything has a beginning, an end, a reason for being in the middle. I smiled, but I felt like saying, "What hoop do I jump through?" Next I saw a travel trailer parked in Helen's yard. "Whose is that?" I asked. Helen's smile got tight. Louisa said, "My mom's. Earl's too, of course." Then Davie's mother—also Louisa's and Helen's, I realize—came out of the travel trailer. "Little Zoe Waverly," she said. "But that's not your name now. And pregnant too. You're a feast for sore eyes."

Louisa said, "*Sight*, Mom. You're blurring clichés again."

Behind her, in the trailer doorway, stood her husband, Earl, who—as Davie once told me—makes a lot of money, spends a lot too, and one day put a lit cigarette down John Senior's shirt collar. No one knows why, not even Earl, who was drunk. But that's why Helen's husband, John Senior, left on a trip during Davie's wedding; he hates Earl. We went inside. My boys were tearing around. I saw Leroy run almost smack into one of Helen's straw flower arrangements she pays fifty bucks a pop for. I pictured the cattails and gay-feathers turning to powder, not to mention the shards of glass vase. But Bruno, a good brother, had him by the collar and stopped him. "Outside," I said, "all three of you. Anything you wreck, you pay for with your allowance." Helen's smile got tighter. She said, "John Junior, take the boys outside."

Davie's mother sorted laundry. "Earl likes his shirt collars snow white," she said, dreamy, "and starch in his jeans. Pork is his favorite meal." She sat down at the kitchen table with a propped-up mirror, a pair of tweezers, and worked on her eyebrows.

"Here I am, just getting out of bed," a voice said. A door off the kitchen opened and a plump woman in a blue-and-mauve kimono walked in. When she smiled, I recognized Aunt Celise of the Hairpieces. She'd once been First Runner-Up for Miss Wisconsin, twirling batons. The Pepsodent sparkle was still there, her lips curving away from her

teeth. My dad used to have a crush on her. Louisa interrupted, tried to get me to go outside. "Don't you want to
see John and Helen's new boat?" she asked.

Aunt Celise said, "Where's the bride?"

Louisa said, "I remember Trudy from the old days. She
had no distinguishing features, not even her hair color.
Davie calls her 'good marriage material.' What does he
mean? That she's a good investment?"

Helen said, "There are worse ways to think."

Davie's mother looked up, tweezers poised, as if she
were torn between sounding like a normal mother who'd
say it takes a practical bent to make marriage work, or her
long-time-in-coming-out real self. She said, "Earl was the
only one for me. God sent him."

Louisa said, "I read that the average person could be
happy with a thousand possible partners."

Her mother said, "I couldn't be happy with anyone but
Earl."

Celise said, "Not a thousand, no. Some are kinder than
others."

Louisa said, "Suppose you had eight qualities in common?"

Celise turned to me. "Zoe, goodness, it's you."

"Nice to see you," I said.

Louisa said, "Come on, Zoe. Let's go outside."

In the yard we looked at John and Helen's boat, upside-
down on sawhorses. Tree branches shook. The smell of
dry leaves blew past. I heard John Junior complaining,
"No fair, no fair." My boys play rough. Louisa turned to
me. "I met him at a professional conference." She started
crying. "I can't say anything that will make it sensible. Or
ethical." She wiped her eyes on her red sweatshirt sleeve.
"But it's good. I mean," she said, "not bad, evil."

Louisa always loves someone. And worries it to a pulp.
Was this different? I said, "Maybe you're on the rebound?"
She said, "No, I had that relationship. It was bitter." I

tipped my head back to look at how the sky sloped from purple on one side to whiter, paler, on the other. I said, "I could use a stiff drink."

Louisa said, "You had a drink or two when you were pregnant before."

Before the stillbirth. "Not now," I said.

She handed me snapshots of a plain man with glasses. First, at a table, turning to the flashbulb light, Louisa beside him, fussy. Next, they stood in front of a museum. Another shot, Louisa in a splashy dress, holding a cocktail. They looked happy, like they'd signed a house mortgage. "These were taken," Louisa said, her voice hushed like she was talking in church, "before, um, I loved him." She started crying again. I saw what she meant. They looked shoulder to shoulder, together. But weren't yet.

"It was meant to be," I said.

Louisa shook her head. "I don't believe in fate."

The sky seemed like water. The clouds like rocks where there'd be women with harps, sitting and singing. My own boys' voices called me back. I looked at Louisa, who acted embarrassed at what she'd just said. I opened my mouth to speak. "What?" she asked.

Once, I'd tried to tell her at her house in Menominee. *I boinked Davie* was how I'd tried to start. She'd acted surprised. Who could I tell then, Aunt Celise? Davie's mother who'd run away with Earl? I thought of Davie's dad who I see buying frozen dinners at the Red Owl, sipping coffee at the cafe. "What are the eight levels of love?" I asked Louisa, half-listening. She said, "Begin, first, with intellectual. Second, we have similar emotional needs. Third, sexual. Fourth, spiritual. Fifth," she said, "a work ethic." She moved onto six and seven, but I stared at the woods, the way light fell in stripes around trees. I thought of the Tarot cards. The man who takes you away from war in a boat with tall blades that stand for trouble. The woman who weeps over a small, empty bed. I thought of Dick, who gives me instructions.

More of *this*. Less of that. I'm close, Zoe. *Close.*

There's a way of knowing someone. Say we'd been to a Chamber of Commerce dinner, and I'd been nervous but came home feeling like the polka-dot dress I'd made was right, and an important person, someone who could help our farm make money, had talked to me, and I'd said smart things and no one could tell I felt shy. I hung up my dress, took off my makeup, shoes, earrings. Dick laid down, arms under his head. "You were brash and mouthy," he said. "I was embarrassed." The first time he did this, he might have dropped a suitcase of precious jewels downstairs, thud thud. I took days getting over it. Noting I looked sad, he made up, gave me uncalled-for compliments. Yet he never took it back. The second time, and third, I came to accept his worry wasn't whether I acted funny or brash, sparkling or mouthy. But whether he did. His nerves had frayed ends. Since I hadn't used him the same way— knocking him low so I could get high—I tumbled out of love. But when?

Louisa put the photos in her purse. "Let's go to town and visit Davie and my dad. Of course, you can't mention this to Dad."

"What?"

"Loving someone who's not available."

I told the boys to get in the Jeep, and I thought about how marriage survives undignified twists. Brawls. You wake up every morning like standing at a gate, yesterday's insults behind. Today ahead, simple. I turned the key, fired the engine, went to town.

I parked on the edge of the gas station lot. I stayed in the Jeep when Louisa jumped out, Bruno and Leroy too. Wayne sat beside me with a toy that's half-turtle, half-man. He's the middle kid. That toy's his friend. "Shit," I said. The baby kicked like a boy. Or a tomboy, I reminded myself to stop the knee-jerking, heart-sinking. When I was pregnant with the girl baby and knew it because of the ultra-sound, I kept saying I could tell because she didn't stomp on my insides like the boys had. It turned out she'd been dead for three weeks, that's why. This baby's fine, though. I don't want to know, yet, if it's a girl. I could see Davie and Louisa by the pumps. They hugged, Davie careful not to smear her clothes. Davie's dad walked over, one hand in his pocket, the other holding a pipe. He's sweet-looking, like Bing Crosby. He tapped on my window. "Taking care of yourself?" he asked. He wanted the real answer. My eyes filled up.

"Yes," I said.

He meant was being pregnant going fine.

Next Davie walked over, Louisa behind him. His face? Was the answer there? Louisa said, "Zoe, Dad's going to watch the station for Davie, and we're going to lunch. You can have an O'Doul's Non-Alcoholic." We ended up at a table in a beer garden. Davie held onto his stein. He smiled, beer taking up room, and it came out not like a smile, but that look you see in the Big Muskie Museum, the breath they take; fish don't have lungs. Once, his arm brushed mine. I could feel afterward where it'd been.

Louisa said, "Where's Trudy?"

He said, "Big plans, her mother, aunt, everyone. Preparation H."

Louisa said, "What?"

"All the Hagens are in on the wedding plans," he said.

Trudy's last name is Hagen.

Louisa said, "That's a bad joke. Where did you meet her?"

"Third grade."

Louisa said, "I mean, when did you start to feel this way?"

Davie said, "Look. She's a good sport."

Louisa said, "You'd be surprised who's a good sport once you get them home."

"Marriage brings out people's temper," I said.

They both stared.

Louisa said, "Yours?"

I said, "People save their best side for public."

Davie stood up. He left his beer on the table next to his burger. "Take it easy." He patted my shoulder. Then Wayne told me Bruno had spilled Leroy's soda pop. A man with long hair and pointed sideburns walked up and said, "We're looking for extras for the movie, and we think you'd be perfect, pregnant in that orange dress." I stared at him. "As part of the background," he explained.

I said, "My dress?"

He said, "The fertile color."

I said, "You mean, like a pumpkin? Go to hell."

Louisa set her drink down. "Zoe."

"I'm gone," I said. But a grand exit should leave some-one stranded. Who? The boys socked each other as we walked back to the Jeep. I drove Louisa to her sister's. "I don't feel well," I explained. Louisa said, "The baby?" And I remembered this made-for-TV movie about a baby that fell down a well, and the mother cried as she waited for the EMS crew. "The baby is stressing my belly button," I said, which was a lie. I thought how Donna Mills had played the mother in a strange way, acting sexy with the paramedics first, worried about the baby's safety second. "I feel like an inflatable toy where you blow the air in. I'm going to burst," I said. I had a picture of myself swooping through a room. Still, I felt nothing, except big. Louisa said, "Do you realize if I don't have a baby in the next few years, I never will?"

"Do you want one?" I asked.

"No," she said, doubtful. I dropped her at Helen's.

As soon as she got out, I took off, thirty-five miles to Couderay. The road—spongy, black tar—zipped around a swamp. The boys hung on. Bruno looking out the window like he had a secret. Wayne, sulky and distant. Leroy, like he might cry. I thought: I'm getting to the bottom of this now. I pulled up in front of the store with the billboard. CANDLE, FLORAL, BOOKS. PALMS READ TOO. "Wait," I told the boys. The woman came to the counter in her checkered dress. "I want to buy my own pack of Tarot cards," I said. She shook her head No. "If you do, don't ask specific questions. Or you'll get yourself in deep," she said.

I went home and called my mother-in-law and asked her to pick up the boys. I felt tired, an excuse. They waited for her in the yard with bedrolls. I lugged plants to the part of the barn Dick had made into a greenhouse. I was toting a clay pot of mums at the end of my stomach when my mother-in-law drove up. "What are you doing?" she asked. I said, "Putting these away before the freeze." She said, "Zoe, try a nap. Or a glass of wine for your nerves."

I went inside, sat down, stared at the phone. Then dialed. I never did before. I'd just show up, close to closing. "Texaco," Davie said. I heard the cash register beep. I was in a rut between two ideas: that even though I was married, if Davie and I had done anything besides make love, he'd call it off with Trudy; or if we'd never done anything besides make love and I wasn't married, he'd call it off. Besides, I was pregnant. Though I loved Dick, I didn't like him. Maybe that made anyone, a gas station attendant, for example, look good. "Texaco," Davie said.

I said, "Could we go somewhere?"

He said, "Zoe?"

"On a trip," I said.

He said, "I go on my honeymoon in three days."

I said, "How about in a month?"

He said, "Zoe, it has to end." The phone line crackled. I slid the receiver away from my mouth so he wouldn't hear me crying. He said, "This is a small town. Someone was bound to notice."

I said, "If I wasn't married, would you?"

He said, "Zoe."

Dick drove into the yard. "I have to go," I said, and hung up.

Dick came in and laid his hat on the table. "I saw my mom with the boys," he said. "Did she take them for overnight?" I looked out the window, and he stood behind me, sliding my dress above my hips. The two years I'd been making love with Davie, lying, or not telling the truth, seemed easy. But at that moment, next to the sink, the fresh-air smell of Dick's skin, gray light coming through the window, I thought he might shake me, call me a whore, cry and say: How could you, the mother of my children? But he kissed my neck, then my mouth in that closed way, not letting me kiss back. I jerked my head down. He stopped. "Don't worry," he said. "Everything's fine. The doctor said." We went upstairs and I shut my eyes and thought that how I felt wasn't Dick's fault. He wants what I want—a house, children, a pantry full of groceries. But his hands felt like trespassers, over the fence without permission. I tried lying on my back and putting my legs like I do with Davie. Dick said, "It'll be better when the baby's here."

And went to sleep.

I stared at the ceiling, the wallpaper with silvery stars. Then I went downstairs and read the pamphlet that came with the Tarot deck. The Queen of Cups is lovely and adoring but, in a tight spot, unfaithful. The King of Pentacles is a reliable owner of large estates but—at his worst—stupid, perverse, mean. The Ace of Swords points to highest heights, also lowest depths. The Page of Wands might break your heart or deliver love. It all depends. I shuffled until the cards blurred. I felt awake, yet sleepy. I turned on the TV, Maury Povich. I remembered how, when I was little, my dad—if he was married or had a girlfriend, if he was married *and* had a girlfriend—came home to sleep, the newspaper over his face, the TV low to blot out noise. Me, my brother, my half-brother. We tip-toed. We lived in Chicago. Our house by the interstate, near a ramp which swooped away like a jet.

In my eggplant-colored house in the middle of plowed fields, I picked toys off the sofa. Watching TV, I remembered standing under the ramp—cars above roared to distant places—and I'd smoke cigarettes I found in the gutter.

My first boyfriend, Brad, had a toy truck he'd speed across dirt. "Pack a lunch," he'd say. "We gotta get someplace." My dad moved the whole family to Wisconsin after I'd been caught shoplifting. Also, one day in the basement, I found a dress my stepmother said used to be my mother's—silky with butterfly-type sleeves—and Brad helped me zip up. I had an idea: what happens if I let the dress fall? My breasts poked out like stones. Your turn, I said; I want to see too. My stepmother heard. But my dad liked Brad and, when we moved north, let him come too. His own mother couldn't afford him. "Never leave them alone," my dad told my stepmother, meaning Brad and me. But it didn't matter because I wanted a new boyfriend by then. Settling down.

On the sofa, my eyelids fell down my face. I tried to stay awake. I looked at Maury Povich. I remembered how, after living with us, Brad joined the Coast Guard. Faraway. Circling the mainland, not letting dangerous ships in. He wasn't coming back. Ever? I got sleepy, thinking Brad was Davie, a man on a boat that bucked black, treacherous waves; he wore a uniform like the one in the photo Brad once sent. But it was Davie's head on top of Brad's shoulders. I opened my eyes and looked out the window at the dark fields. The big silos, their silver caps gleaming. The Knight of Swords means misfortune: coming or going. Until you know which—coming or going—it's hard to tell if you're having misfortune. Or its opposite, joy. One day my dad and I drove Brad to the airport where he'd fly to Coast Guard training. I'd told my dad that morning I was marrying Dick, and I didn't want to wait. I stayed in the car as my dad took Brad, and his pitiful suitcase, to the ticket counter. Brad looked back a last time. When my dad returned to the car, he said, "Honey, I can't say I've understood your taste in boys. But do what you want, including marry your farmer." My dad died seven months later, heart trouble.

I fell asleep. This is where we're headed. I couldn't

breathe, walking on one of those underground things like
an escalator but flat: a sidewalk that moves. The air was
steamy. My stepmother—I haven't seen her in years—
walked with me. The walls slid by. Somewhere, airplanes
roared. I heard Brad talking. *We gotta get someplace.* Then I
saw bouncers, thugs, clamping down handcuffs, hauling
Brad away. Next to him, someone was getting cuffed and
dragged off too. I said to my stepmother, "Brad's arrested."
She touched my arm. "They've got Davie too. Say good-
bye." I got off the moving sidewalk, switched sides, went
back. Everyone in the tunnel, I saw, was dead, or leaving. I
passed a shop that sold cigarettes; the boy behind the
counter was Skeeter from third grade who'd died of
leukemia. Next, on a barstool, I saw my real mother, like
Patsy Cline, a flashy smile; she didn't know yet death was
arriving. My dad on a couch, frowning. Brad in handcuffs.
Davie, a lanky stride, his blond head, his face gray as dust.
What did he say? *Save yourself.* I looked around. Ahead, the
exit that would take me upstairs. Outside. Behind, everyone who'd died or been pushed aside. *Go back.*

Which way?

It'd be easy, being a mermaid, singing a man off-course.
But once I got him where I wanted, foundering, did I have
to stay? I woke, stumbling through the house, staring at
empty beds, their flat blankets. I got scared until I remembered the boys were with Dick's mother. I thought of the
baby in my stomach. How, in a short, narrow time, she'd
pass out of that warm pool to here, earth, where air would
enter her lungs like ice. Light would sting. I went upstairs,
laid my stomach on its side, backed my hips into Dick.
The night shone through the window. I stared at the wallpaper that's been on the wall a hundred years. I thought of
all the ancestors who'd made love here—made babies—
and considered my dream about the tunnel with the dead
and missing, how my old neighborhood in Chicago was a
war zone; the boys I'd smoked cigarettes with were in
prison now, at best. I hadn't explained to Dick I got mar-

ried to be safe. Now I wanted out. A contradiction is hell. Outside, dew turned to frost. Snow would fall soon. I'd never—I decided, hugging the blanket—wander away again.

What I thought when I opened my eyes was: lies come true. My belly button did hurt. Its aching woke me. I said it, and now I had it. Psychosomatic. I got the idea from TV—that if something's wrong with your brain or soul you can't admit, your body gets sick so you'll allow yourself some tenderness. Louisa calls talk like this *Oprahic*, meaning we heard it on *The Oprah Winfrey Show* first. She's right. When I say *self-esteem* or *codependent*, I feel sad that my heartache sounds common, my complaints like everyone else's. Once Donahue had a show titled "Women Who've Settled." The same day, on Arsenio, a British actress said how lucky we are, getting self-help from TV for free. I got out of bed, my hand on my belly, and looked at Dick. He combed his hair, put underwear on, then laid garlic pills in a row on the bed, swallowed them one at a time. They promote long life. I thought what a grouch he'd be, old, and smelling like garlic. But I didn't want to fall out of love over that. I limped past in a red housedress his mother bought me in Acapulco. My foot hurt. I sat down—hard to do—and looked at it. I said, "You gave me athlete's foot." He said, "What?" I said, "You gave me athlete's foot." He said, "What?" I said, "I got your athlete's foot, damn it." He stared. "Whatever, Zoe. Whatever makes you happy."

I put slippers on, then went outside and got the curved saw with the ten-foot pole. I trimmed the maple. Next the elm by the fence. Dick, on the porch, drinking coffee, said, "What the hell, Zoe?"

I said, "I'm trimming trees."

He said, "I'm worried."

I said, "About money?"

He said, "You're going through a bad phase. My mother explained."

I turned around.

He said, "You're afraid for the baby."

The skin on my stomach felt tight. I checked: Was the baby moving?

He said, "But I tell you this. Once the baby's here, get a grip."

I said, "What?"

He said, "I took you away from a run-down trailer house."

Yes. Talk I'd heard before. I picked up the saw.

Dick said, "I took you away from crazy people." I hooked the blade around a branch and pulled it back and forth. "Your old man couldn't make ends meet if they were tied in a knot," Dick said. Sawdust sifted down. "The least you could do is act happy." I didn't answer. The times I had—yelling my family wasn't crazy, getting red in the face, crying—he shook his head and said, "See? See what I mean?" The branch splintered and fell. Dick walked away.

I sawed, remembering how, a long time ago, I thought Dick was wise. That he'd make plans to keep us safe. But he took trips and didn't tell me. Once he had to go to Minneapolis for a Cargill Seed convention, and Wayne fell downstairs and broke his arm, and I called the hotel, but Dick wasn't there. He came home three days later. He'd been fishing. Why didn't he tell me? Because he'd chartered a boat for Lake Superior, and if he'd told me I would have said not to spend the money. True. His parents paid us a lean salary then. Meanwhile, I'd called his mother, crying, telling her I didn't know where he was. She said, "Zoe, you need to grow up." I said, "But what if he's with a woman?" She said, "And?" Four years later in my housedress and slippers, clipping branches, I wondered. If he was—had been—did I *care?* I would have then. But now? I pictured Dick with a woman, pretty as a doll, and thought about the cramped way he kisses, how he puts his hands on my head and pushes it down, down. I decided: I didn't.

The phone rang.

I ran, bobbing, towards the house. I picked it up.

It was Louisa who said she wanted me to go with her to the Hair and Nail Salon. She wanted her nails painted for when she manned the guestbook at Davie's wedding. "Can you believe it," she said, "I had to buy a bridesmaid dress, a hundred and ten dollars, to stand over a book?"

I hung up, got dressed.

When Louisa pulled into the yard, she gave me a five-dollar bill. "Do you mind?" she said. "I want to use your phone." She went inside, paced, stared at the phone. Finally, she picked it up and moved to the combination-sewing-room-and-office, and shut the door.

Its old latch popped. I watched Louisa, chin in her hands, flirting, chatting. Scowling. Then she stood up, shook her head no. I remembered how, when my dad had girlfriends, he got lovesick, bewitched. Once he hired a male secretary. "It'll be simpler this way," he said, but he looked blue. If Dick had a lover, she was serviceable, discreet. If I did . . . I did, I realized. But Davie seemed like family. A brother? No. My belly button ached. Louisa walked into the living room, pursing her lips like she did the whole five years she was married to Dale. "What happened?" I asked. She said, "Nothing. Not quickly either." The phone rang again, Dick's mother. "Bruno and Wayne are at school," she said, "and Leroy's watching TV. He has a sore throat."

Leroy's grades are like Dick's used to be. I thought about arguing, saying Leroy was a good actor, too much TV. But I said, "Fine," and hung up. I got in my Jeep with Louisa, who talked about Jarvis.

She said, "He's rented an apartment—to move into, to leave his wife—and he told me about the high ceilings, the old-fashioned bathtub, how he pictures me there. Romantic talk, sure," she said, her voice flat. "But then he got worried that there weren't curtains. I told him that there rarely are in rental places, and I realized he's never lived alone. His wife tends to details, makes the budget, writes the checks." Louisa twisted in her seat. "I'm starting to feel like a voice on the phone, Zoe, a projection. Not a flesh-and-blood woman. He rented this apartment months ago, but hasn't moved in. He's had a plane ticket for weeks, but can't decide to come and visit. He's extracted a commitment, a promise." I slammed on the brakes. Roadblocks crossed Main Street. "Chrissake," Louisa said. Actors in costumes. Cameras on wheels. She said, "I told him that by the middle of November we have a future or not. He fishes or cuts bait."

We edged into the parking lot of the Hair and Nail Salon.

"A deadline," I said, "is practical."

We got out. Louisa opened the door to the salon. "Zoe," she said, "I love him." She started crying again. I thought how every day she goes to her job, typing news into a computer. At night she comes home to a dark house. The conference where she met Jarvis was more like a party than anywhere she'd been in years. "It's impossible," she said, "living in this purgatory of love-talk and no action. I have a headache. I've had hives for weeks. I got food poisoning because I was so distracted by Jarvis, his indecision, that I didn't buy groceries or notice I'd eaten old sausage. November the fifteenth," she said, "I move on."

We sat down, dipped our fingernails into Solution #1. The manicurist put on her pink and lime green gas mask, which is manufactured by Revlon expressly for women who do nails. She handed me one. "Where whan too," she said, muffled through the tube. "Fooms are bad for the baby." Louisa talked about her private life. We don't here—a small town, too much gossip—unless what used to be secret turns into a big fact, and busts out. Louisa said, "It isn't a deadline for Jarvis as much as for me."

"You'll forget him?" I said, my words clogged behind the gas mask.

Louisa laughed. "You sound like the teacher on one of those Charlie Brown TV specials." I looked at her smile, creased deep. She used to have dimples. I thought how durable she was, falling off another cliff into love. How many times? Ten? More? For me, counting Brad (we were kids) and Dick (who I picked out for my husband) and Davie: three times, total. I turned around because Louisa was talking to someone behind me. Her Aunt Celise, who put her hand on my shoulder. "How are you doing, Zoe, honey?" Next to Celise—I shrank—stood Trudy, staring. At first, I thought she didn't recognize me but of course she did. I sat next to Louisa, my stomach sticking out in the middle of my yellow-striped maternity dress. I don't like Trudy's looks, her hair the color of liver, her eyes beaming a message: nothing's fun. She said, "Hello."

I pulled off my gas mask.

Aunt Celise said, "The movie people have turned on fire hoses and flooded Main Street to make it look like a river—right under the Big Muskie Museum. They've got a fishing boat tied next to it."

Trudy said, "I *would* get married the week Bremmer turns into Hollywood."

The manicurist's phone beeped. She answered it, then put her hand over the receiver and said, "Zoe, it's your mother-in-law. She needs you to come when you can. One of your boys is sick." The room seemed like a swamp. Trudy still stared at me. I felt myself blush, my neck to my head. Did Trudy know? "I don't feel good either," I said, standing up. I thought about Leroy at my mother-in-law's, making his throat gravelly and raw on purpose. He likes the attention. Louisa looked at me. "Zoe? Are you all right?" I said, "Yes." But I thought about the little girl inside me, ready to be delivered. "See you later," I said, and left.

I got in my Jeep. I pulled around sawhorses onto the street. On the edge of town, I looked at my gas gauge, *E.* I hadn't filled up yesterday—or thought of it—as I sat in the driver's seat at Texaco and stared at Davie. I turned the Jeep around, headed to Tote-a-Poke, the other place in town that sells gas. But I didn't have cash. I drove toward the bank, but people were sitting in front in canvas chairs as two actors punched each other. Water from Main Street burbled into the gutter. I thought, Fuck it. I pulled up at Davie's Texaco and tried not to think of our phone conversation when I'd asked him to go away, and he talked about his honeymoon. I got out, unlocked my gas cap, pumped. I kept my back turned to the station. I planned how to act when I went inside. I'd push my credit card across the counter. When I had to meet his eyes, I would: like years had passed and he'd become my beloved memory, a figment from bygone days, an ex-. The door opened.

He came out, washed my windshield. Then the window on the driver's side. Only two inches between Davie and me. Then no inches at all. He hunkered behind my Jeep as cars passed. He grabbed my arm, pushed his face into mine and, bumping the gas lid shut, said, "One last time. I swear to God, Zoe." We went inside.

He locked the front door. I'd left my keys dangling in the gas cap lid, the door on the driver's side open, that bell behind the dash going ding, ding. We went in his office. He shut the door. Outside, my lavender Jeep; everyone could see. At first it hurt.

Like I was a virgin.

Electric shock, a lilt and jolt.

But before I could think *pain*, I felt swollen and ready. Pleasure began, colliding and rocking. What was the feeling? Familiar. But what? We didn't use a condom. We didn't if I was pregnant. Davie leaned toward me. *Angles*, I thought. Forty-five degrees. Or ninety. I opened my eyes. The office seemed gloomy and subterranean. The cinderblock walls, the gray desk, the grease-smeared sofa. I heard a faraway, gurgling noise. I remembered how, when I was in grade school, I'd read a book that didn't have pictures, and it told about a girl who got lost in the

woods. *Angels* led her home. I'd never heard of angels. I
wrote the word on a piece of paper and asked my dad what
it meant. Either I couldn't spell, or he couldn't. Because
he squinted and said, "It's like the side of a triangle,
honey. A corner." I tried to picture the side of a triangle, a
corner, leading a girl home. I couldn't.

Davie rubbed his nose with the back of his hand.
Breathing, he said, "Good-bye. I swear it, this time. Good-
bye." I heard a bell chime. Someone driving past the gas
pumps. Davie moved quicker. Up down, up. Water fell on
my shoulders. He was crying. The bell chimed again.
Naked and soaking wet, Davie sighed. I thought of Leroy
at my mother-in-law's, homesick and weary. Trudy down
the street getting her hair styled, her fingernails painted.
Bruno and Wayne on the school bus. Dick in a backhoe,
digging a ditch. A few blocks away, Main Street ran like a
river; a boat floated on asphalt. I wondered for a minute if
the real river was dry and cars drove there now. If my real
life was here, inside these walls, or at home in my eggplant-colored house and—in years to come—in my new
house, my anniversary gift with straight beams and a solid
basement. I heard cars, voices, the sounds of daytime outside. Moving and holding still. Was I treading water? I
reached for my dress. Davie put his hands around my face,
pulled me near, started over again.

In the morning I noticed my fingernails—spongy and
yellow. Yesterday, I'd dipped them in Solution #1, but
not #2. I sat on the edge of the bed. I heard Dick in the
kitchen, giving the boys cereal. When he feeds them or
stays home when I go somewhere, he calls it baby-sitting,
which makes him seem like a grouchy hired hand. I heard
him slap bowls on the table. "Goddamn," he said. He was
hardest on Bruno. "Who cares if it's Captain Crunch?
You're too old for cereal." I sat for a minute. I had pangs in

my hips. When I'd come home last night, I felt like I'd been dusted with fingerprint powder—touched, bruised, and you could see where and who did it. I'd be in trouble if I let on. I got out of the car, drifted through the house, past Dick, who'd picked up Leroy, past Bruno and Wayne, who'd watched cartoons for hours. Now they were watching a show about real cops who arrested real people. "Glad you could make it," Dick said, leaning against the counter.

I floated past to the bathroom. I took off my clothes and stuffed them in the hamper. I smelled like a fish, like I'd been in deep water. "I don't feel well," I yelled through the door. I didn't like the high-pitched tremble in my voice. Dick stood outside. The shower rained hot. He said he didn't care for Louisa, never had, the way she made me act. But when I turned the water off and opened the door, his brown eyebrows crinkled to a frown. "If you're sick," he said, "you'd better go to bed." Even in the shower I'd noticed the feeling wasn't going away. I might shiver into an orgasm any minute. My belly button stretched and pulled.

I put on my bathrobe, made sandwiches, and opened a can of beans—no dinner to win a prize for. Leroy pretended he couldn't help but walk into the refrigerator, bumping his head. Wayne got upset because I forgot he didn't like cheese. Bruno helped Leroy put his pajamas on. Dick watched TV. "Don't say I didn't warn you to lay down," he said. He went to bed. I stayed up, shuffling my Tarot cards. I thought how the lady at the the store said not to tell my own future—I'd get myself in deep, injecting hope. Wishes fulfilled. I could tell someone else's, for instance (even without the cards), Louisa's: she'd wear herself out loving Jarvis, then quit, claim it was Jarvis who conked out, and when he finally left his wife, she'd call him a wimp. I laid down the Queen of Cups. Me! Two cards on top, and eight around it.

The cards said this: I was waiting for a ship to come in. But I felt distracted by a devil who had a pair of lovers with white, lumpy bodies chained to his black hips. Carnal desire. Too many love messages had come too soon. I'd find courage but lose earthly goods. My friends say to Stay Put. Next, I laid the cards down for Davie. He'd lately come to realize he'd stolen something. But he'd thought he'd been waiting for a gift. There'd been bragging and destruction. Love had been served. Could Davie pick up the cup and drink? I laid the cards again, and they said Davie's family liked me. But I'd keep him chained to the devil with black hips. Next the cards said Davie was raking gold coins into a pile. Next, they said my beginning had turned against me. I put the cards back in their box. I wondered: In three years, where would I be? In thirteen? Or thirty?

All that, last night.

I'd stumbled to bed to wake like this, staring at the wall, remembering how I'd once arranged my mind to think of Davie as a stand-in. Like when one of the boys' teachers gets sick, the school hires a sub. When I'd realized the time I spent with Davie had helped me smile as I went about my chores, canning tomatoes, mending overalls, I thought: *I've got a sub.* But I'd moved inch by inch, I saw, from getting help from Davie, a little relief, to thinking he'd be mine forever. Not Trudy's. And I understood we can't tell the future because the future is what we want. And that changes. Louisa made herself sick—food poisoning and hives—racking her brain about whether Jarvis was a good risk and the evidence for it, being in love on different levels: spiritual, intellectual, sexual, emotional. And it turned out she wasn't going to want Jarvis anyway because the real Jarvis had ended up not the same as the one she'd dreamed in her head. All we know for sure is now. *Now.* I love Davie. I thought of myself, pregnant. I love Davie. Forever. Maybe. And I felt sure, this time, I'd have a girl. An invisible line separates hope from belief.

I remembered how I'd felt sure last time. In the drugged haze, the silvery light of the delivery room, the doctor's voice grew tense, angry. The baby came out a girl. Sure. But dead, the color of wax. The doctor told me not to look. Later, the nurse said she'd let me see the baby once, before they took her away. I thought, also, about yesterday, being with Davie in his office that seemed like a cave, a secret. One last time: had it shed light? Davie cried. Over what? I thought of the devil, the shackled lovers. What you wreck, you pay for. Would I get to the bottom? I looked around the bedroom Dick and I had slept in for twelve years. My stomach felt blown up like a schoolroom globe, all that blue water, the knotty, bumpy continents. It could be something I ate, I realized. Did I eat last night? Getting to the bottom meant landing on top of some new place I hadn't known existed. All this climbing and sinking. I felt tired.

I heard noises downstairs, the boys cleaning up after breakfast. A car pulled in the driveway. The back door opened. Another voice, Louisa's. "Zoe," she called out. To Dick, she said: "Where's Zoe?" I came downstairs. Louisa had been crying, but not like yesterday. Chewing her lip, she said, "I've had the most annoying day." The veins in her neck stood out. Her eyes widened. She said, "To begin with, I ate breakfast with my stepfather, who talks about his genitals." This last bit surprised Dick and me. We looked at each other. I said to Louisa, "Pardon me?" She said, "He calls them 'Big Earl and the Twins,' a pet name."

I said, "What does he say about them?"

She threw her hands up. "What doesn't he say? He takes a shower and says, 'Big Earl and the Twins are washed up and ready to go.' He rearranges his pants and says, 'Big Earl has shifted.' Yesterday, he said, 'Your mother has a special place in her heart for big Earl and the Twins.' Like any daughter wants to hear that. I can't imagine what my mother likes about him unless it *is* Big Earl," Louisa said. She looked at the boys who were standing in a row, staring. "Oops," she said, "sorry. Little pitchers."

"Don't worry," I said. I felt full, like a boat floating. Air kept me on the surface. I looked at Dick, who gave Louisa the once-over. When she's not here, he calls her stuck-up.

Once she asked us to dinner, and Dick sneered, "She can't cook." She can, but not food Dick's heard of. He puts her down because he knows there's not—never could be—a chance in hell she'd be interested back.

Louisa kept talking. "After breakfast with Earl," she said, "I got the idea that if I didn't actually wear the ugly bridesmaid dress I could return it. So when Trudy came by, I mentioned that it didn't seem essential for the person behind the guestbook to wear the same dress as the bridesmaids, and that I'd brought along a nice pleated skirt and matching velour tunic. But Trudy is a control freak," Louisa said. "Then Helen started yelling because of course she's the matron of honor, and she likes the ugly dresses, and . . ." Louisa stopped talking and rubbed her face on her sleeve. "That's not the worst of it," she said. "I had a wicked, terminal conversation with Jarvis, who is a wimp." She ran in the bathroom, and I heard her running water and blowing her nose.

Dick rolled his eyes. "All these female hormones gone haywire."

Louisa's dad pulled up in the yard.

He came to the door. "Knock, knock." He stepped into the kitchen. He nodded at Dick, "Hello." To me, he said, "I guessed I'd find Louisa here. She seems so upset this week. Helen said she ran out of the house crying and saying she wouldn't go to the rehearsal dinner. Of course, she has to—Davie's her brother. Family ties don't mean what they used to," he said. He shook his head.

Louisa came out of the bathroom. "Helen is a liar," she said. "I did not run out. I will attend the rehearsal dinner, though I hardly see what I have to rehearse. Holding a ballpoint pen?"

Dick thought that was funny. "Ha."

Louisa said, "Dick, please, you and Zoe come to the rehearsal dinner."

Louisa's dad looked at Dick, then me. I was in my

bathrobe. I hadn't combed my hair. He said, "Dinner's on me. Thick, juicy T-bones."

I said, "No." Everyone stared.

I said, "We can't leave the boys alone." I thought about watching Davie and Trudy practice getting married. "I'm under the weather."

Louisa said, "Make one excuse, not two. You sound like a liar."

Dick said, "I haven't had a T-bone in months. My mom will take the boys. As for feeling sick—you won't have to cook tonight."

I looked at Louisa, who'd worked herself up. At her dad with his hands in his pockets. At Dick. I thought how Davie once said he worried about going to heaven—it seemed like a rough crowd. "Please," Louisa said, "I've had the worst day ever." I said, "No way."

Sitting in a pew in the Lutheran church, shivering, watching the minister pace around in a white-sleeved robe to chat with Trudy and the bridesmaids, I thought how I never know I've had a bad day until it's over. Tomorrow I might wake and say: My word, yesterday seemed long. Three weeks from now, or three years, I'd say: True, going to Davie's wedding rehearsal was stressful. I looked at the mint green walls, the varnished pews, the pale, ugly candles. Today tallies up bad. Yes. In a minute, Davie would walk through the door with his family, take a look at me in the back pew, and wonder if I was deranged. Or if maybe I didn't understand etiquette: never attend your lover's wedding rehearsal. There's also the going-numb part. I don't have time to notice a bad day if it's under way. I soak up details—for instance, the soft nap of my dress, the scent of my good perfume, Knowledge, wafting from a pulse point. I looked at Dick, his skin polished and handsome like it is on days he dresses up. Louisa sat next to me. "What, if anything," she said, "did Trudy have done at the salon?"

I heard Davie's dad in the entryway.

Behind him, ducking his head as he passed through the door—Davie, his hair still wet from the shower. When he saw me, he turned white, the color of candles. Dick shook Davie's hand. "Hey," Dick said, "ready to strap on the ball and chain?" Davie blinked.

Davie's dad said, "He doesn't feel well."

Louisa said, "I hope you don't mind I brought Zoe and Dick."

Davie stared. That's when I noticed the rubber pad on my shoe was missing.

Louisa said, "I don't know anyone here."

At Louisa's wedding, a woman in high heels slipped and fell.

Louisa said, "I needed company, see?"

But didn't hurt herself. Davie nodded.

And I thought about yesterday, Davie. The feeling I was at the end of a tunnel, coming out. Up down, up. I looked at the stained glass, the altar. Now? I'd remembered being naked and making love *now?* Someone once told me it's a sin to look back. Davie stared at Dick, eyes narrow and exhausted. Dick stared at Louisa. Trudy stood in front, giving directions. "No," she said to the minister, moving his hands which held the Bible, "like this."

The minister said, "We don't usually rehearse the photos."

Trudy said, "I want things to go off without a hitch."

The front door opened and Aunt Celise came in. "Whew," she said, "what a day." Next, Davie's mother and Earl walked in. They stood ten feet away. I noticed Earl was drunk—I smelled it. My father's scent: whiskey overriding a cold, north wind. Davie's dad and Earl eyed each other. "Hello," Earl said. "Hello," Davie's dad answered.

Davie once told me how his dad brought Earl home for dinner, bragging he'd married the sweetest woman, a good cook. This went on for months. Then Earl came for dinner by himself. "How's business?" Davie's dad asked. Earl said, "Couldn't be better." Davie's mother straightened the lapels on Earl's coat. "There now," she said. "That's nicer. Behave."

She went to the front of the church.

Earl said, "In fact, I'm putting in a swimming pool."

"Is that so?" Davie's dad nodded.

Louisa sat next to me. "Eight levels of love," she said. "I must have been deluded. I'd known him six weeks. Only two in person. Four by way of the phone. But people do fall in love. Right?"

"People fall?" Celise said. "Are we talking about swimming pools?"

Trudy walked toward us. She stopped beside Davie, put her face near his to be kissed. I didn't look. "In addition to the ceremony," she said, "I'd like to run through a list of photos we'll have taken tomorrow. One of the bridal party. One of the bridesmaids only. Then the groomsmen. Then the Hagens. Then the Hagens with Davie. Then the groom's family." She stared at Davie's relatives clustered in a corner. "This is complicated," she said. "But first we'll have one of Davie's family with Earl. Then one of Davie's family without Earl—with his dad." She turned and stared. "What are you doing here?" She meant me and Dick.

Davie's dad said, "I invited them for Louisa."

Trudy said, "I thought it would be just family."

Earl said, "I see your point."

I looked at the ceiling—how it curves to a dome. I read somewhere that it helps launch souls into heaven. But the church seemed unmysterious, like a miracle couldn't happen: two becoming one.

Davie's dad said, "We're not so formal as that."

Trudy's eyebrows shot up.

Earl said, "Family's family."

Davie's dad said, "If it comes to that, maybe you should leave."

Earl jerked his head. "You have something to say?"

Dick stood up. "Take it easy."

Davie said, "Dad. Earl. Please. Not tonight."

Trudy tossed her head. "We should rehearse."

Davie's family moved to the front of the church—one of Trudy's brothers, a Hagen, helped everyone to a pew. Louisa sat with her dad, Davie's mother with Earl. The soloist started her song, "Forever." The minister stood under the dome. His white sleeves fluttered. He said, "The best man here. Davie, here," his voice making ordinary words sound pretty as church words, like: *Take, eat, this is my cup given so you won't perish on this continent.* Words like that. The bridesmaids came in a row. Next a gap. Then Helen, matron of honor. Then another gap. Then Trudy inched up the aisle. "Slower," the minister said. She kept coming, her short hair flat like a helmet. She pretended she held a bouquet, a handful of air. I felt a twinge—Dick wiggling his arm under mine, holding my hand. He had tears in his eyes. He'd cried at our own wedding. Davie stood faraway, like a doll, a man on a cake. I got this sudden picture in my head about a big fish, like in this book I read in high school where a man lost his leg trying to fight a white whale. The whiteness, the teacher said, stands for everything we can't control. The minister said, "The ring."

Davie fumbled in his coat pocket. Trudy looked perturbed. I've known her since seventh grade. She looks attractive perturbed.

The minister looked around, smiling. "Is everything clear?"

We left for dinner.

In the car, I told Dick I wasn't hungry. He pulled up in the parking lot of the steak house. He held my hand as we went inside. Orange fishnets hung from a black ceiling. Candles in basins burned on tables. A band in the next room played. I couldn't hear the words but I felt the bass in my bones, thump-tap thump-tap.

I stared at my steak, redder, more bloody, than I'd figured. Louisa said, "Check it out." She was talking to me but looking with one eye, head tilted, fork poised. Like a fish, considering bait. "It's that guy from the movie crew." The man with pointy sideburns—who'd asked if I'd pose like a pumpkin in my orange dress—raised his glass and nodded. Louisa nodded back. The steak seemed like a slab. Dick cut his into chunks, his knife squeaking across the plate. I thought how dull he was not to see Davie wouldn't meet his eyes, that every two minutes Trudy looked my way and sniffed. She knew, she must. Unless my brain was unsteady and I imagined it. Davie's dad stood up, put his coat on. Earl sat in the middle of the table, chewing, laughing. I thought about Davie's dad going home to an empty house, about the times I see him at the Red Owl. Once, after his wife left, he stopped me and asked how to make a BLT. I started to say it was a sandwich with B, L, T, and mayonnaise. But then I realized he didn't cook much, and I told him that when the bacon's frying is a good time to put the toast down, slice tomatoes, wash lettuce, so on. He'd thanked me, wheeled his cart away, and I felt like crying.

The guy with pointy sideburns sat down. "First the orange dress. Now this one, the color of pine trees. You look fertile. Evergreen. Are you sure you won't be in the movie?" I said, "No." Dick said, "Who the hell is this?" No one answered. Louisa pursed her lips, set her elbows on the table to sip her cocktail. "So," she said, "tell me the movie plot. How does the big fish fit in?" The guy started to answer. She said, "I can't hear," and leaned closer. I thought again how strong she seemed, putting Jarvis behind her. Except I noticed from the way she threw her head back when she laughed, the hunted look in her eye, she felt sad. If I didn't know her like I did—for twenty years—I'd think she was vivacious, sending a signal. I wanted to leave. I saw Davie out of the edge of my eye, a sideways angle, cornered. And I felt the bottom give out, everything turning on its side, the world sliding through a small chute. My first contraction.

At 1:00 A.M., Dick said we should time them. "Time what?" I said. "They're not steady. They're the Braxton Hicks things." I sat propped on the couch. The TV droned, Maury Povich talking about liver pâté, geese who were force-fed. "Braxton what?" Dick said. "Hicks," I answered. "With Leroy, I had them for three weeks." But in the restuarant—sitting across the table from Louisa, watching her flirt with the guy from the movie crew, knowing Davie was in the corner if I wanted to look—I'd thought the first contraction was real. Slow. Big. Growing. Then I didn't have another. Two hours later, I felt a twinge, like someone pulling a string. A charley horse. Dick yawned. He said, "Whatever," and went upstairs to bed. I tried to sleep but kept staring at the clock shaped like a sunburst. Today Davie would get married. My mother-in-law had bought a new dress for the wedding. She wanted Dick to drive. Dick wanted to stay home and plow. He'd said, on the way home from dinner, "Hell, I saw the rehearsal. It's not like a book where I haven't read the last chapter. She'll say 'I do.' He'll say 'I do too.' Isn't that it?"

We'd pulled into the driveway.

Inside, Dick's mother told us Bruno had balked at going to bed. Wayne was sleeping with a turtle. Leroy had hogged the remote control. Dick drove her home. When he came back, I had the TV on. He said, "If it's false labor, you can still take my mother to the wedding. She'll help tend the boys." I thought about having the boys in church, whispering, tearing up pamphlets, Leroy zooming a toy truck across someone's back; Dick's mother next to me in double-knit brocade, frowning. I pictured Louisa in her Quiana bridesmaid dress, a turtleneck with a halter-back, an odd combination of prim and bare, a Lutheran version of sexy. I didn't think of Trudy's white dress. Trudy, a thirty-five-year old virgin. I thought instead of the picture of Queen Elizabeth in the encyclopedia, her low forehead and black teeth. I thought of Davie in a tux, his ruffled shirt, cummerbund riding up, hair combed back. I lay on the couch pretending—like I do if I can't sleep—that I'm at the house my dad bought to get me away from Chicago. My half-brother lived there, my stepmother, and, for a while, Brad, who'd started to seem like my brother. They're gone now.

But they made noise back then. I'd get out of bed, go down to the lake, listen to waves hit the pier. Slap. Tap. Slap. But, now, my stomach hurt. I couldn't sleep. I thought of water. I thought, too, about the basement for the new house, the hole in the ground getting stacked, brick by brick, into a home. Mine, Dick's too. A home far from a lake. No ship would come in, except by trailer. I pictured a boat with sails and tall poles lurching over the potato fields. I shivered, worrying about Davie's wedding. The only way not to go would be to pretend I felt real contractions starting. But I had chores, so much to do. I fell asleep; I woke a few minutes later. I'd been having a dream in which I'd tried to make soup in a deep, narrow pot. The boys had to eat some or we couldn't go to the wedding. Every time I stirred, a mouse floated on top of the broth. I'd yank it out, throw the soup in the trash, start over. But I'd stir the soup again and there'd be more mice, swimming. I looked at the clock over the TV. 3:00 A.M. Four, five, six. Three hours until dawn.

I woke, the sun in my eyes, Leroy asleep on the couch beside me, sucking his thumb. Bruno and Wayne sat on the floor, playing Old Maid. "We didn't want to wake you," Bruno said, smiling with a blank face. It's how he looks when he's worried. Dick came downstairs. "Are you in labor?" he asked, hooking the straps of his overalls. I said, "Real contractions are eight minutes apart. Then less." I realized that if I meant to get out of going to Davie's wedding, I'd missed my first chance. Dick picked up his tractor keys from the hook by the door. "You know where to find me."

I made Cream of Wheat for the boys.

The phone rang. I held it under my chin as I stood near the stove. Louisa said, "I called to see what time you're going to the wedding. I stayed at my dad's last night because Helen is mad at me. I invited that man to the wedding—the assistant to the producer. For sure, it'll piss off Trudy. You want to meet us there?"

I started my lie. "I'm in labor," I said.

Louisa let out a noise like a blown tire. "Dad," she said. "Zoe's having her baby." I heard him coughing, fussing. I pictured him with his hands in his pockets, saying: "Is that a fact?"

"Mild labor," I told Louisa. "I don't think I'll deliver today."

She said, "Are you going to the doctor?"

Complicated, I thought, lying. "Yes."

She said, "I'll drive."

I said, "No."

She said, "You know that idea you could fall in love with a thousand possible partners? Well, maybe. If you traveled a lot."

My labor *was* under way. And mild. Like a barrette clipped too tight in my hair, tweaking my scalp. Tweaking my hips. Braxton Hicks contractions don't hurt much. But they seem like they'll go on forever. "I'll have to get back to you," I told Louisa.

She said, "You're going to the doctor."

I said, "Yes." I hung up. I set bowls on the table. "Eat," I told the boys. My mother-in-law called next. "What time do we leave?"

I said, "I'm in mild labor."

She said, "Dick was just here. He said it was false."

I said, "There's no such thing as false labor."

She said, "Well, they have a fancy word for it now."

I said, "I'm going to the doctor."

She said, "On a Saturday?"

My back hurt; no one cared, except Bruno. I said, "I called ahead."

She said, "Why don't you get yourself and the kids dressed? The labor might stop. Of course, I could go by myself to the wedding."

"Right," I said.

"But I like your company."

I hung up. I found the keys to the Jeep. I had on the maternity sweatsuit I'd changed into when I got back from the rehearsal dinner last night. The boys still wore their pajamas. Bruno said, "Where are we going?" I said, "For a drive." We headed down the road, past Dick's mother's. She stood in the window, straightening curtains. "Can we stop and see the new house?" Leroy asked. I pulled off the road. Wayne held onto his toy that's half-turtle, half-man. "Where are the carpenters?" he asked. I explained that it was Saturday, they had the day off. "Are the carpenters going to the wedding?" Wayne asked. The hole in the ground had started to look like a house. Brick walls. You could huff and puff and never blow them down. "This is my bedroom," Bruno said. "Mom, you and Dad will sleep over here." We got back into the Jeep and drove to Bremmer, past sawhorses, barricades, actors. The guy with pointy sideburns wheeled a camera to the Big Muskie Museum. I thought of Louisa at her dad's, lint-brushing her velour tunic, tweezing her eyebrows. I looked at my sweatsuit. "Where are we going?" Bruno asked. I'd take a lesson from Louisa. When something's done, stick a fork in it.

Dig deeper. Once, when Louisa came back from a trip to visit her mother, she said, "I grieve for her," because her mother had changed, being married to Earl. This was the same year Louisa got divorced. She asked me how I'd done it. "Learned to live without family."

I thought about my real brother, Willy. When my dad

died, I'd called Willy to tell him about the funeral. "I don't want any truck with the old days," he'd said. My half-brother couldn't be reached. People brought casseroles, sent flowers. But the day after the funeral—no one warns you how bad you'll feel—I put Bruno, who was a baby, into my Volkswagon that had holes in the floorboard. I remembered how Willy had said, long-distance: "Sorry, Small Fry, but no." I pictured my half-brother, who I hadn't seen in years, so in my mind he was still a boy. It hurt to be the last member of a family. But a family with a single member isn't one, I'd realized, gripping the wheel. Rain fell. After that—though I had days of wishing for, let's say, a Sunday dinner where I cooked my dad's favorite food and it made him so happy he cried, or Willy pulled my hair and cracked jokes—in the end, giving up on my family wasn't harder than quitting cigarettes. I clamped down my jaw, cleaned a closet, mowed the lawn, decided not to crave something that made me worse, not better.

But the day after the funeral I couldn't stop thinking my dad was still alive: in his messy office in Chicago, or sitting on a bar stool in that tavern near our house at the lake. I also thought how when Willy was twenty, and I was four-teen, I saw him so rarely, his tall, suave self; I had a crush. And Brad—who my dad liked so he let him live with us—I saw so often he got on my nerves. Driving my Volkswagon, Bruno in the car seat next to me, the puny windshield wipers slapping, I got angry about my family, my brother who'd seemed like a boyfriend, my boyfriend who'd seemed like a brother. I thought about Dick, who'd never understood any of us. I thought about Louisa, who had a fa-ther, a sister, a brother. A real mother until she was twenty. What else did she want? I kept driving until the pine trees vanished and we were in low hills. *Rommel drove deep into Egypt,* I remembered from history class. What for? I had no idea. The rain didn't let up. It leaked through the floor, around the seal on the edge of the windshield. The wind-shield got steamy. I'd keep going, I decided, until I left Wis-

consin, entered Illinois, then down to Mexico, Venezuela,
Peru, finally. Would they have roads the whole way?

"Do you mind if I ask where we're going?" Bruno,
eleven years old, said. "I mean, we're still in our pajamas." I
slowed down. We were on the tar roads by Couderay.
"We're out for a drive because Grandma thinks we're at
the doctor," I said. I turned the Jeep around. I'd turned the
Volkswagon around all those years ago; I ran out of gas,
money. "I'm too old to be going out in public like this,"
Bruno said, gritting his teeth. He looked like Dick.

Driving, I hadn't had a contraction.

At home, I said, "Get dressed. No, everyone take a
shower." I wanted us ready. Wayne and Leroy took showers first. Then Bruno. "Please help your brothers," I asked
Bruno as he came out, a towel around his waist, his crew
cut spiky and gleaming. "Leroy, wear the plaid sportscoat
with the polka-dot tie. Wayne, you wear the navy blue
blazer." Next, I showered. I washed my hair with pearly
shampoo. I shaved my legs and under my arms. I dabbed
perfume. This, I thought, slipping into my new red dress
with its neck shaped like a valentine. I imagined myself
driving to Davie's dad's, marching across the lawn, my red
shoes crunching dry leaves, saying to Louisa, finally: I
can't go to the wedding. I love Davie. We used to, you see,
boink. Of course, the boys shouldn't hear; I'd leave them in
the Jeep. Davie's dad shouldn't hear either. I'd ask Louisa
to step outside. We'd stand in the yard, next to the garage.
But why did I need to wear this dress? I pulled its flounce
over my head, down my hips. Because I might change my
mind and end up at the wedding. Because if I tell the wild
truth for the first time in my life I'd better look sweet. Besides, I'd drive to my mother-in-law's, drop off the boys,
and say: I got dressed, I tried, but I'm sick. And I'd make
waves, almost.

I put makeup on. Red lipstick. Pale eyeshadow. Mascara,
bottom lashes first or I'd get tracks. I didn't have panty-
hose, I realized. I'd stop at Tote-a-Poke. They don't carry

Maternity. But sometimes Queen-Size fits just fine. We got back in the Jeep. We drove to Davie's dad's house, by-passing Texaco. I didn't know who'd be working. Not Davie, not the day of his wedding. I looked in the rearview mirror and saw my hair was styled, but I hadn't picked it with the big comb. Too curly. I'd also forgotten to put mascara on the top half of my eyes, which gave me a vacant look like a tired clown. I parked in front of Davie's dad's. I pulled the brake on. "You boys wait," I said.

I knocked on the door, shivering in my short dress, my bare legs stuffed into suede pumps. Davie's dad answered. I asked, "Is Louisa here?" He said, "No, she's shopping for some last-minute item for her toilette." Behind me, Wayne said, "Is her toilet broken?" I turned around. All three boys had gotten out of the Jeep. "I thought I told you to wait," I said. But what was the point? I had nothing to say. I felt deflated, letting go.

Davie's dad said, "How do you feel?"

Before I could answer, a car pulled up. Aunt Celise got out. She flashed her white teeth. "How cute the boys look in their little suits," she said. Leroy smiled back, flirting. Wayne hung onto his turtle-toy and stared. Bruno rolled his eyes. I looked at the sky, shifting, turning dark. One side gray and cloudy; the other side, lavender. Davie's wedding day. I felt the dull throb in my hips that had grown so constant I'd accommodated it. *Expecting:* it causes pain. I felt a twinge. "I'm having those Braxton Hicks things," I said, because lying was hard. "They're not serious. Last time, I had them for weeks."

Celise said, "Goodness, Zoe, they are serious. Your body's telling you to get ready. You need to put your feet up, plump a pillow." And I remembered that, in addition to being First Runner-Up for Miss Wisconsin, Aunt Celise had been a stewardess, a nurse too. Davie's dad's phone was ringing. "I'd better get that," he said.

Celise said, "It's probably Helen. John came home drunk from his fishing trip and got into a fight with Earl, who's also drunk. Plus, Earl has hurt feelings—something to do with family photos." She shook her head. "Good-bye, Zoe, sweetie." She went inside.

I felt stalled.

Then Louisa drove up. "Boys, get in the Jeep," I said. I cleared my throat. "Louisa," I called out, as she opened her door.

"You wore that to the doctor's?" she said. "Pretty sexy." Then: "My God, it's crazy at Helen's house. John's drunk. John hates Earl. Earl is drunk. My mother is a lunatic." The front door opened. "Louisa," her dad said, "your sister wants you on the phone." Louisa said, "Zoe, I'll be right back." And went inside.

I got in the Jeep with the boys. I stared at the fence around Davie's dad's yard, old-fashioned posts with round balls on top. Down the street, pine trees, elm trees, light poles, fire hydrants. Over and over, I thought. Wands. The King of Wands—friendly, passionate—stands for good marriage. The Ace of Wands, a stick with bees hovering near its bulb-tip, means a baby is coming, a new family forming. I decided to call the Tarot lady. I started the Jeep. Bruno said, "Are we going to this so-called wedding?"

"You are," I said, "to keep Grandma company." I drove to Tote-a-Poke. I hunched in the phone booth, dialing Information. "Couderay, please." I pictured the Tarot lady, her glass counter with stones and books. I'd drop off the boys at my mother-in-law's, tell her to take them to the wedding, and if she was afraid of driving, to go slow. A long time ago, I'd hoped she'd be my friend. But it came to this. Dialing for Information. Dialing for guidance from a woman who wore a wig and too much jewelry with her plaid pantsuit. All my hankering after Kings, Queens, Knights, Pages. After the Emperor. His wife, the Empress. After the Ten of Cups, the card where a man, a woman and two children dance in front of a home, a rainbow of blessings overhead. Sometimes, when the weather turned sunny and I puttered in the garden, the boys playing beside me, I felt happy, like the sky gave permission. Then Dick came home and spoiled it with angry talk: The house wasn't clean. Why had I skipped chores to plant flowers?

The voice on the phone said, "Hold for the number, please." The recording came on, 434-2222. I pictured the shop in Couderay. CANDLE, FLORAL, BOOKS. PALMS READ TOO. I dug in my purse for change, thinking that what I needed was simple, voluntary. To live where I wanted with someone I liked and, failing that, alone with the boys and the new baby. I looked at my big stomach. I thought of the first card in the deck. *O.* Zero. The Fool. Wise or stupid, daring or brash. He steps off a cliff. He'll float or sink. *Divers lust*, I thought. I turned around to check on Bruno, Wayne, and Leroy. What I saw instead was this: Black pin-stripes. Satin lapels. A cravat, not a tie. Trudy picked it out, of course; I like a modern tuxedo. Davie, his blond hair combed back, lurching between aisles of cars in the park-ing lot. The Groom. He looked like he should wear a top hat. *Oh.* He should row a boat, my old-fashioned lover. He's drunk, I thought. He waved a flask. "Wedding pre-sent," he said. "You look gorgeous." He leaned close, and frowned. "What's wrong with your eyes?"

I hung up, put my hand to my face. I didn't have nail polish on either. "I didn't finish my makeup," I said, wish-ing I could go into Tote-a-Poke, buy Maybelline Great Lash, and finish up right there. Davie stepped forward, put his face in my neck. Everyone could see, even the boys. "Your skin is white," he said, his voice muffled, "like snow, like marshmallows." I remembered once, in the gas sta-tion, I'd told him I'd just had my fortune read, that I was the Queen of Cups. "Yes," he'd answered, his hands on my breasts. But outside the Tote-a-Poke, I noticed the darken-ing sky. A six o'clock wedding. "Shouldn't you go to the church?" I said. "Shouldn't you?" He pinched my leg. "The Hagen boys took my car—to tie tin cans to the bumper." He opened the door to the Jeep. "Can you get in back," he asked Wayne, "and let your mom in front?"

He drove to Main Street. We got jammed behind the movie. Sawhorses. Actors. Props. A woman wheeling a rack of clothes. Three men pushed cameras over bumpy asphalt. I looked for the guy with pointy sideburns and realized he was at a motel, putting on aftershave, smoothing his hair into a ponytail, getting ready for his date with Louisa. I looked at the clock over the bank. The time. The temperature. "We need to get to the church," I said. Davie pushed the clutch in. A man stumbled past with tall light poles. The Jeep drifted. "The polite thing," Davie said, "would be to cancel." I stared. His eyes seemed like water, like I could slide in. Or a mirror: deep-seeming, but I'd smack the surface.

"Cancel?" I said.

"It's wrong to say so," he said.

"But get it off your chest." Under my lungs, my stomach twisted.

"In that case," he said, "I wish your kids were mine."

"Quiet," I said, "they're right here." I turned around to look at the three of them, listening but pretending not to. Bruno stared out the window. Wayne revved a toy truck beside Leroy, who sucked his thumb. I remembered a day, years ago, when Leroy was a baby and had the flu. There was shit on the car seat and when I stopped to fill gas, Davie came out with warm water and dabbed Leroy's fat legs, cupping his hand on Leroy's head, saying, "There, there, buddy." Had he wished it then? "Of course, they're not," Davie said. "Not a chance. You were so careful. I should turn this Jeep around." He wiped his face on the back of his hand. "Go to the church—" Even the boys could hear him crying now. "—and say I can't do it. But Trudy is organized, practical. Bossy," he said. "Hell, I don't remember proposing." I stared at a camera in front of the Jeep, its electric cords dangling.

"There," I said. To no one. To all of us. Leroy had crawled into my lap. We cruised to the end of the street, to the Big Muskie Museum with its green stripes, its stucco fins flexed, mouth open to reveal the little balcony. Actors walked through the double doors in its belly. All of a sudden, I wanted to be inside, climbing the stairs to the fish's mouth. You can see for miles, to the next county. Someone knocked on the Jeep, a woman with her hair cut short like Bruno's; I'd seen her at the pizza parlor. I looked at her tattoos. One arm said: *Transcend.* The other, *I Love Keith.* "Are you extras?" she asked. Davie shook his head no. "Sightseers?" She stared at Davie's tux, the boys in their suits. "Then you need to park," she said. "You'll be blocked in for an hour." Davie pulled the brake on. He said, "I wish we had some popcorn." Bruno tapped my arm. He loves me. But he loves his dad. He said, "Are we crazy?" Davie said, "I feel crazy. I wake up every night at three o'clock." And my stomach ached.

I remembered stories about babies being born in cars. I thought of Davie at the Texaco in a pit underneath engines, his tools flashing. Would he help me? I thought of the half-built house. Dick would complain I'd picked a bad time—crops in the field, a baby coming, the new home almost done. A divorce costs money, he'd say. Money doesn't flow through pipes. Actors walked toward the big Muskie which curved into the sky. I remembered being a girl, smoking cigarettes under the ramp to the interstate, traffic above roaring. Davie put one hand on my neck, the other on my stomach. Wayne and Leroy sat behind me. "I want us to be together," Davie said. Bruno stared, his lips creased. It won't be easy, I thought. "Mom, look," Wayne said. Because the sun had slid behind trees. The crew opened hydrants which gushed to the pavement. Tall lights flickered on, and water rippled down Main Street as a boat inched its lonely way. Cameras glided to the Big Muskie Museum. I thought of heroines who roll their eyes and want love; if they can't get it, they want to be alone. A spotlight shone into the fish's mouth, the balcony where two actors embraced, arms angling. I'd been waiting to be taken, I realized. Away.